PARADOX GIRL

FIRST CYCLE

PUBLISHED BY TOP COW PRODUCTIONS, INC.
LOS ANGELES

PARADOX GIRL
FIRST CYCLE

WRITTEN BY CAYTI ELLE BOURQUIN
ILLUSTRATED BY YISHAN LI
EDITED & PRODUCED BY PETER BENSLEY

ADDITIONAL ART BY
HARLEY WILLIAMS
SUZANNE ELIZABETH MILLER
STUART WALLACE MILLER

COMIC SHOP LOCATOR SERVICE
888-COMICBOOK
888-266-4216

To find the comic
shop nearest you, call:
1-888-COMICBOOK

Want more info? Check out:
www.topcow.com
for news & exclusive Top Cow merchandise!

For Top Cow Productions, Inc.
For Top Cow Productions, Inc.
Marc Silvestri - CEO
Matt Hawkins - President & COO
Elena Salcedo - Vice President of Operations
Henry Barajas - Director of Operations
Vincent Valentine - Production Manager
Dylan Gray - Marketing Director

IMAGE COMICS, INC.
Robert Kirkman—Chief Operating Officer
Erik Larsen—Chief Financial Officer
Todd McFarlane—President
Marc Silvestri—Chief Executive Officer
Jim Valentino—Vice President

Eric Stephenson—Publisher/Chief Creative Officer
Corey Hart—Director of Sales
Jeff Boison—Director of Publishing Planning
          & Book Trade Sales
Chris Ross—Director of Digital Sales
Jeff Stang—Director of Specialty Sales
Kat Salazar—Director of PR & Marketing
Drew Gill—Art Director
Heather Doornink—Production Director
Nicole Lapalme—Controller

IMAGECOMICS.COM

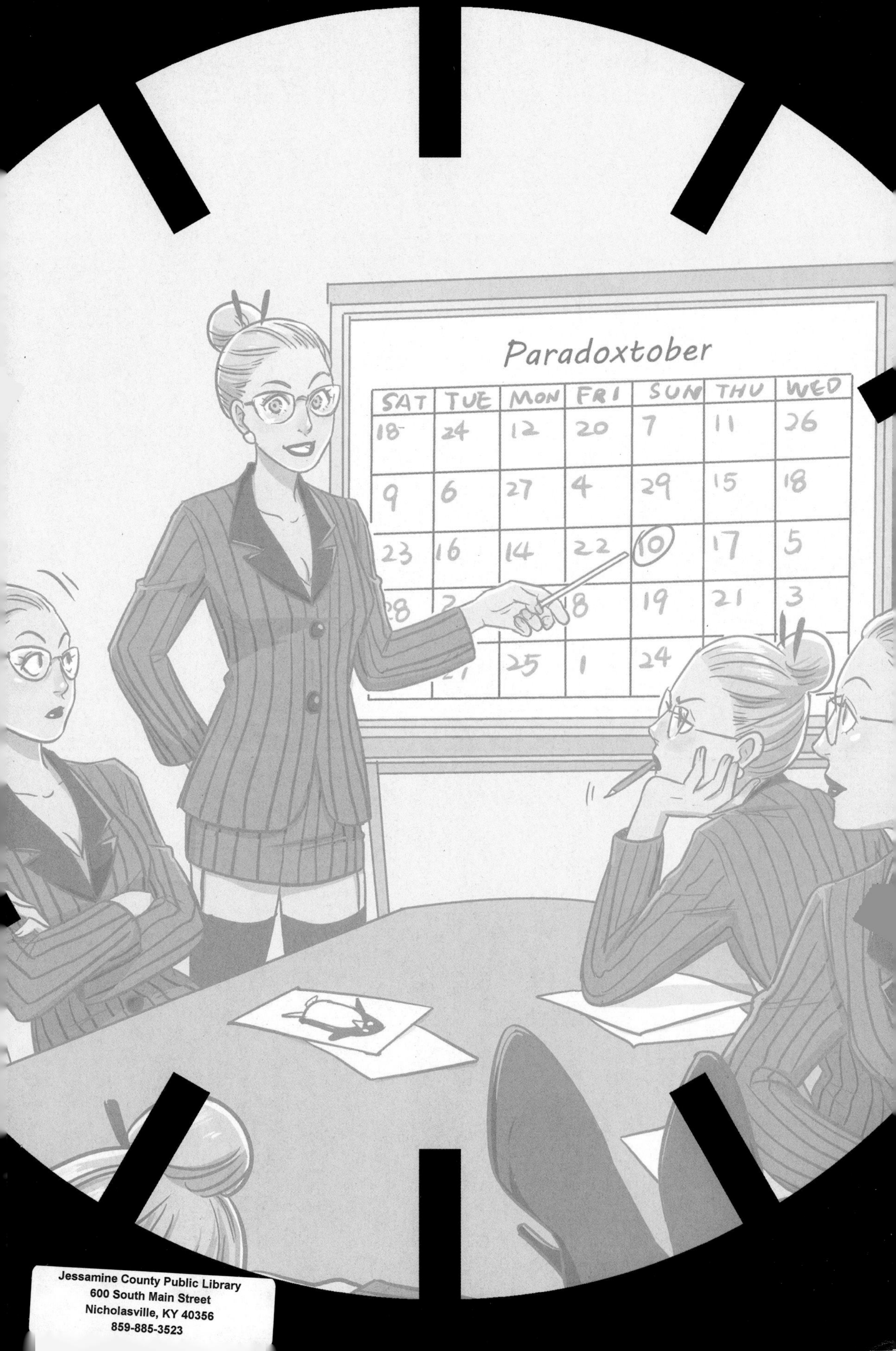
Paradoxtober
SAT TUE MON FRI SUN THU WED
18 24 12 20 7 11 26
9 6 27 4 29 15 18
23 16 14 22 10 17 5
28 8 19 21 3
25 1 24

CHAPTER 1

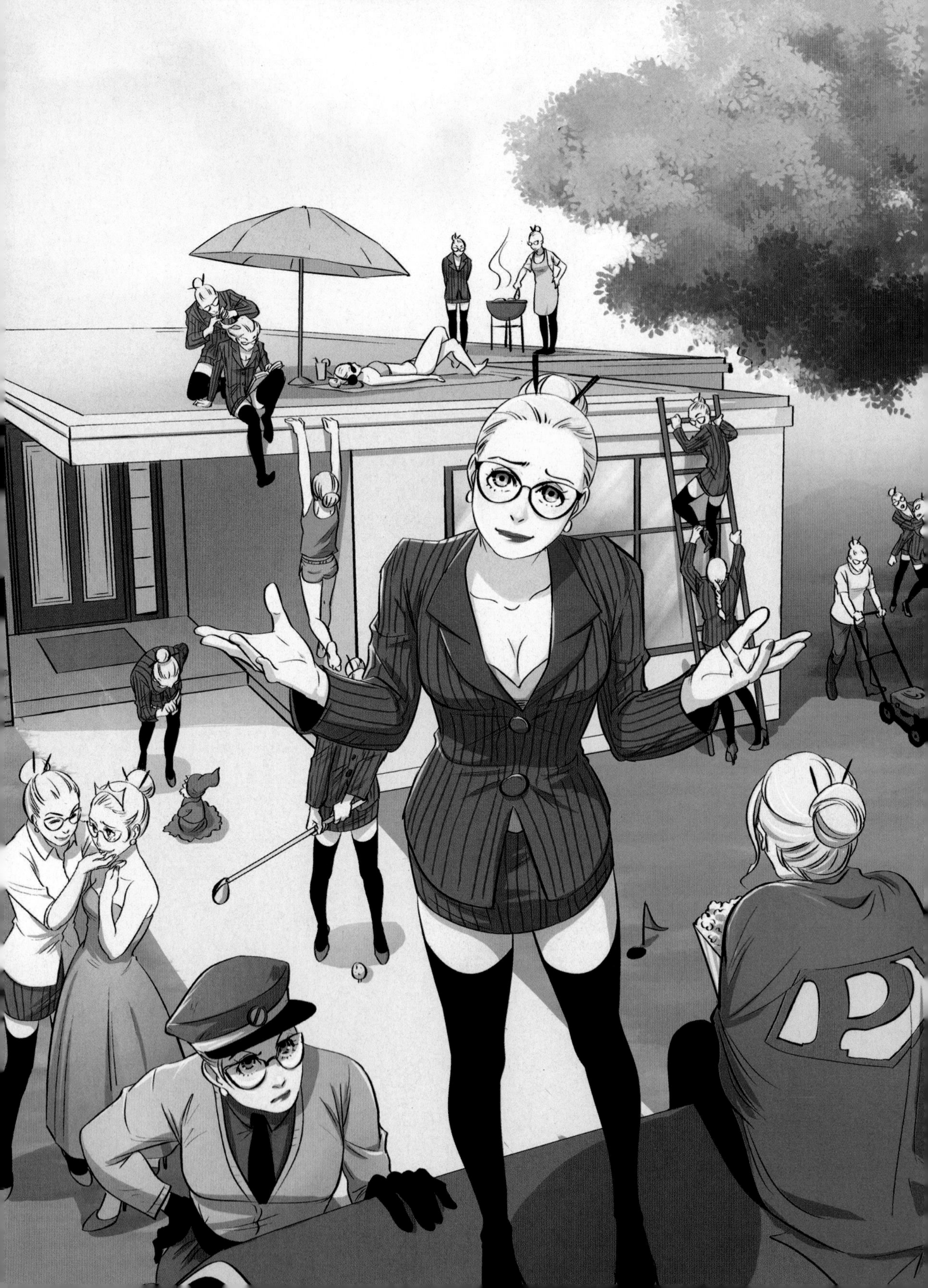

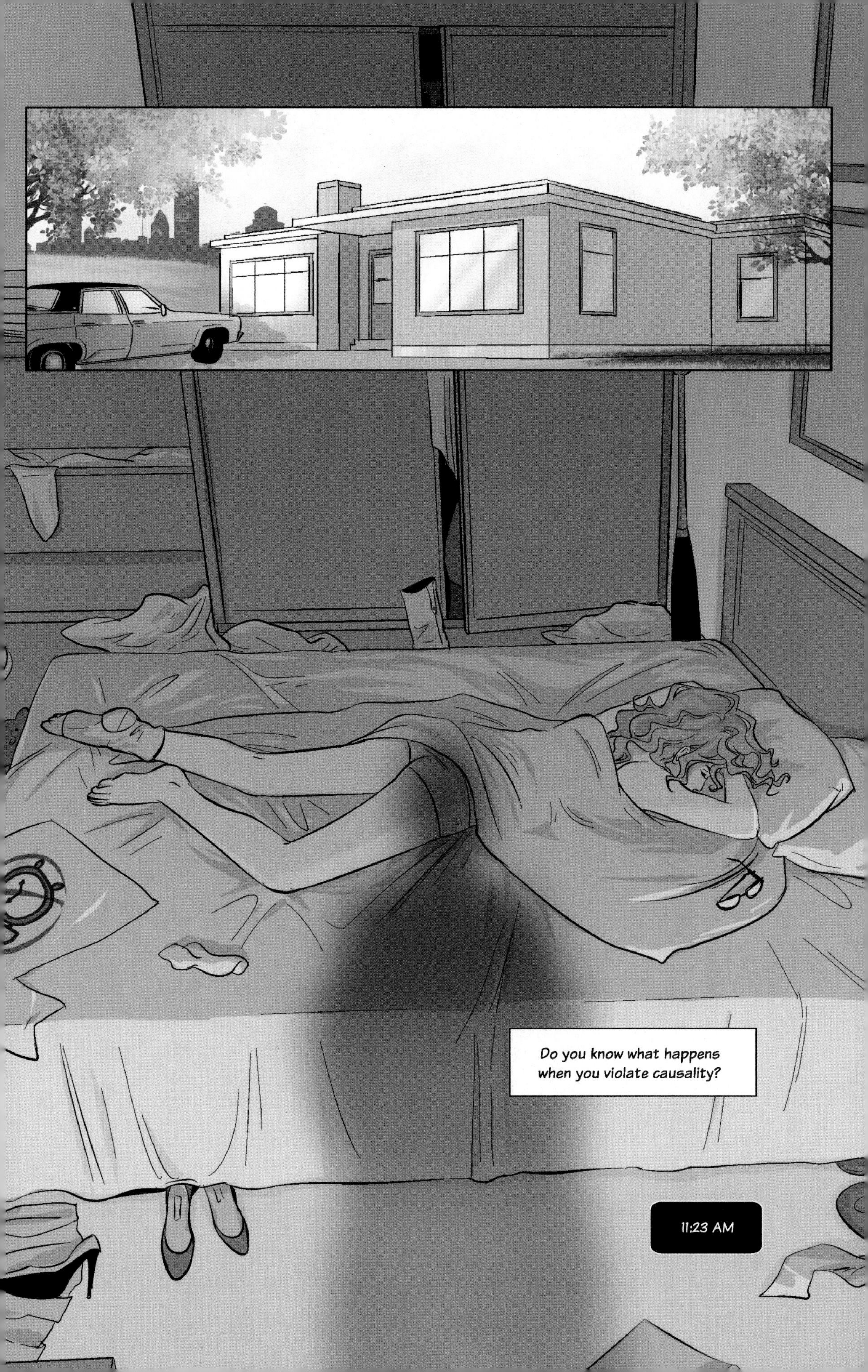
Do you know what happens when you violate causality?
11:23 AM

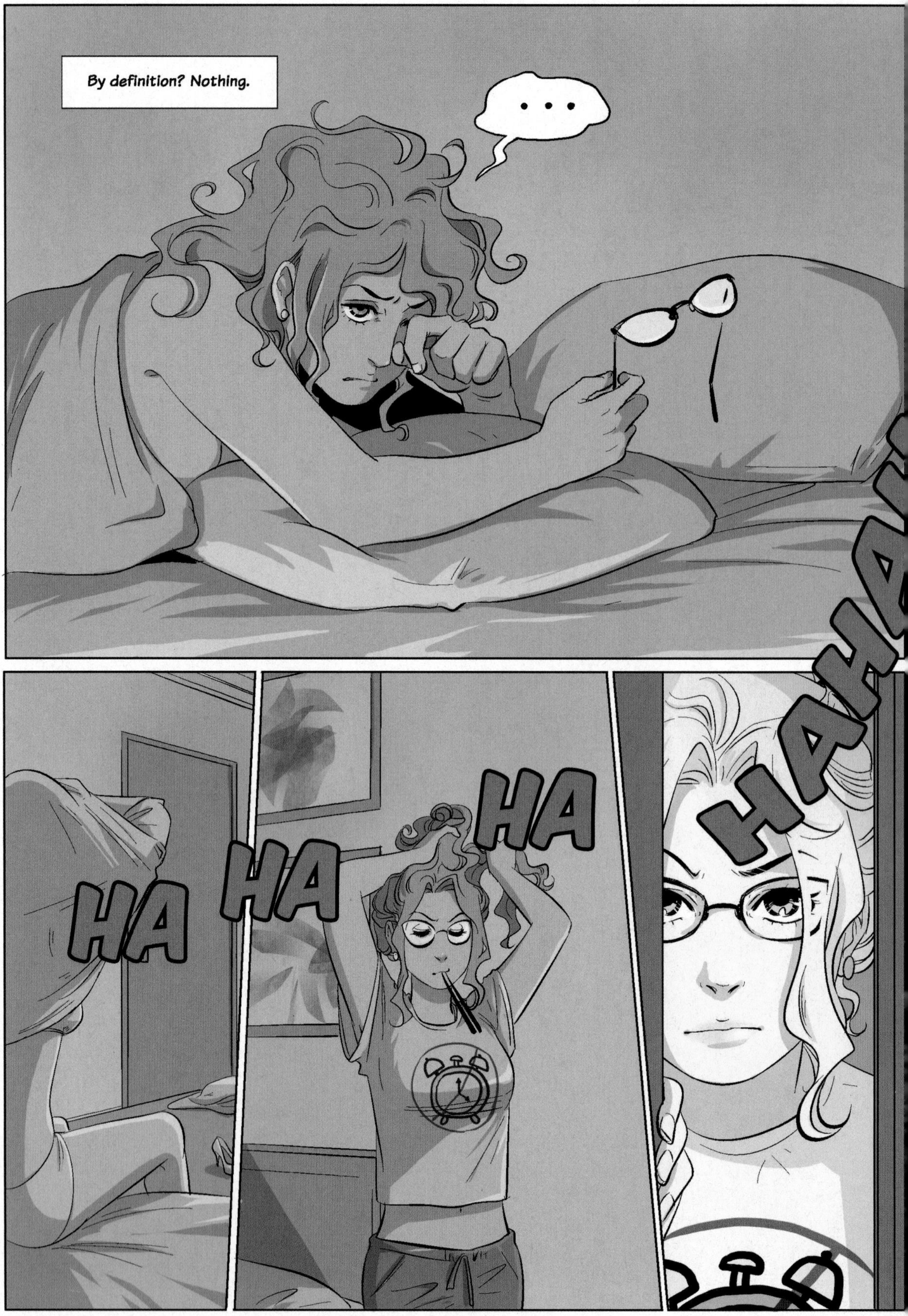
By definition? Nothing.
. . .
HA
HA
HA
HAHA

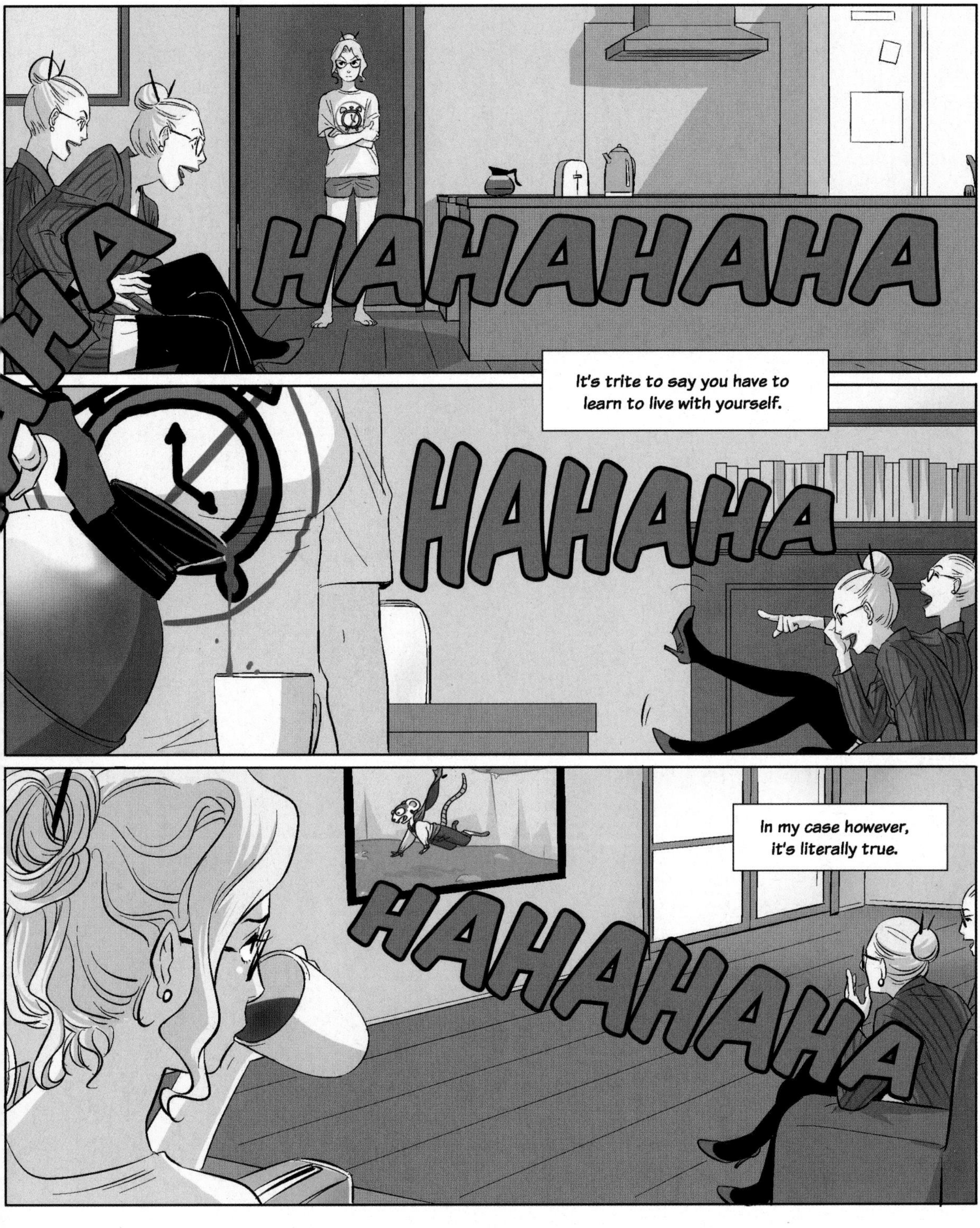
HAHAHAHA
It's trite to say you have to learn to live with yourself.
HAHAHA
In my case however, it's literally true.
HAHAHAHA

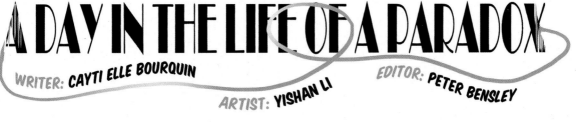

A DAY IN THE LIFE OF A PARADOX

WRITER: CAYTI ELLE BOURQUIN
ARTIST: YISHAN LI
EDITOR: PETER BENSLEY

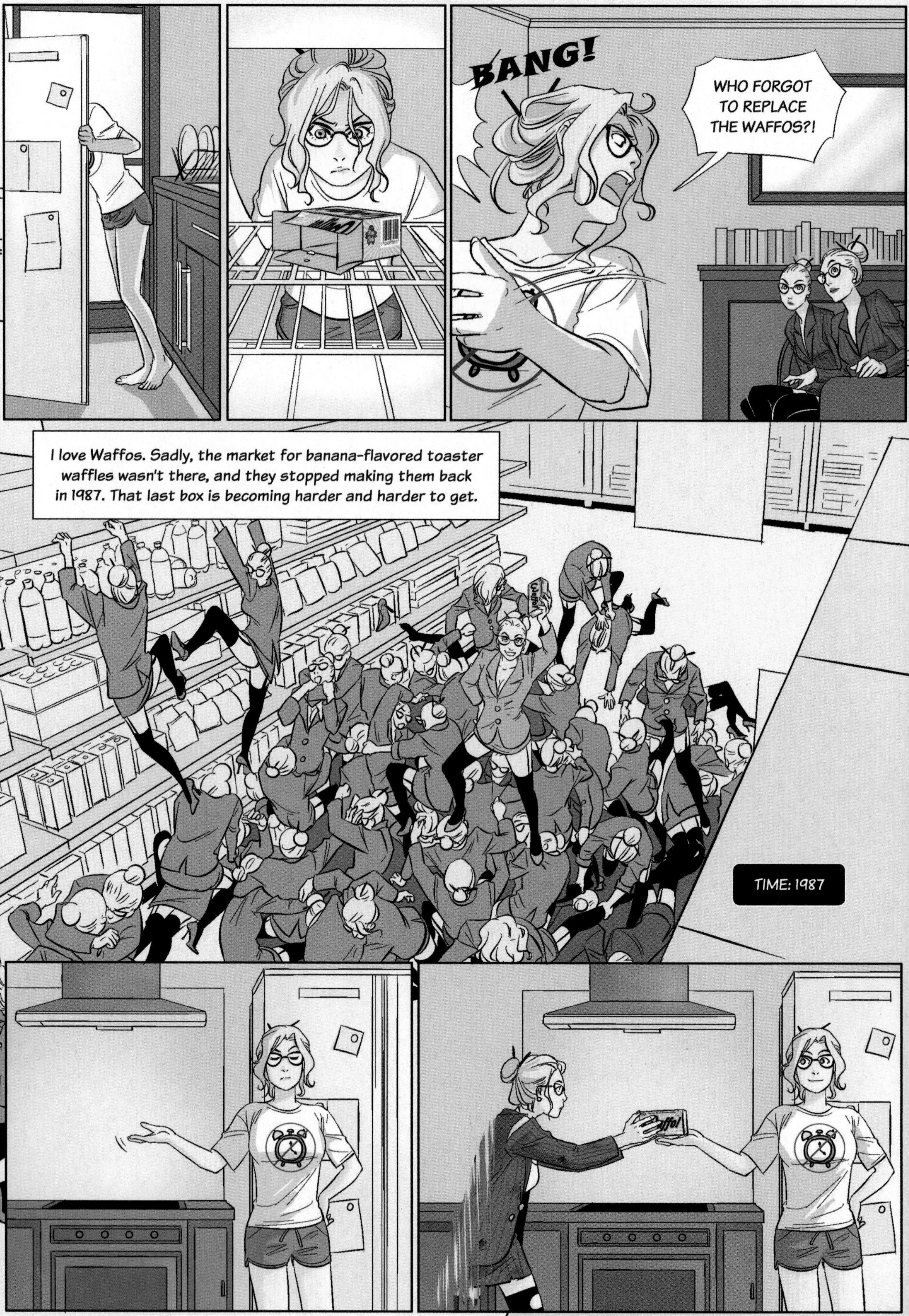
BANG!
WHO FORGOT TO REPLACE THE WAFFOS?!
I love Waffos. Sadly, the market for banana-flavored toaster waffles wasn't there, and they stopped making them back in 1987. That last box is becoming harder and harder to get.
TIME: 1987

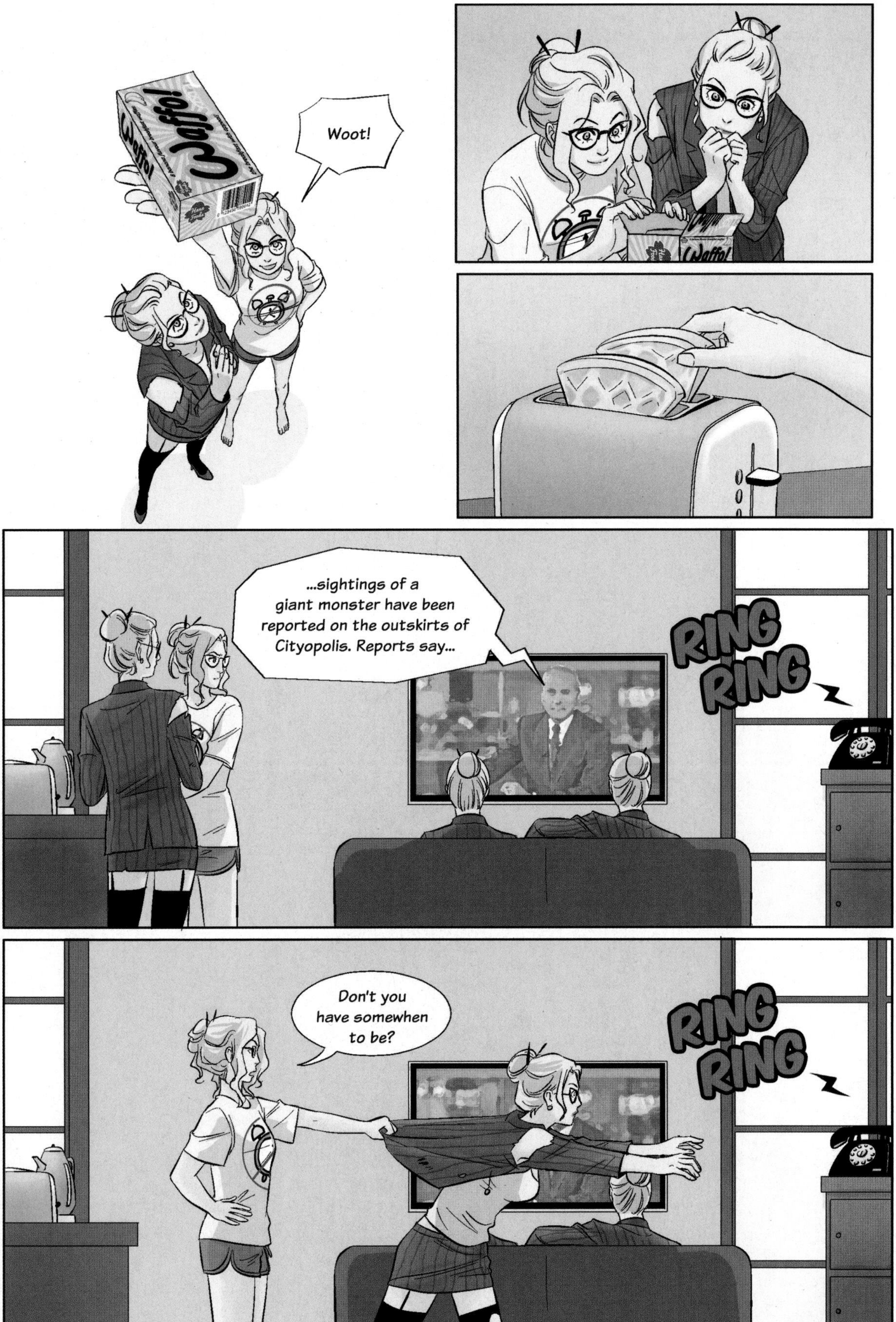
Waffo!
Woot!
...sightings of a giant monster have been reported on the outskirts of Cityopolis. Reports say...
RING RING
Don't you have somewhen to be?
RING RING

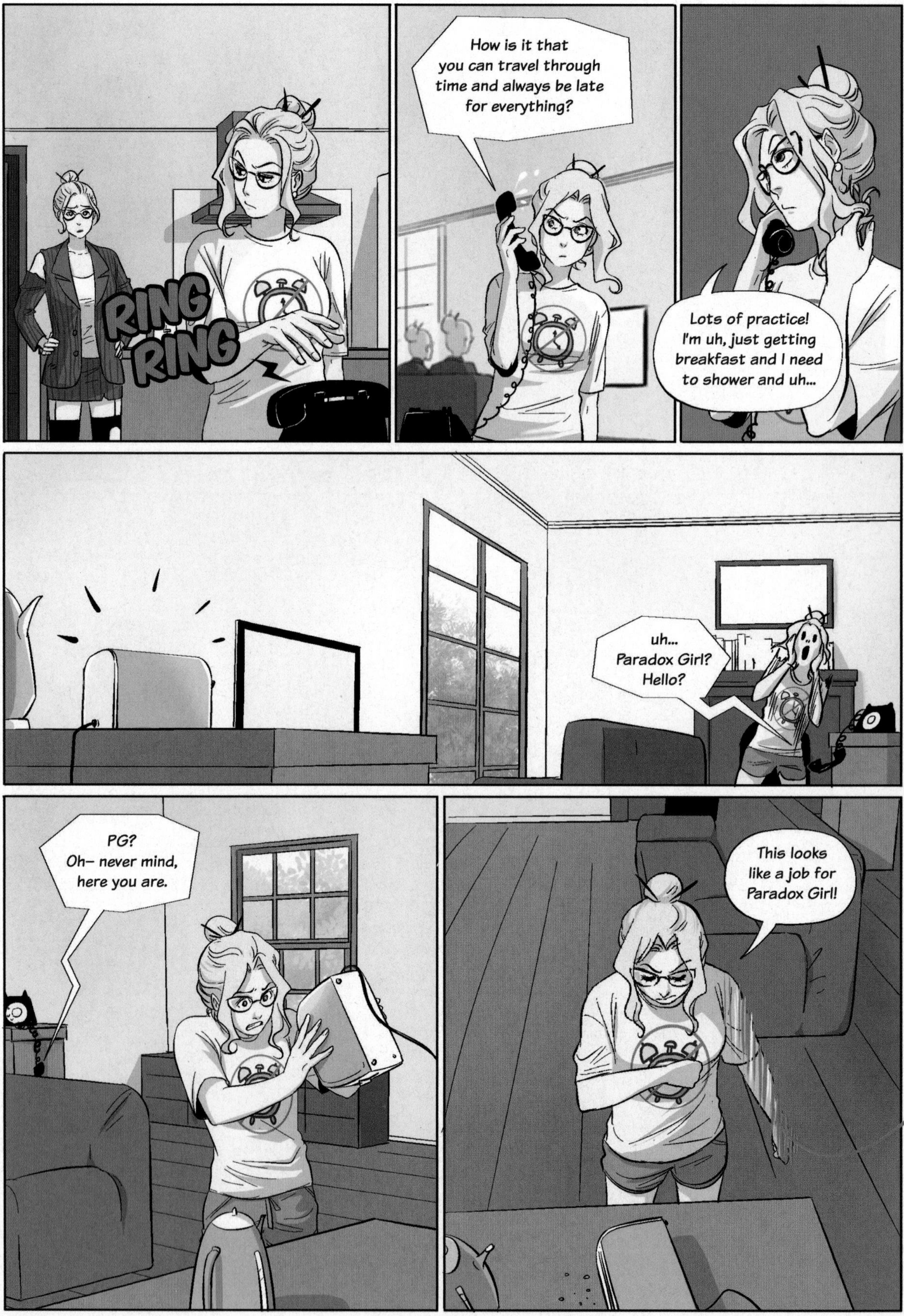
RING RING
How is it that you can travel through time and always be late for everything?
Lots of practice! I'm uh, just getting breakfast and I need to shower and uh...
uh... Paradox Girl? Hello?
PG? Oh– never mind, here you are.
This looks like a job for Paradox Girl!

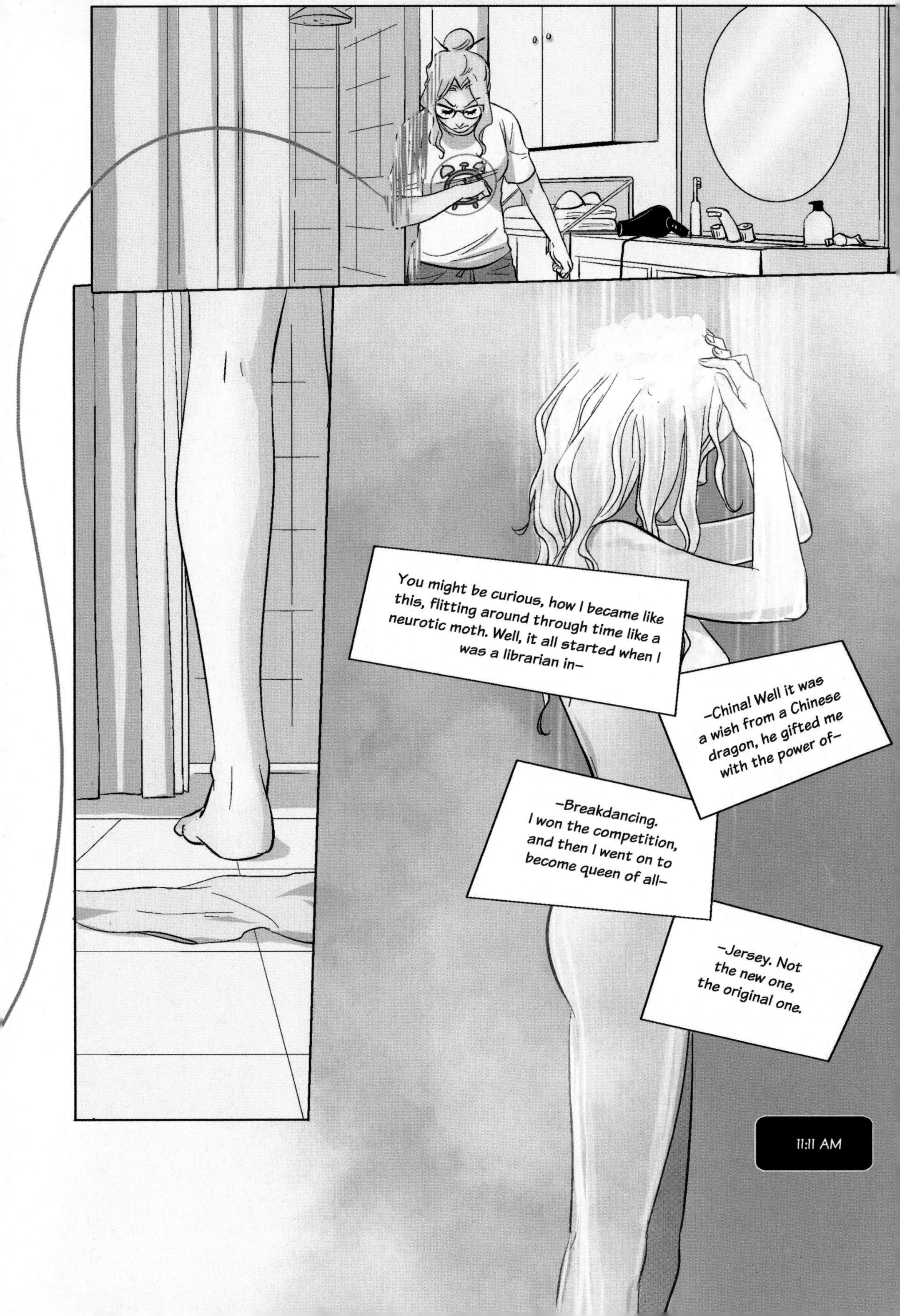
You might be curious, how I became like this, flitting around through time like a neurotic moth. Well, it all started when I was a librarian in–
–China! Well it was a wish from a Chinese dragon, he gifted me with the power of–
–Breakdancing. I won the competition, and then I went on to become queen of all–
–Jersey. Not the new one, the original one.
11:11 AM

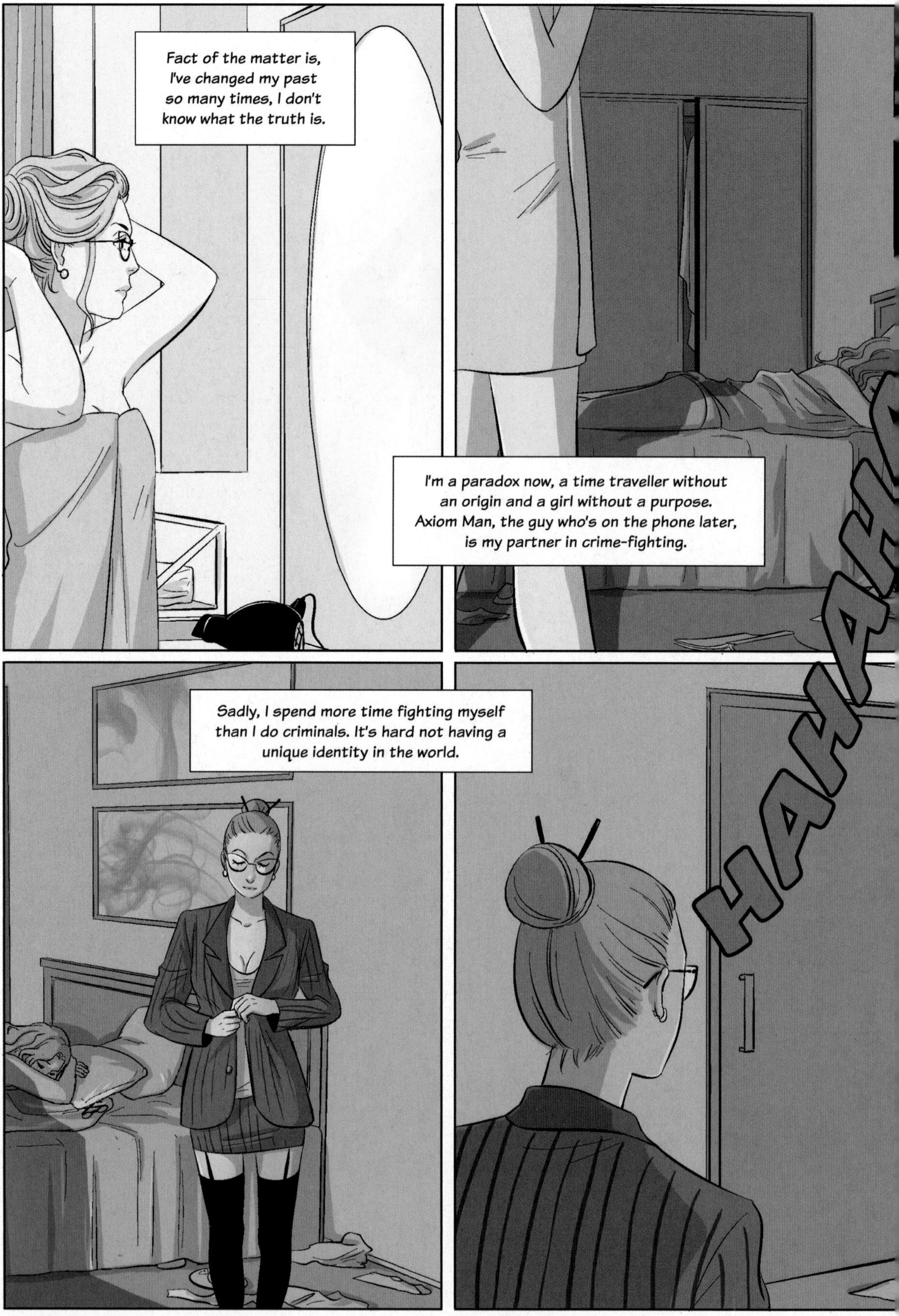
Fact of the matter is, I've changed my past so many times, I don't know what the truth is.
I'm a paradox now, a time traveller without an origin and a girl without a purpose. Axiom Man, the guy who's on the phone later, is my partner in crime-fighting.
Sadly, I spend more time fighting myself than I do criminals. It's hard not having a unique identity in the world.

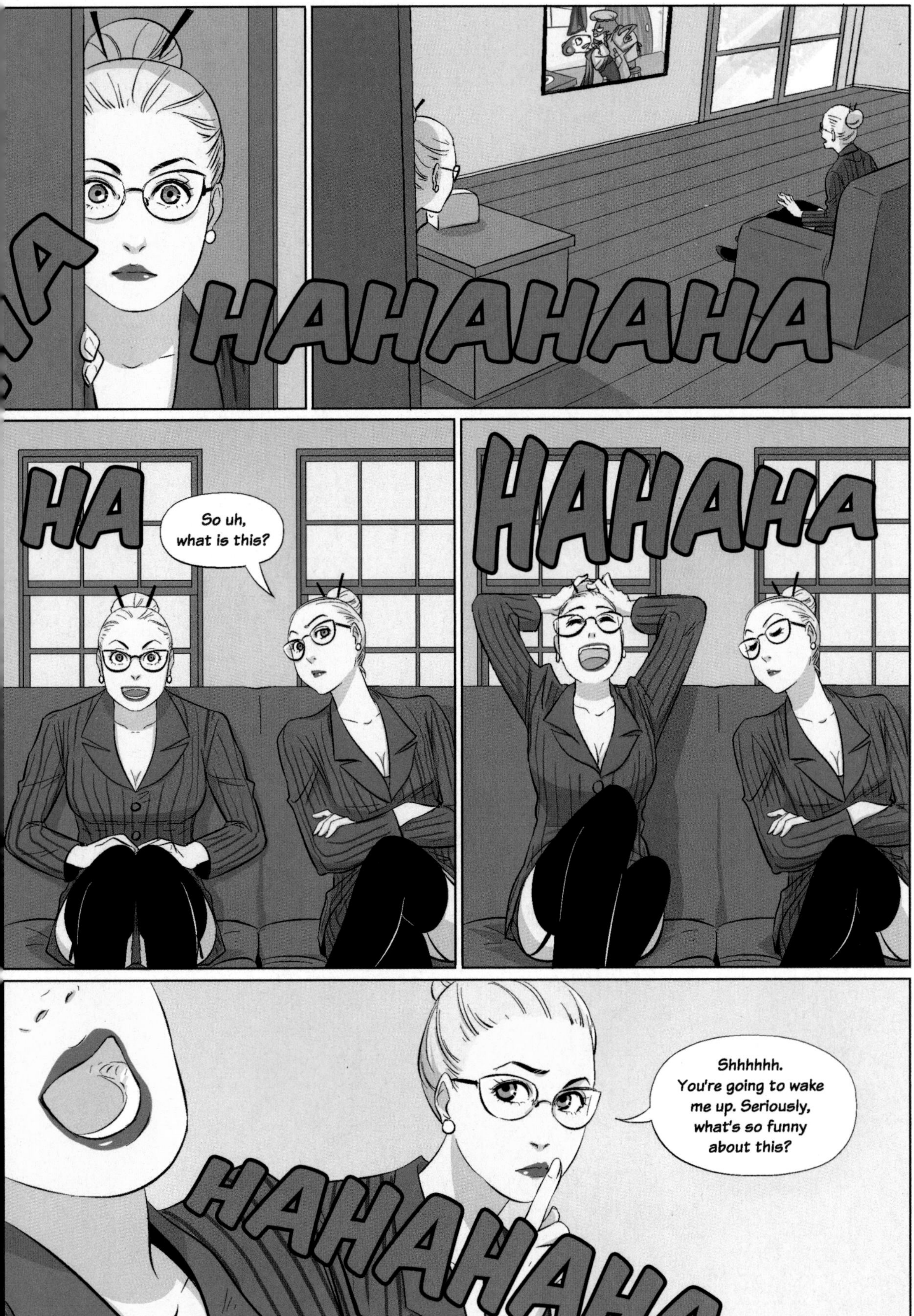
HA
HAHAHAHAHA
HA
So uh, what is this?
HAHAHA
Shhhhhh. You're going to wake me up. Seriously, what's so funny about this?
HAHAHAHAHA

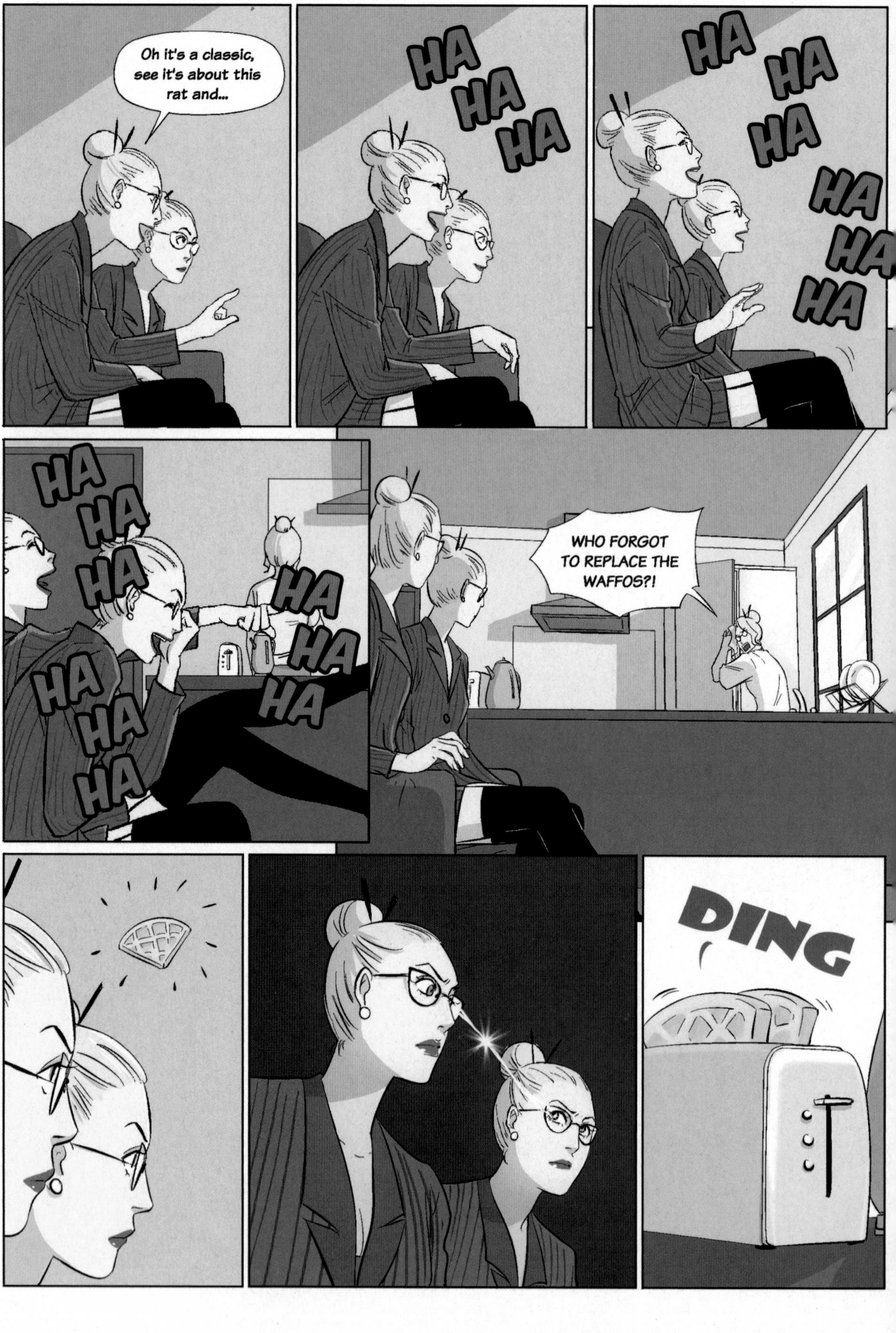

Oh it's a classic, see it's about this rat and...
HA HA HA
HA HA HA HA HA HA
HA HA HA
HA HA HA
HA HA HA
WHO FORGOT TO REPLACE THE WAFFOS?!
DING

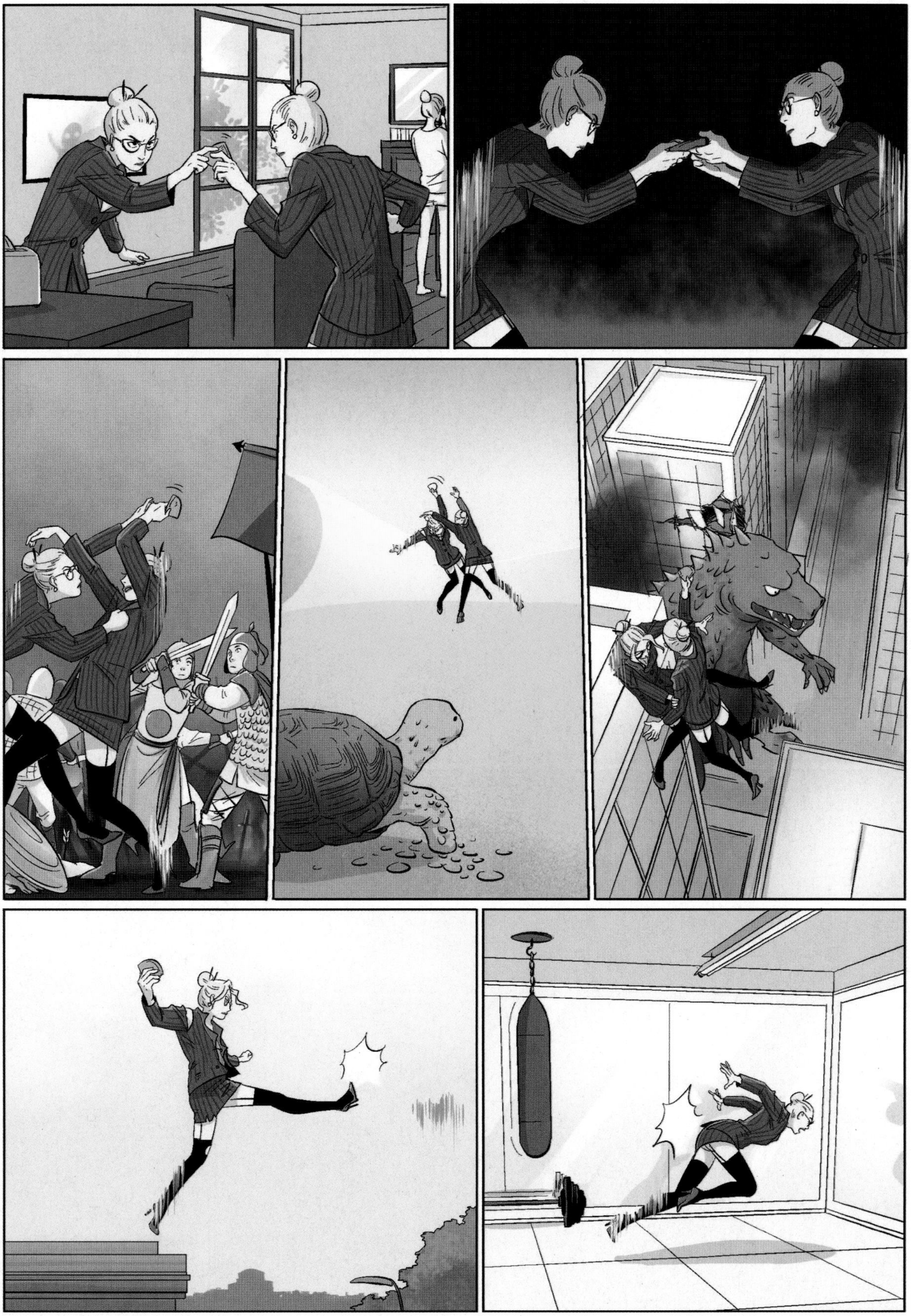

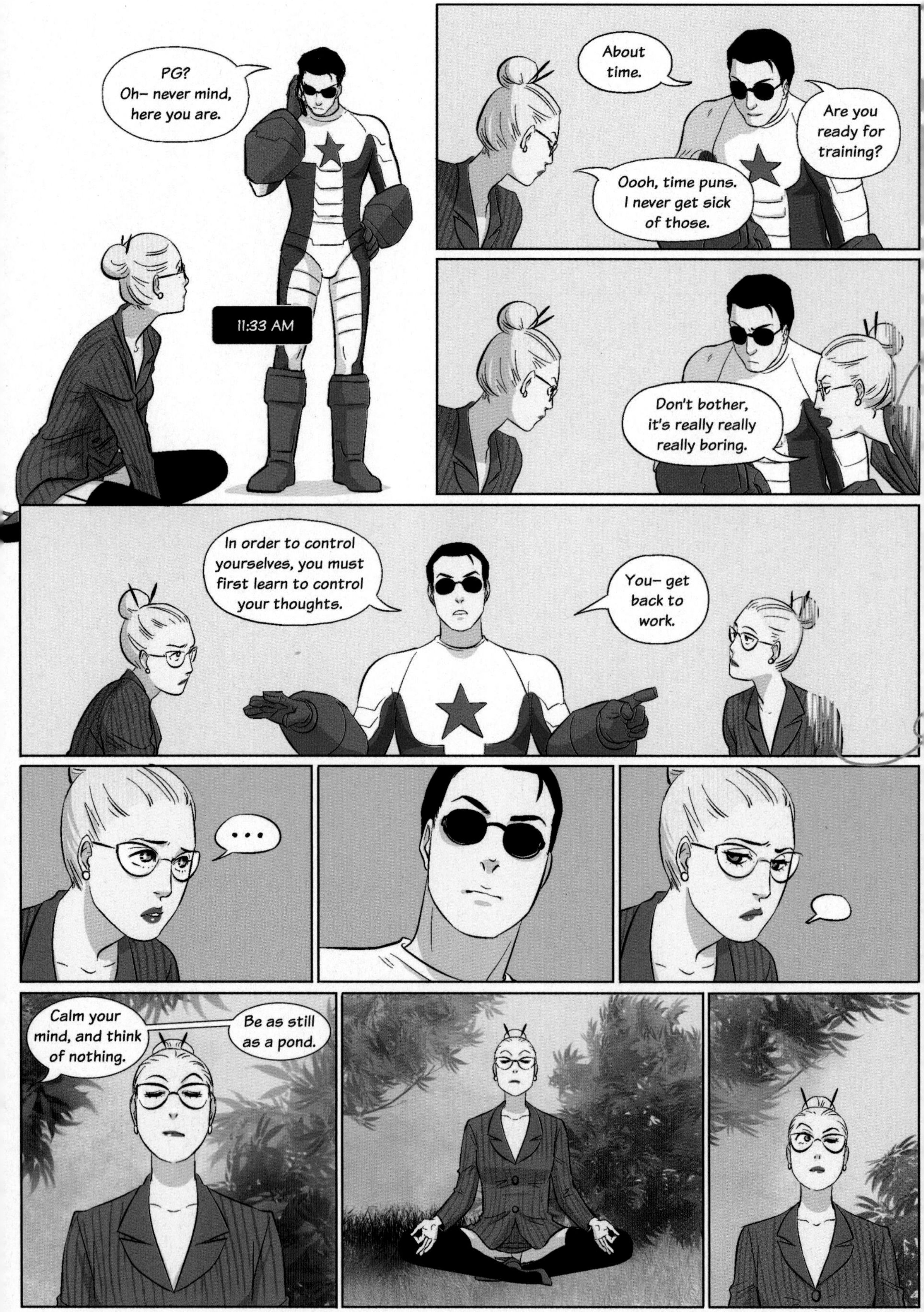
PG? Oh– never mind, here you are.
11:33 AM
About time.
Are you ready for training?
Oooh, time puns. I never get sick of those.
Don't bother, it's really really really boring.
In order to control yourselves, you must first learn to control your thoughts.
You– get back to work.
...
Calm your mind, and think of nothing.
Be as still as a pond.

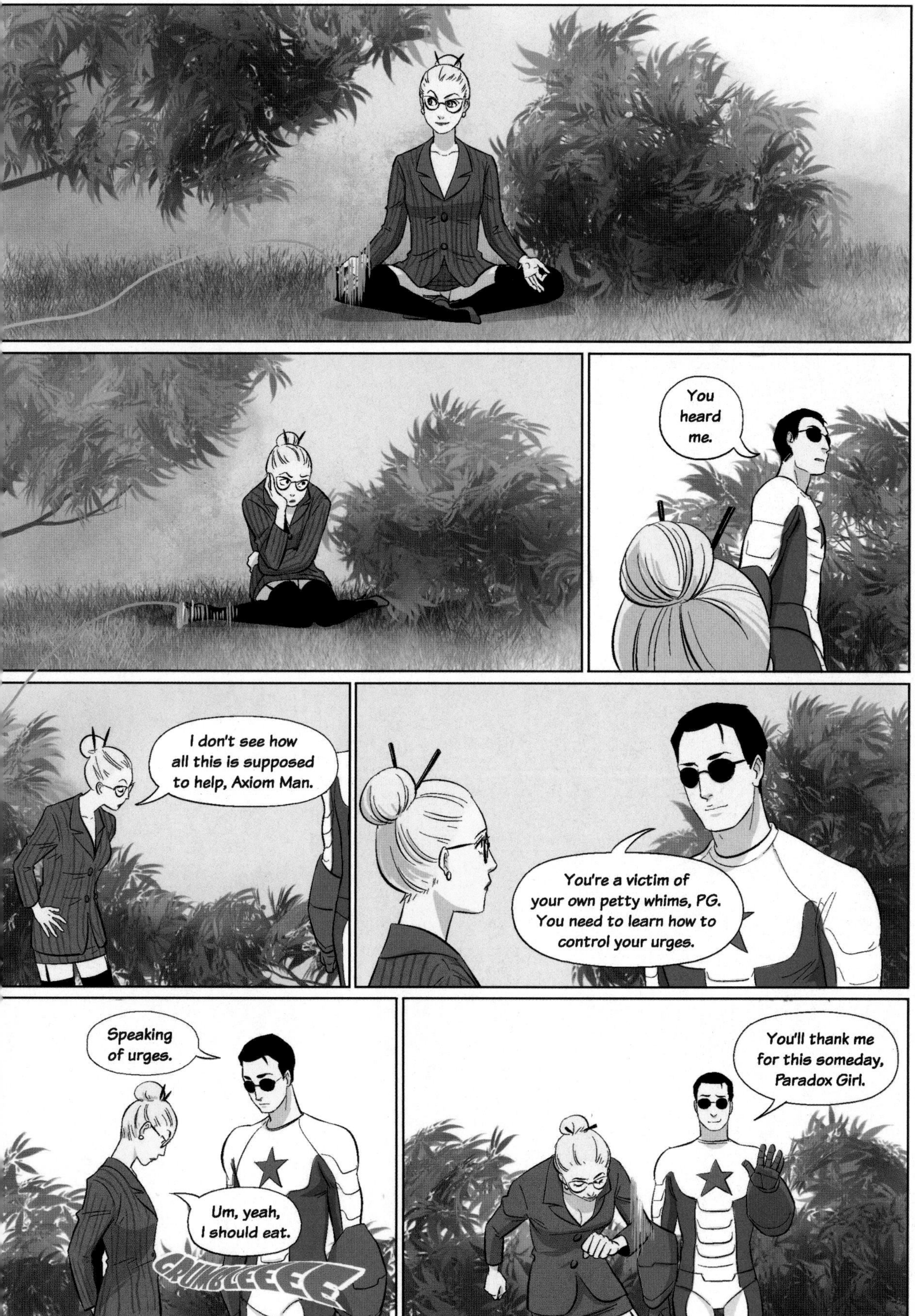
You heard me.
I don't see how all this is supposed to help, Axiom Man.
You're a victim of your own petty whims, PG. You need to learn how to control your urges.
Speaking of urges.
Um, yeah, I should eat.
GRUMBLEEEEE
You'll thank me for this someday, Paradox Girl.

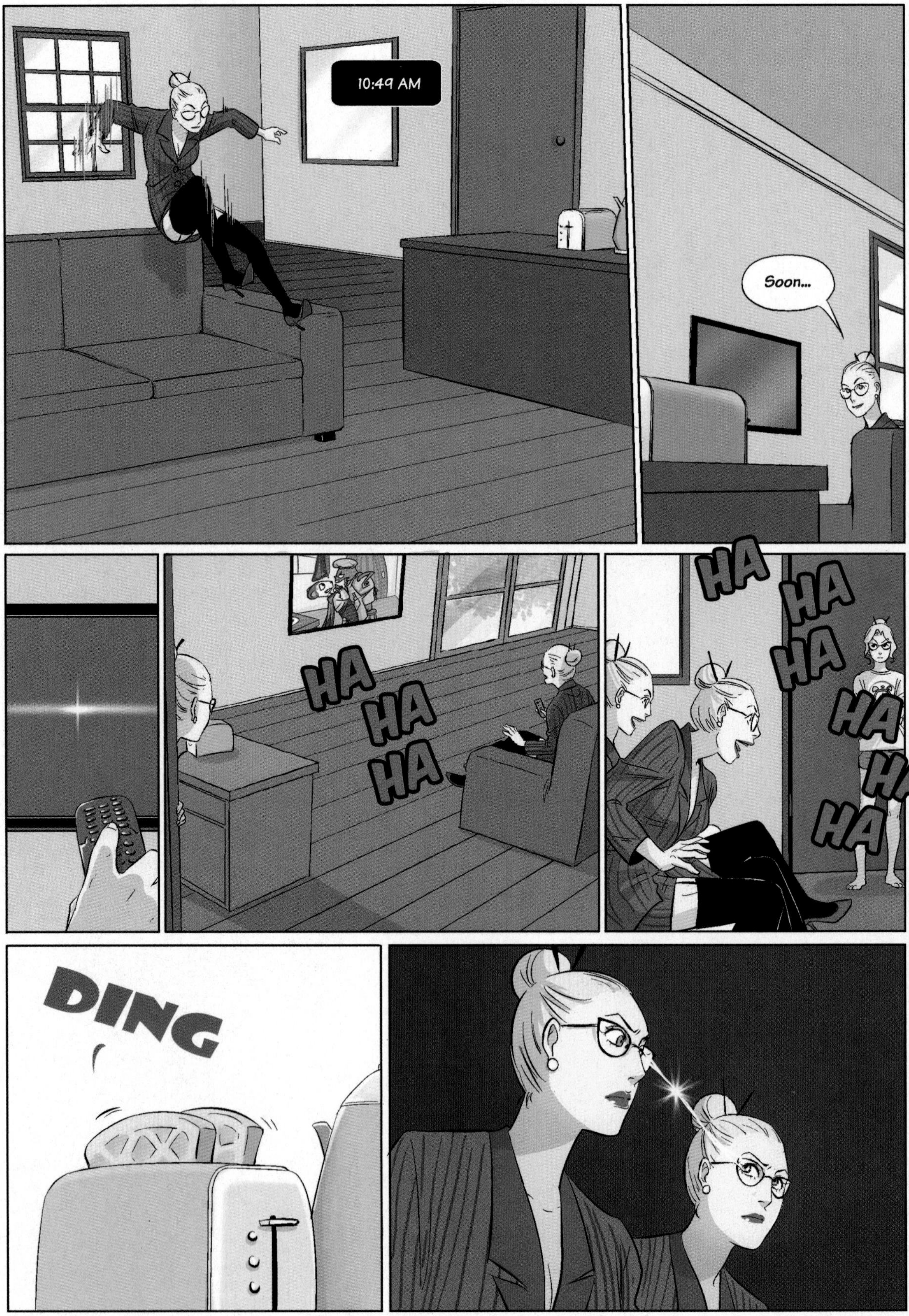
10:49 AM
Soon...
HA
HA
HA
HA
HA
HA
HA
HA
HA
DING

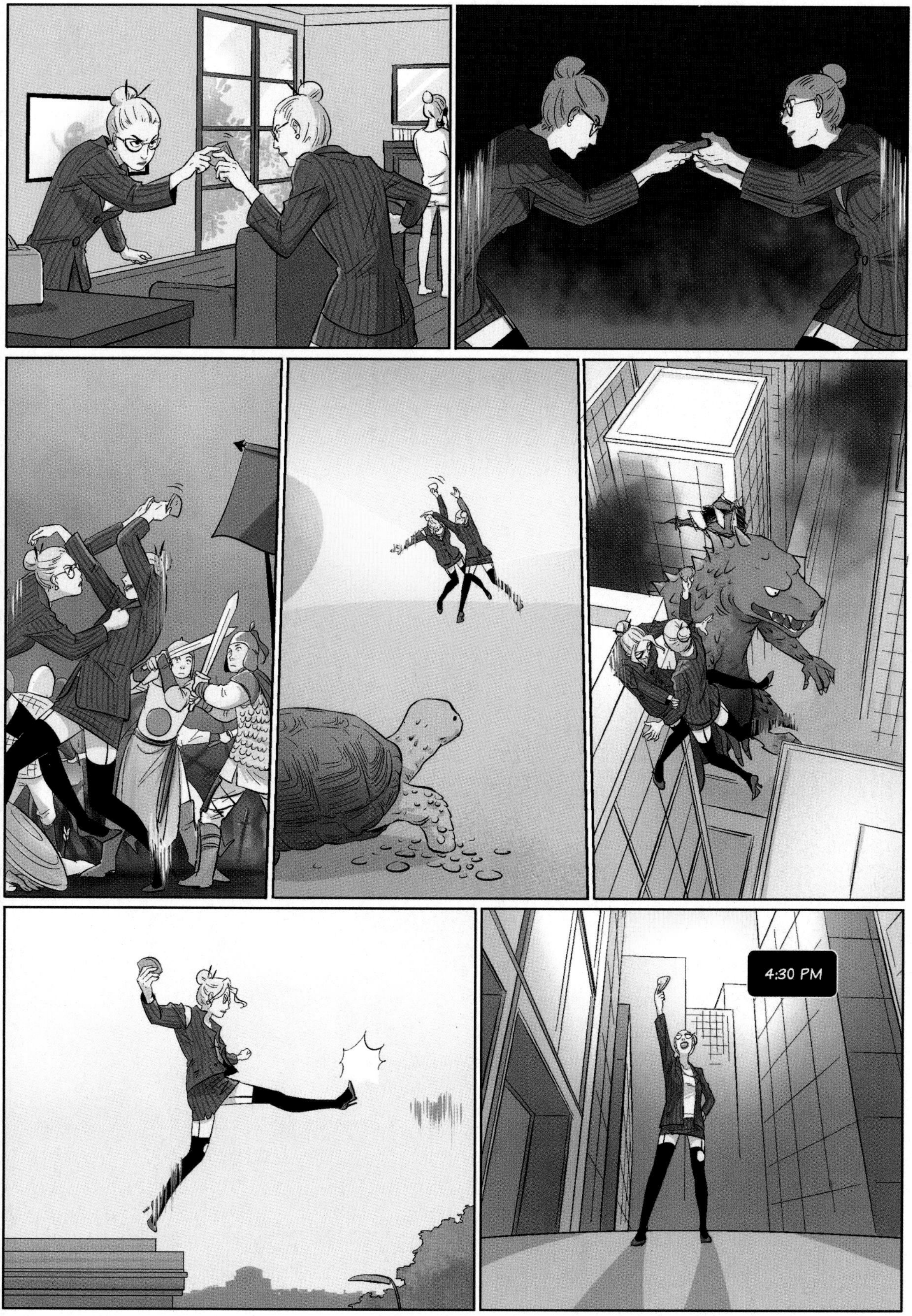
4:30 PM

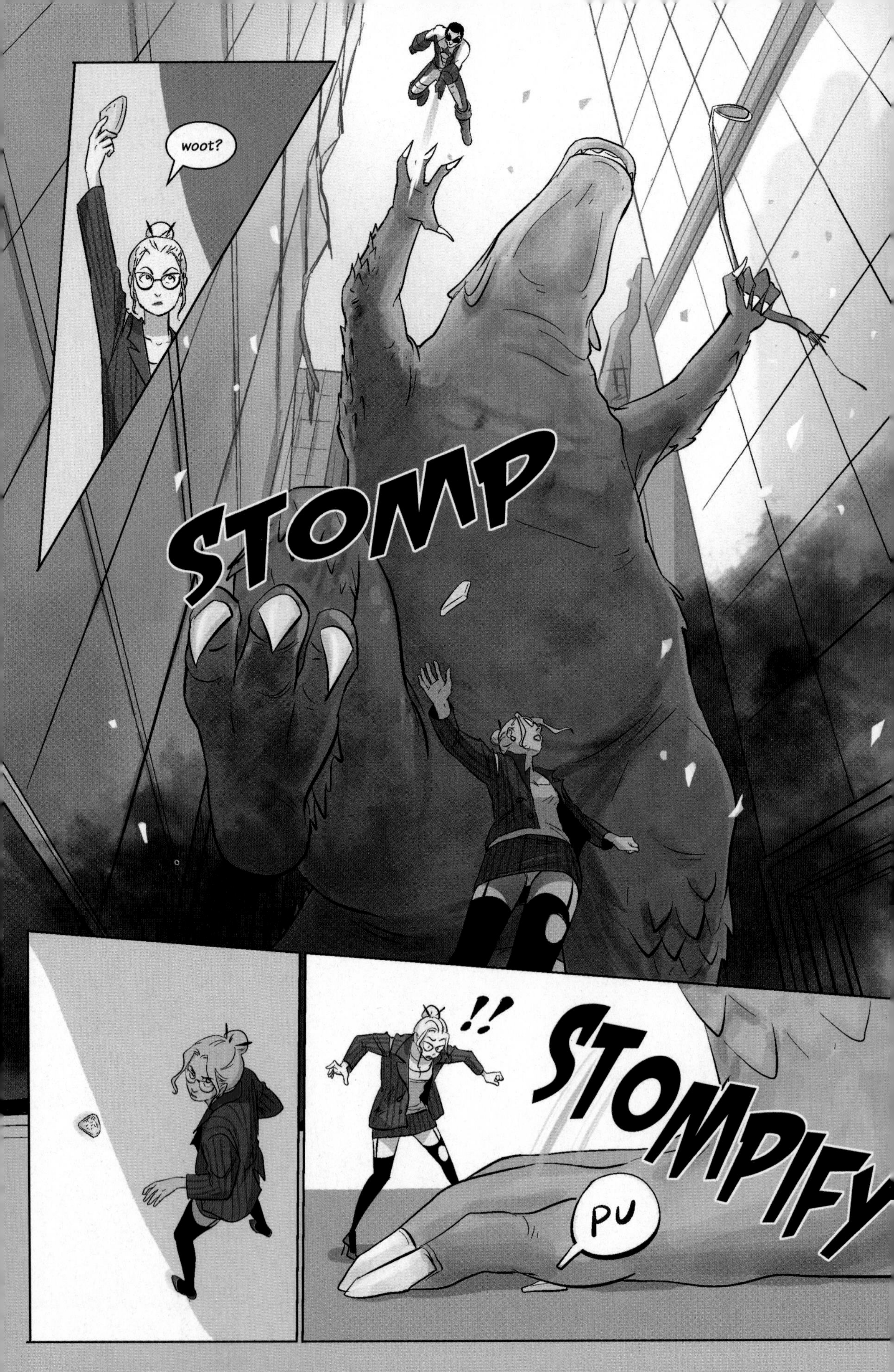
woot?
STOMP
!!
STOMPIFY
PU

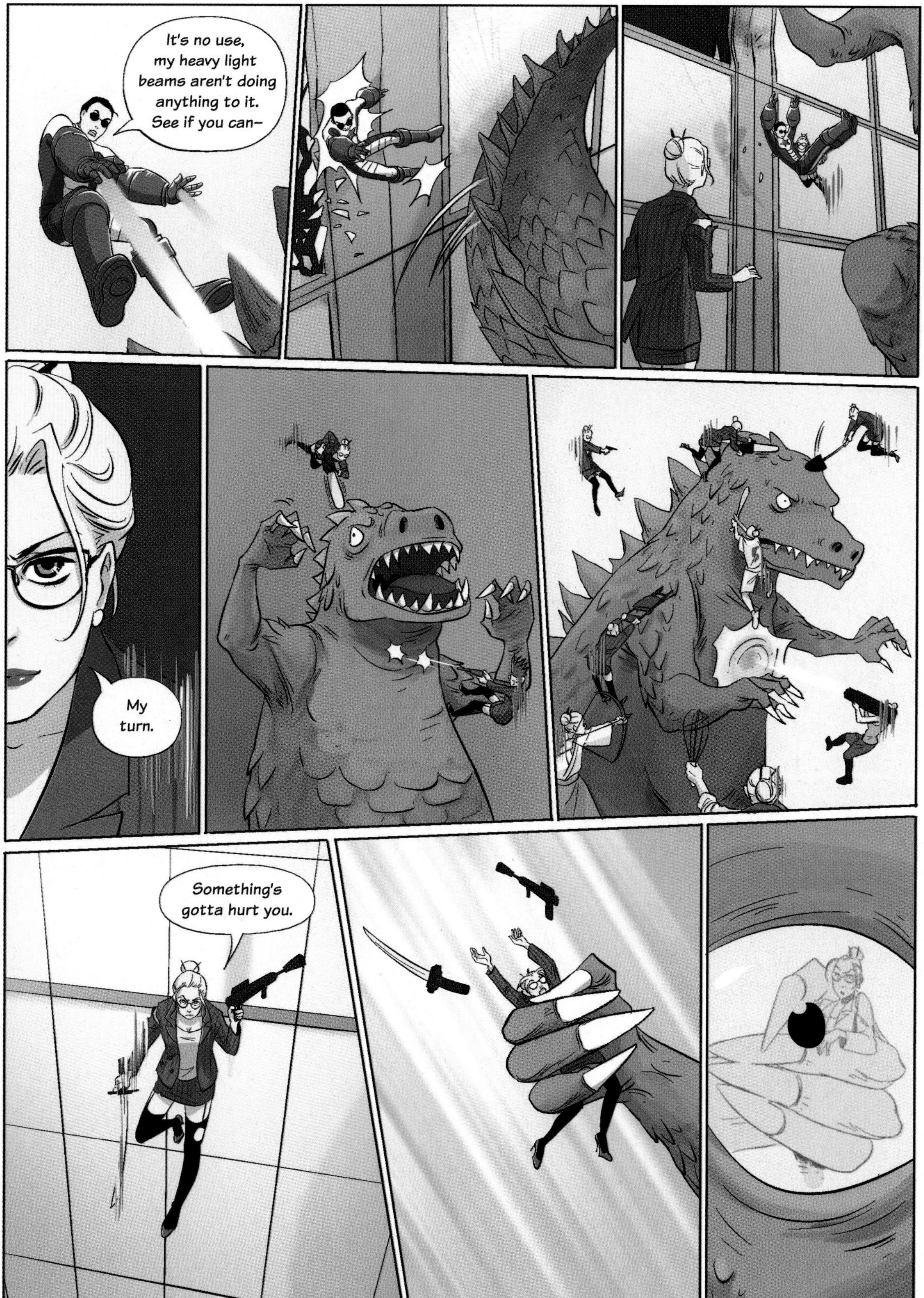
It's no use, my heavy light beams aren't doing anything to it. See if you can–
My turn.
Something's gotta hurt you.

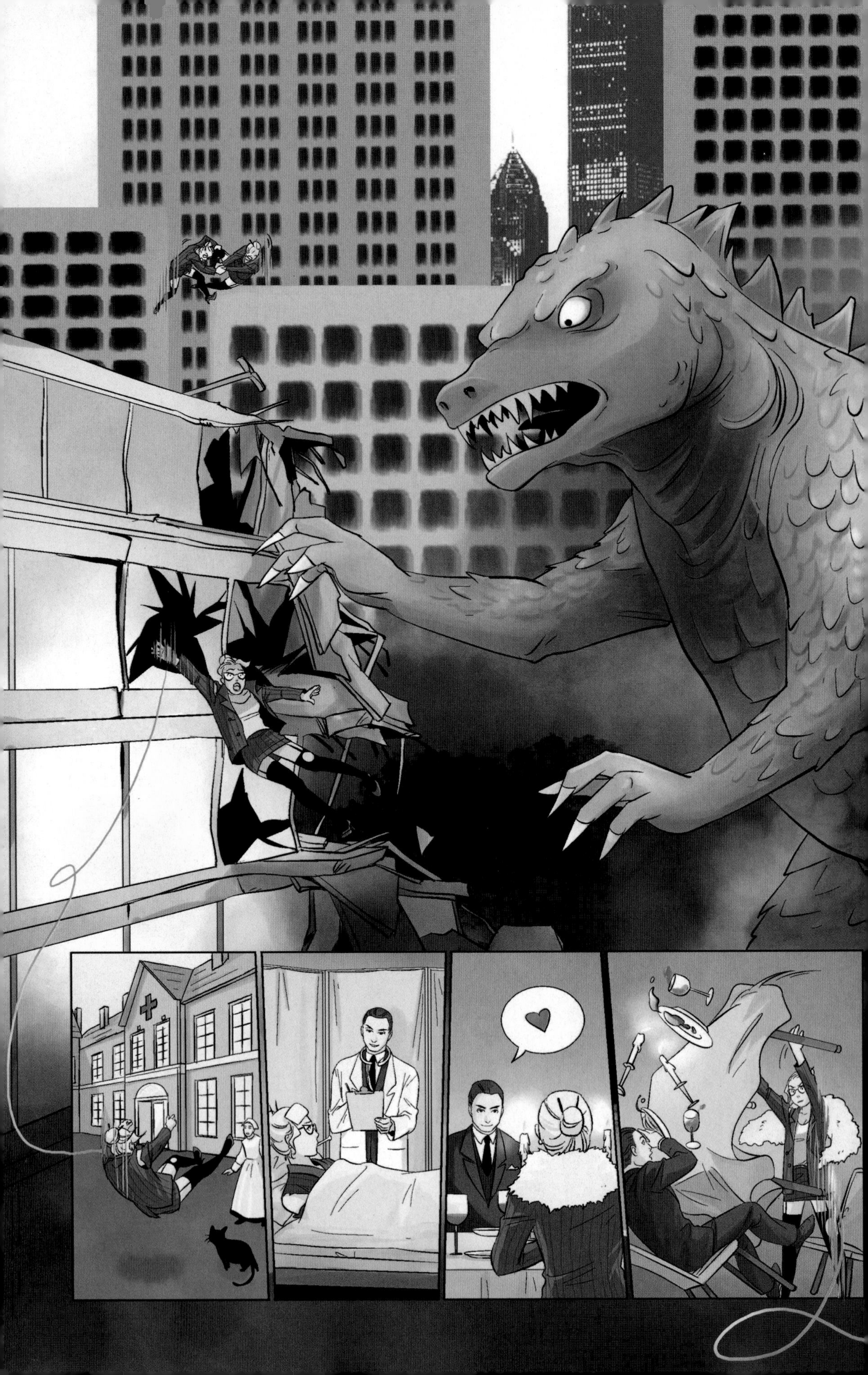

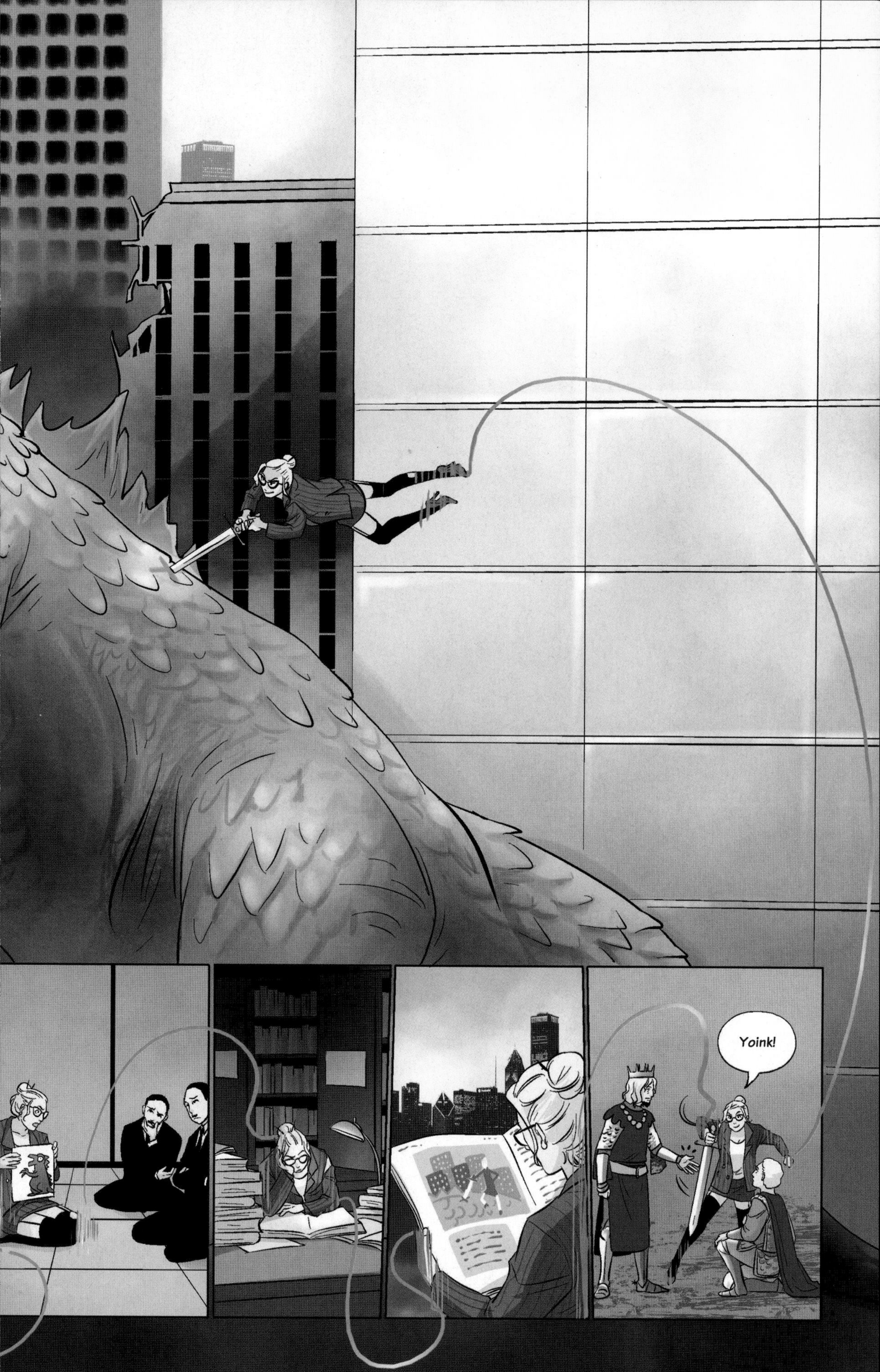
Yoink!

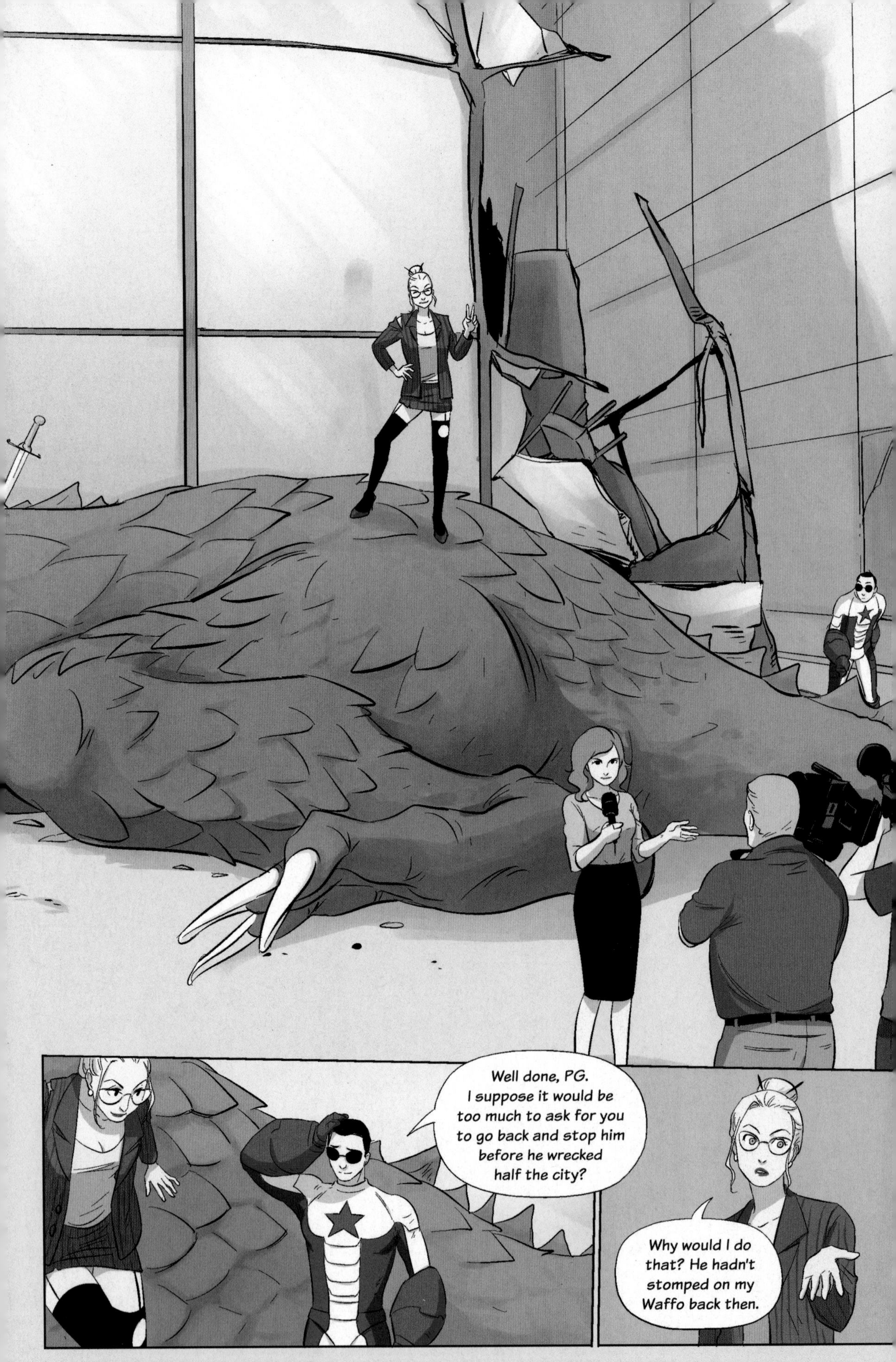

Well done, PG. I suppose it would be too much to ask for you to go back and stop him before he wrecked half the city?
Why would I do that? He hadn't stomped on my Waffo back then.

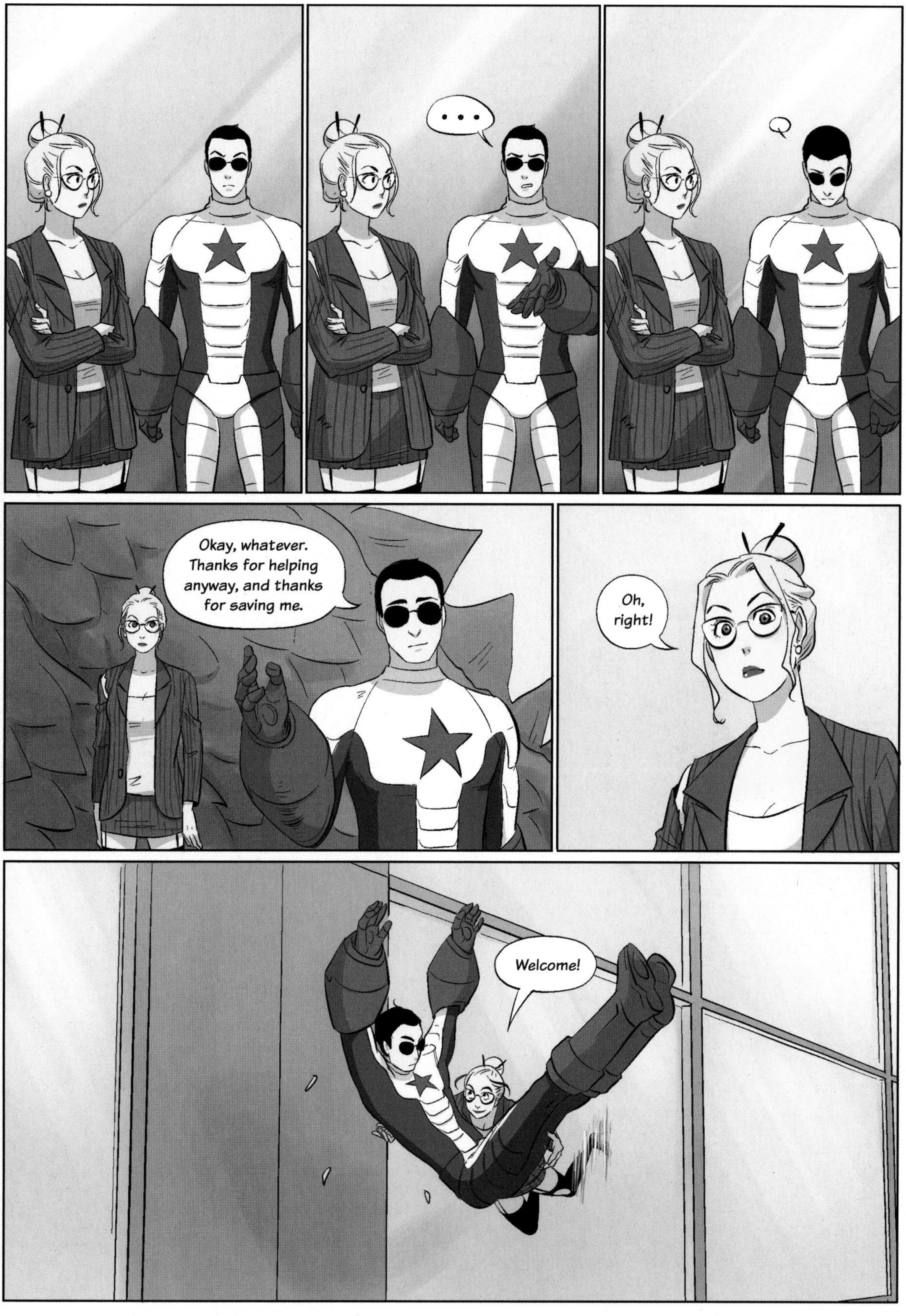
...
Okay, whatever. Thanks for helping anyway, and thanks for saving me.
Oh, right!
Welcome!

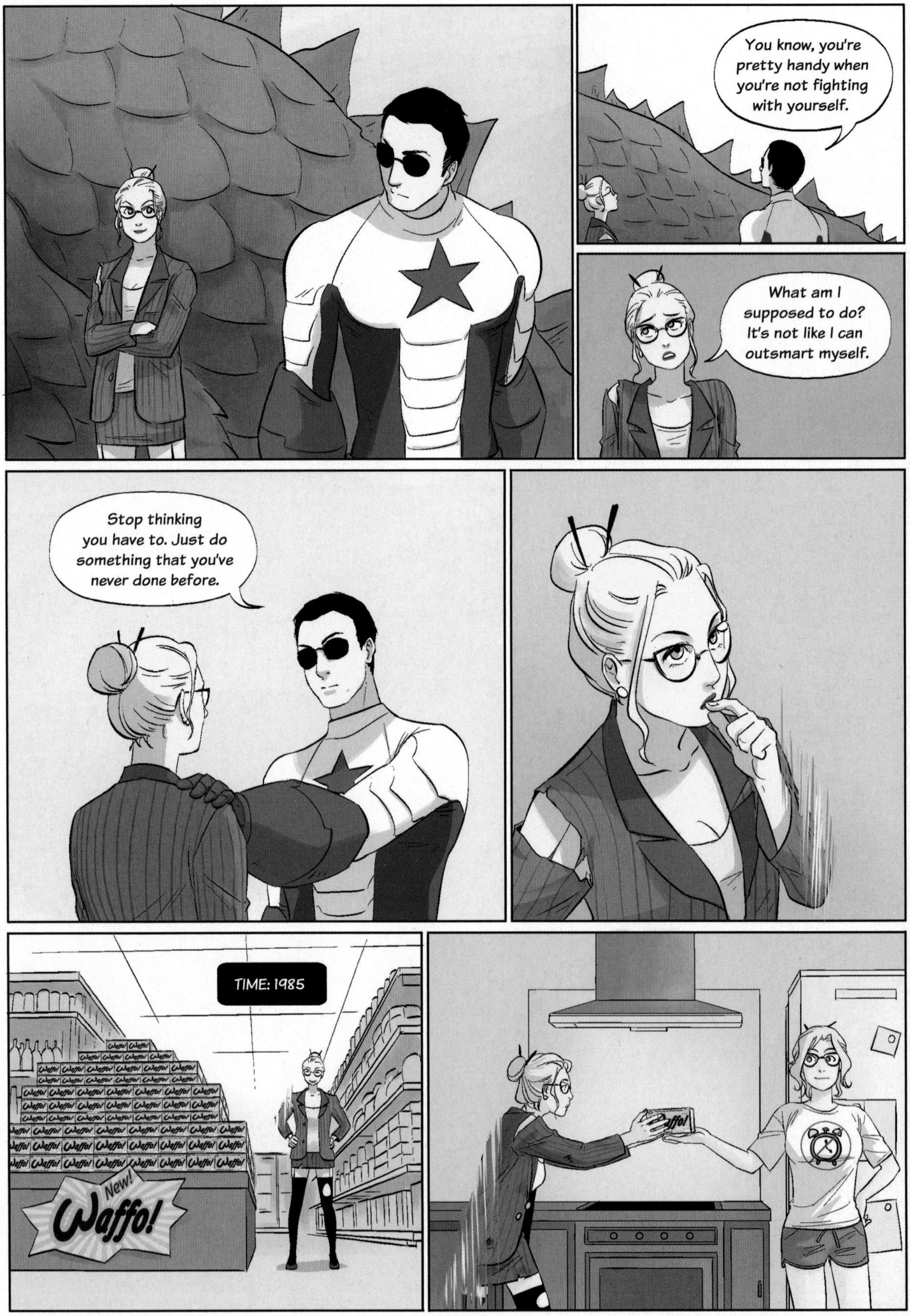
You know, you're pretty handy when you're not fighting with yourself.
What am I supposed to do? It's not like I can outsmart myself.
Stop thinking you have to. Just do something that you've never done before.
TIME: 1985
New!
Waffo!

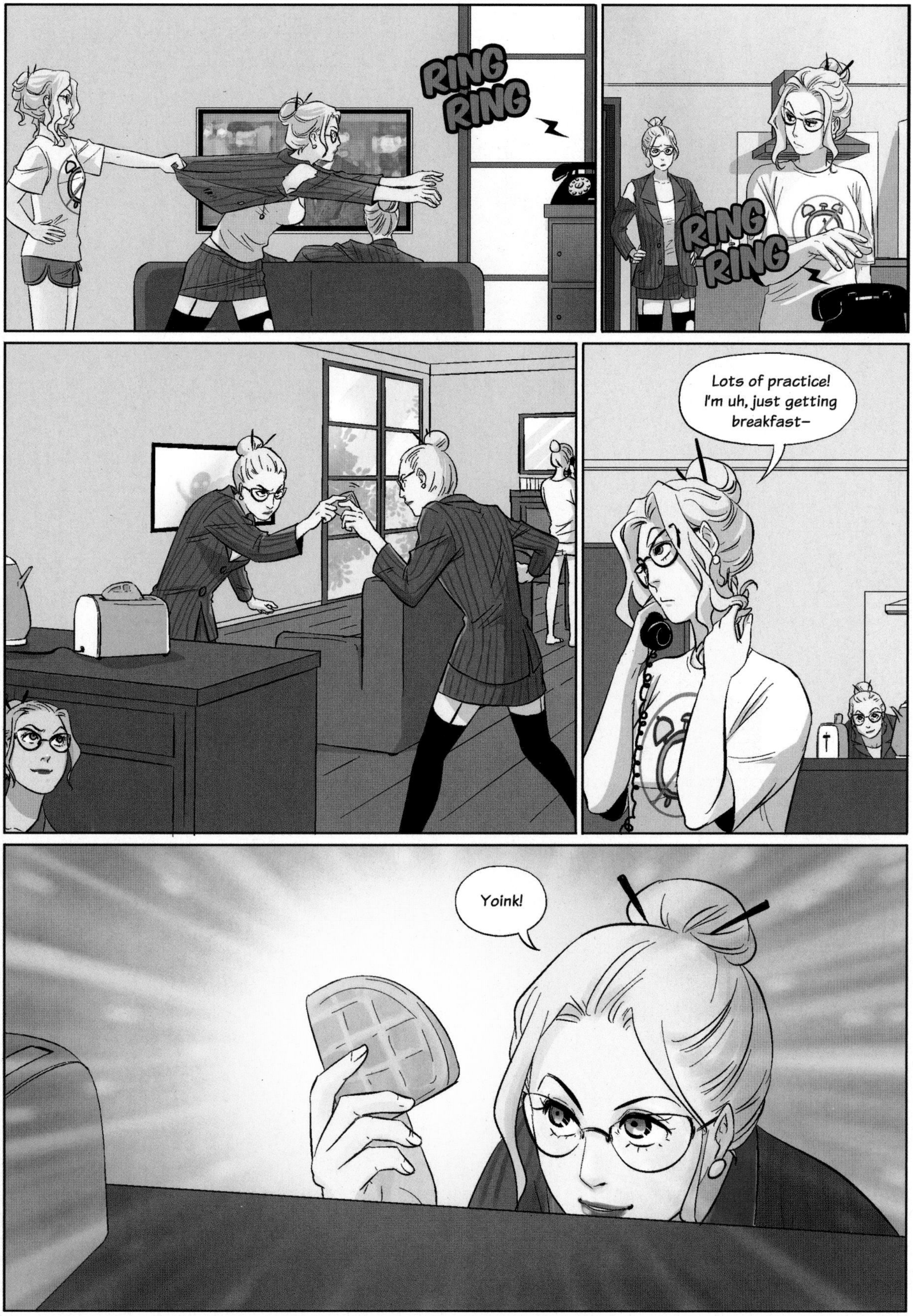
RING RING
RING RING
Lots of practice! I'm uh, just getting breakfast–
Yoink!

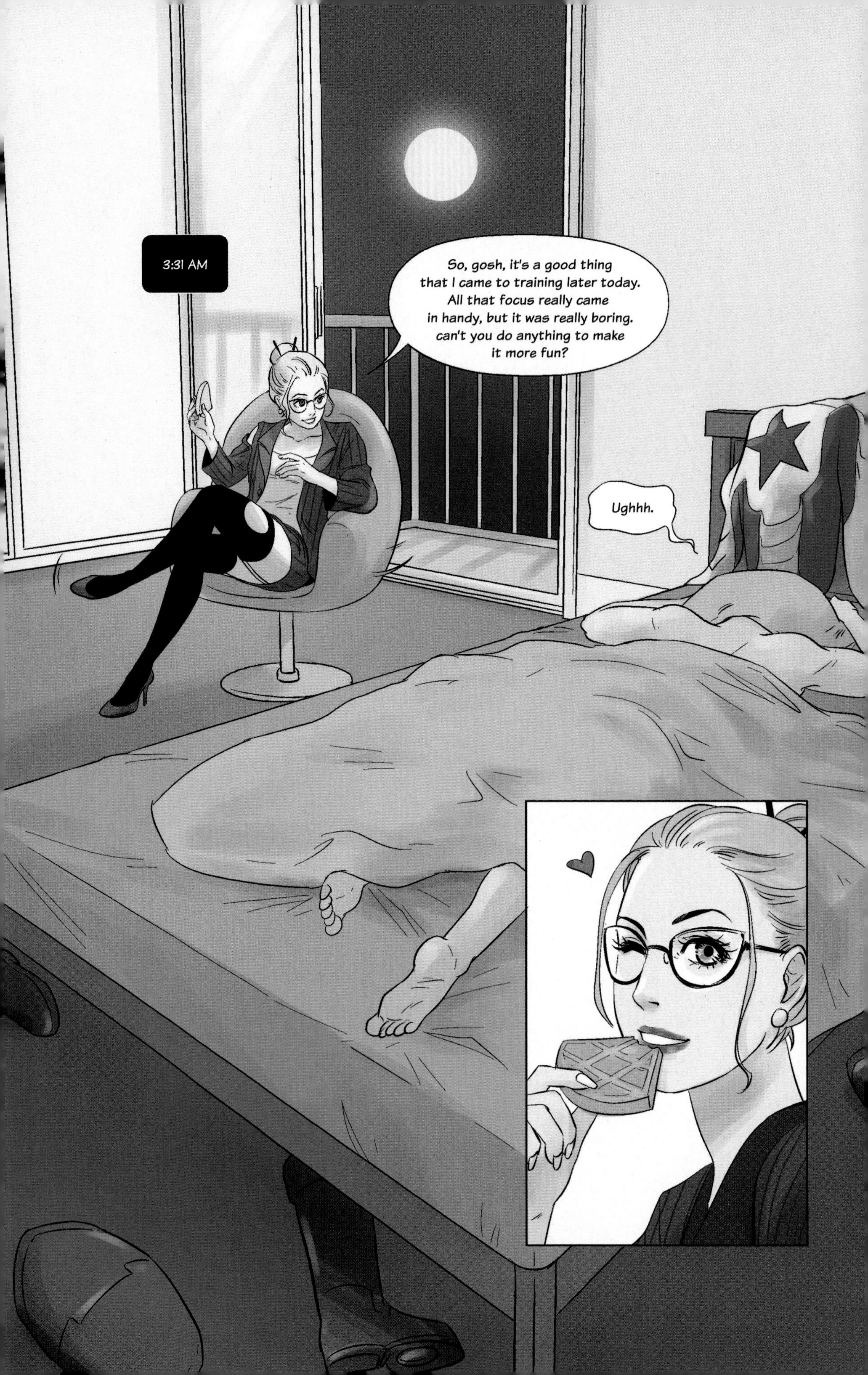
3:31 AM
So, gosh, it's a good thing that I came to training later today. All that focus really came in handy, but it was really boring. can't you do anything to make it more fun?
Ughhh.

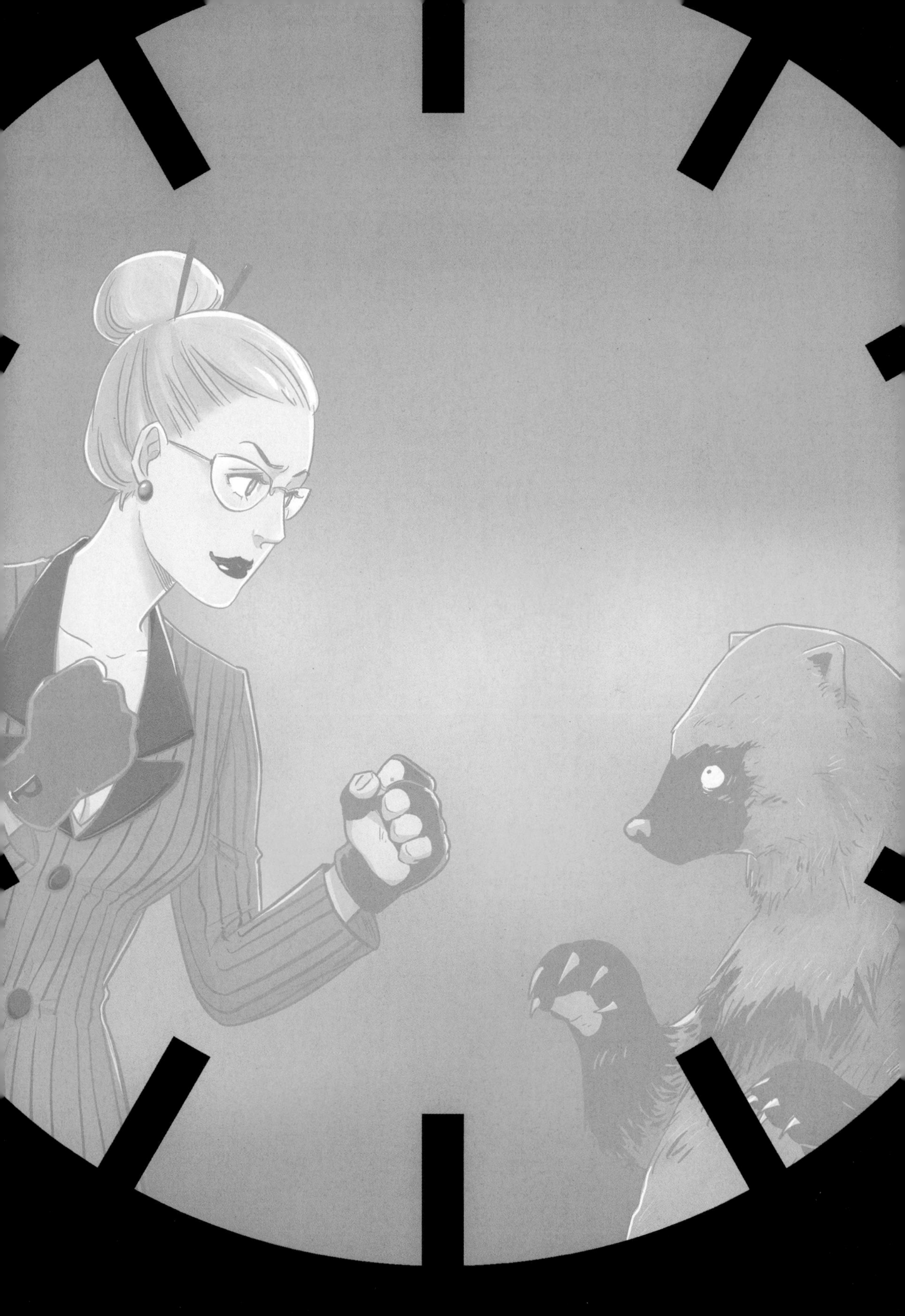

CHAPTER 2

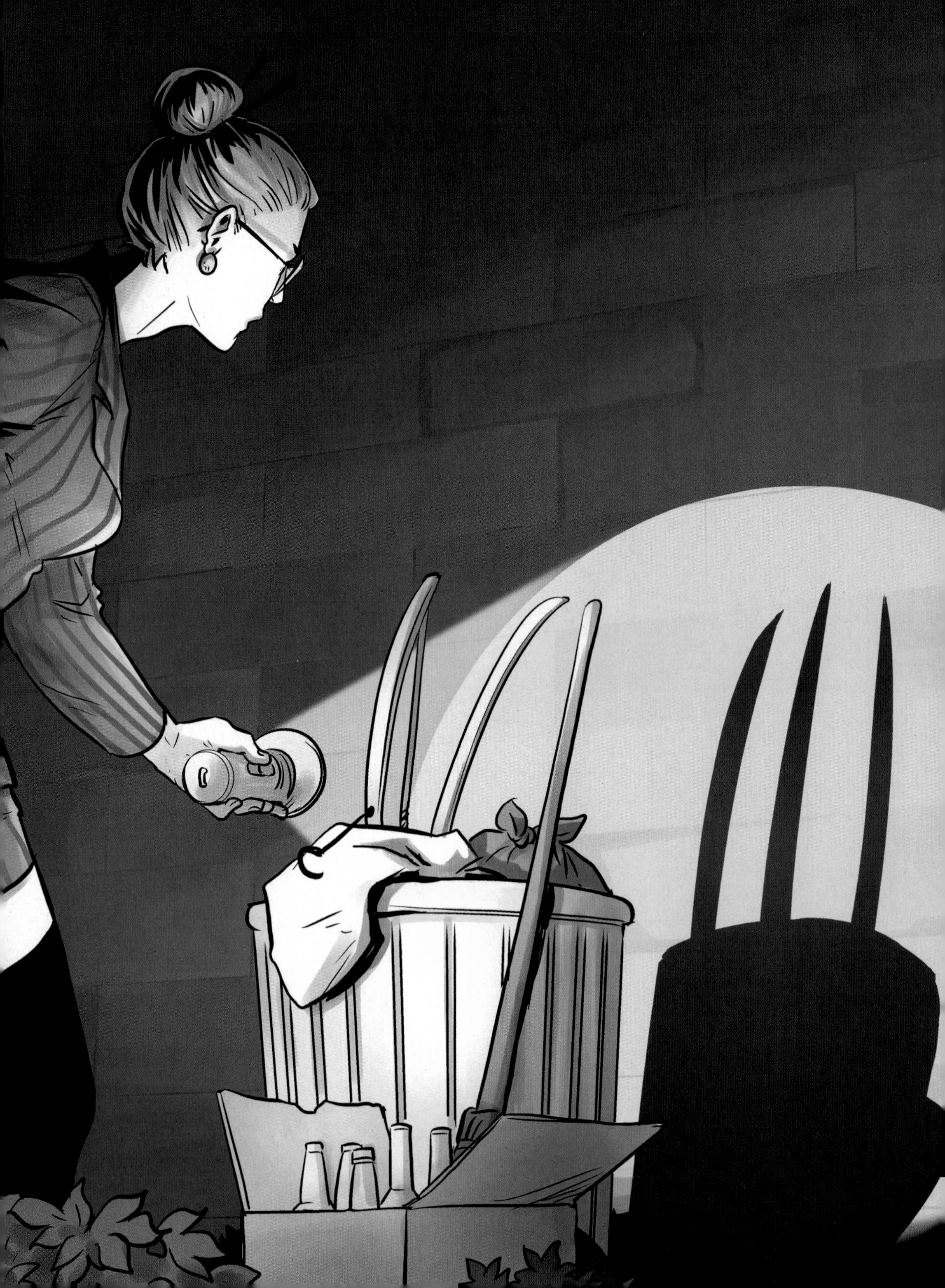

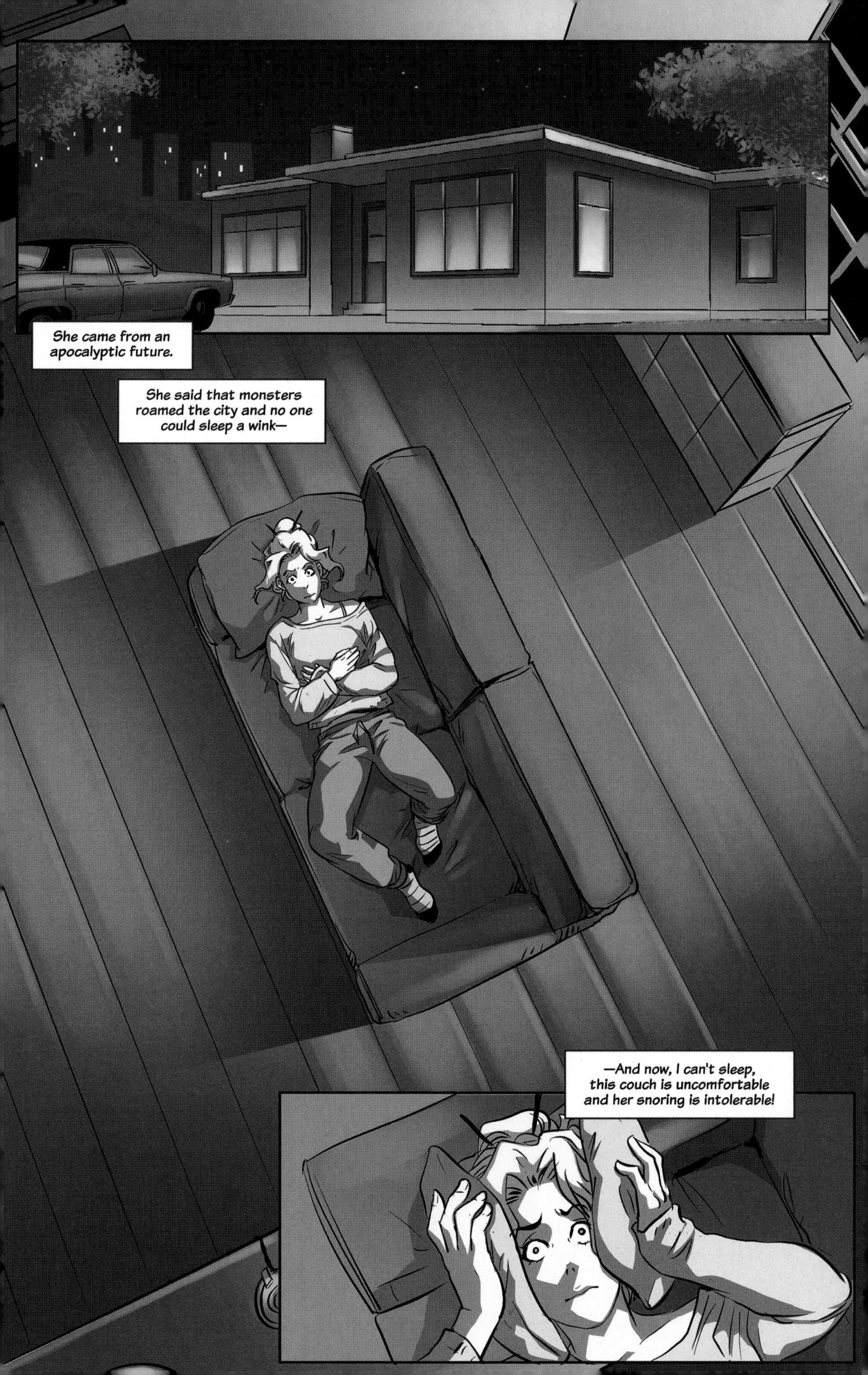
She came from an apocalyptic future.
She said that monsters roamed the city and no one could sleep a wink—
—And now, I can't sleep, this couch is uncomfortable and her snoring is intolerable!

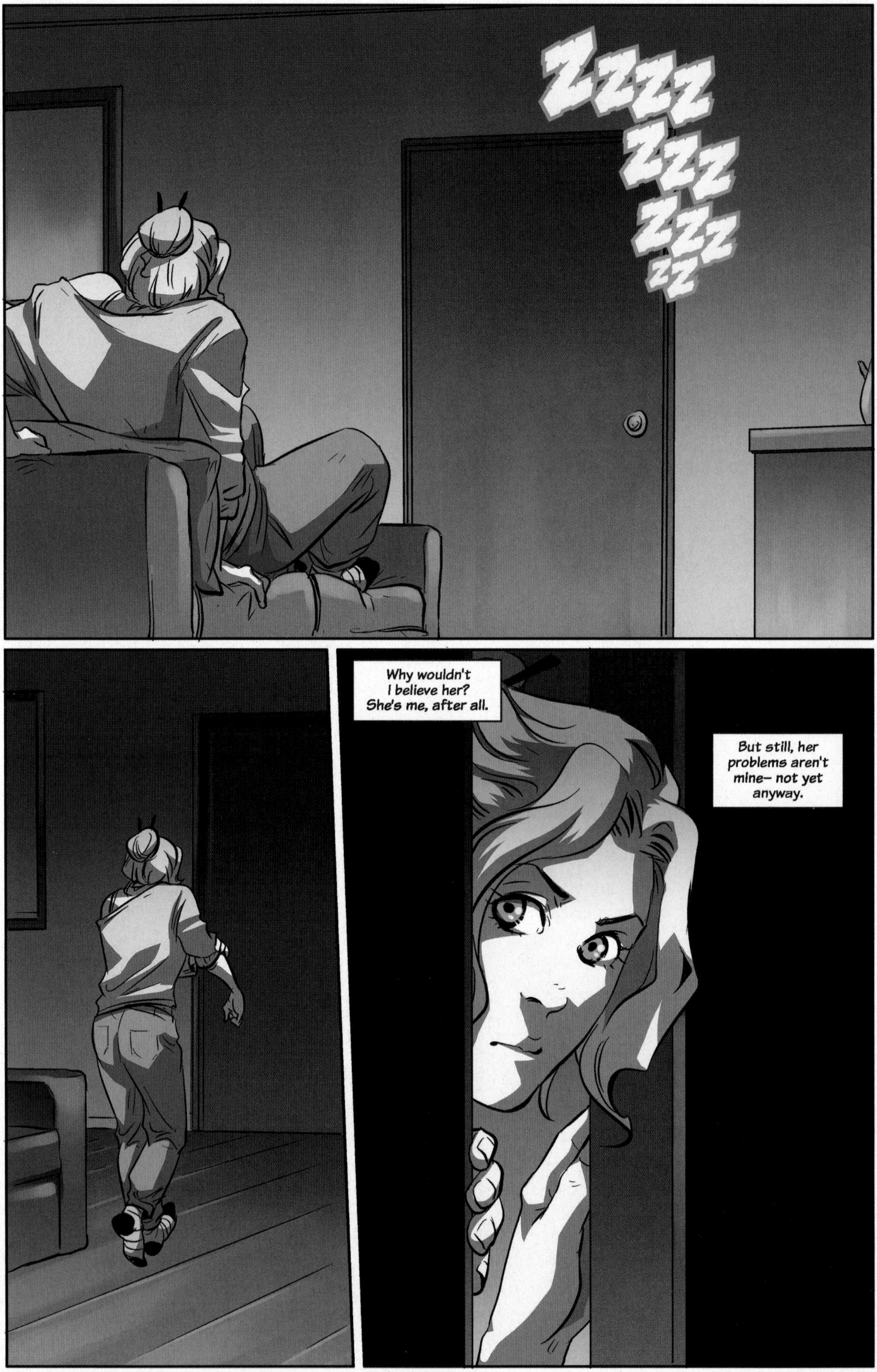
ZZZZ ZZZ ZZZ ZZ
Why wouldn't I believe her? She's me, after all.
But still, her problems aren't mine– not yet anyway.

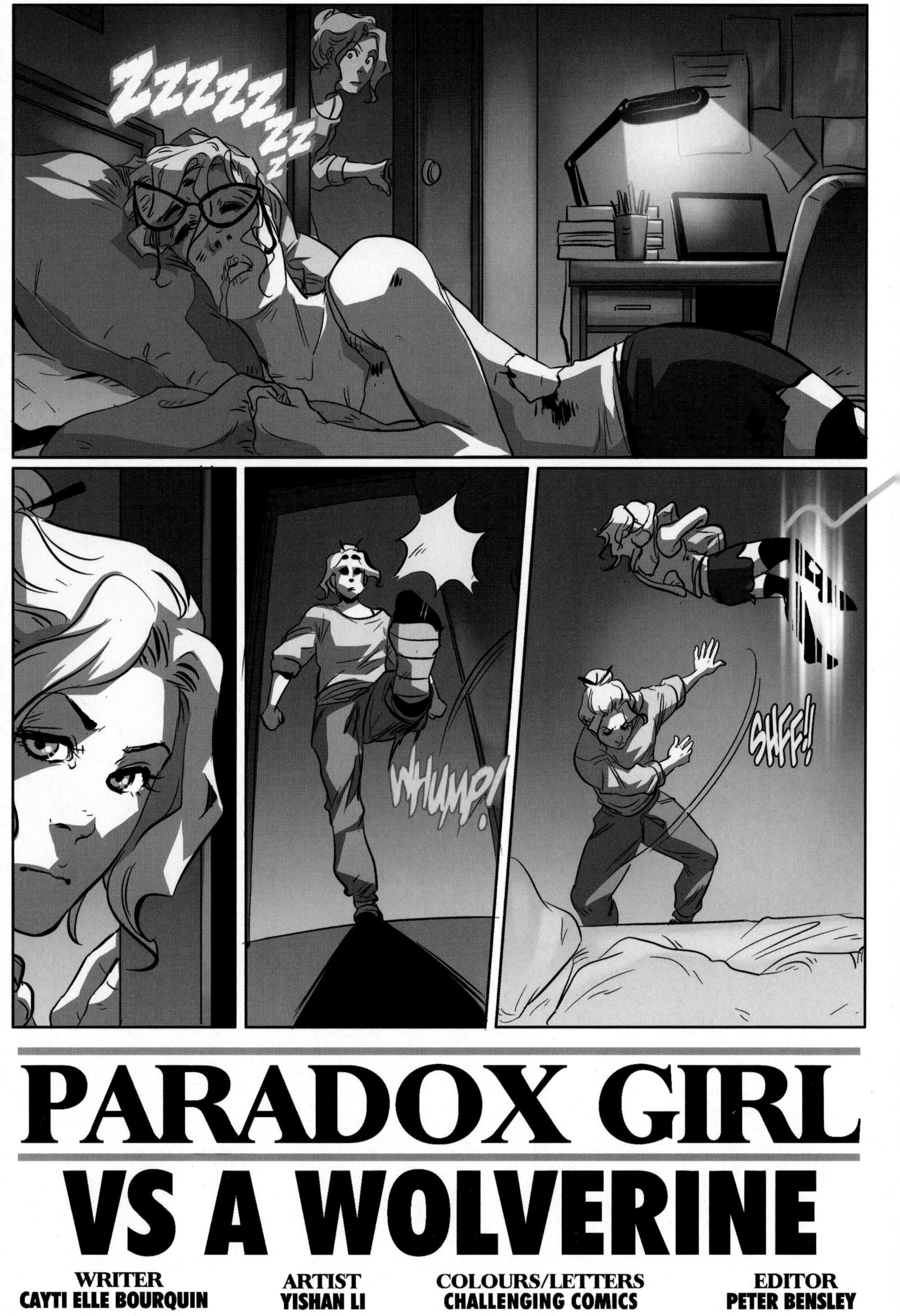
ZZZZZZZZZ
WHUMP!
SHFF!!

PARADOX GIRL

VS A WOLVERINE

WRITER
CAYTI ELLE BOURQUIN

ARTIST
YISHAN LI

COLOURS/LETTERS
CHALLENGING COMICS

EDITOR
PETER BENSLEY

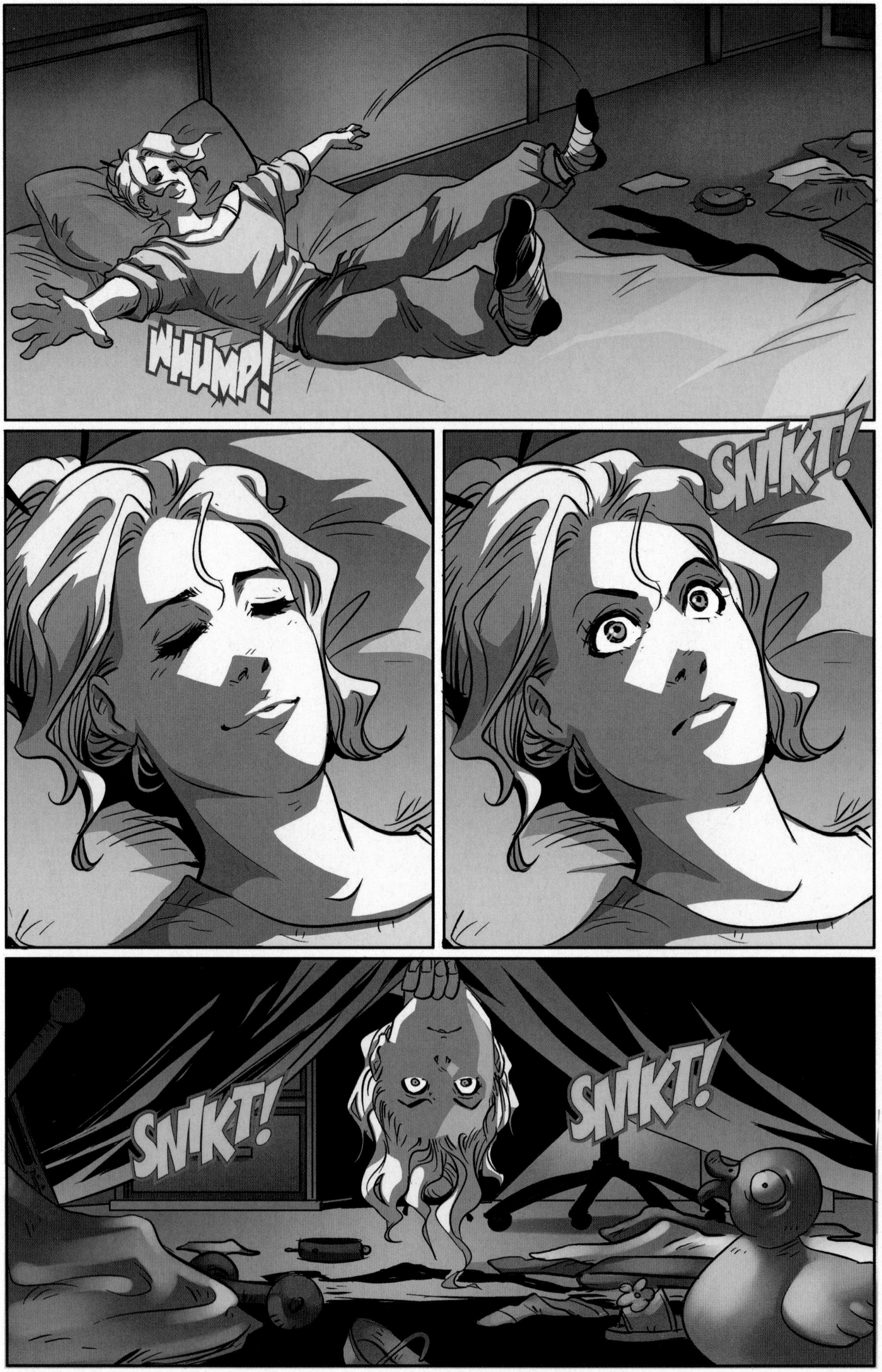
WHUMP!
SNIKT!
SNIKT!
SNIKT!

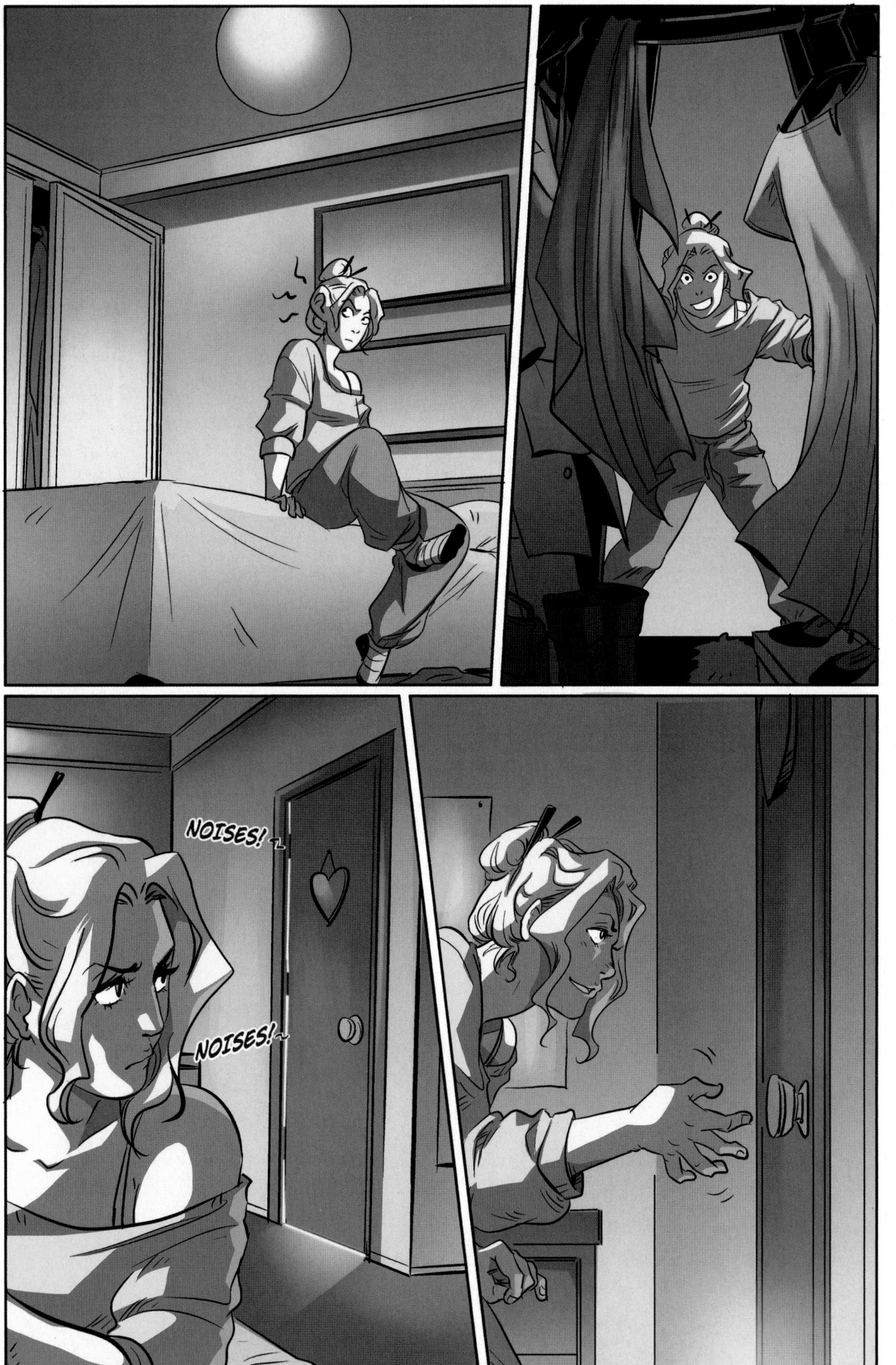
NOISES!
NOISES!

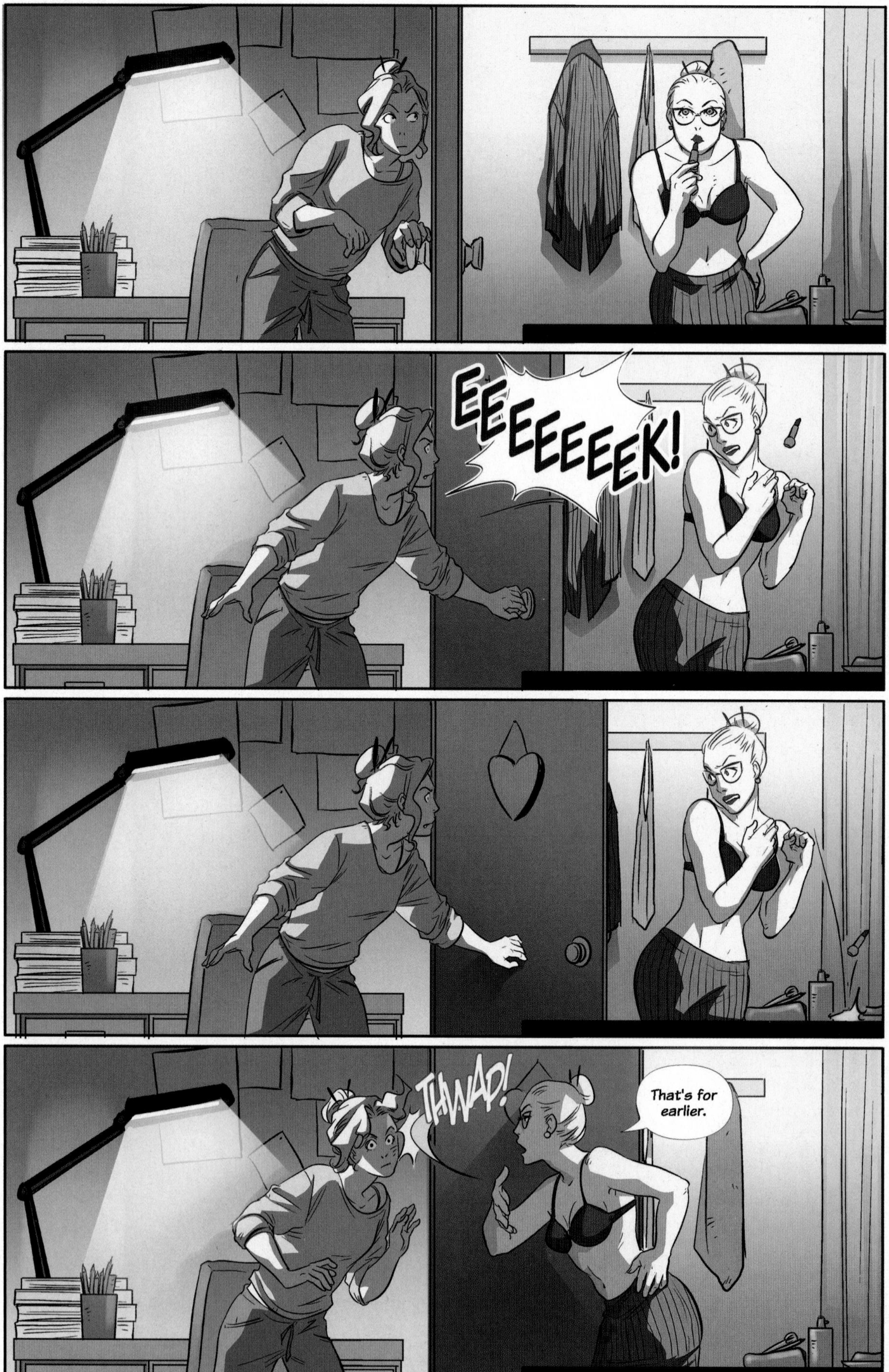
EEEEEEEEK!
THWAD!
That's for earlier.

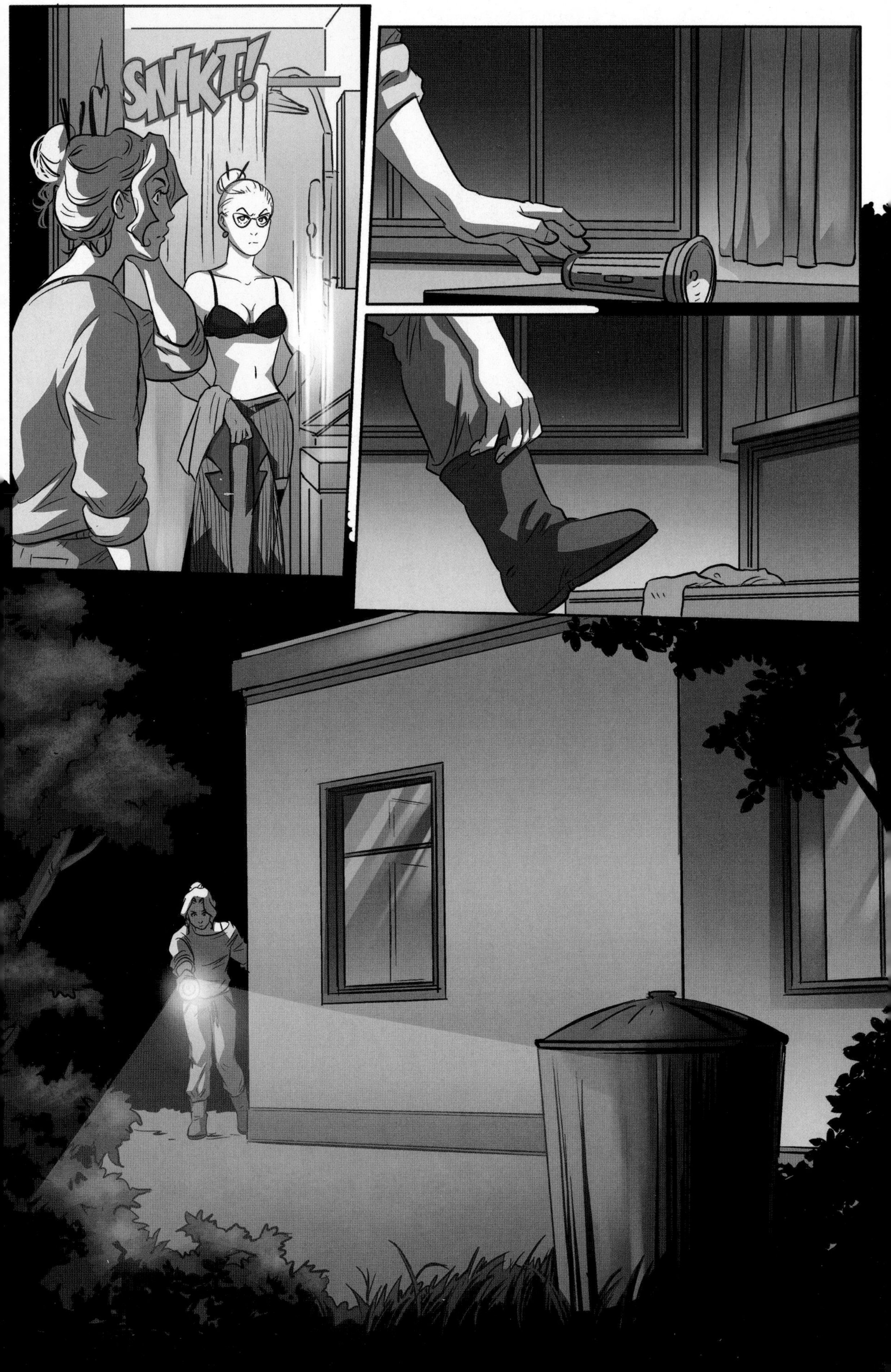
SNIKT!

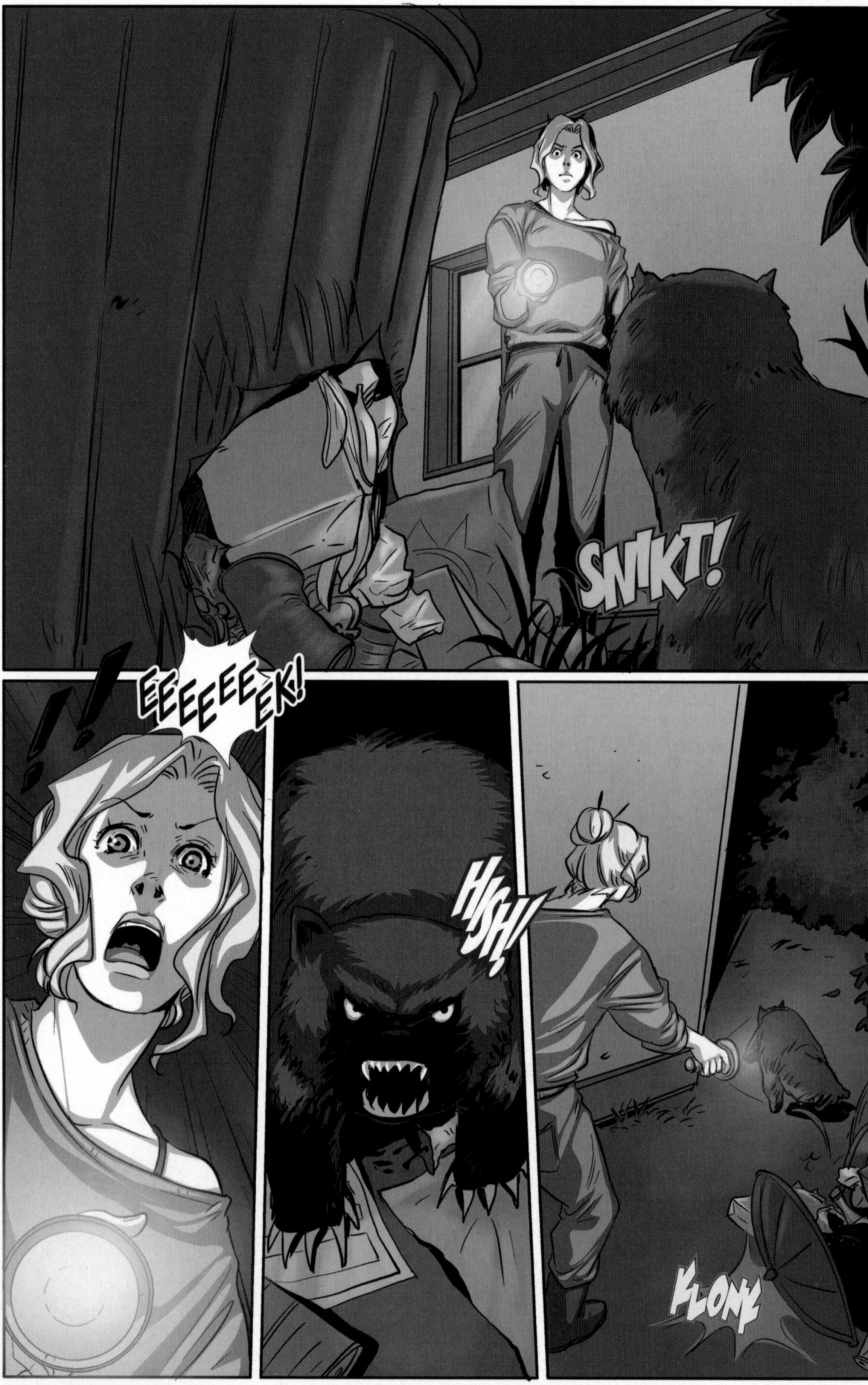
SNIKT!
!!
EEEEEEEK!
HISH!
KLONK

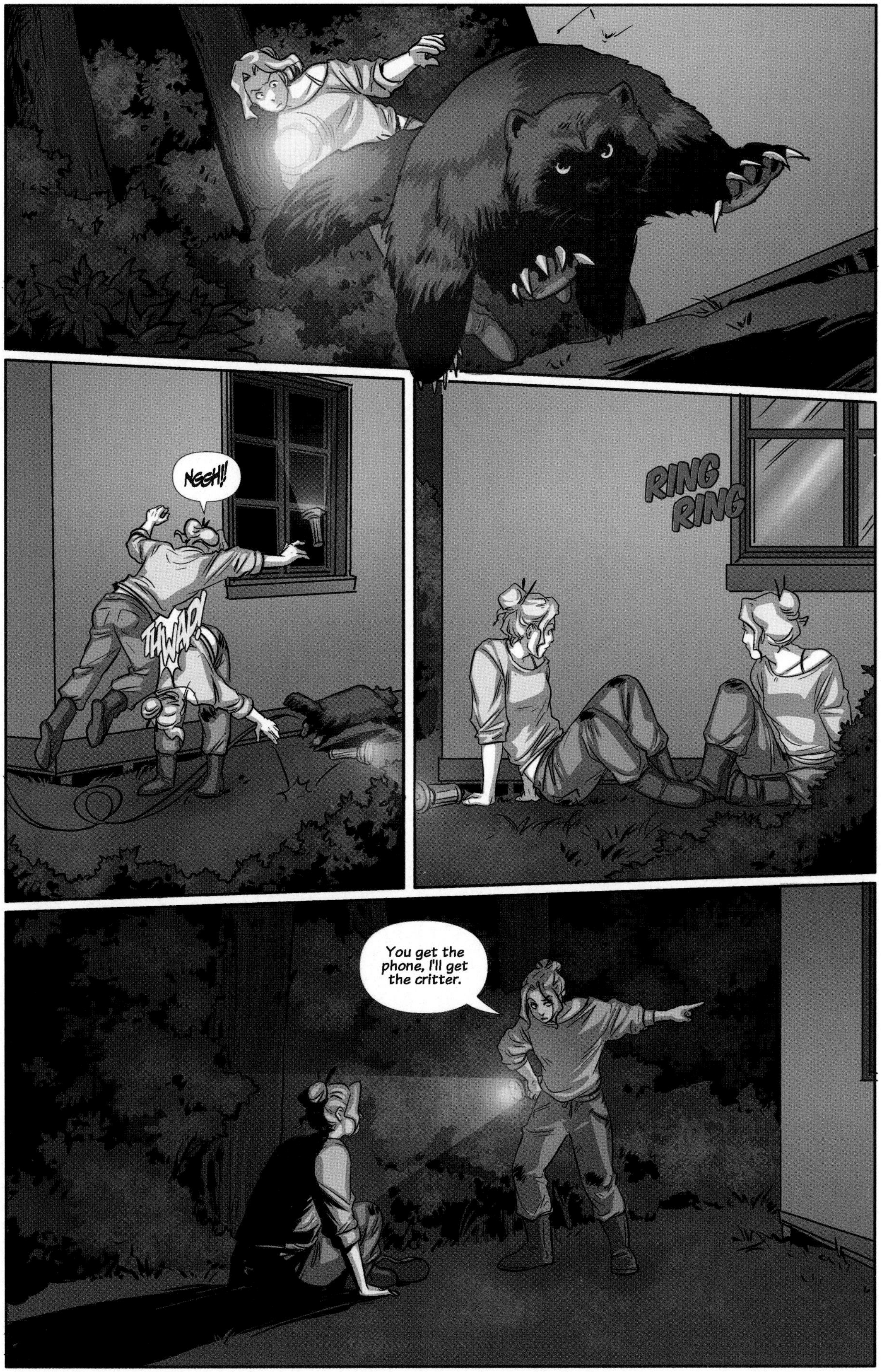
NGGH!!
THWAP!
RING
RING
You get the phone, I'll get the critter.

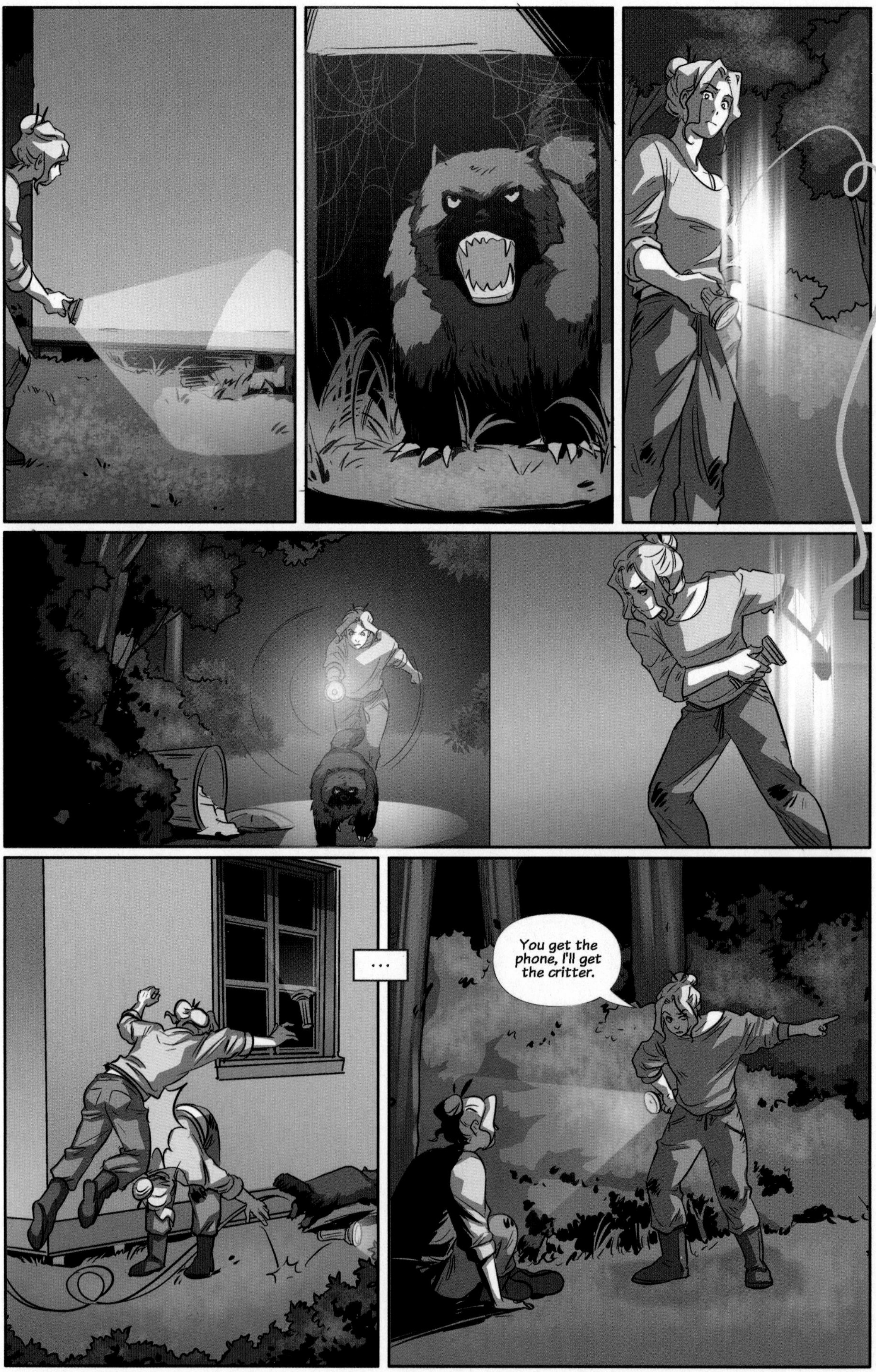
...
You get the phone, I'll get the critter.

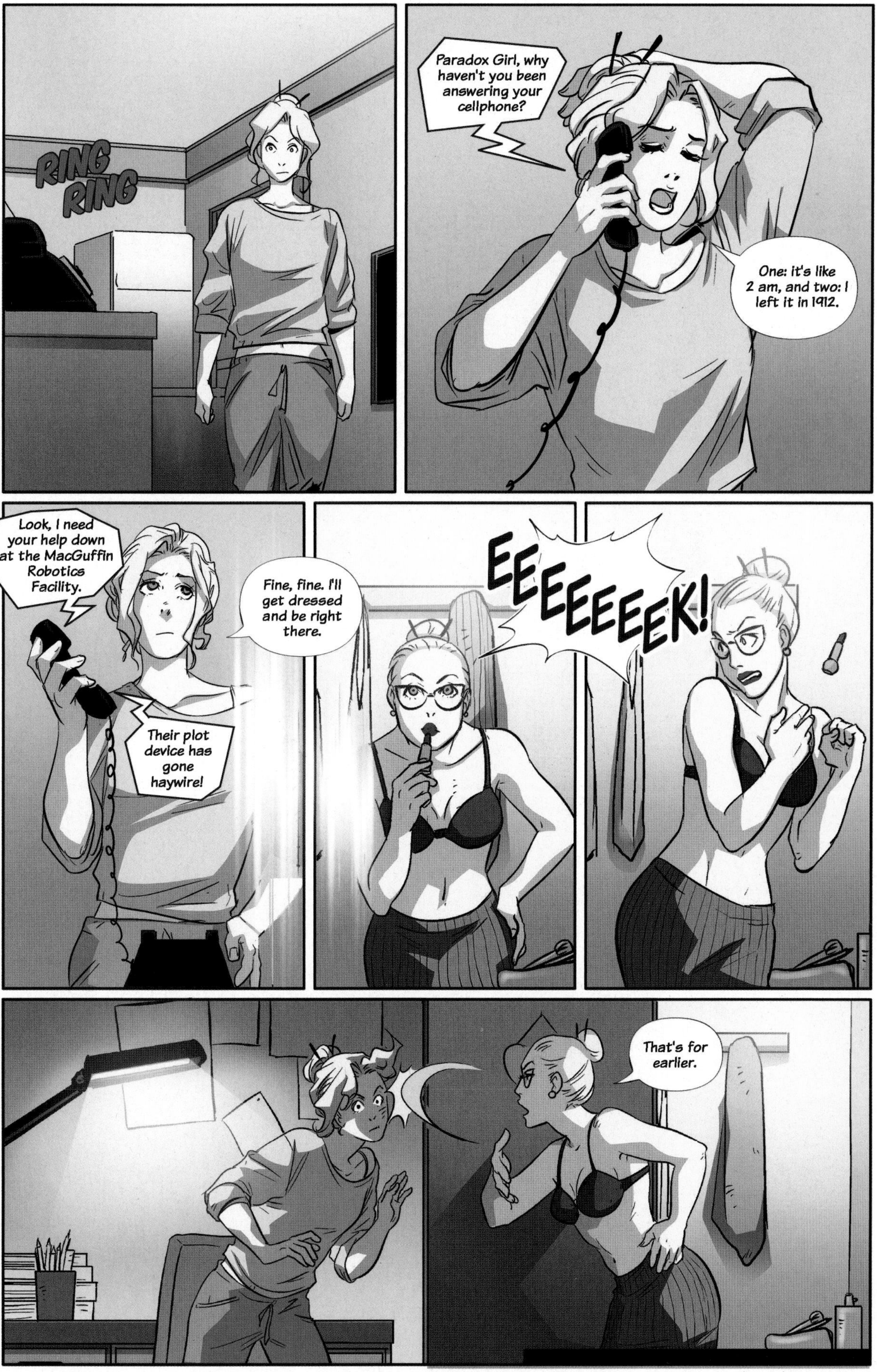
RING RING
Paradox Girl, why haven't you been answering your cellphone?
One: it's like 2 am, and two: I left it in 1912.
Look, I need your help down at the MacGuffin Robotics Facility.
Fine, fine. I'll get dressed and be right there.
Their plot device has gone haywire!
EEEEEEEK!
That's for earlier.

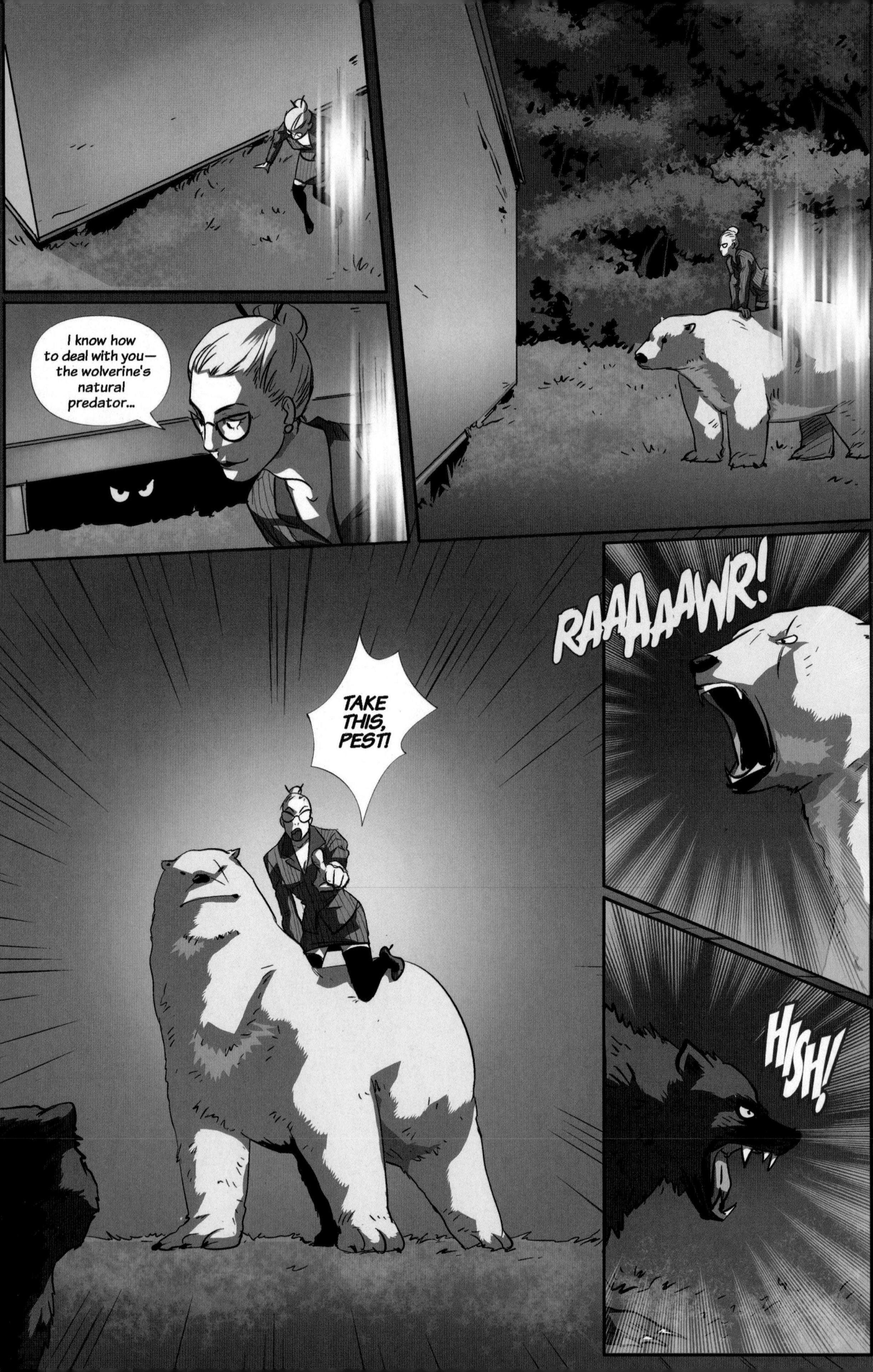
I know how to deal with you— the wolverine's natural predator...
TAKE THIS, PEST!
RAAAAAAWR!
HISH!

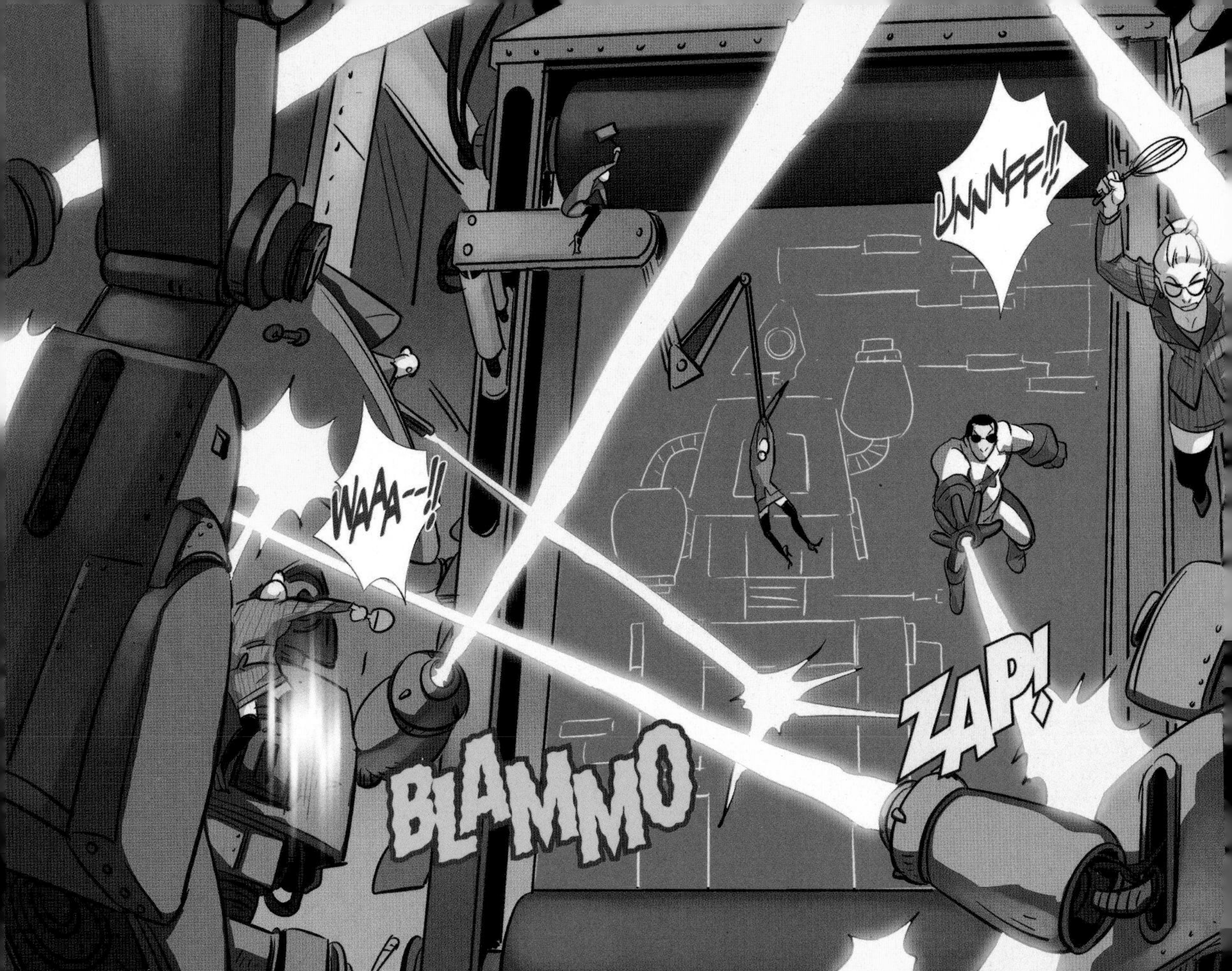
UNNNFF!!!
WAAA--!!
ZAP!
BLAMMO
LAAAAZOR

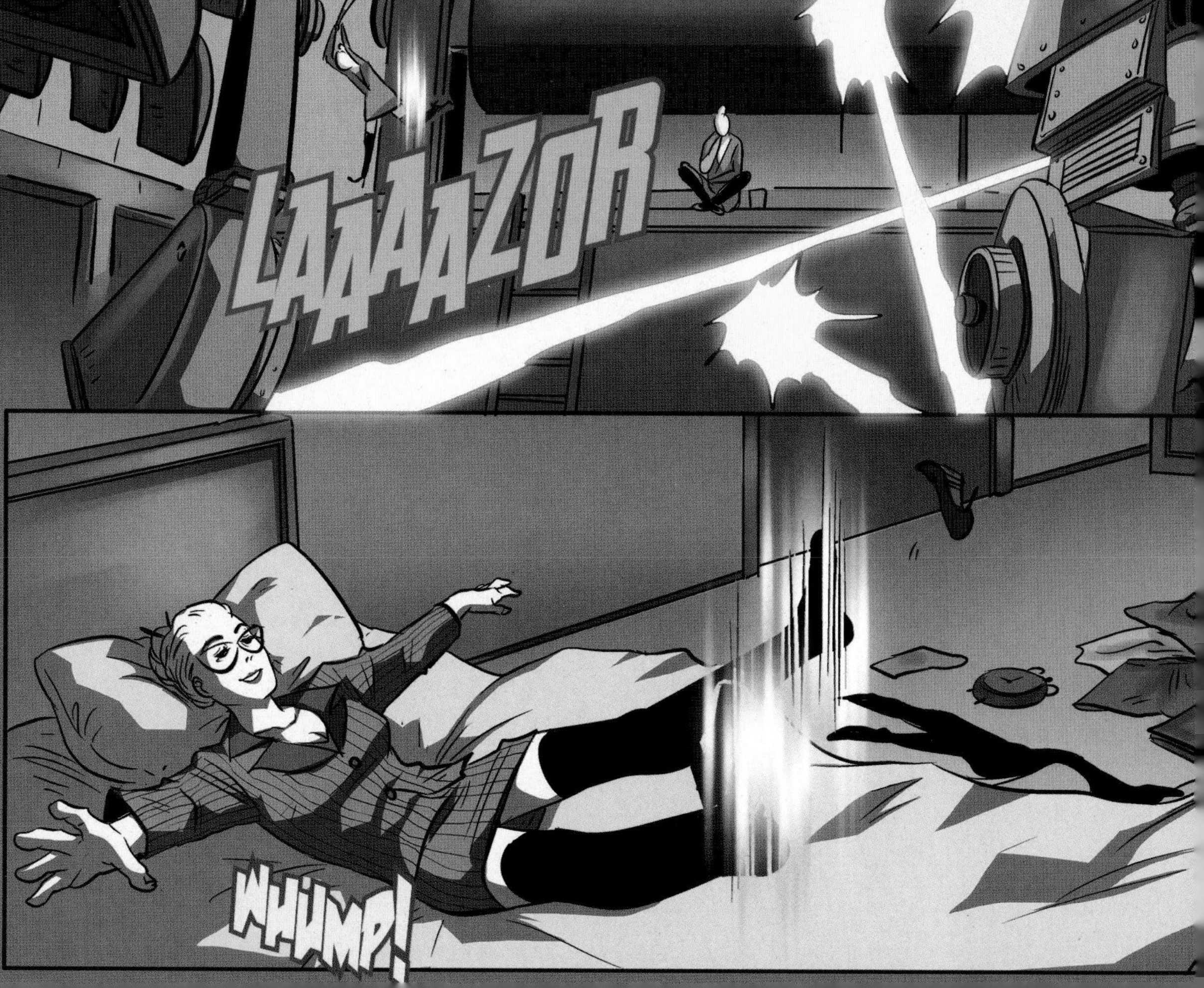
WHUMP!

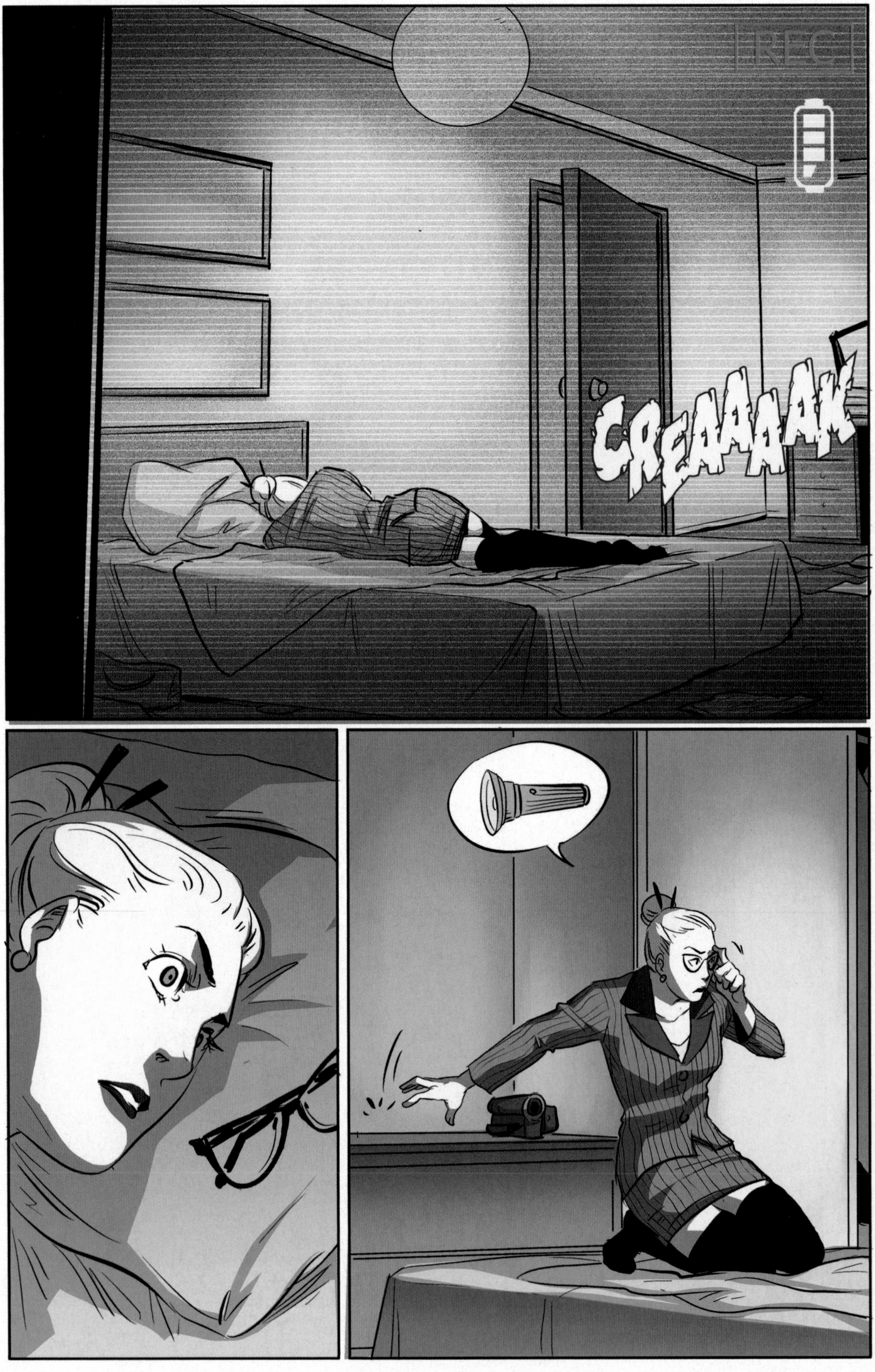
[REC]
CREAAAAK

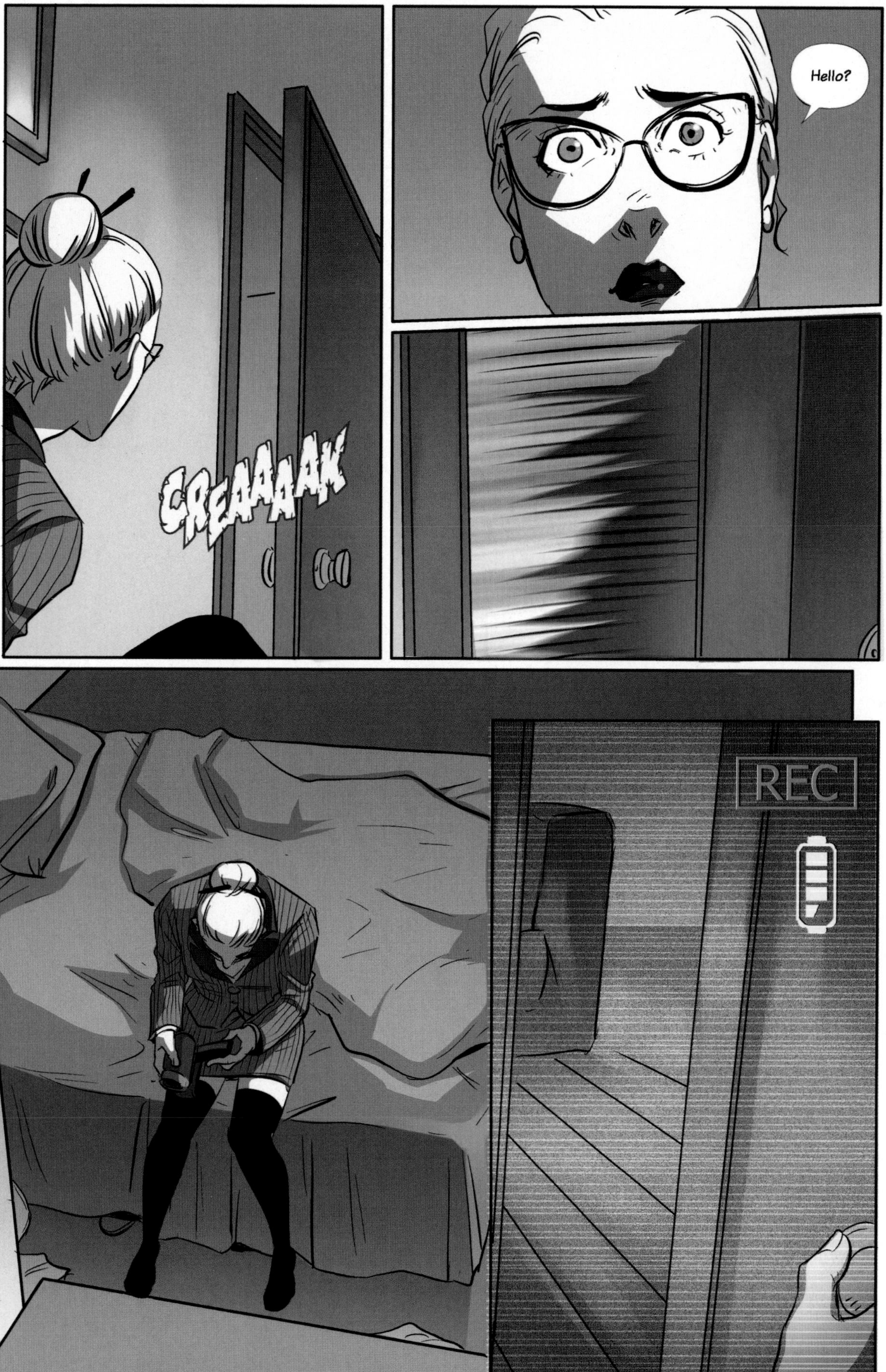
CREAAAAK
Hello?
REC

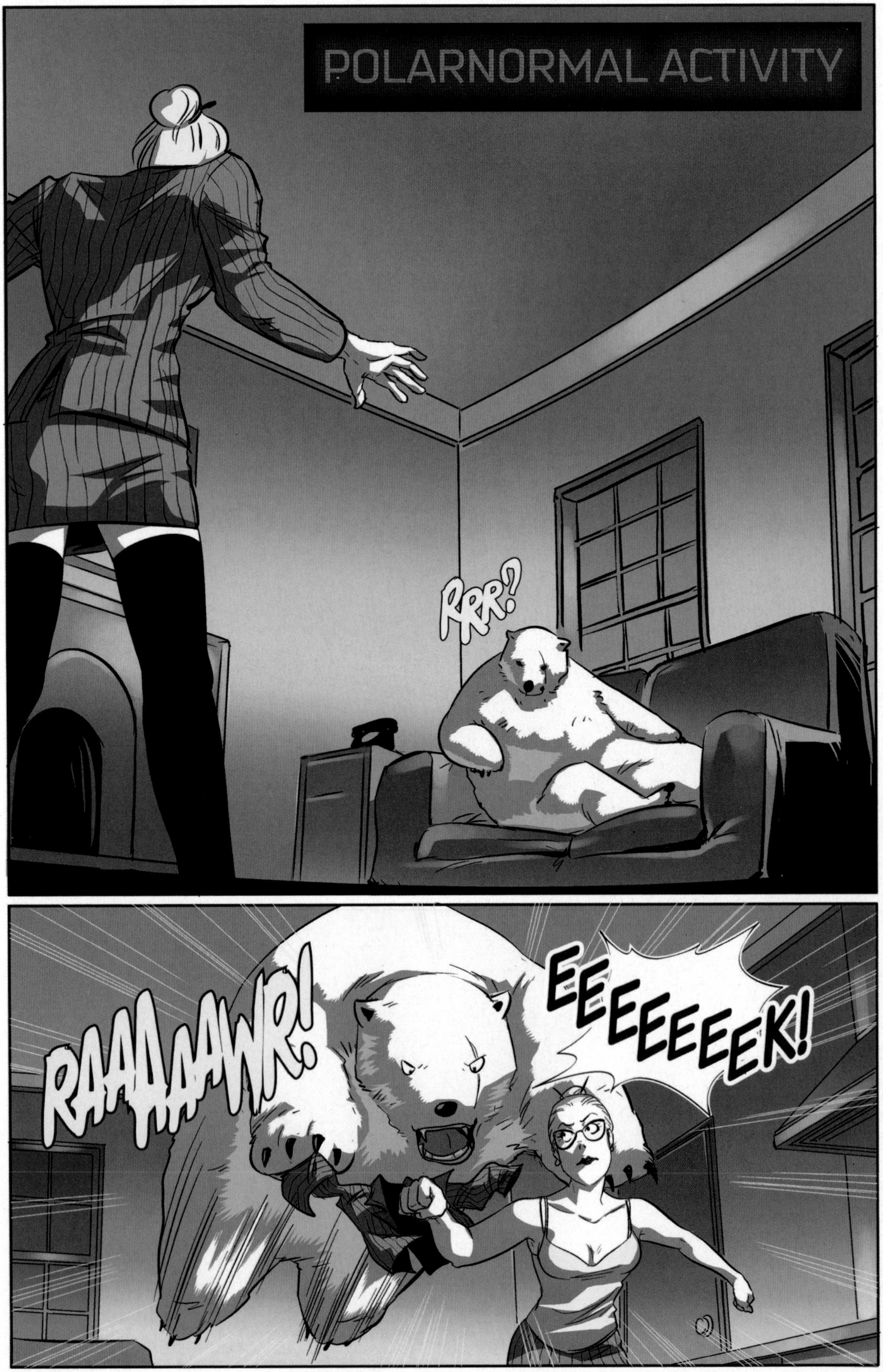
POLARNORMAL ACTIVITY
RRR?
RAAAAAWR!
EEEEEEEEK!

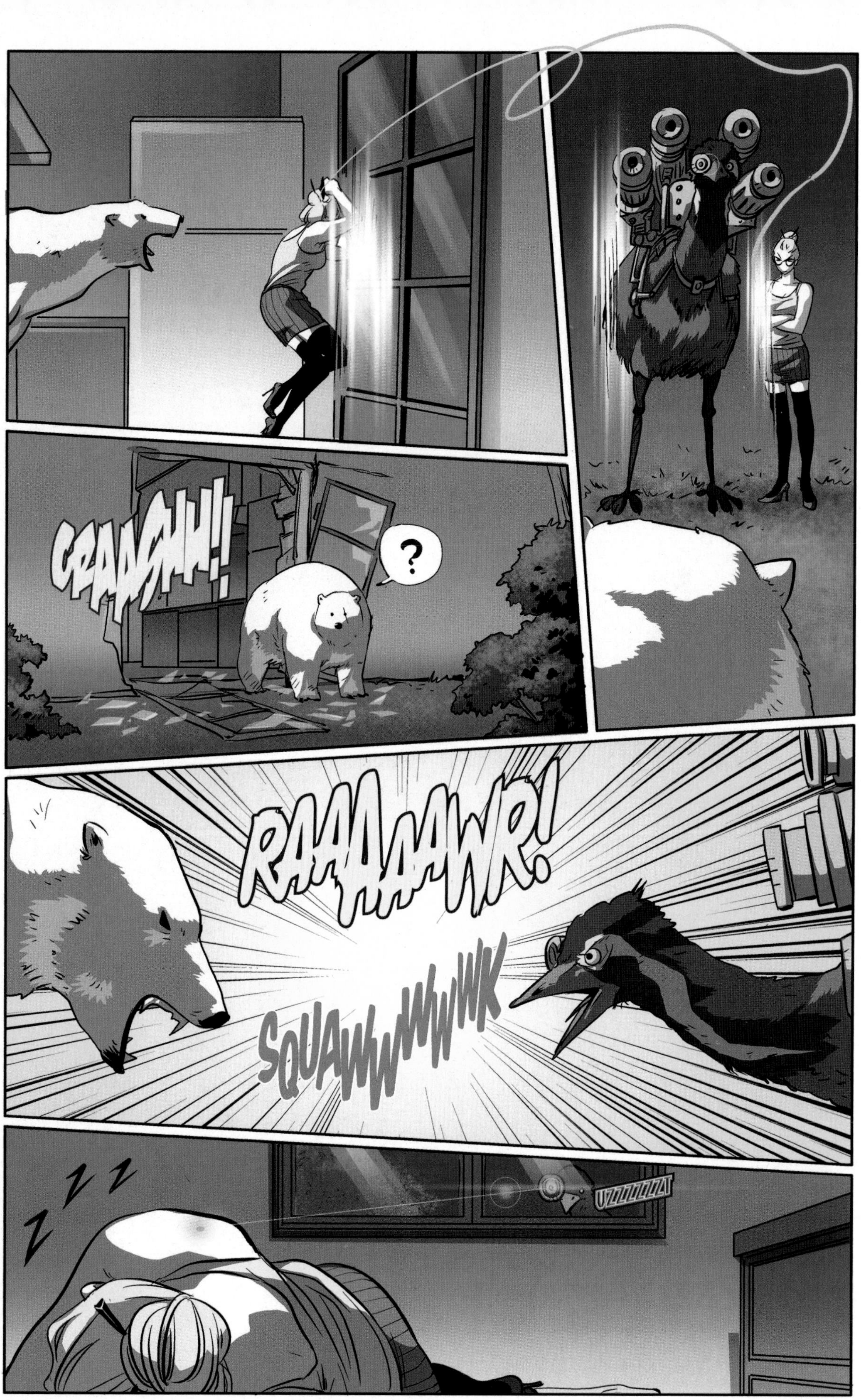
CRASHH!!
?
RAAAAAWR!
SQUAWWWWWK
Z Z Z
UZZZZZZZT

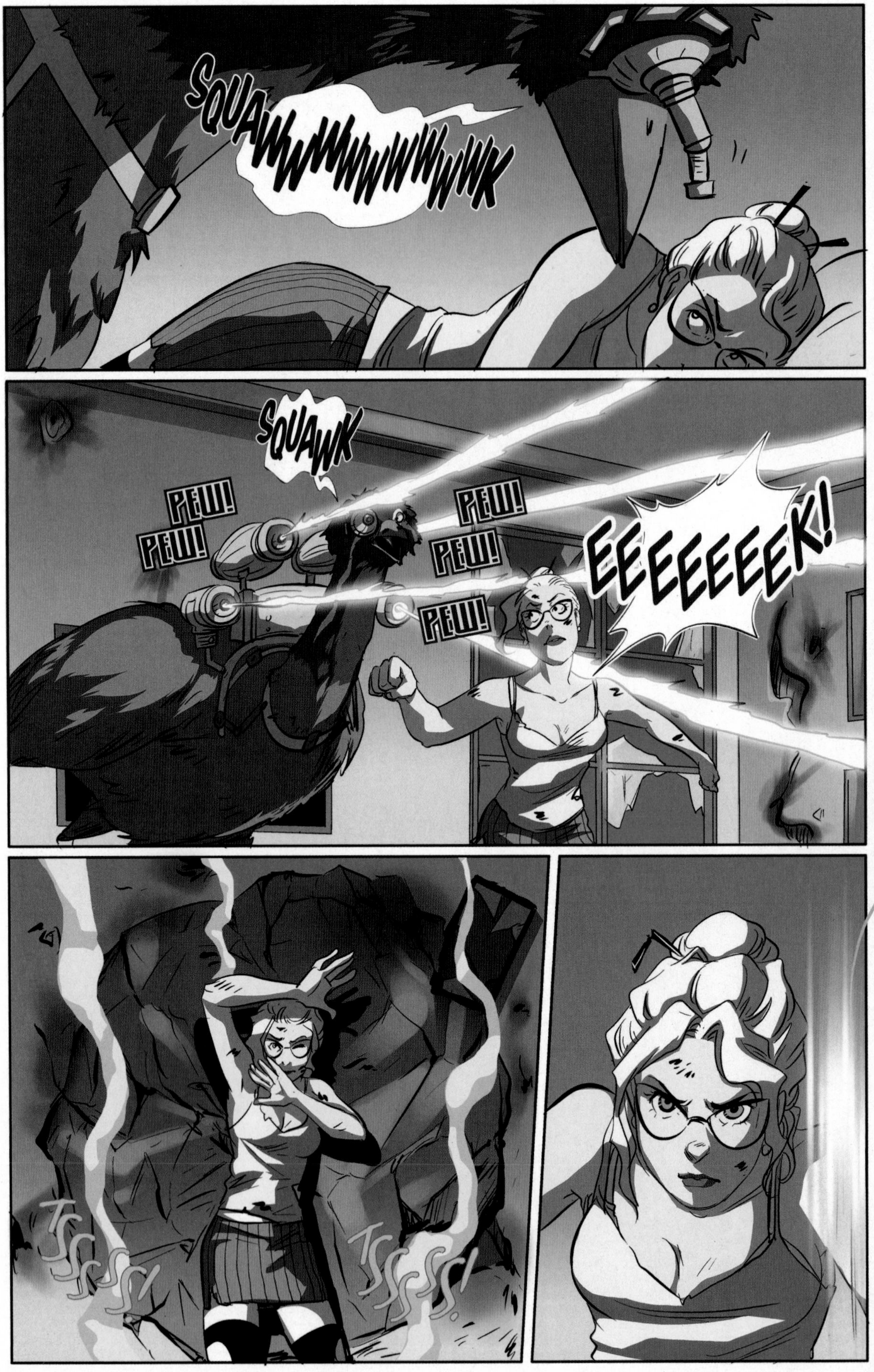
SQUAWWWWWWWWWWK
SQUAWK
PEW!
PEW!
PEW!
PEW!
PEW!
EEEEEEEK!
TSSSS!
TSSSS!

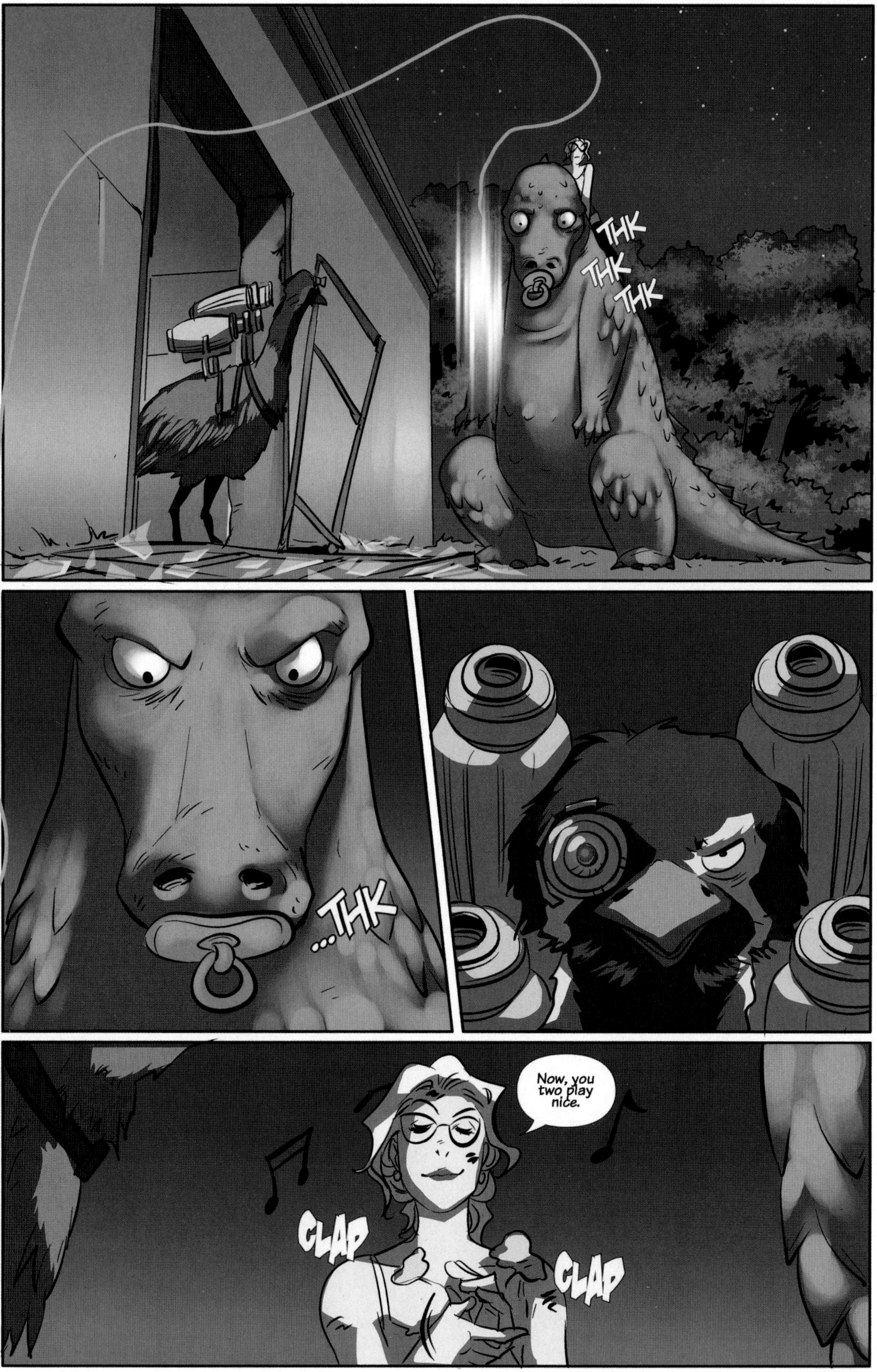
THK
THK
THK
...THK
Now, you two play nice.
CLAP
CLAP

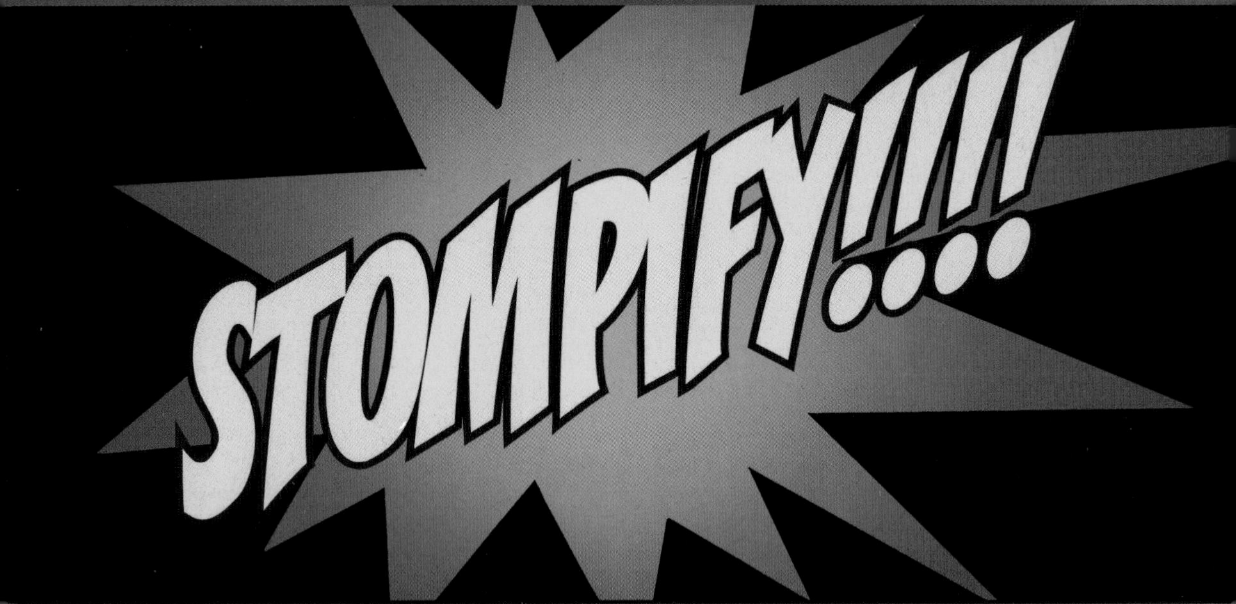
STOMPIFY!!!!
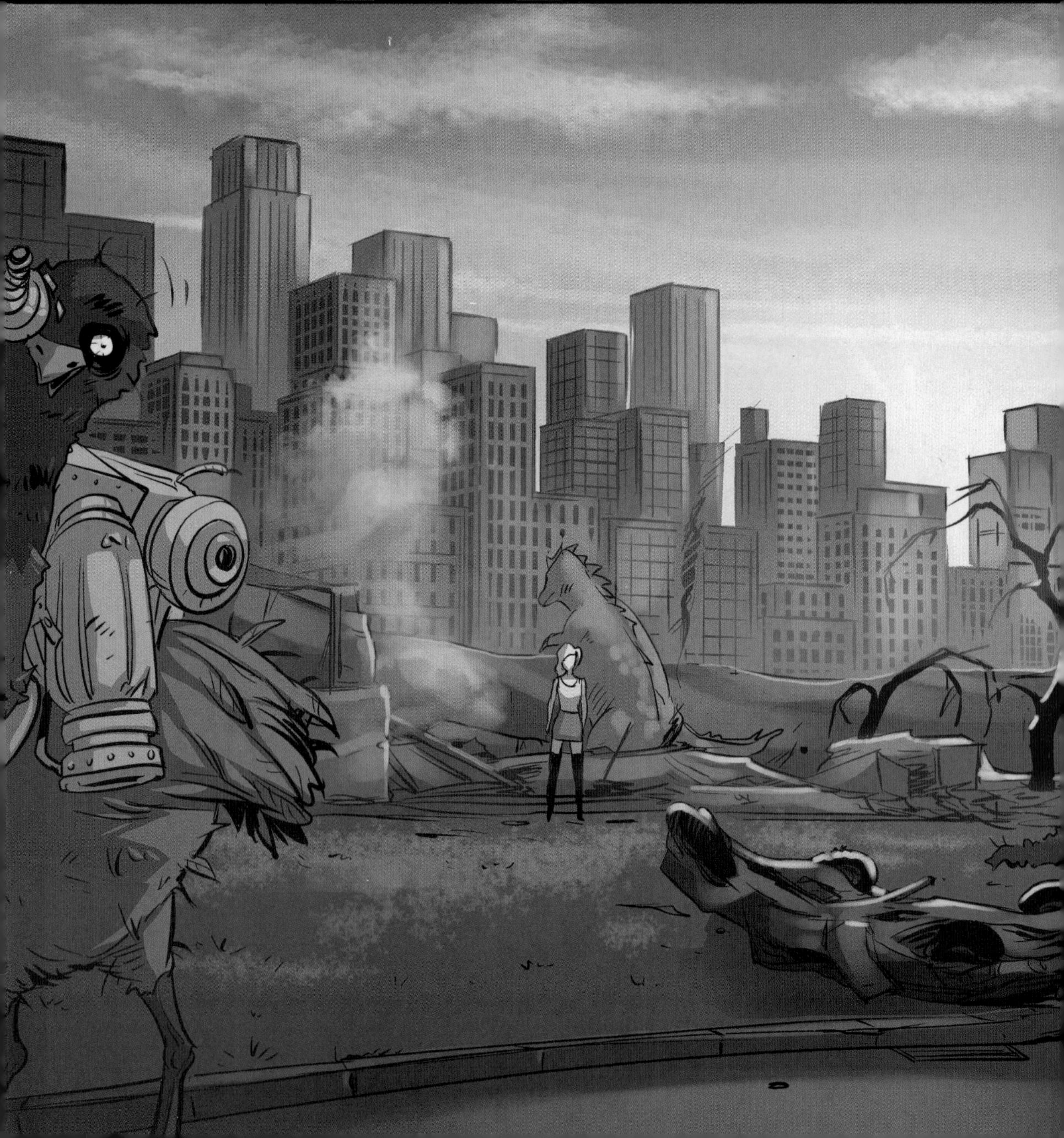

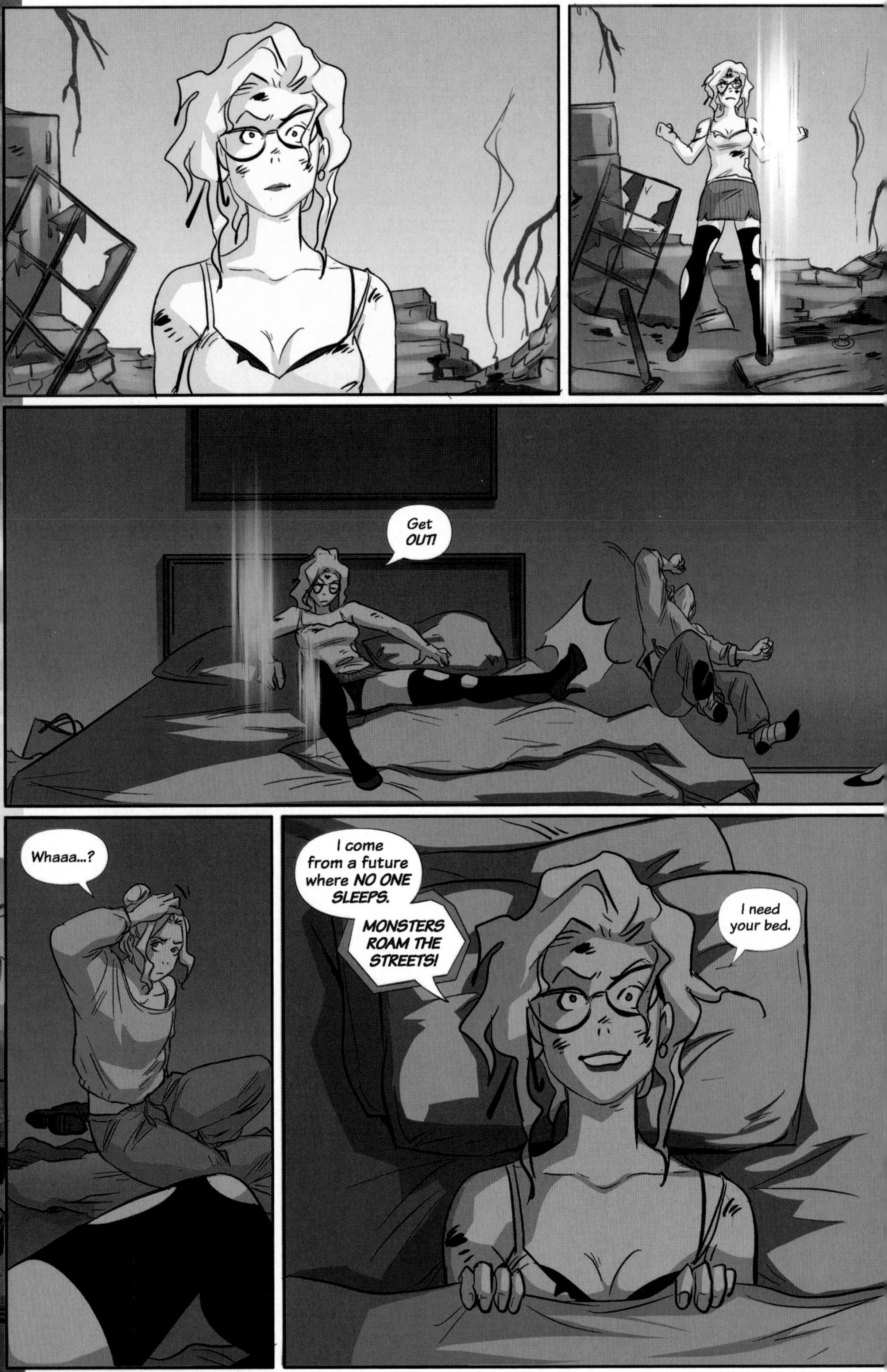
Get OUT!
Whaaa...?
I come from a future where NO ONE SLEEPS.
MONSTERS ROAM THE STREETS!
I need your bed.

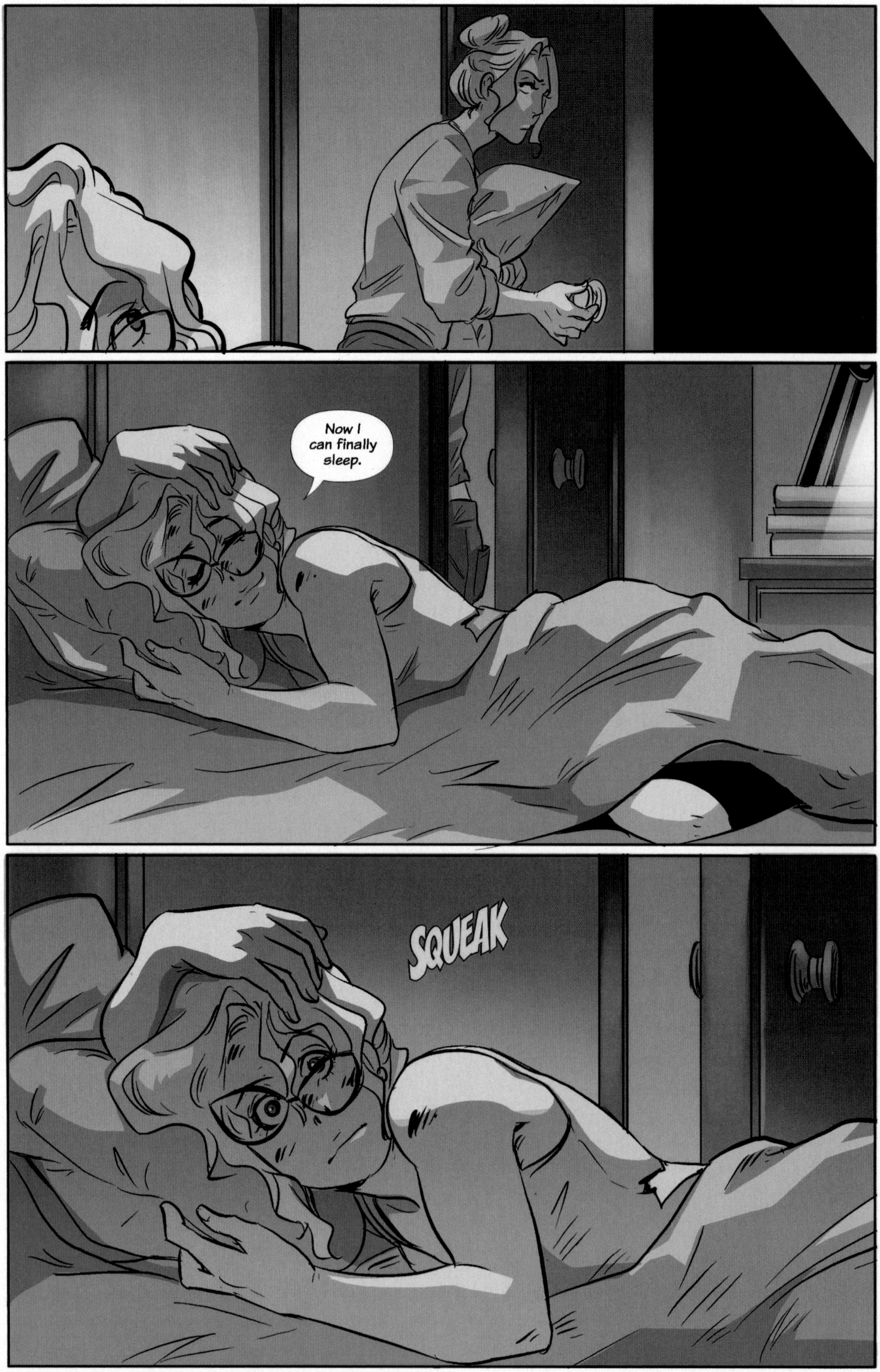
Now I can finally sleep.
SQUEAK

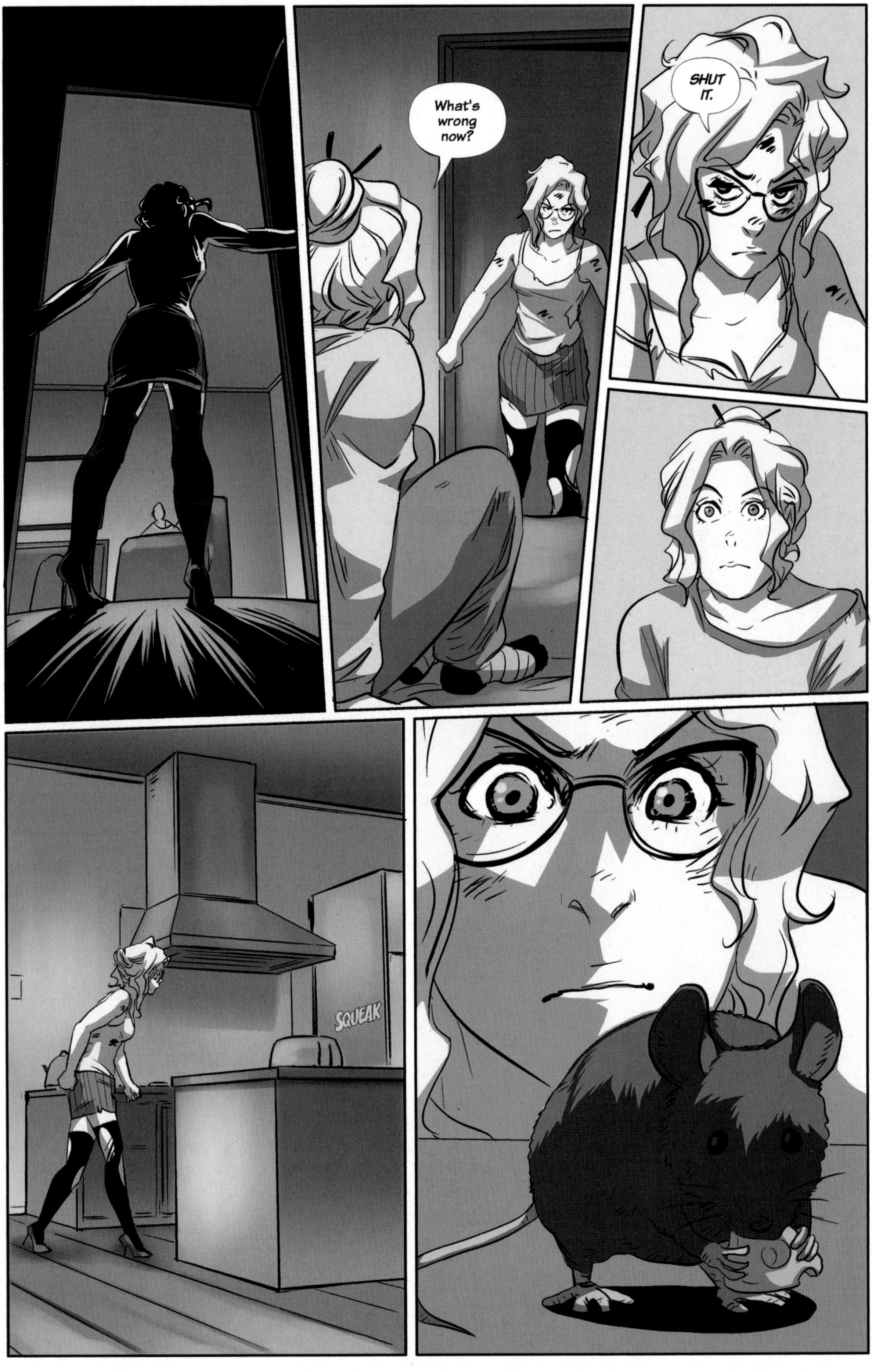
What's wrong now?
SHUT IT.
SQUEAK

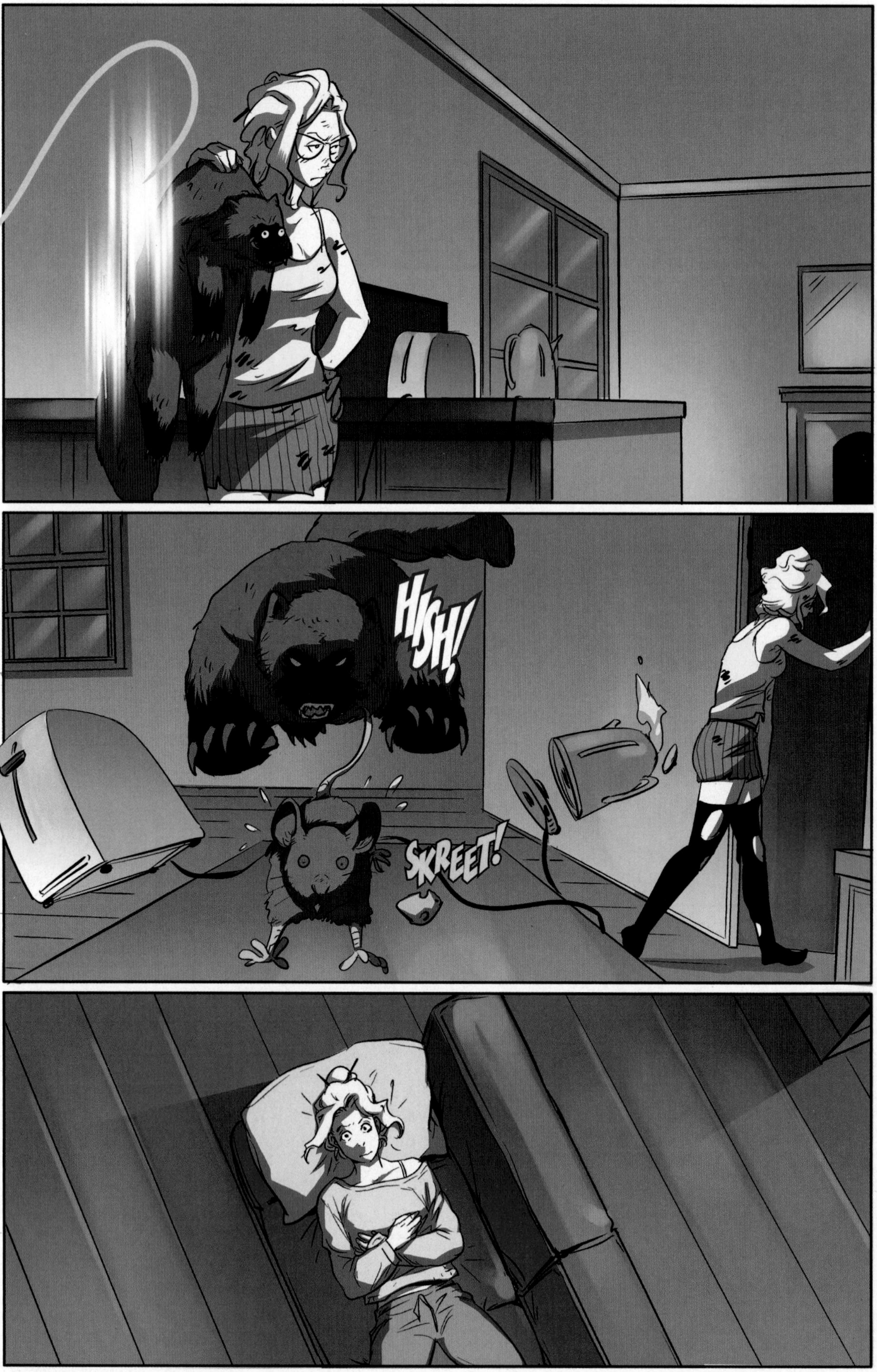
HISH!
SKREET!

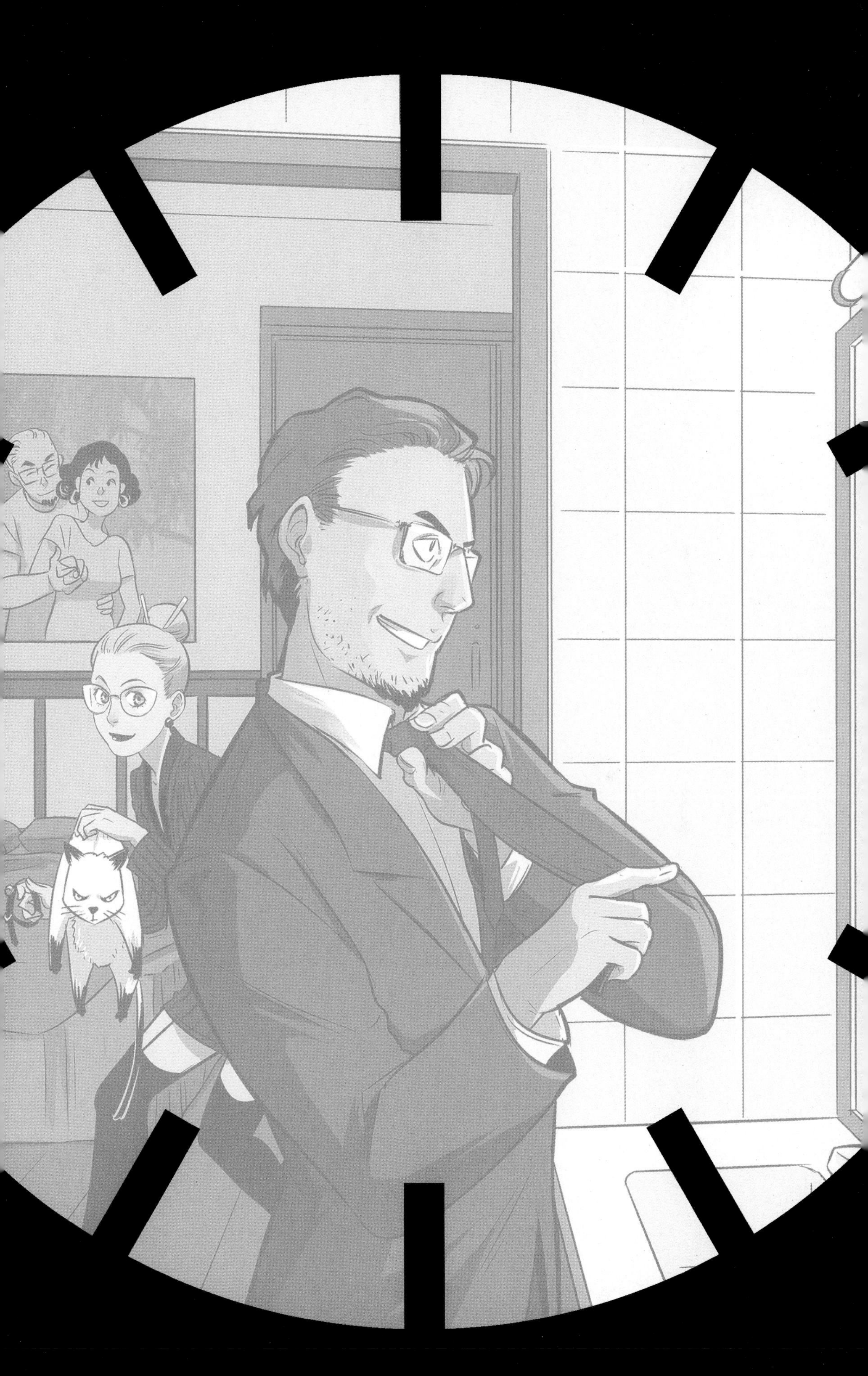

CHAPTER 3

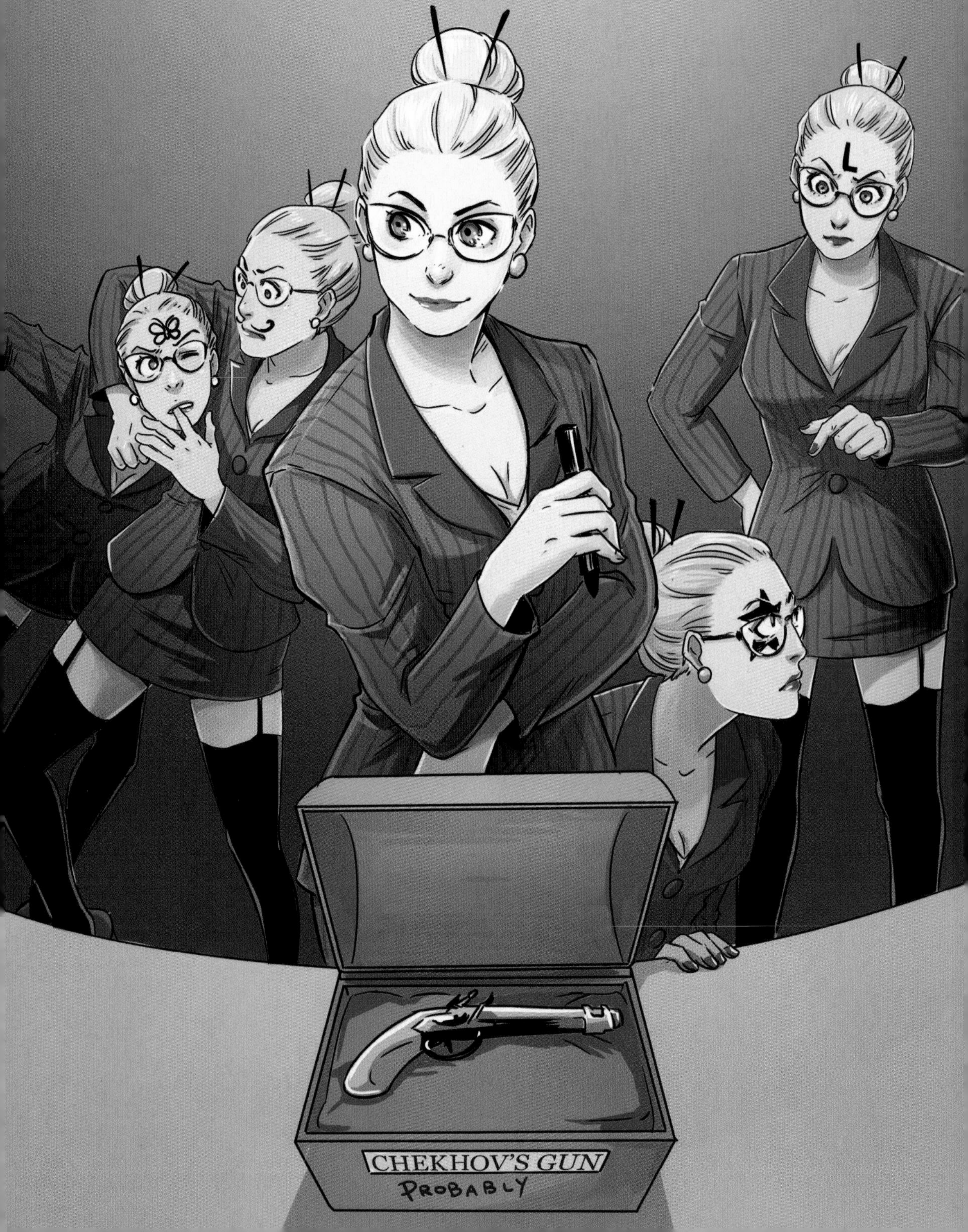
CHEKHOV'S GUN
PROBABLY

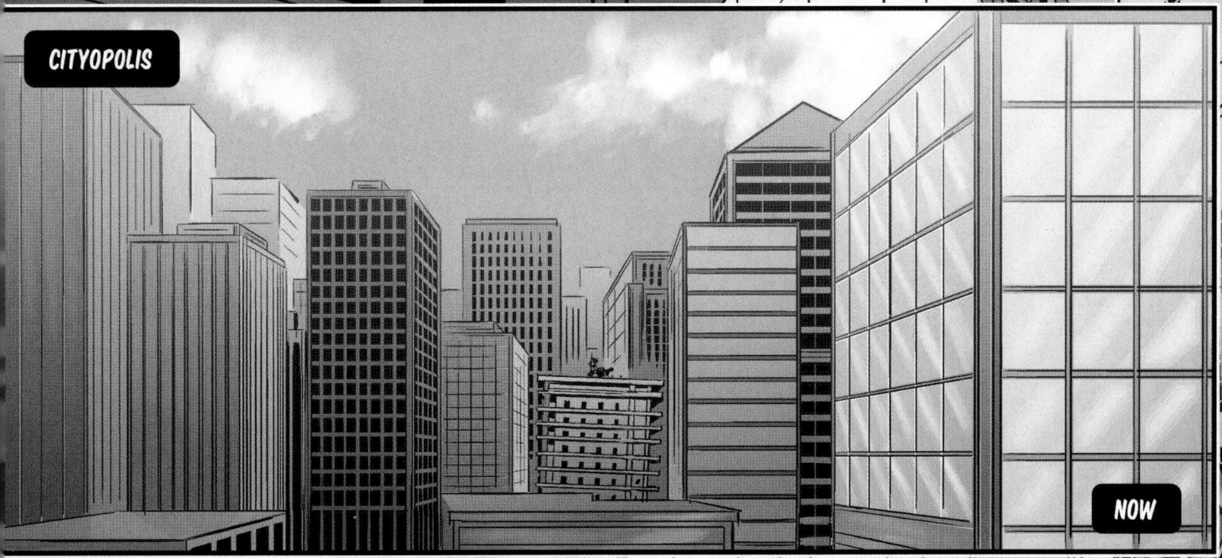
CITYOPOLIS
NOW

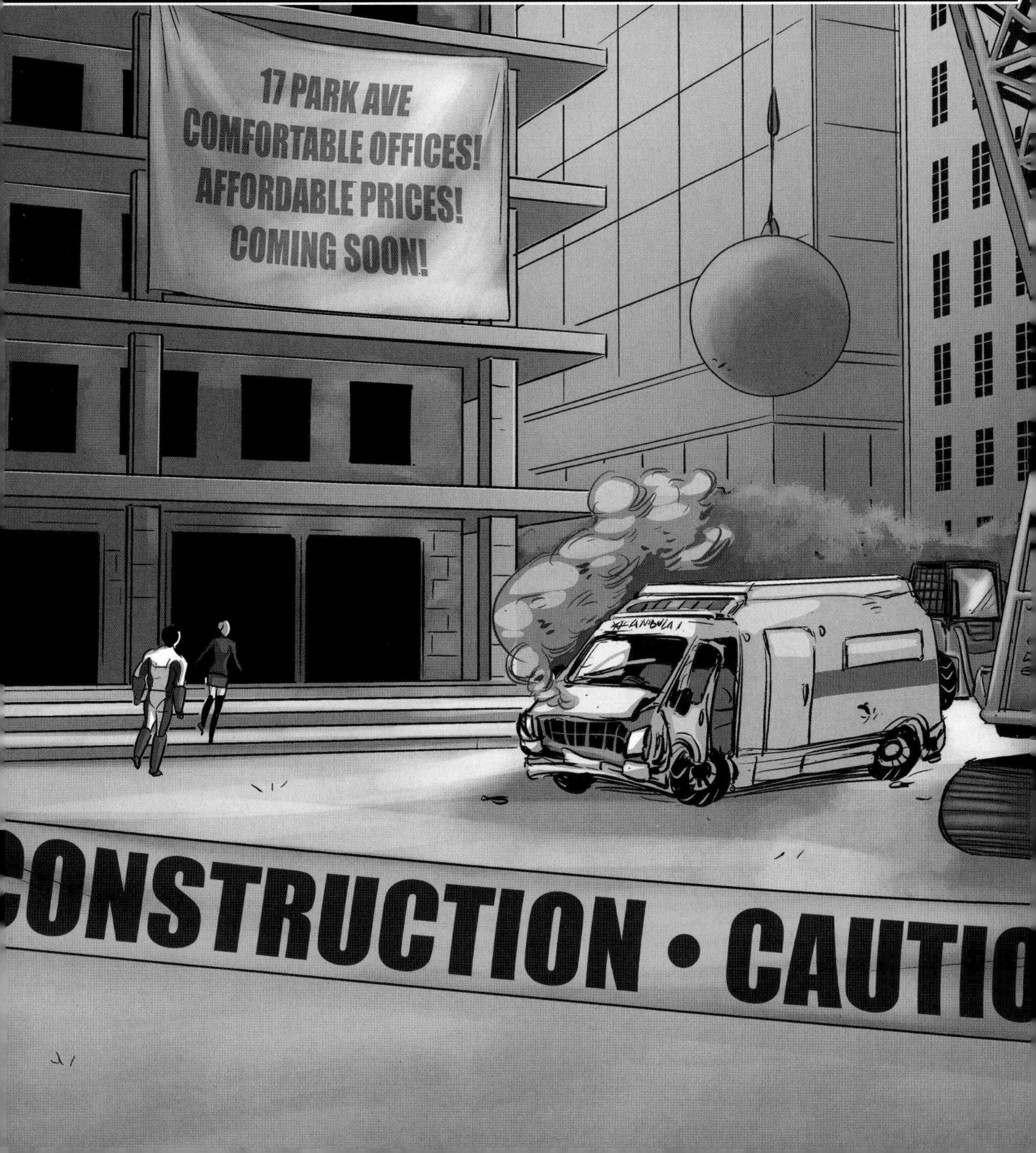
17 PARK AVE
COMFORTABLE OFFICES!
AFFORDABLE PRICES!
COMING SOON!
CONSTRUCTION • CAUTIO

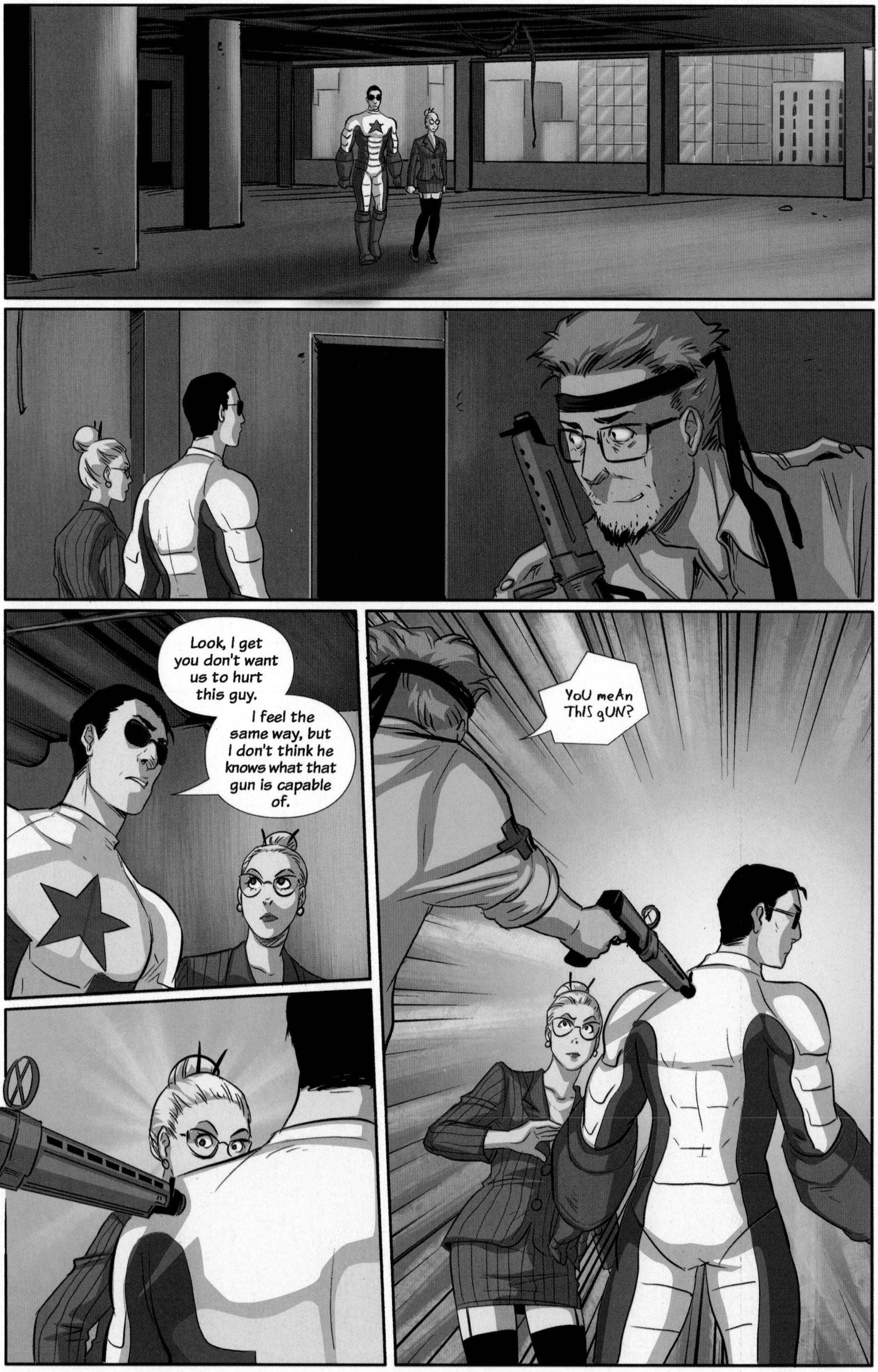
Look, I get you don't want us to hurt this guy.
I feel the same way, but I don't think he knows what that gun is capable of.
YoU meAn ThIS gUN?

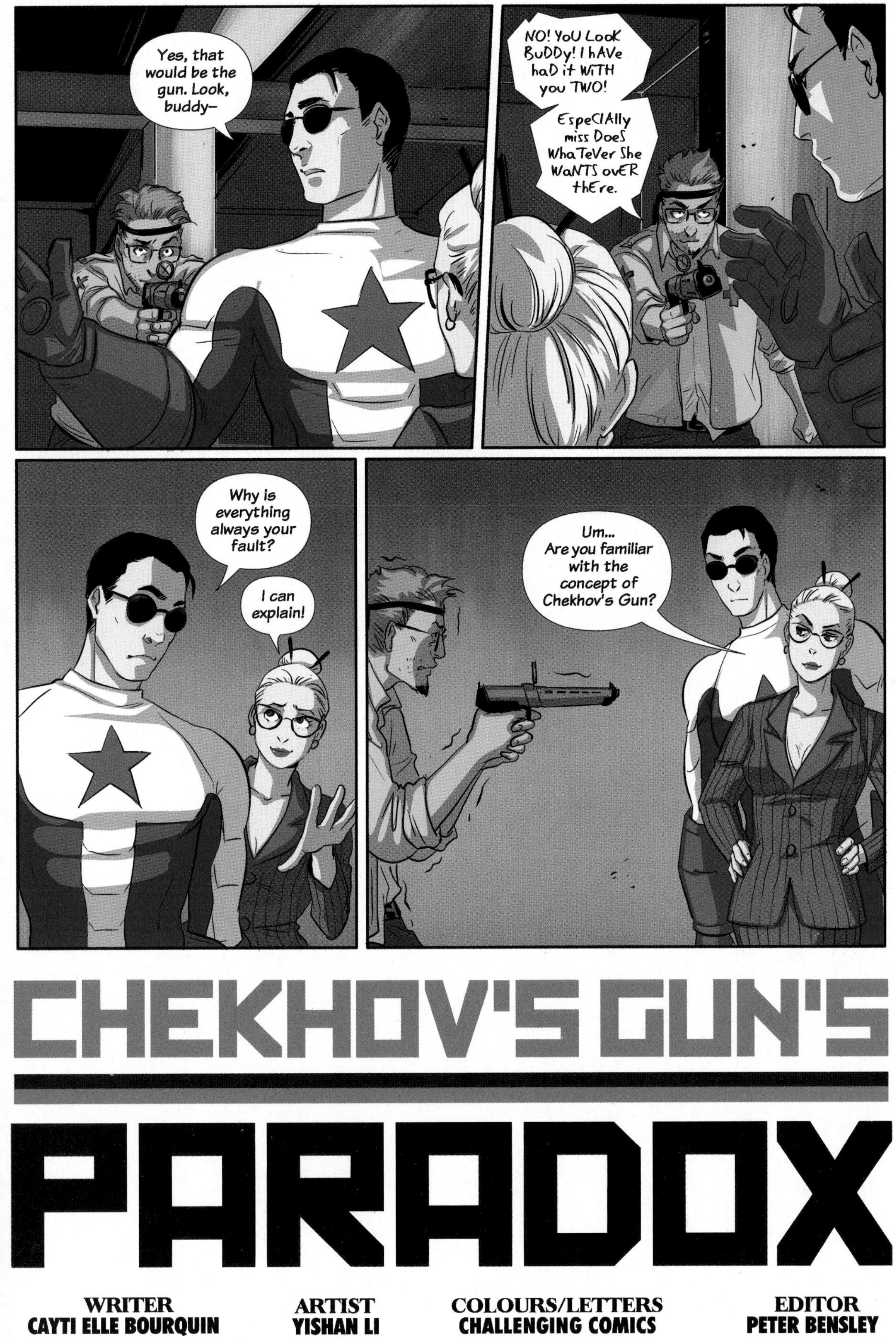
Yes, that would be the gun. Look, buddy–
NO! You look buddy! I have had it WITH you TWO!
Especially miss Does Whatever She Wants over there.
Why is everything always your fault?
I can explain!
Um... Are you familiar with the concept of Chekhov's Gun?

CHEKHOV'S GUN'S PARADOX

WRITER CAYTI ELLE BOURQUIN

ARTIST YISHAN LI

COLOURS/LETTERS CHALLENGING COMICS

EDITOR PETER BENSLEY

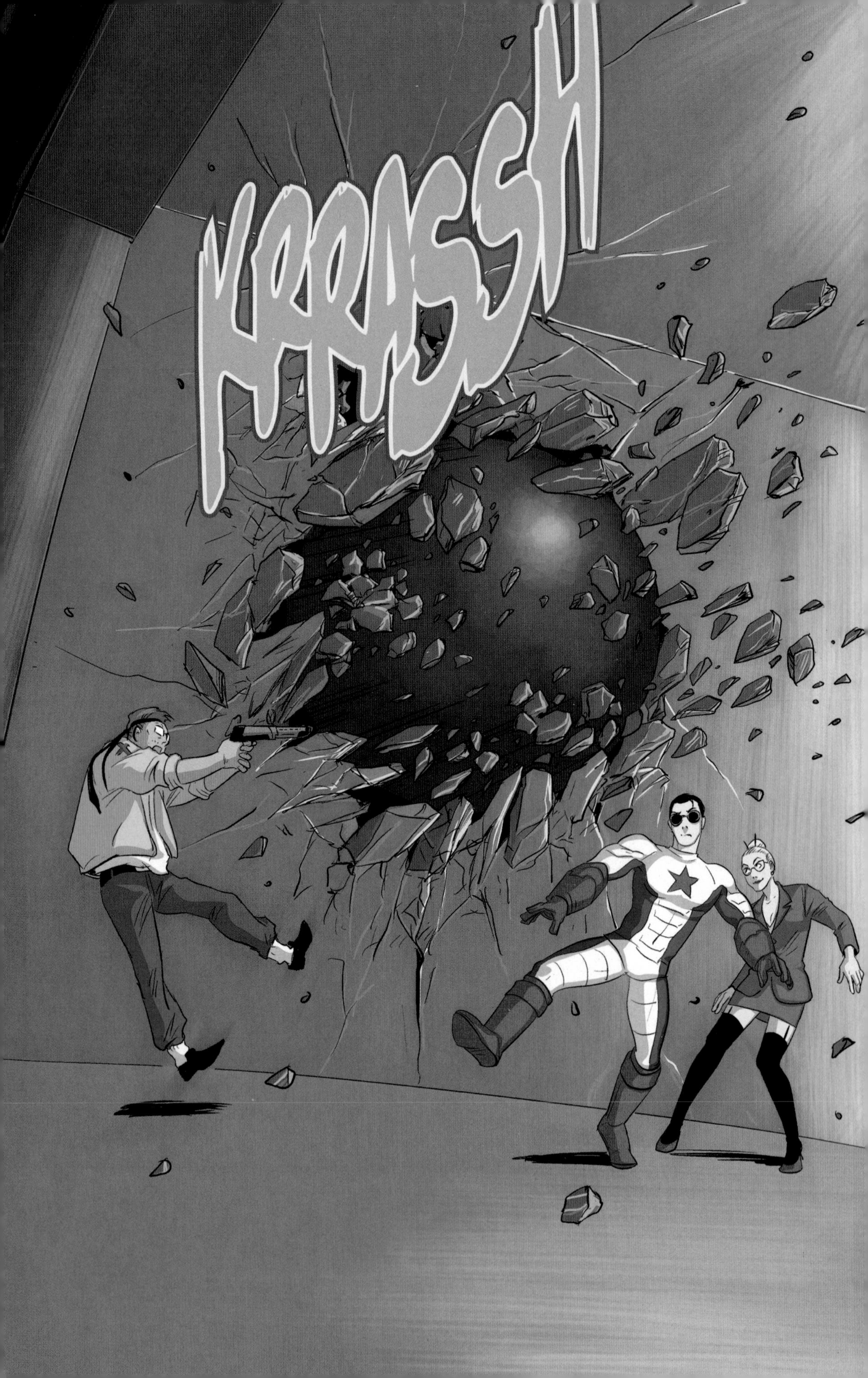
KRRASSH

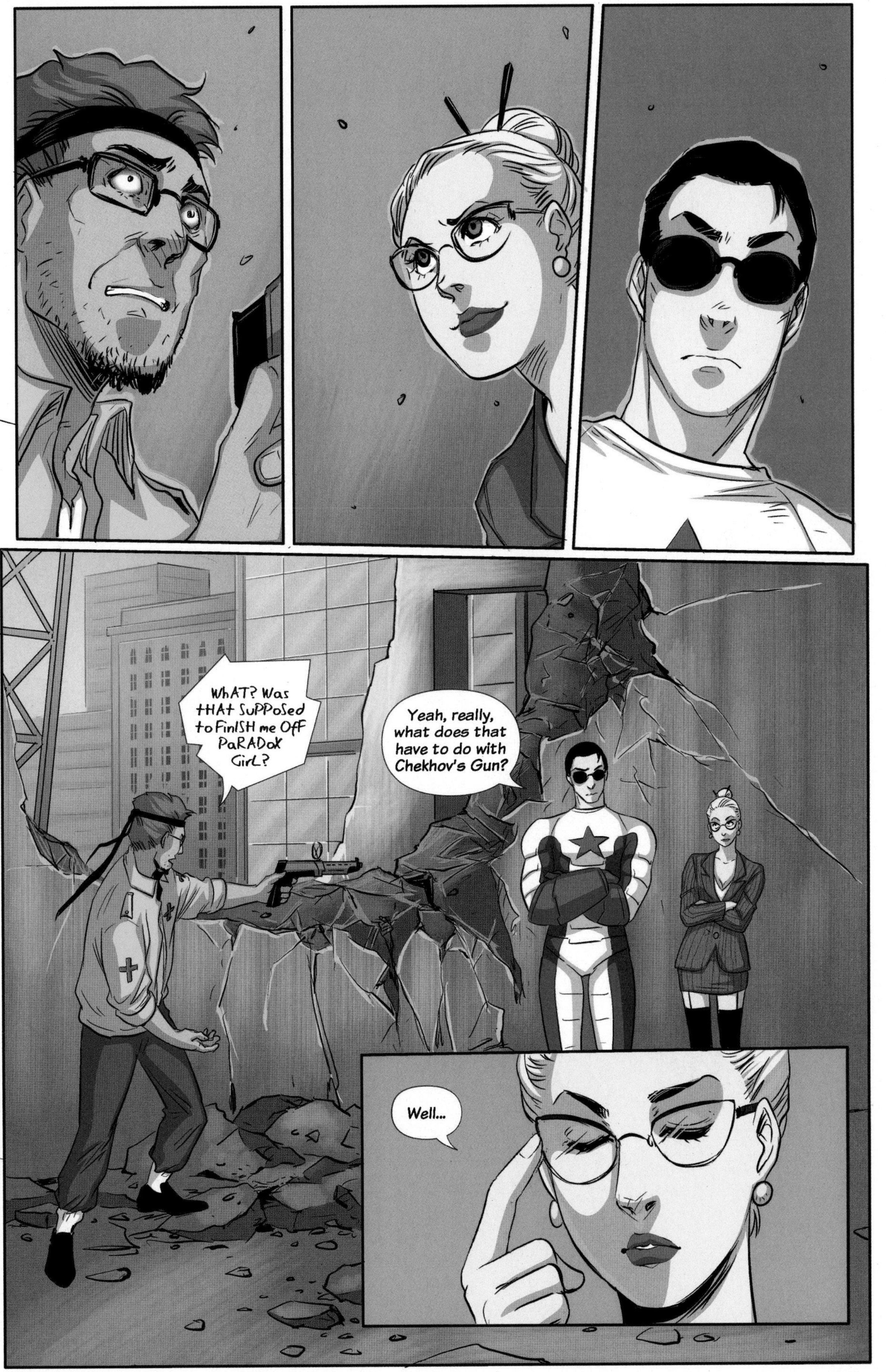
WHAT? Was THAT SUPPOSED to FINISH me OFF PARADOX GIRL?
Yeah, really, what does that have to do with Chekhov's Gun?
Well...

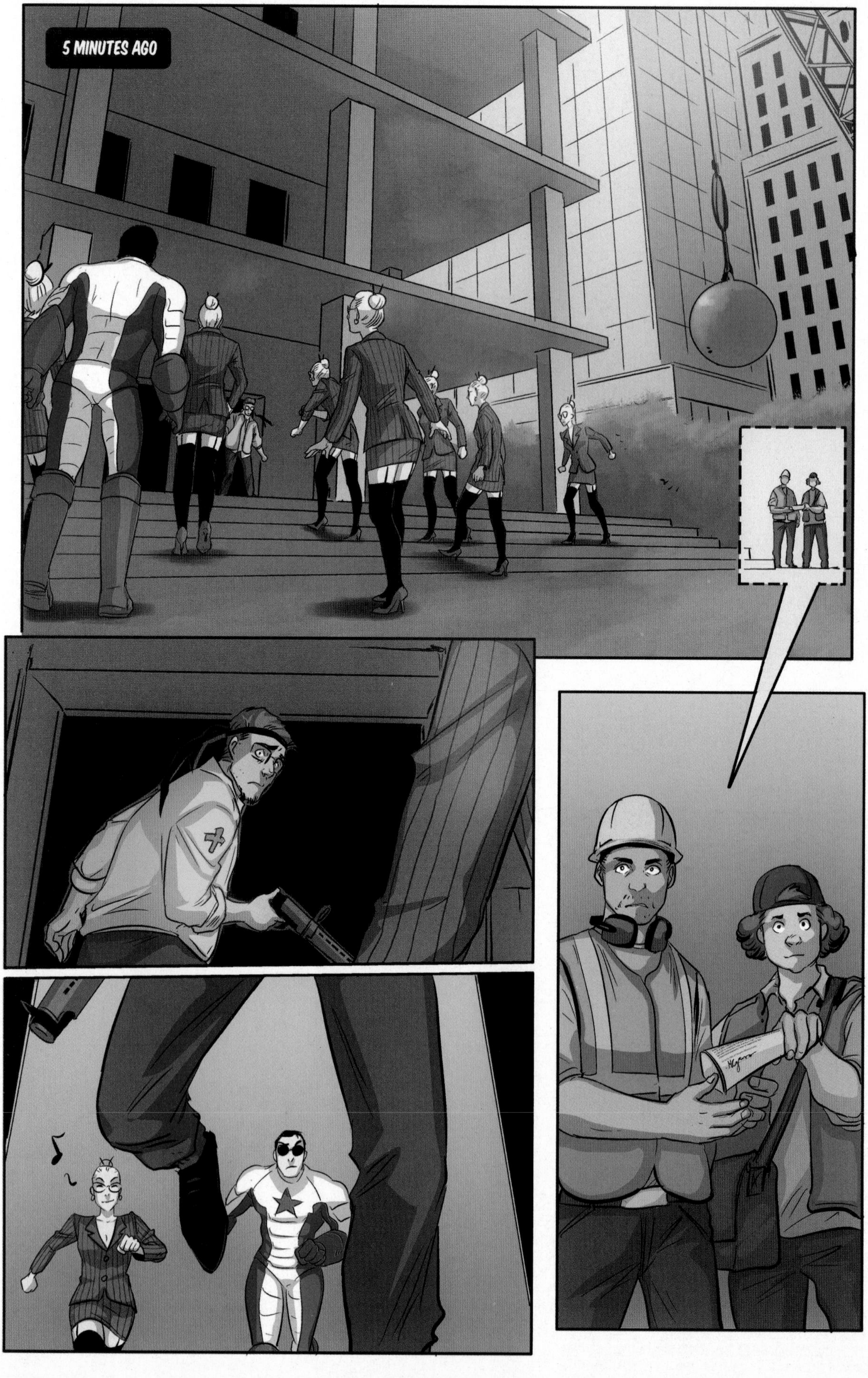
5 MINUTES AGO

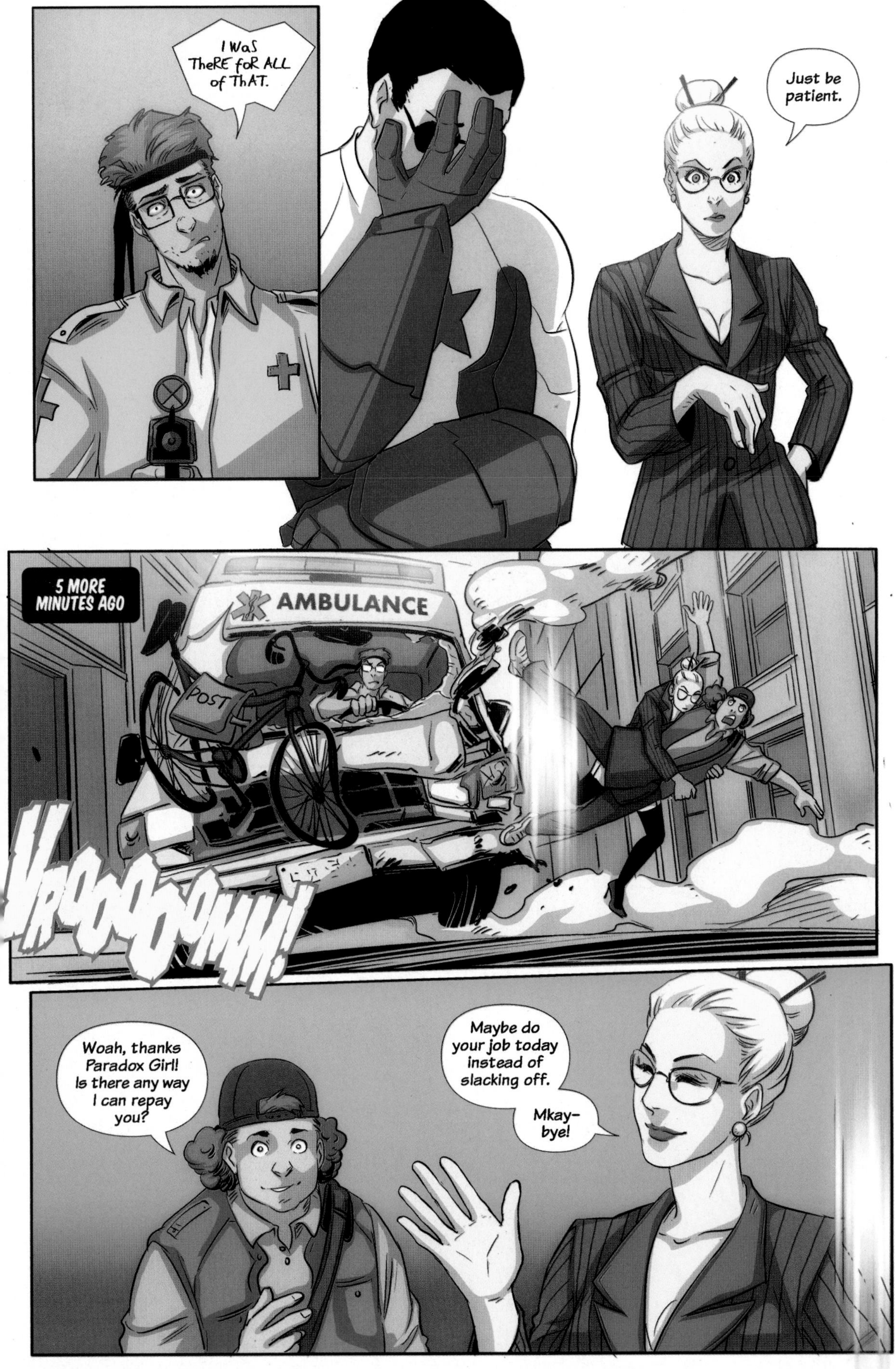
I WaS ThERE foR ALL of ThAT.
Just be patient.
5 MORE MINUTES AGO
AMBULANCE
POST
VROOOOOMM!
Woah, thanks Paradox Girl! Is there any way I can repay you?
Maybe do your job today instead of slacking off.
Mkay-bye!

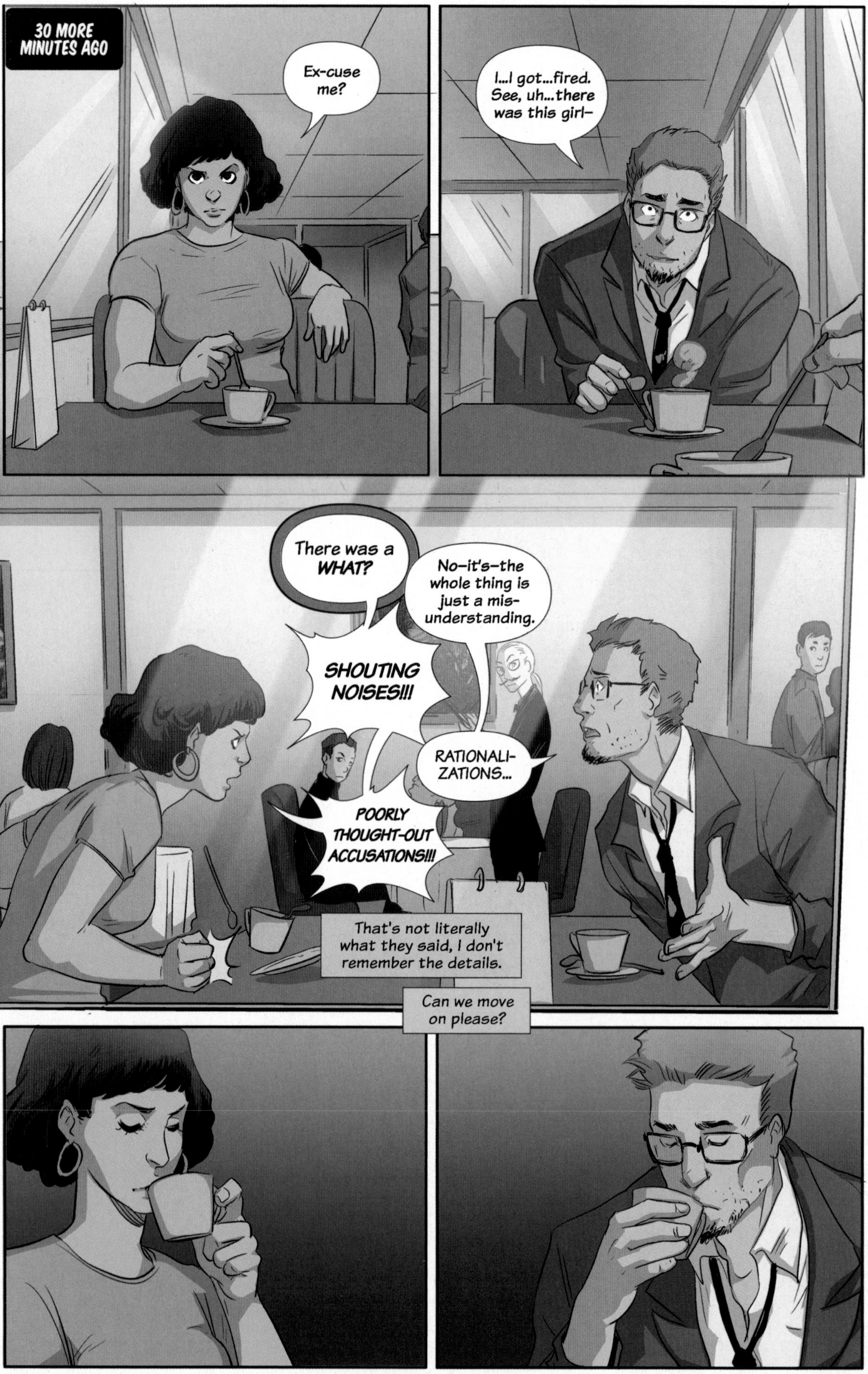
30 MORE MINUTES AGO
Ex-cuse me?
I...I got...fired. See, uh...there was this girl–
There was a WHAT?
No–it's–the whole thing is just a misunderstanding.
SHOUTING NOISES!!!
RATIONALIZATIONS...
POORLY THOUGHT-OUT ACCUSATIONS!!!
That's not literally what they said, I don't remember the details.
Can we move on please?

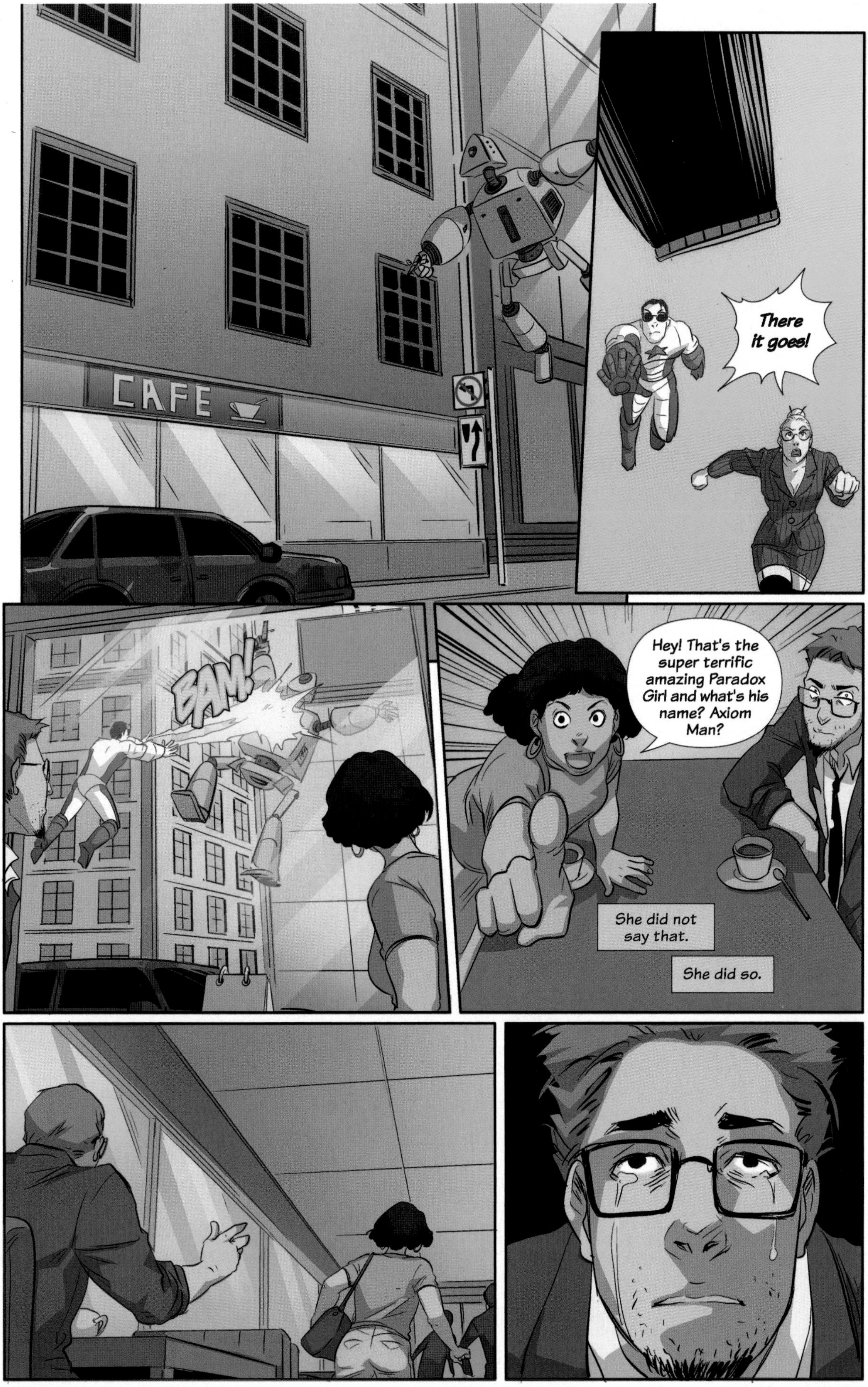
CAFE
There it goes!
BAM!
Hey! That's the super terrific amazing Paradox Girl and what's his name? Axiom Man?
She did not say that.
She did so.

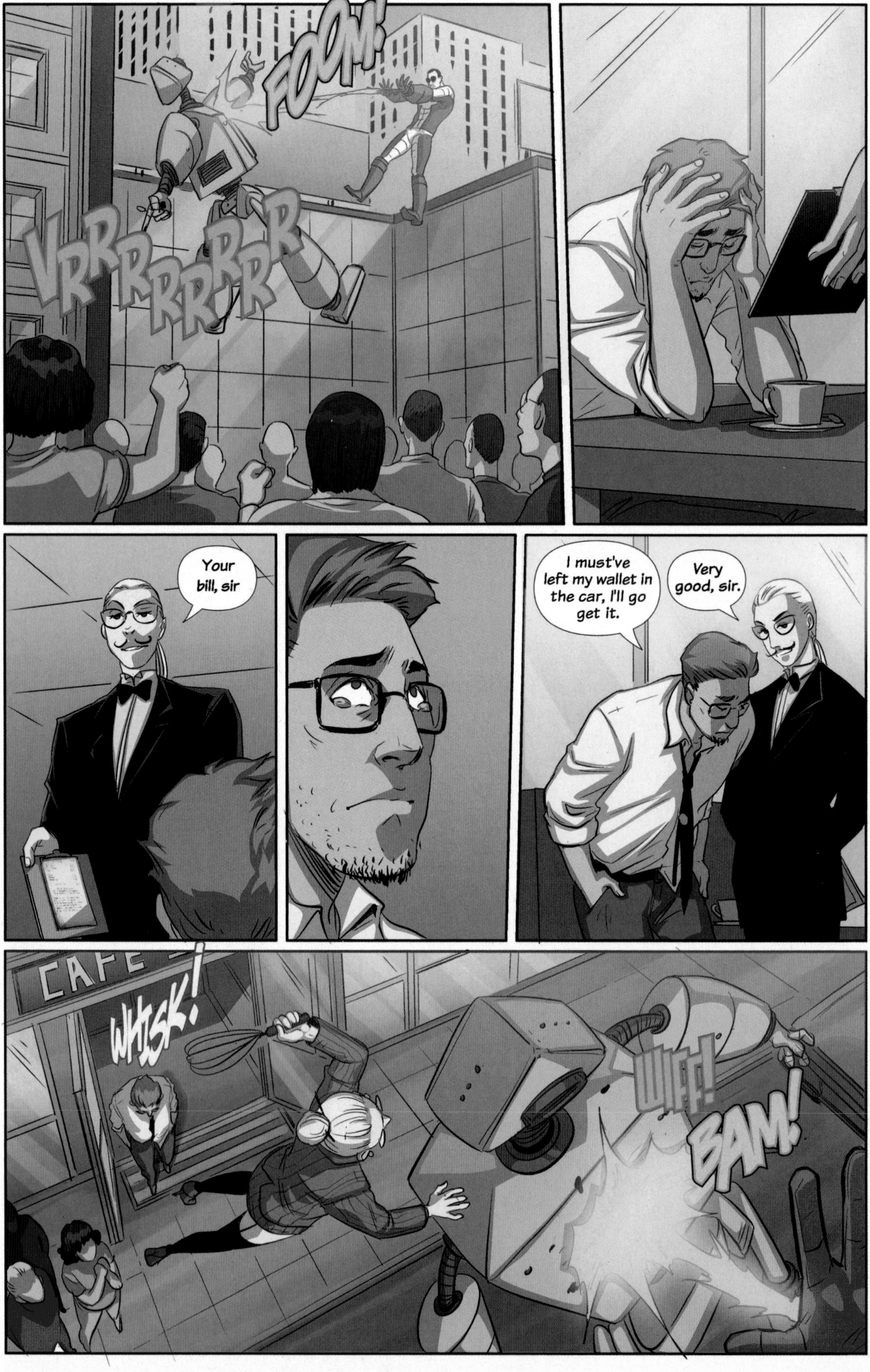
FOOM!
VRRRRRRRRR
Your bill, sir
I must've left my wallet in the car, I'll go get it.
Very good, sir.
CAFE
WHISK!
WIFF!
BAM!

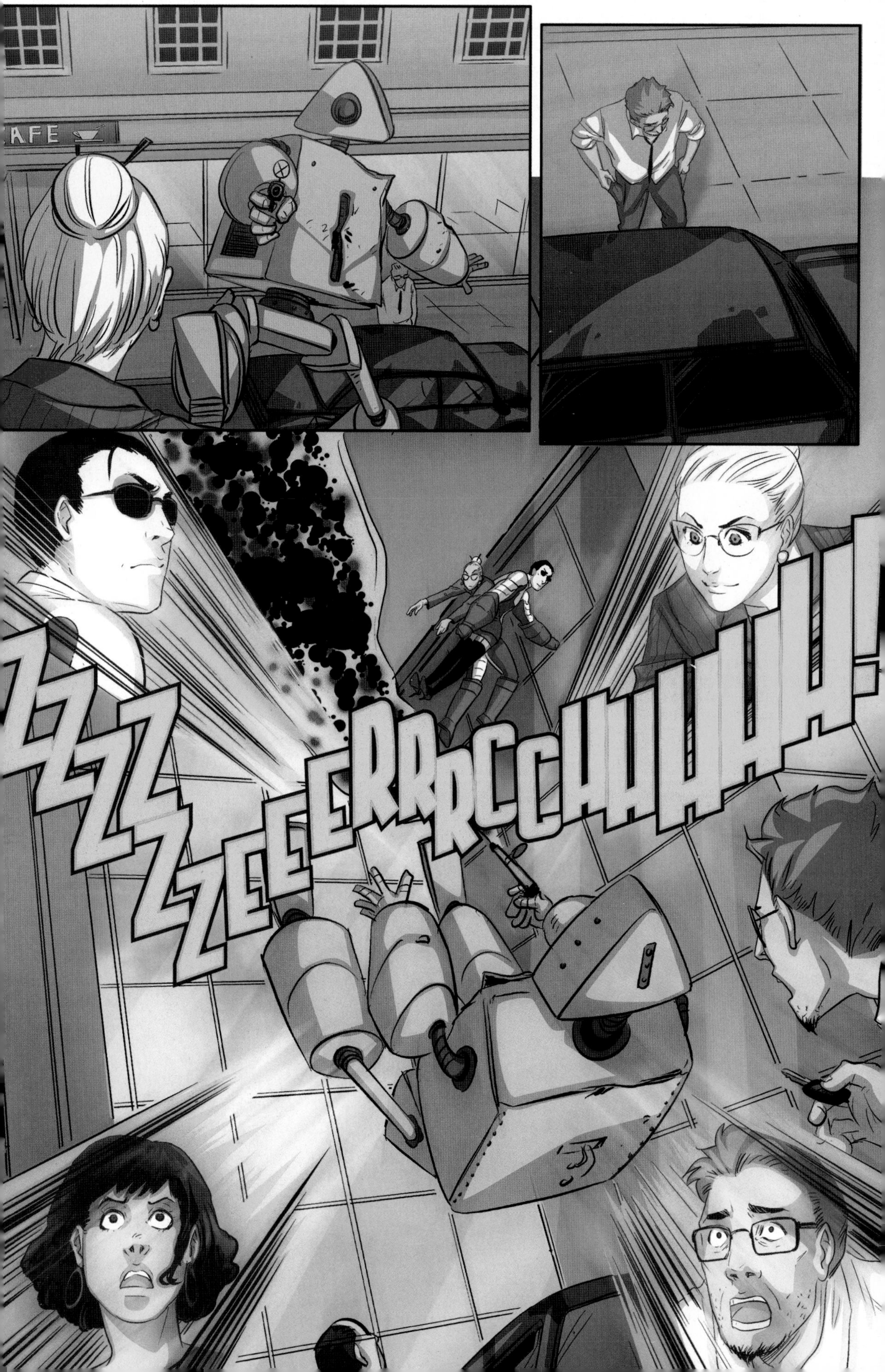
AFE
ZZZZZZEEERRRCCHHHHHH!

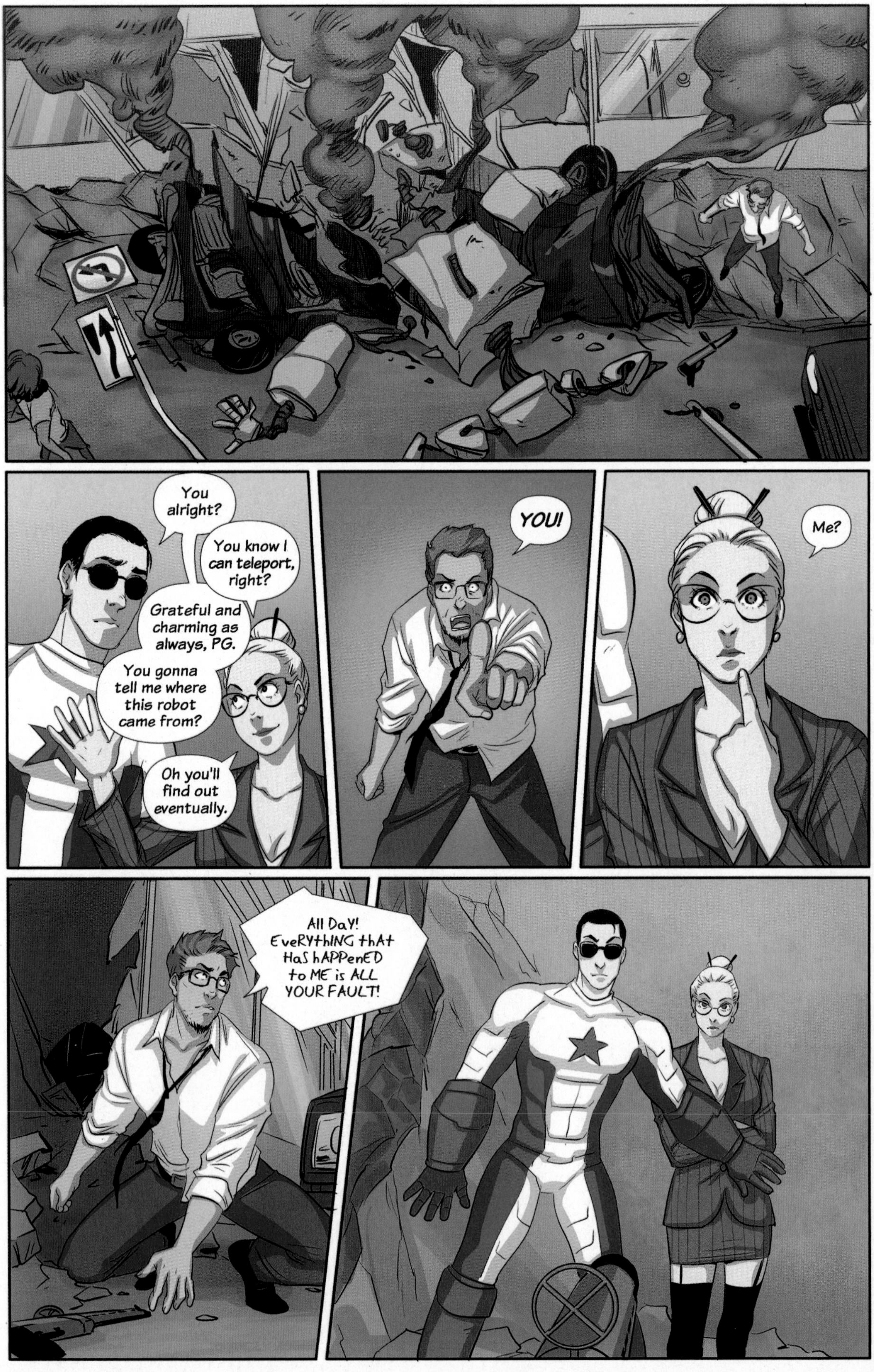
You alright?
You know I can teleport, right?
Grateful and charming as always, PG.
You gonna tell me where this robot came from?
Oh you'll find out eventually.
YOU!
Me?
All Day! EveRYthING thAt HaS hAPPenED to ME is ALL YOUR FAULT!

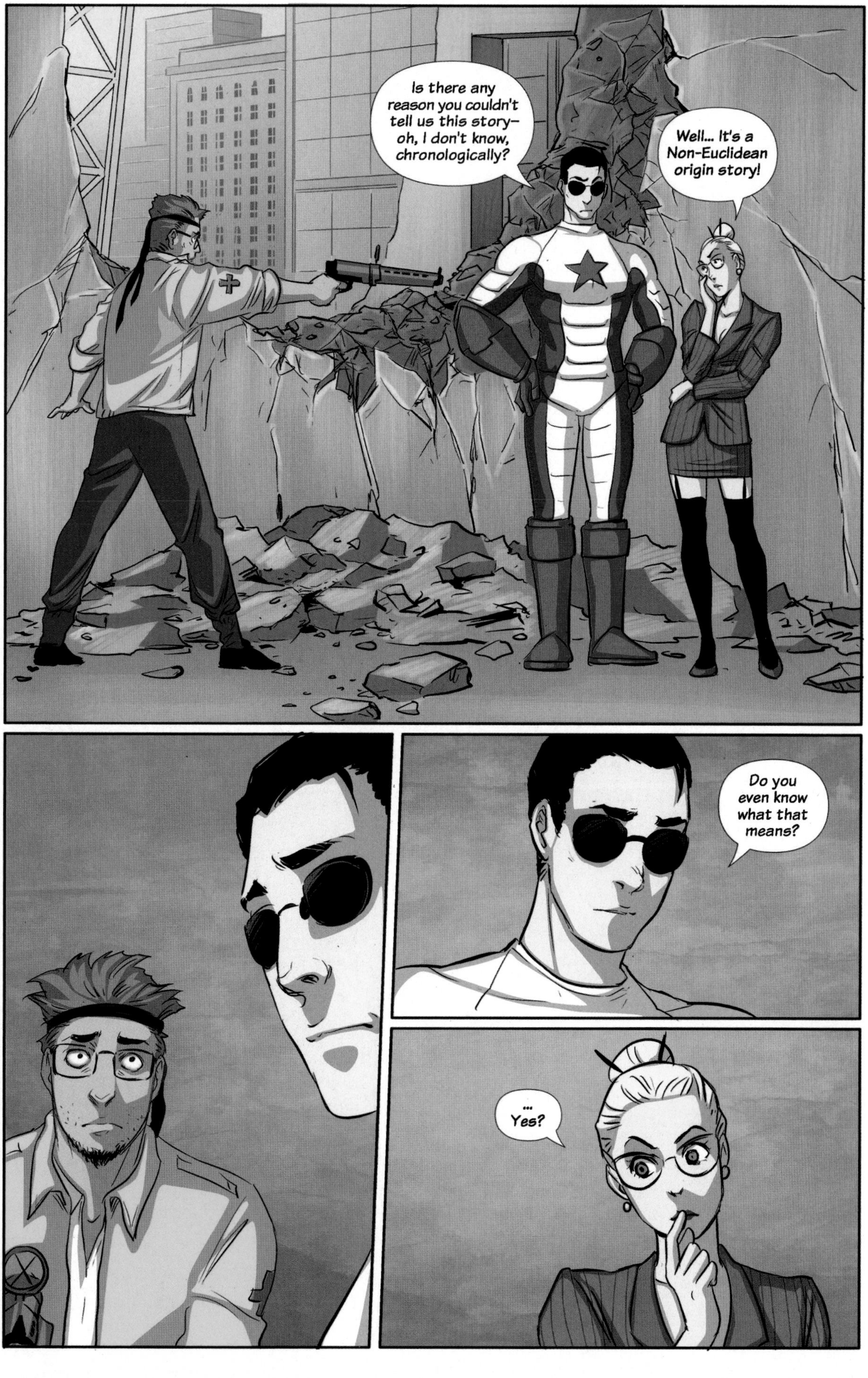
Is there any reason you couldn't tell us this story— oh, I don't know, chronologically?
Well... It's a Non-Euclidean origin story!
Do you even know what that means?
... Yes?

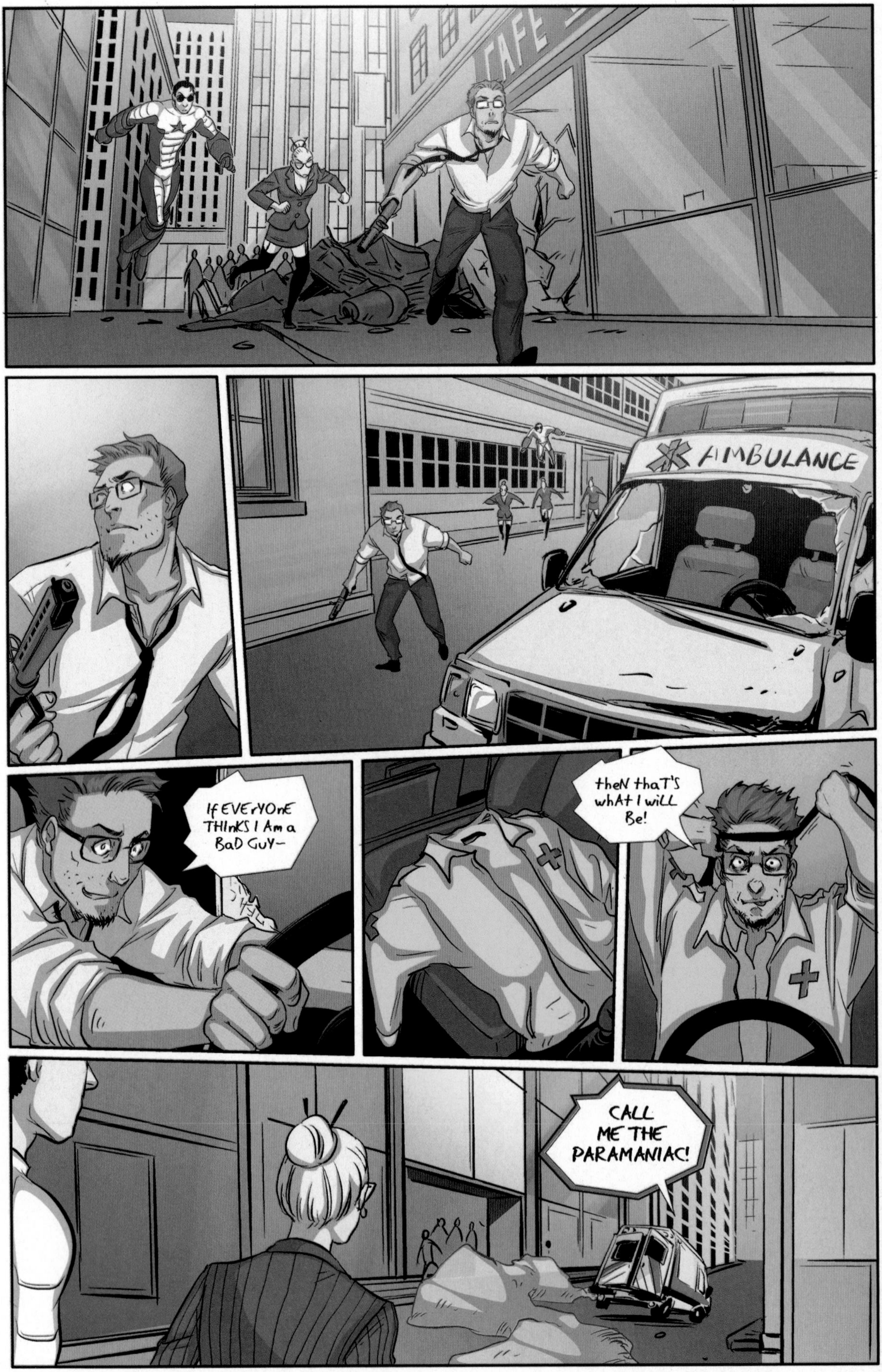
CAFE
AMBULANCE
If EVERYONE THINKS I Am a BaD GUY—
theN thaT'S whAt I wiLL Be!
CALL ME THE PARAMANIAC!

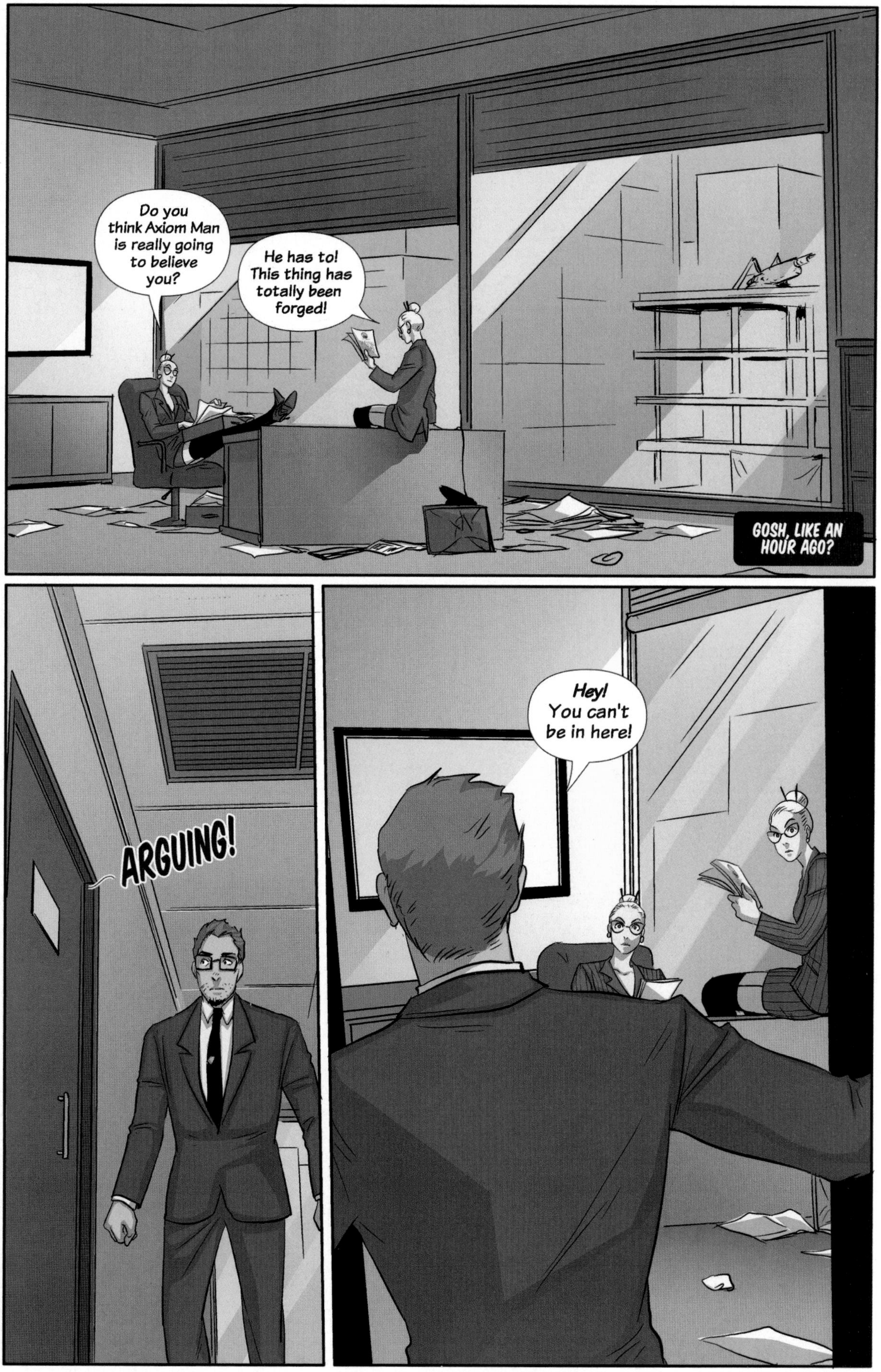
Do you think Axiom Man is really going to believe you?
He has to! This thing has totally been forged!
GOSH, LIKE AN HOUR AGO?
ARGUING!
Hey! You can't be in here!

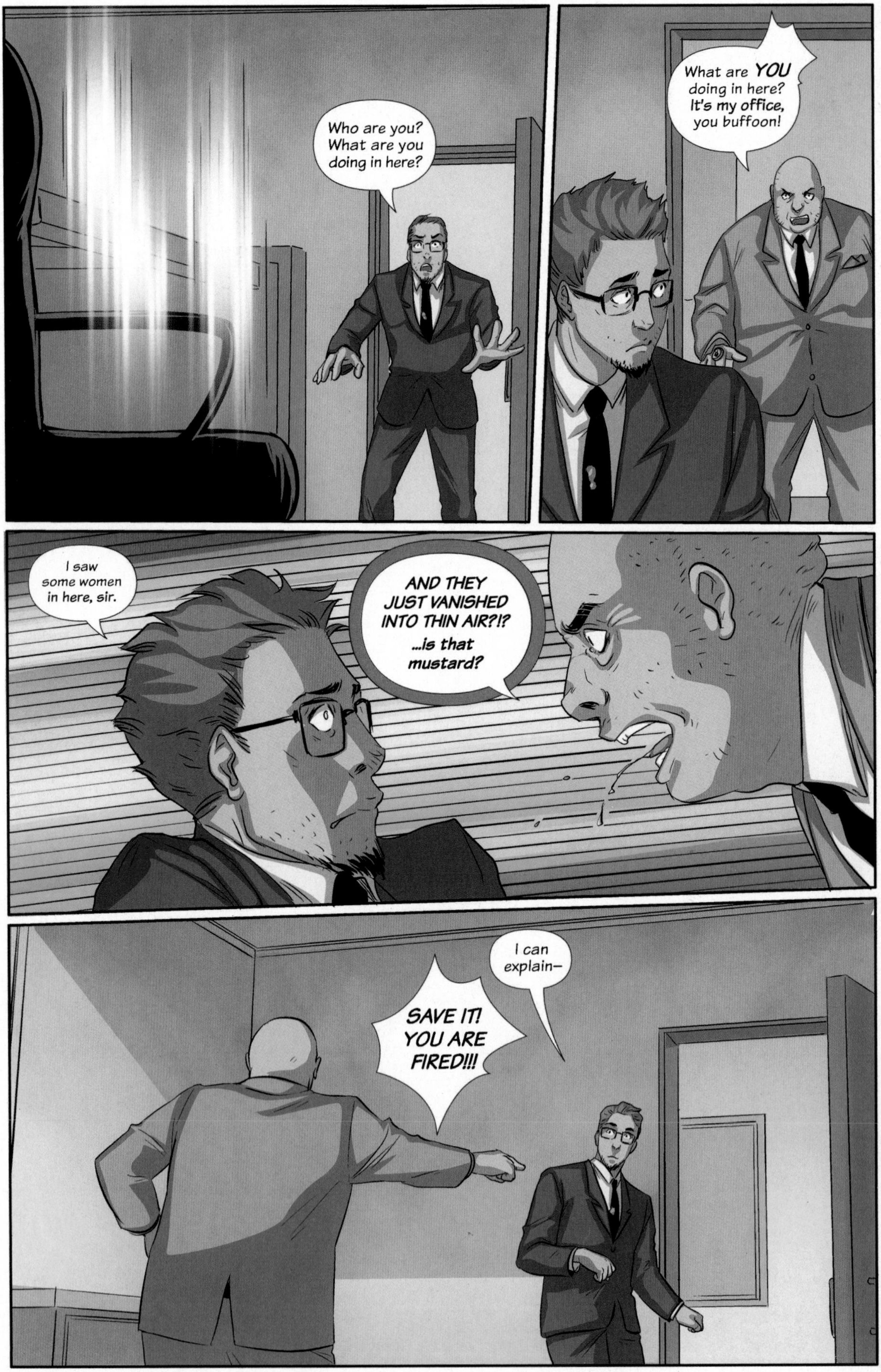
Who are you? What are you doing in here?
What are YOU doing in here? It's my office, you buffoon!
I saw some women in here, sir.
AND THEY JUST VANISHED INTO THIN AIR?!?
...is that mustard?
I can explain–
SAVE IT! YOU ARE FIRED!!!

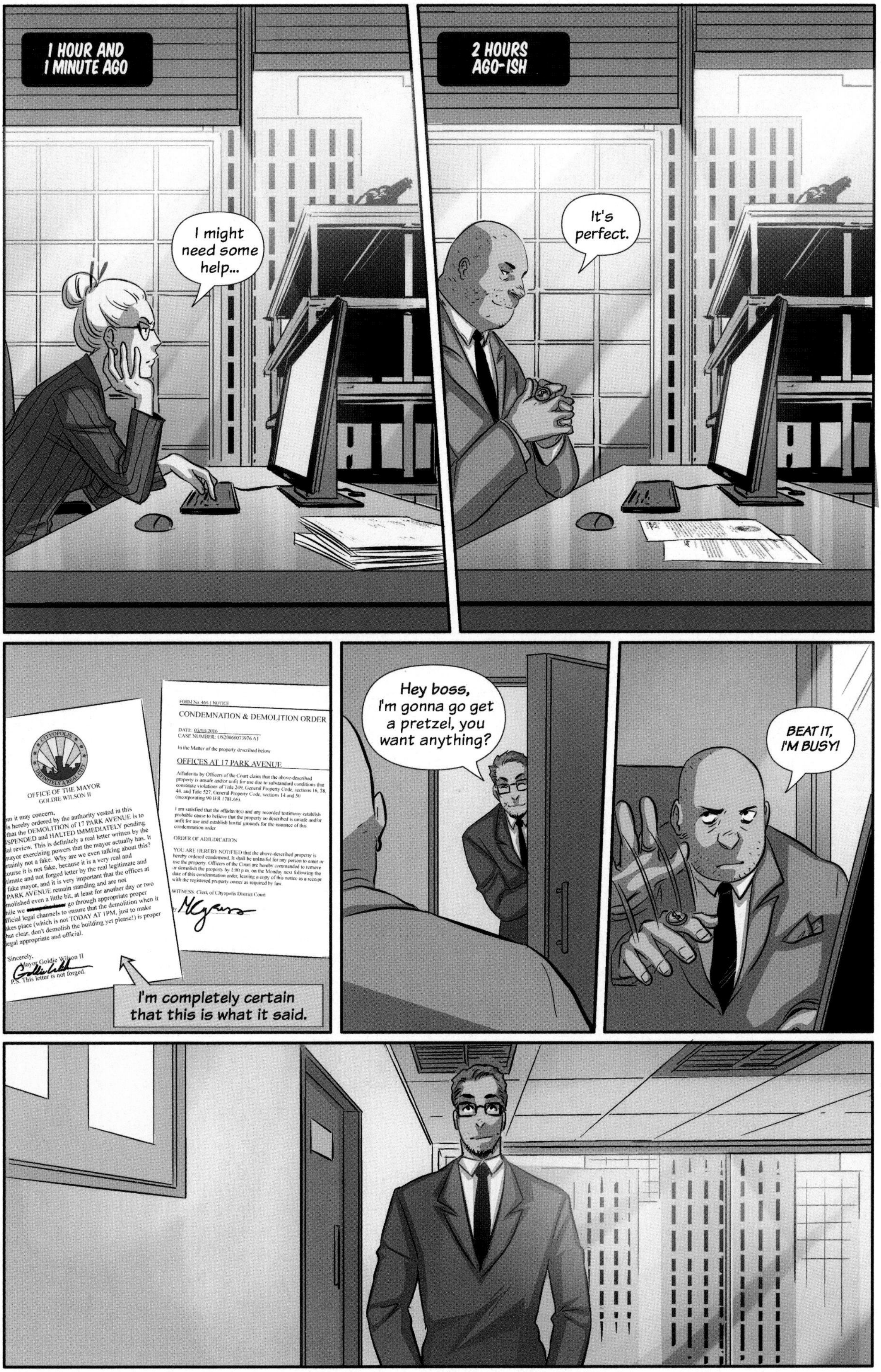

1 HOUR AND 1 MINUTE AGO
I might need some help...
2 HOURS AGO-ISH
It's perfect.
CITYOPOLIS
DEFINITELY A REAL CITY
OFFICE OF THE MAYOR
GOLDIE WILSON II
om it may concern,
is hereby ordered by the authority vested in this
that the DEMOLITION of 17 PARK AVENUE is to
SPENDED and HALTED IMMEDIATELY pending
ial review. This is definitely a real letter written by the
mayor exercising powers that the mayor actually has. It
rtainly not a fake. Why are we even talking about this?
ourse it is not fake, because it is a very real and
timate and not forged letter by the real legitimate and
fake mayor, and it is very important that the offices at
PARK AVENUE remain standing and are not
molished even a little bit, at least for another day or two
hile we [redacted] go through appropriate proper
fficial legal channels to ensure that the demolition when it
akes place (which is not TODAY AT 1PM, just to make
hat clear, don't demolish the building yet please!) is proper
legal appropriate and official.
Sincerely,
Mayor Goldie Wilson II
P.S. This letter is not forged.
FORM No. 464-1 NOTICE
CONDEMNATION & DEMOLITION ORDER
DATE: 03/03/2016
CASE NUMBER: US20060073976 A1
In the Matter of the property described below
OFFICES AT 17 PARK AVENUE
Affadavits by Officers of the Court claim that the above-described property is unsafe and/or unfit for use due to substandard conditions that constitute violations of Title 249, General Property Code, sections 16, 38, 44, and Title 527, General Property Code, sections 14 and 50 (incorporating 90 IFR 1781.66).
I am satisfied that the affadavit(s) and any recorded testimony establish probable cause to believe that the property so described is unsafe and/or unfit for use and establish lawful grounds for the issuance of this condemnation order
ORDER OF ADJUDICATION
YOU ARE HEREBY NOTIFIED that the above-described property is hereby ordered condemend. It shall be unlawful for any person to enter or use the property. Officers of the Court are hereby commanded to remove or demolish the property by 1:00 p.m. on the Monday next following the date of this condemnation order, leaving a copy of this notice as a receipt with the registered property owner as required by law.
WITNESS: Clerk of Cityopolis District Court
I'm completely certain that this is what it said.
Hey boss, I'm gonna go get a pretzel, you want anything?
BEAT IT, I'M BUSY!

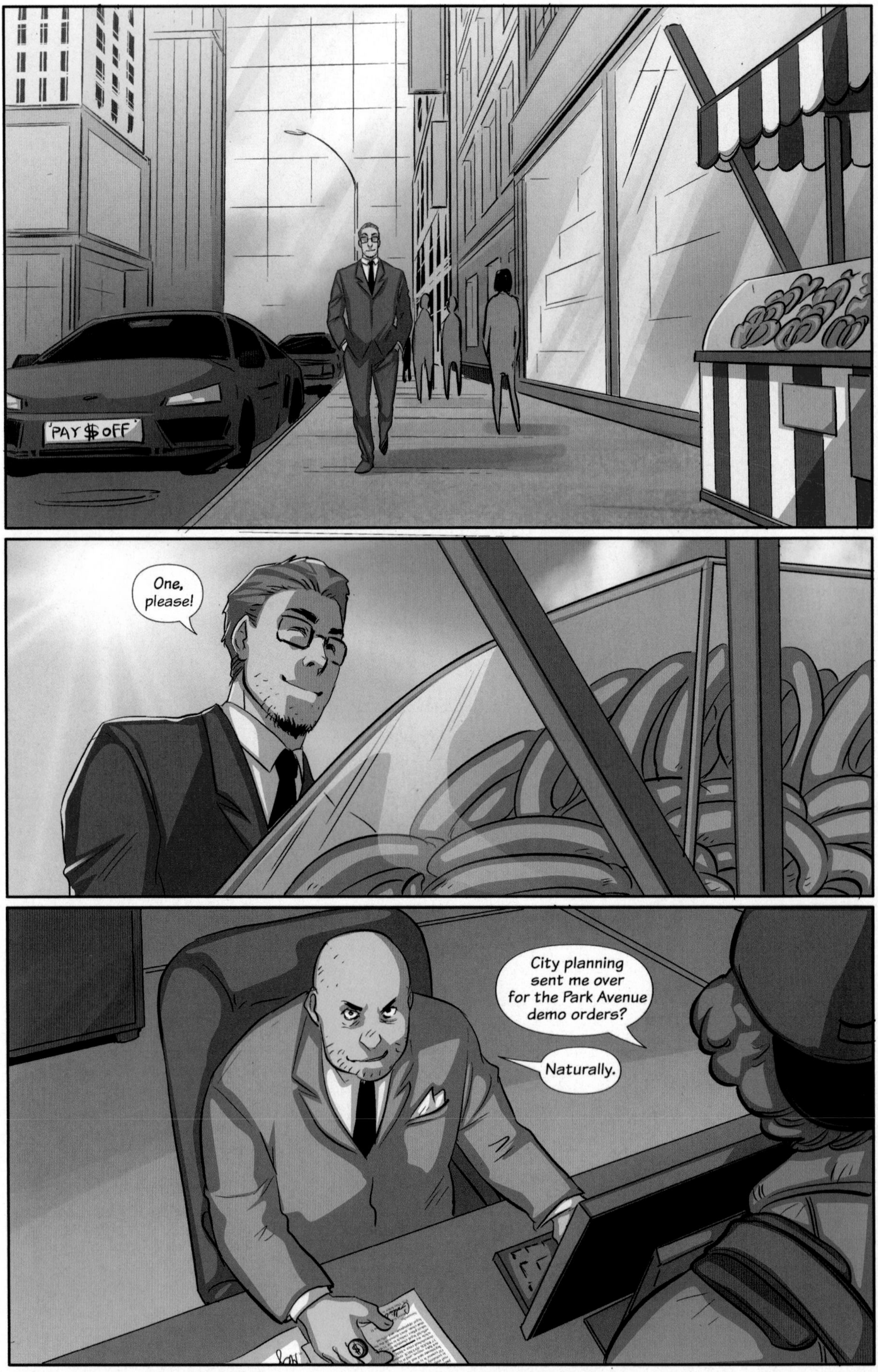
PAY $ OFF
One, please!
City planning sent me over for the Park Avenue demo orders?
Naturally.

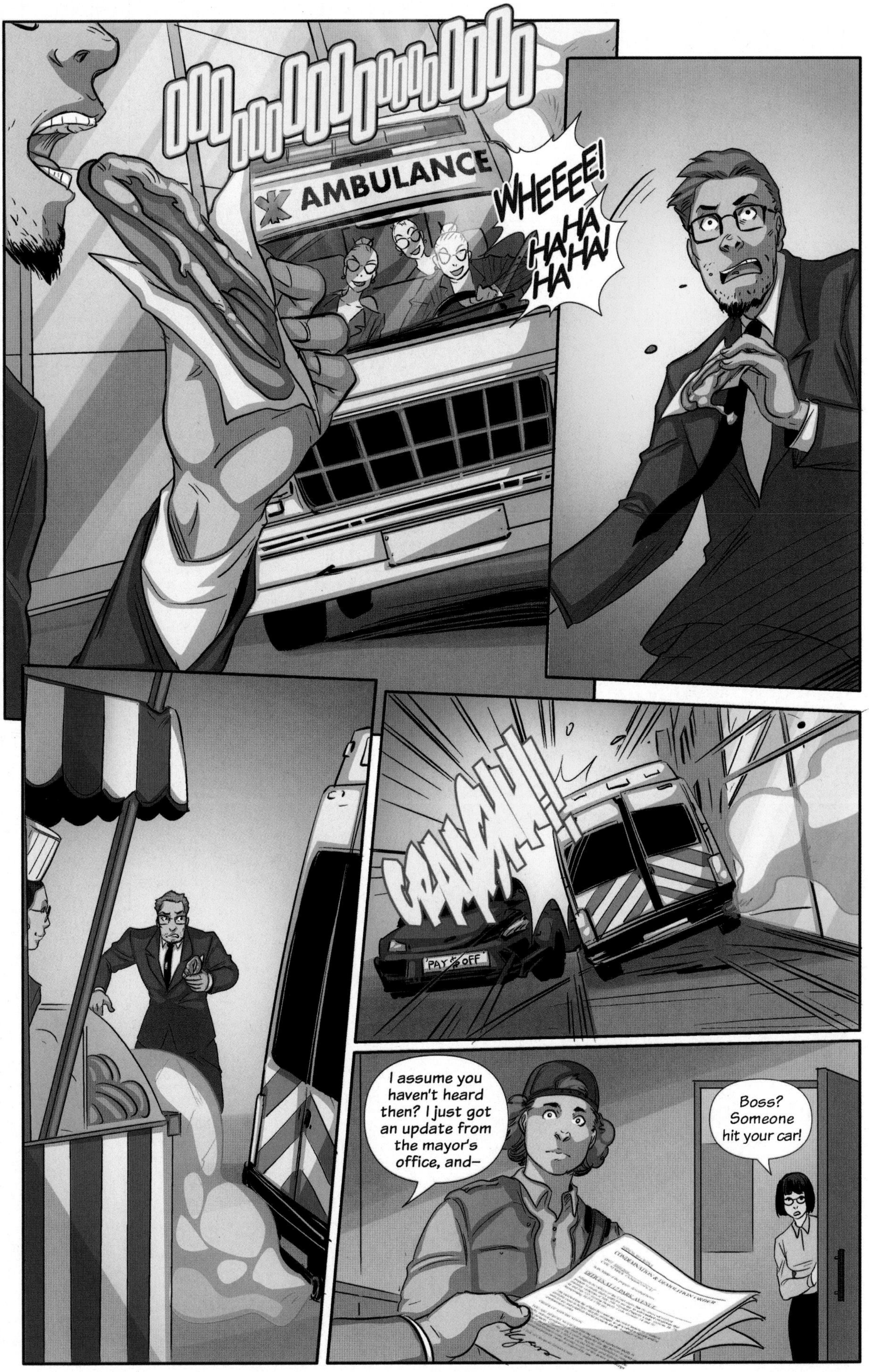
OOOoooOOOOooooOOOO
AMBULANCE
WHEEEE!
HAHA HAHA HA!
I assume you haven't heard then? I just got an update from the mayor's office, and–
Boss? Someone hit your car!

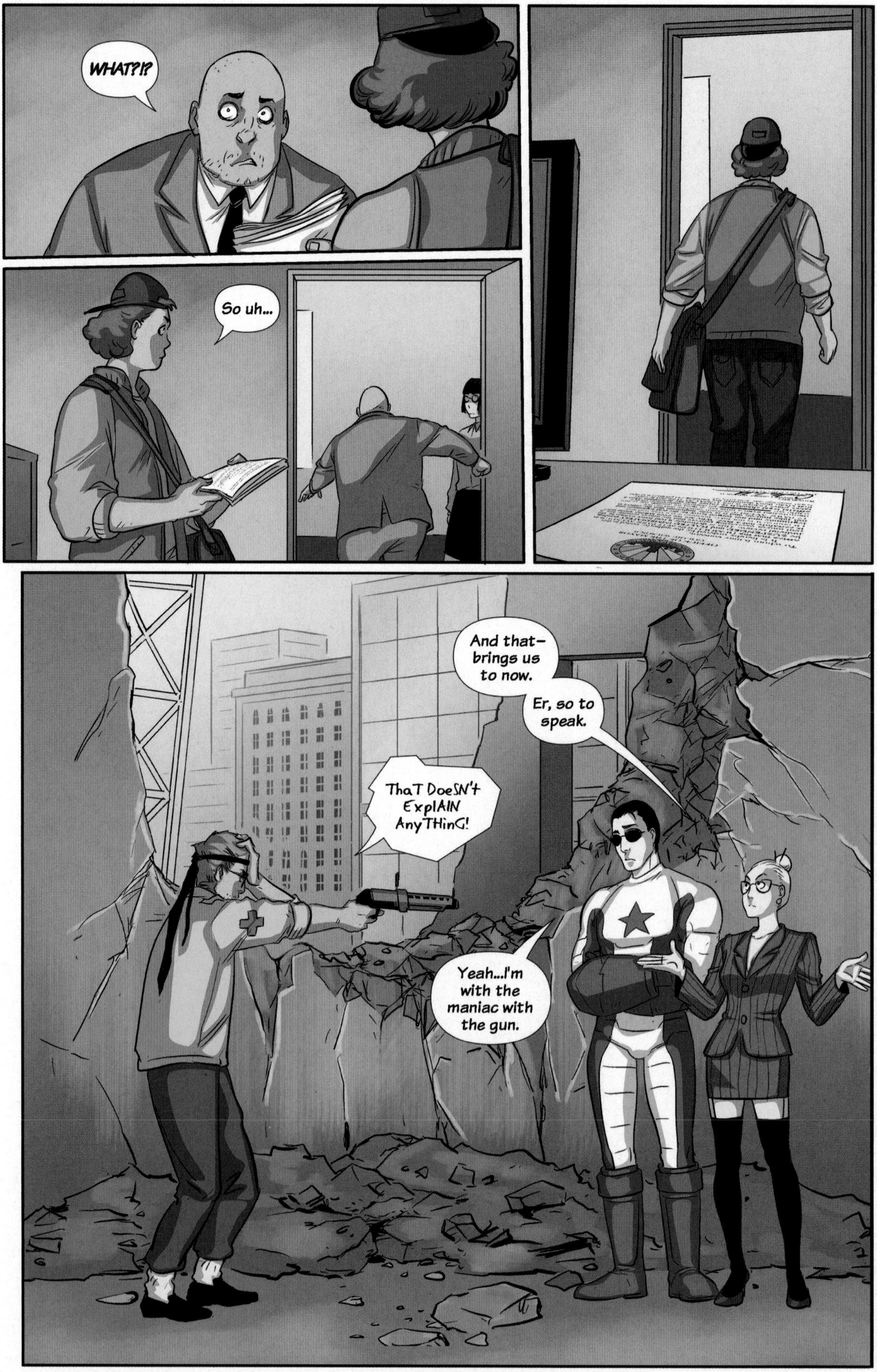
WHAT?!?
So uh...
And that-brings us to now.
Er, so to speak.
ThaT DoeSN't ExplAIN AnyTHinG!
Yeah...I'm with the maniac with the gun.

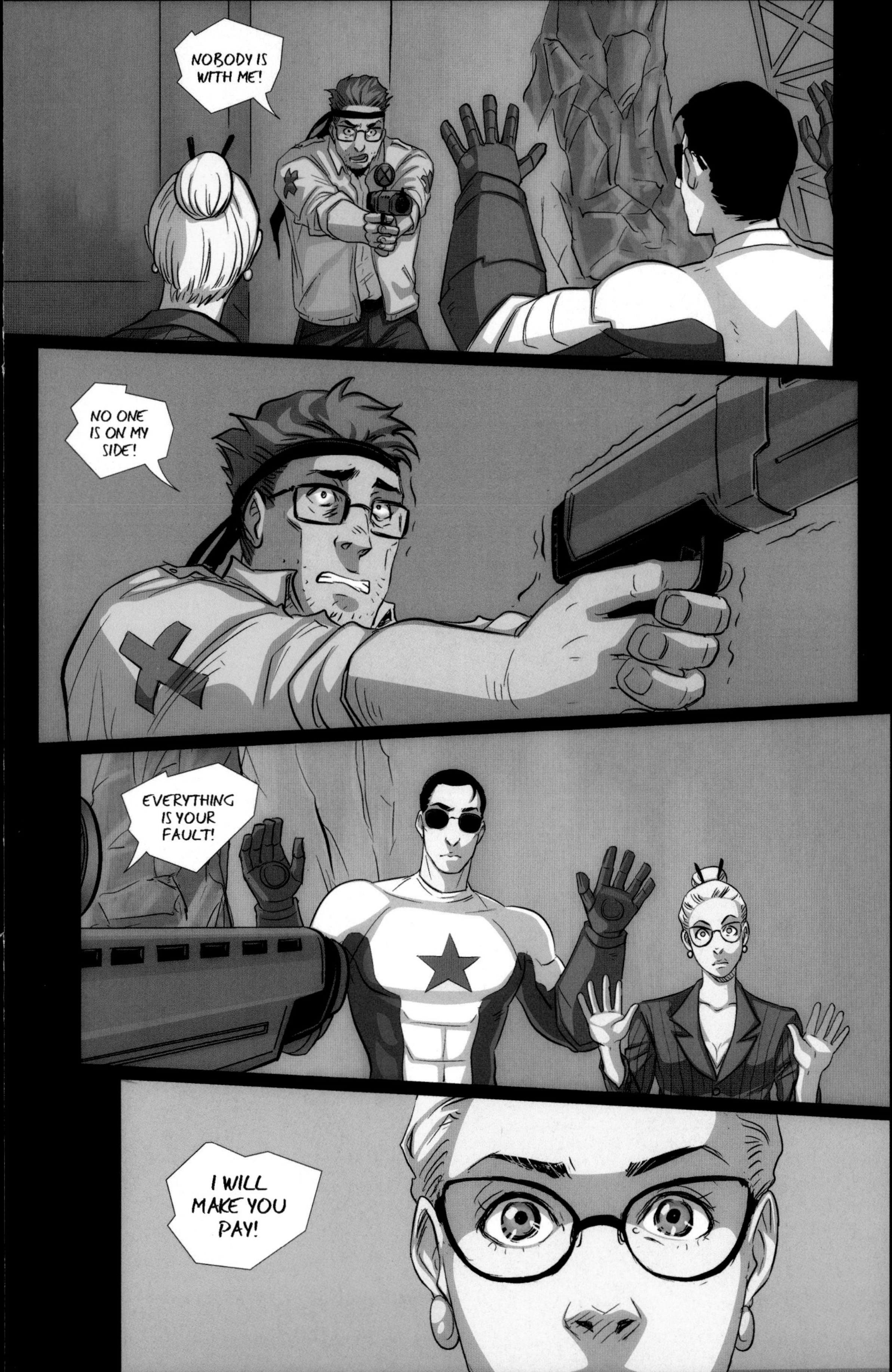
NOBODY IS WITH ME!
NO ONE IS ON MY SIDE!
EVERYTHING IS YOUR FAULT!
I WILL MAKE YOU PAY!

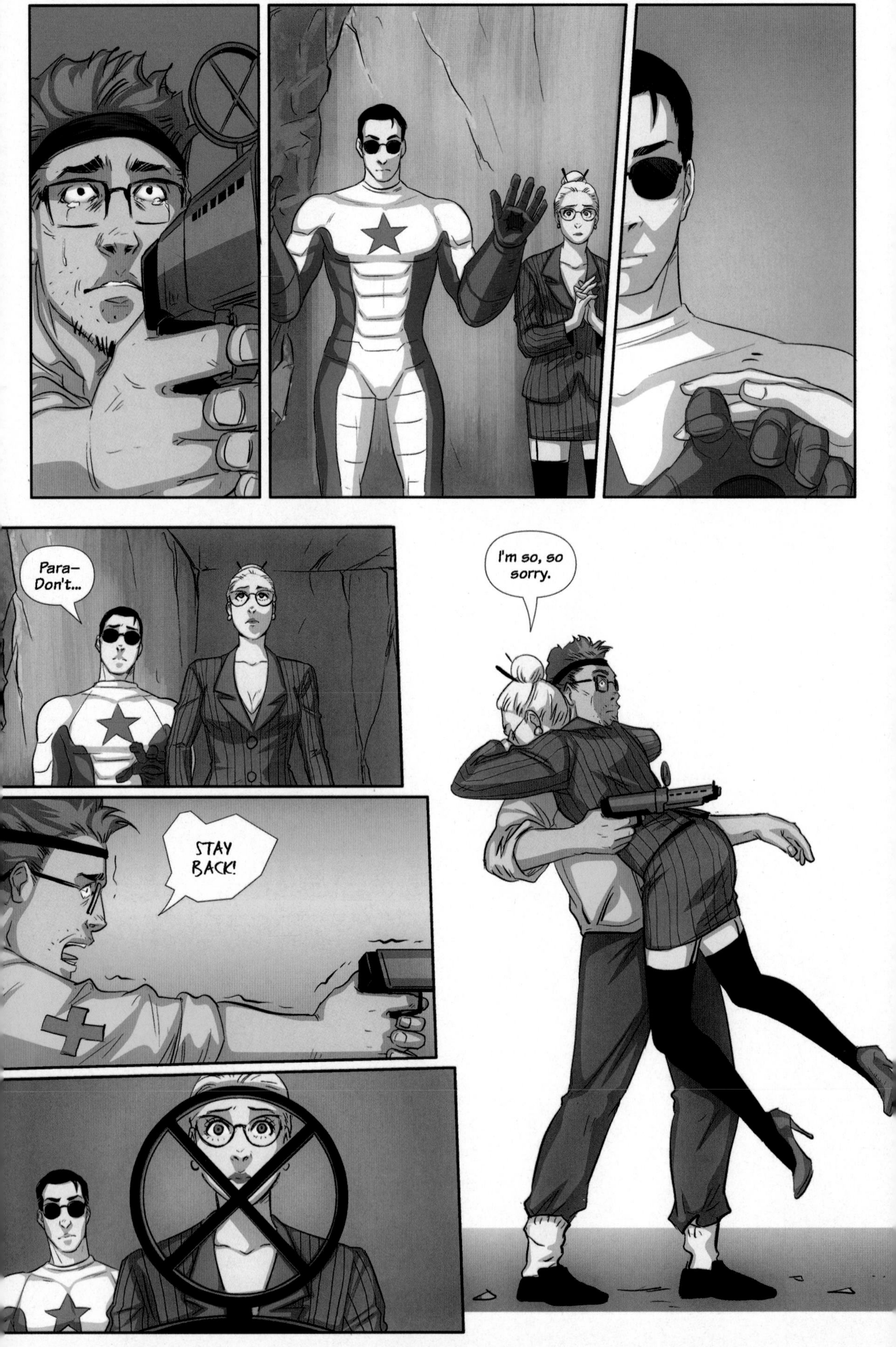
Para-
Don't...
STAY BACK!
I'm so, so sorry.

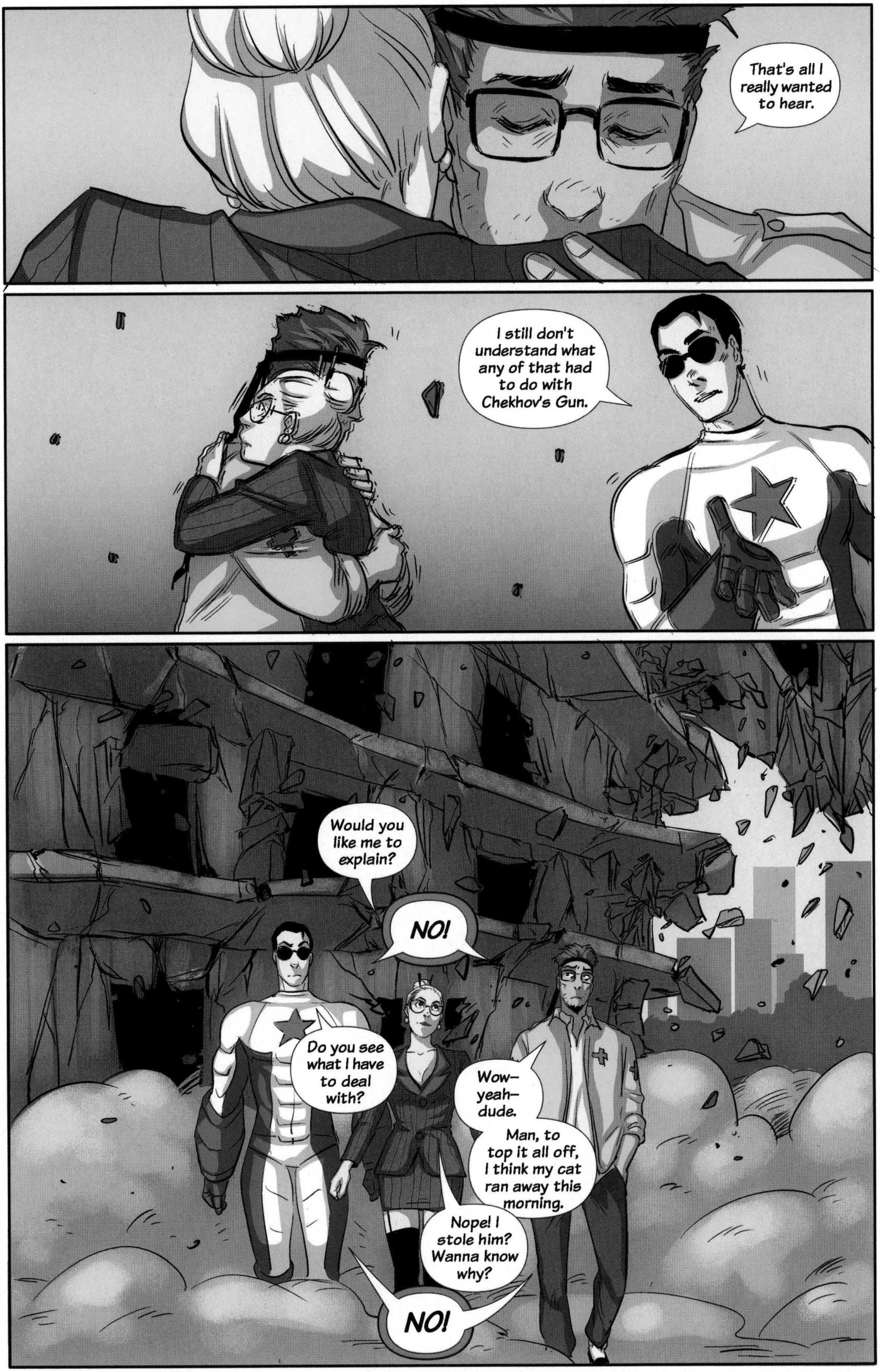
That's all I really wanted to hear.
I still don't understand what any of that had to do with Chekhov's Gun.
Would you like me to explain?
NO!
Do you see what I have to deal with?
Wow— yeah— dude.
Man, to top it all off, I think my cat ran away this morning.
Nope! I stole him? Wanna know why?
NO!

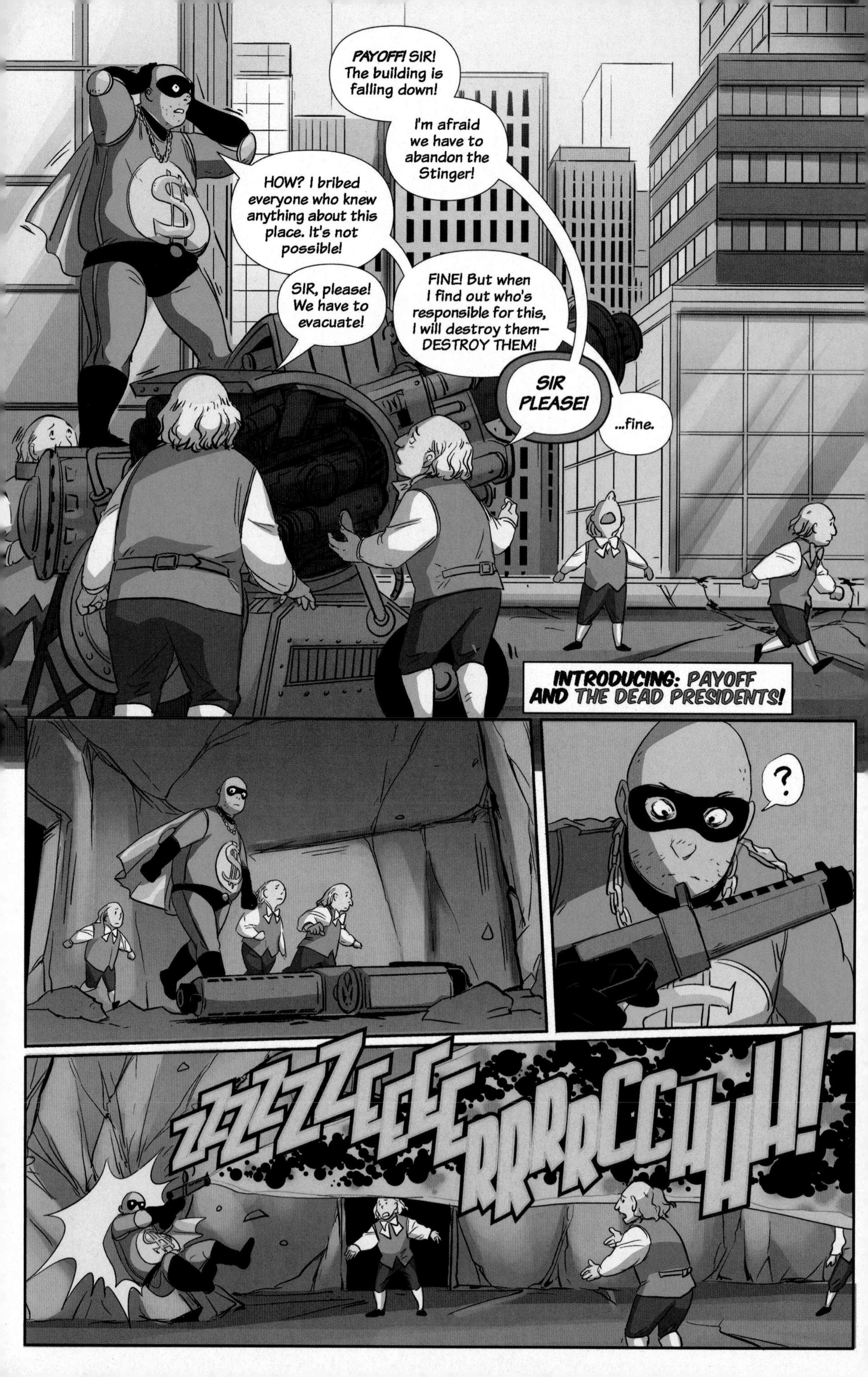
PAYOFF! SIR! The building is falling down!
I'm afraid we have to abandon the Stinger!
HOW? I bribed everyone who knew anything about this place. It's not possible!
SIR, please! We have to evacuate!
FINE! But when I find out who's responsible for this, I will destroy them—DESTROY THEM!
SIR PLEASE!
...fine.
INTRODUCING: PAYOFF AND THE DEAD PRESIDENTS!
?
ZZZZZZEEEEERRRRRCCHHH!

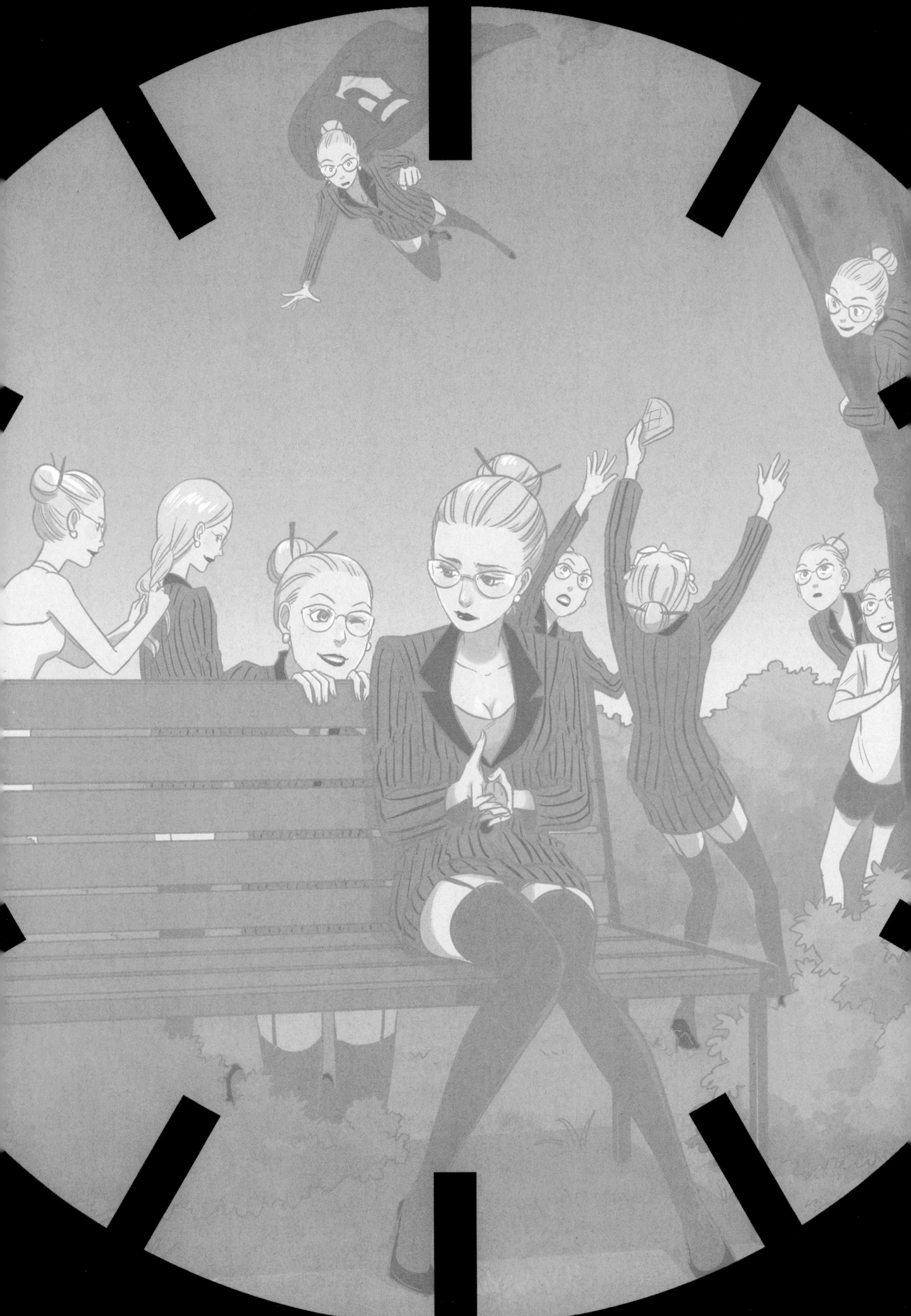

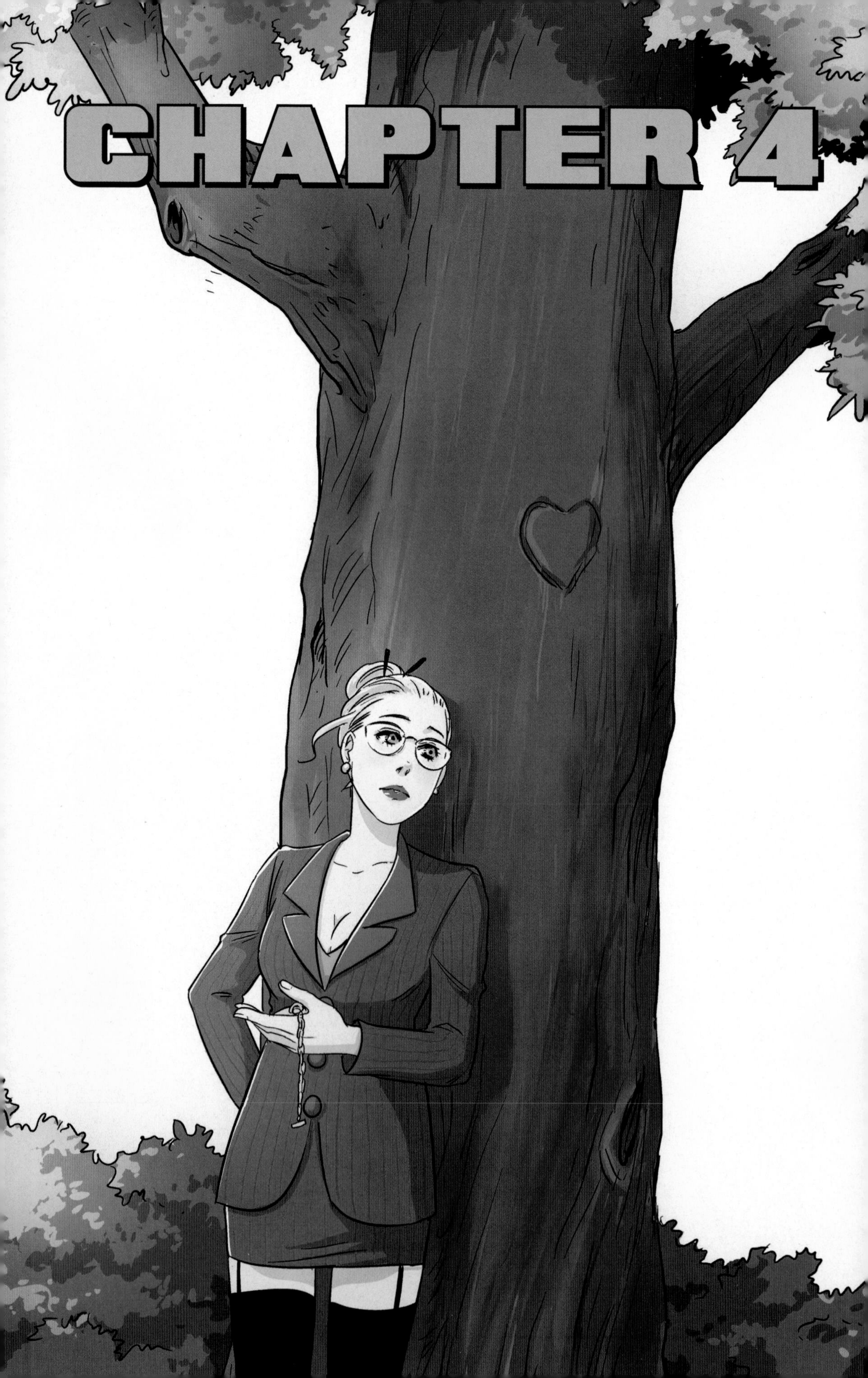
CHAPTER 4

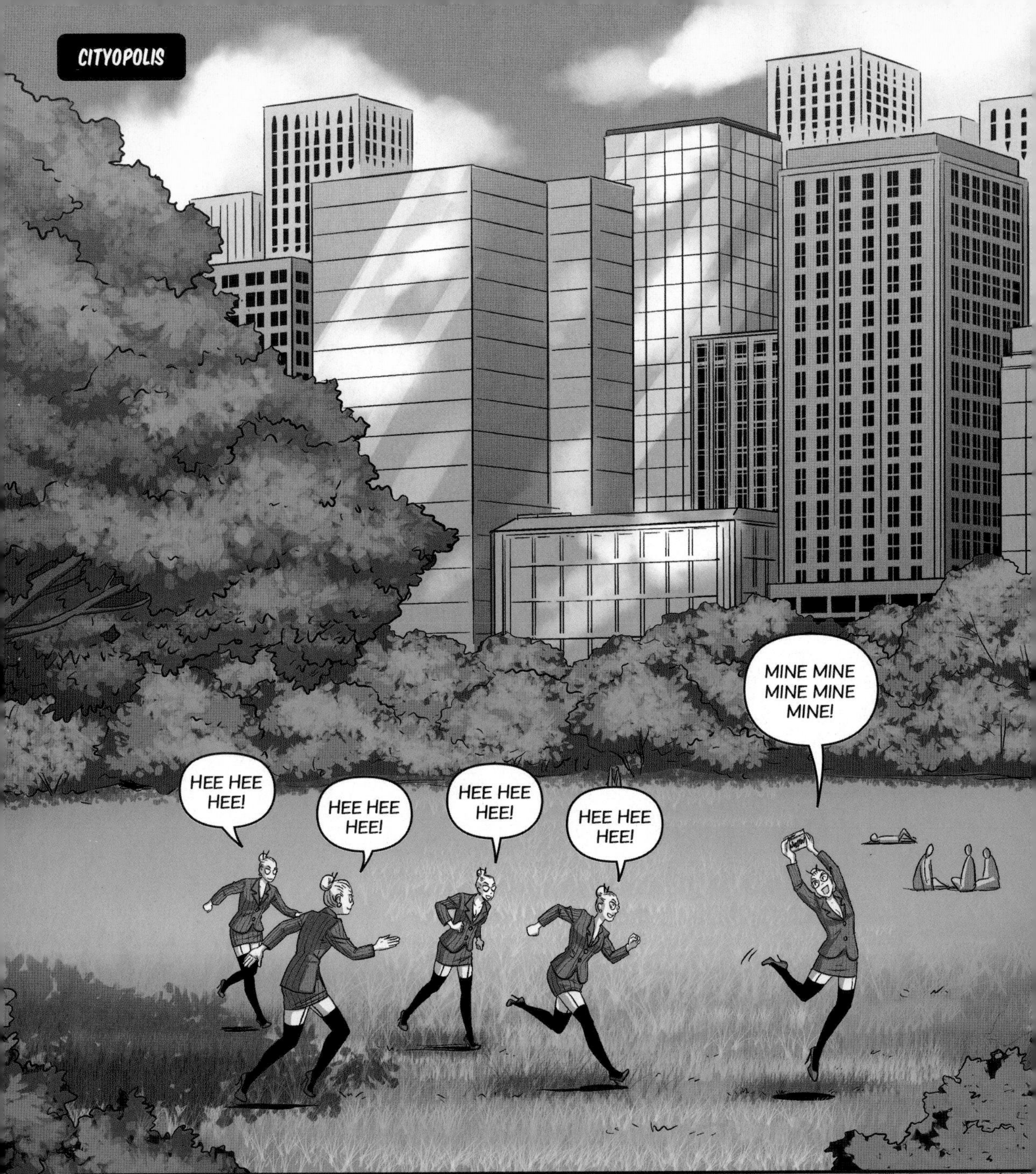
CITYOPOLIS
MINE MINE MINE MINE MINE!
HEE HEE HEE!
HEE HEE HEE!
HEE HEE HEE!
HEE HEE HEE!

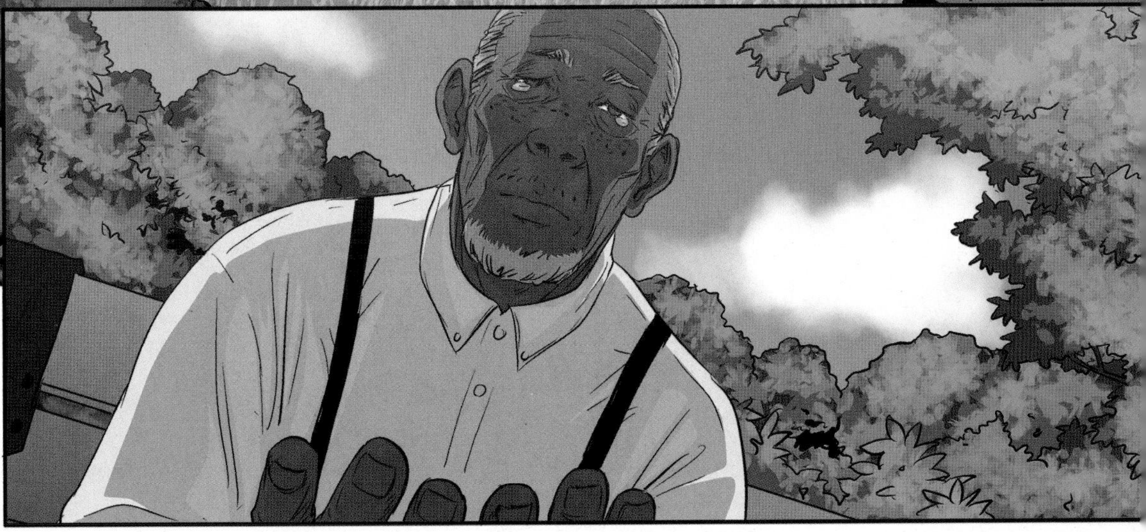

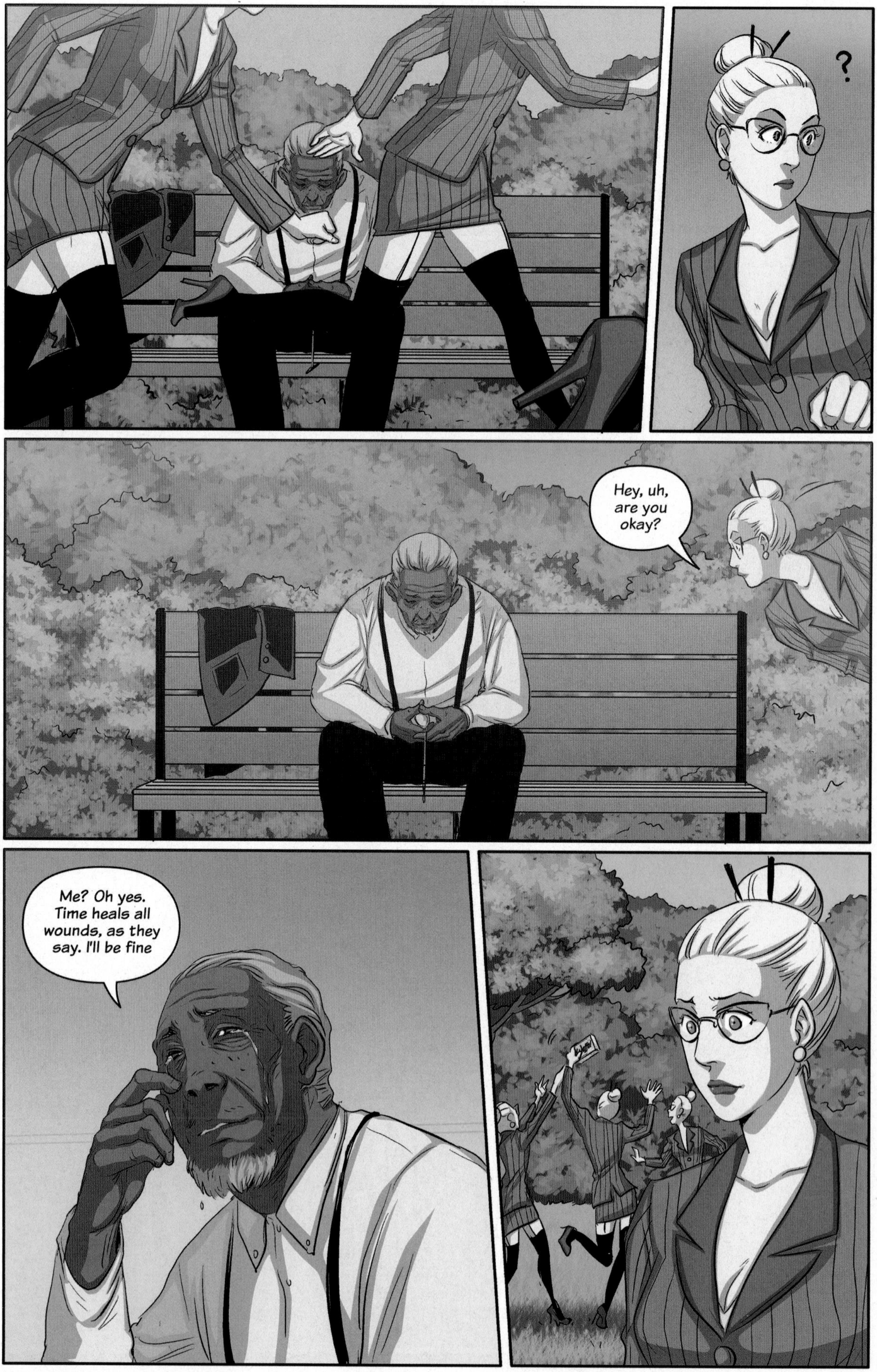
?
Hey, uh, are you okay?
Me? Oh yes. Time heals all wounds, as they say. I'll be fine

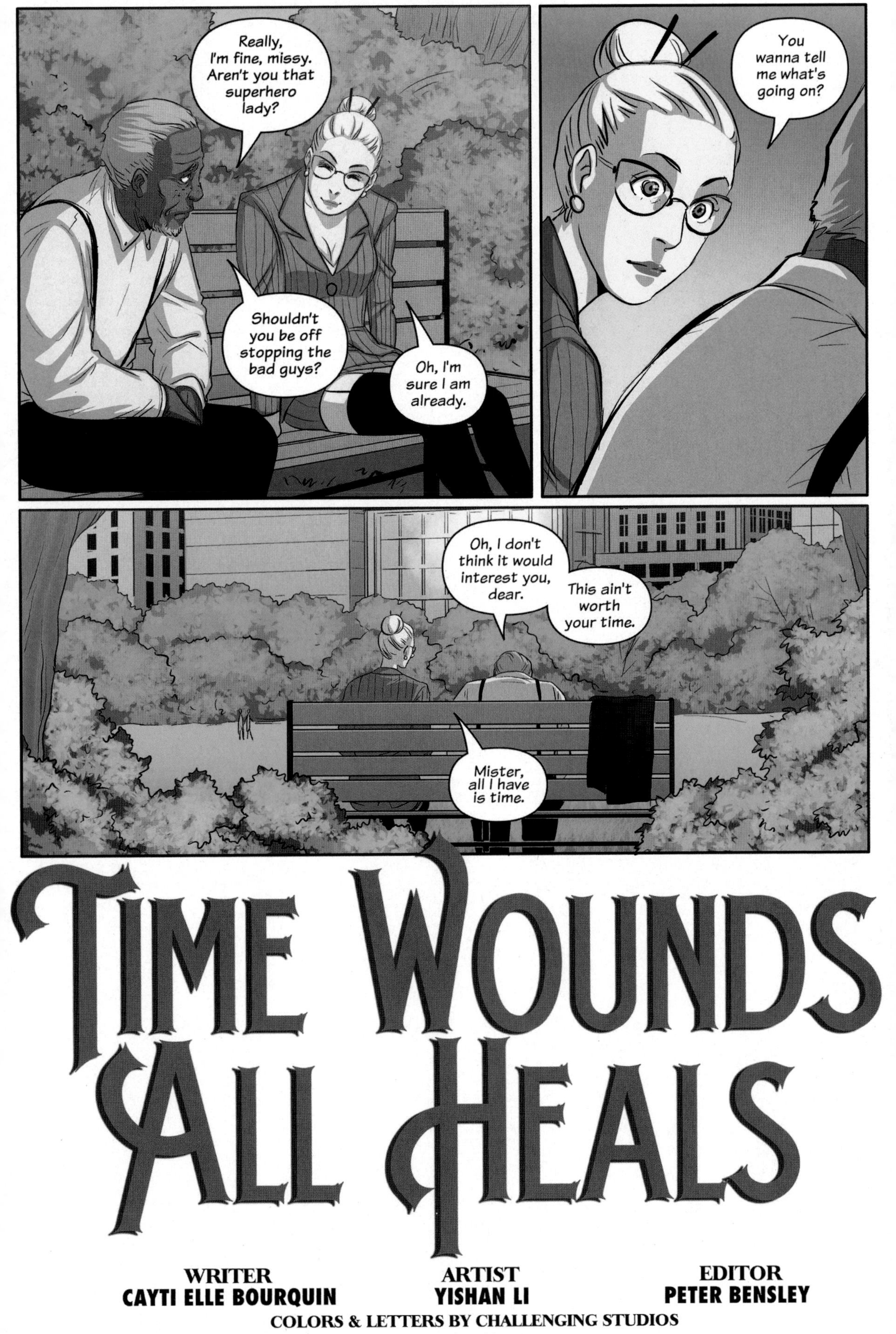
Really, I'm fine, missy. Aren't you that superhero lady?
Shouldn't you be off stopping the bad guys?
Oh, I'm sure I am already.
You wanna tell me what's going on?
Oh, I don't think it would interest you, dear.
This ain't worth your time.
Mister, all I have is time.

TIME WOUNDS ALL HEALS

WRITER
CAYTI ELLE BOURQUIN

ARTIST
YISHAN LI

EDITOR
PETER BENSLEY

COLORS & LETTERS BY CHALLENGING STUDIOS

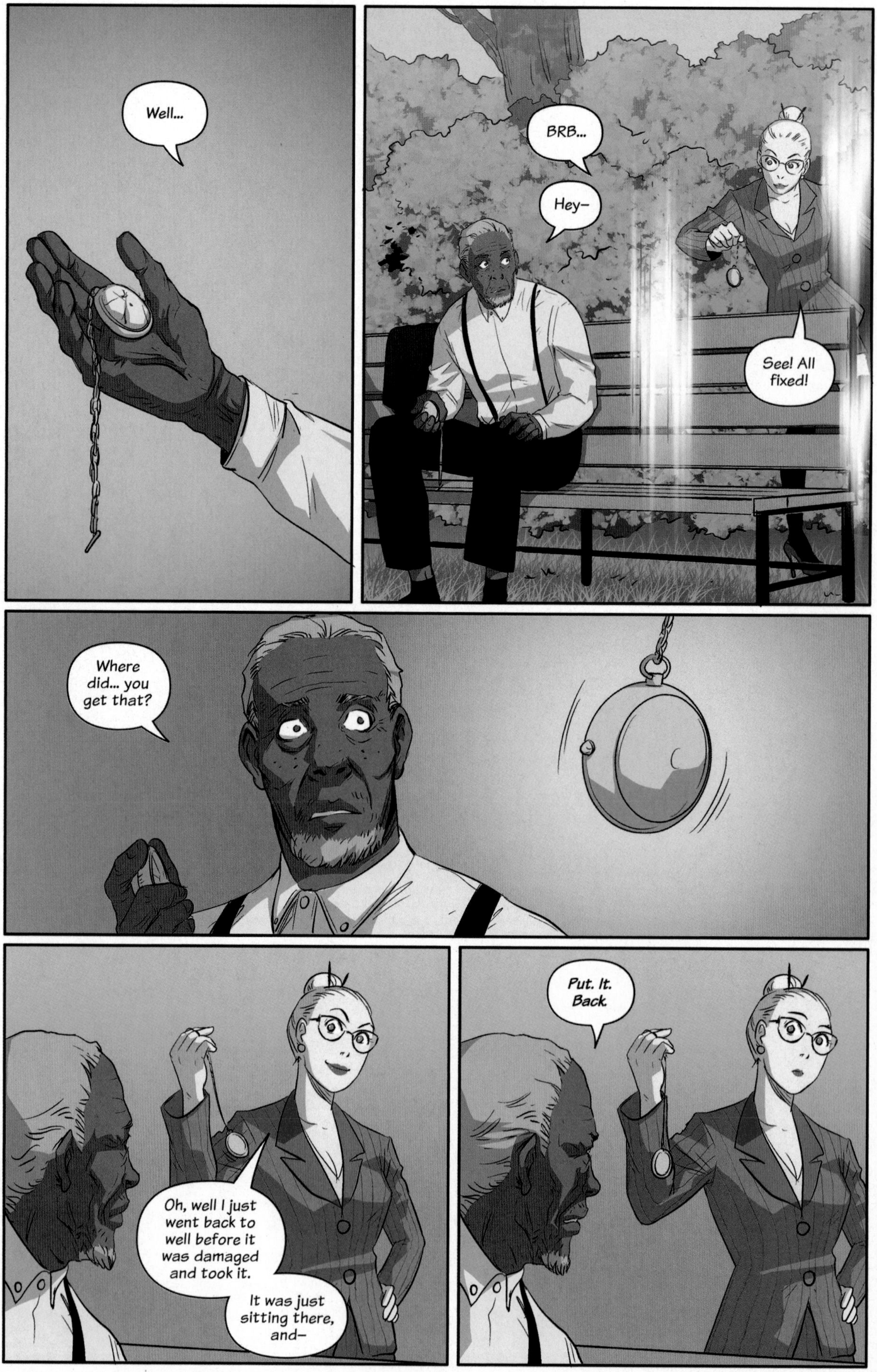
Well...
BRB...
Hey–
See! All fixed!
Where did... you get that?
Oh, well I just went back to well before it was damaged and took it.
It was just sitting there, and–
Put. It. Back.

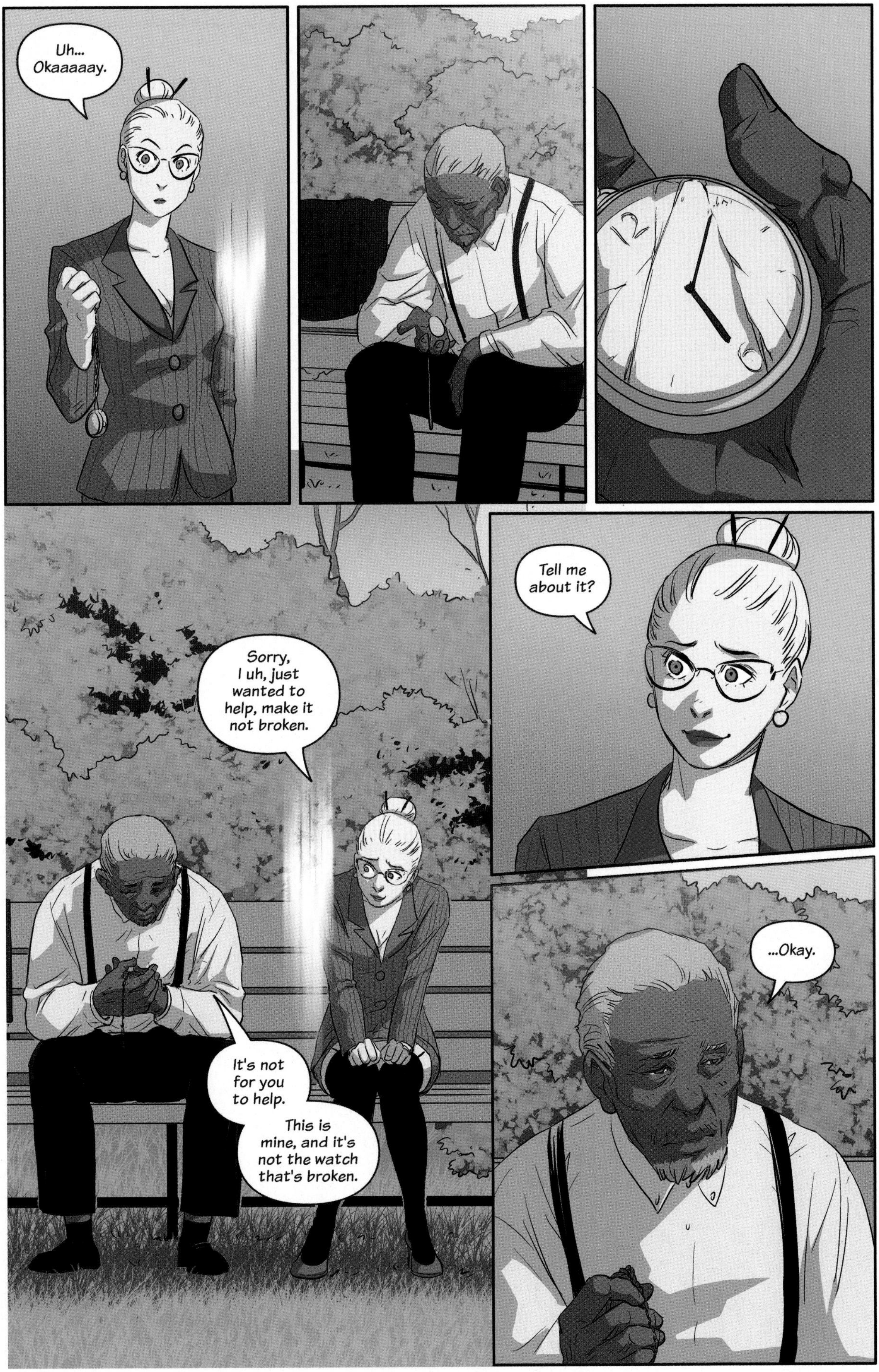
Uh... Okaaaaay.
Sorry, I uh, just wanted to help, make it not broken.
It's not for you to help.
This is mine, and it's not the watch that's broken.
Tell me about it?
...Okay.

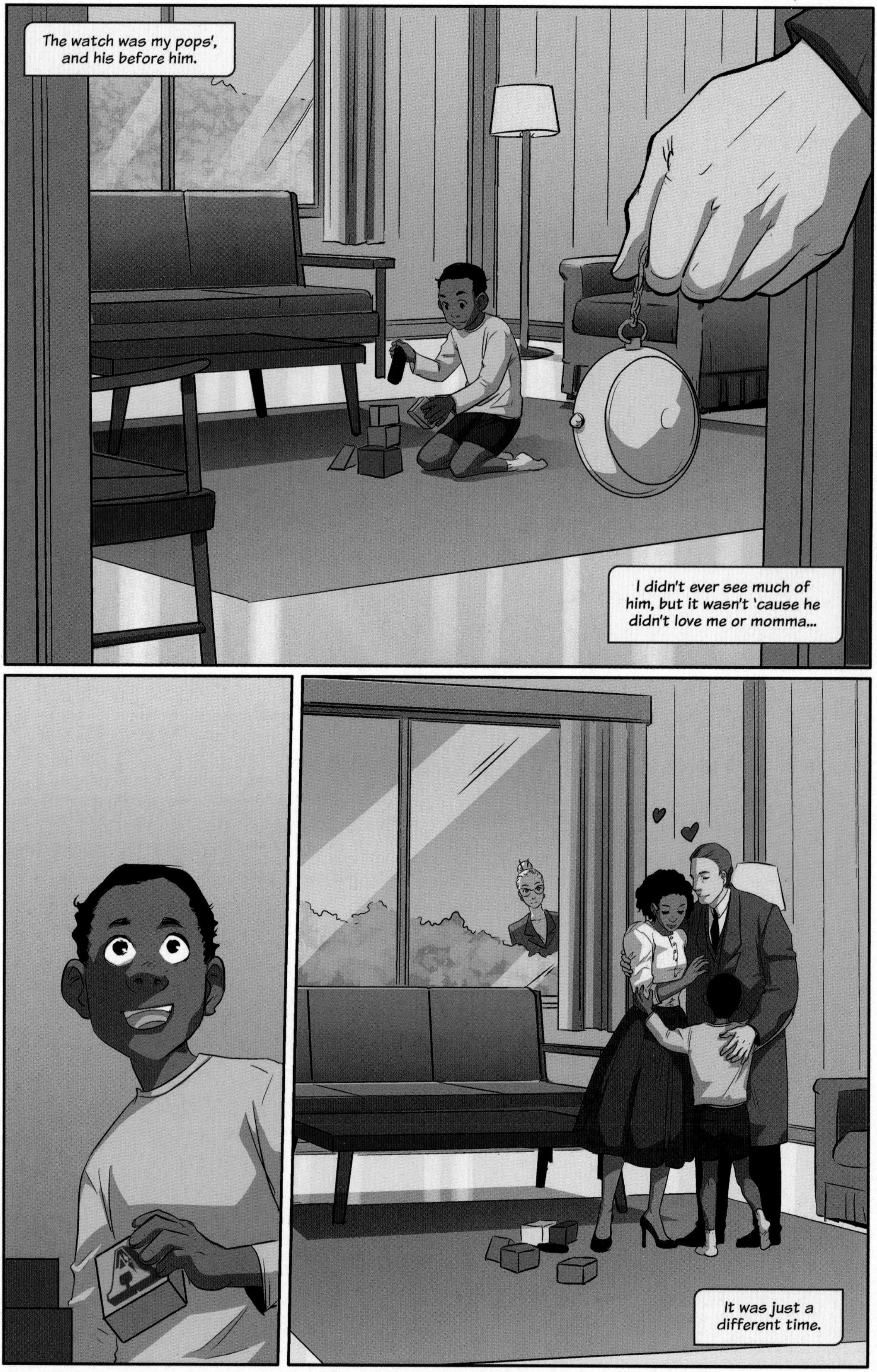
The watch was my pops', and his before him.
I didn't ever see much of him, but it wasn't 'cause he didn't love me or momma...
It was just a different time.

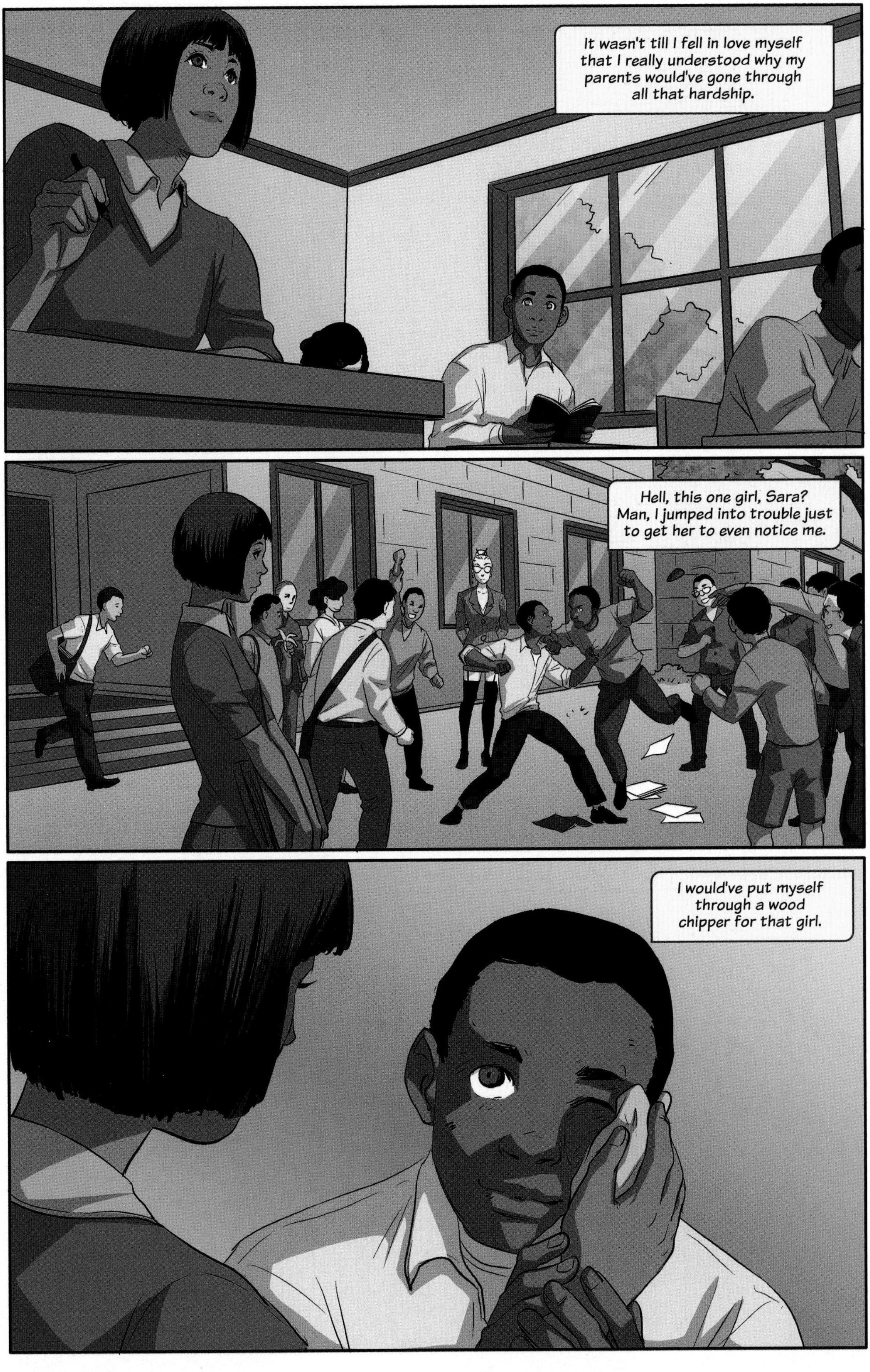
It wasn't till I fell in love myself that I really understood why my parents would've gone through all that hardship.
Hell, this one girl, Sara? Man, I jumped into trouble just to get her to even notice me.
I would've put myself through a wood chipper for that girl.

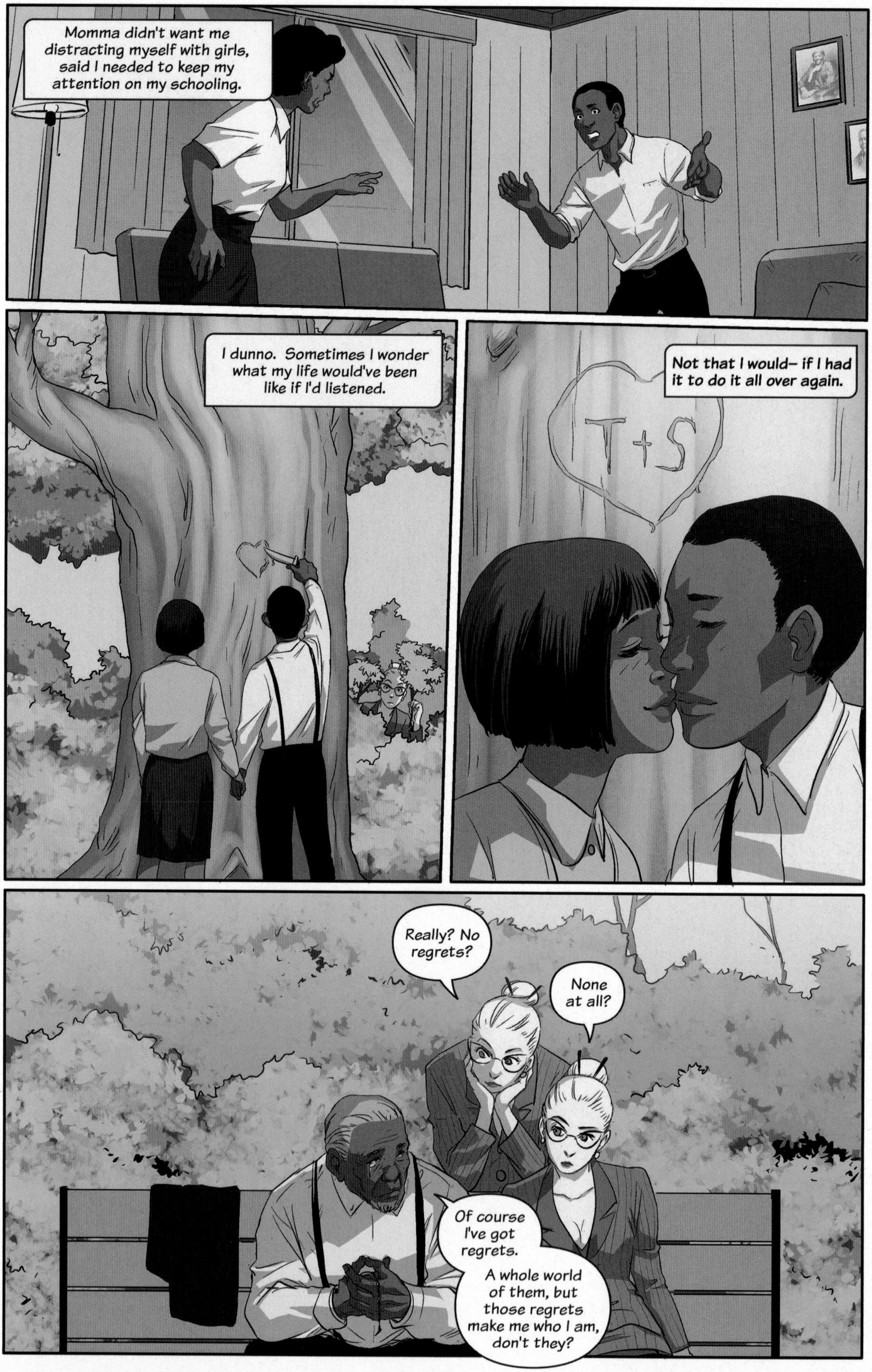
Momma didn't want me distracting myself with girls, said I needed to keep my attention on my schooling.
I dunno. Sometimes I wonder what my life would've been like if I'd listened.
T+S
Not that I would- if I had it to do it all over again.
Really? No regrets?
None at all?
Of course I've got regrets.
A whole world of them, but those regrets make me who I am, don't they?

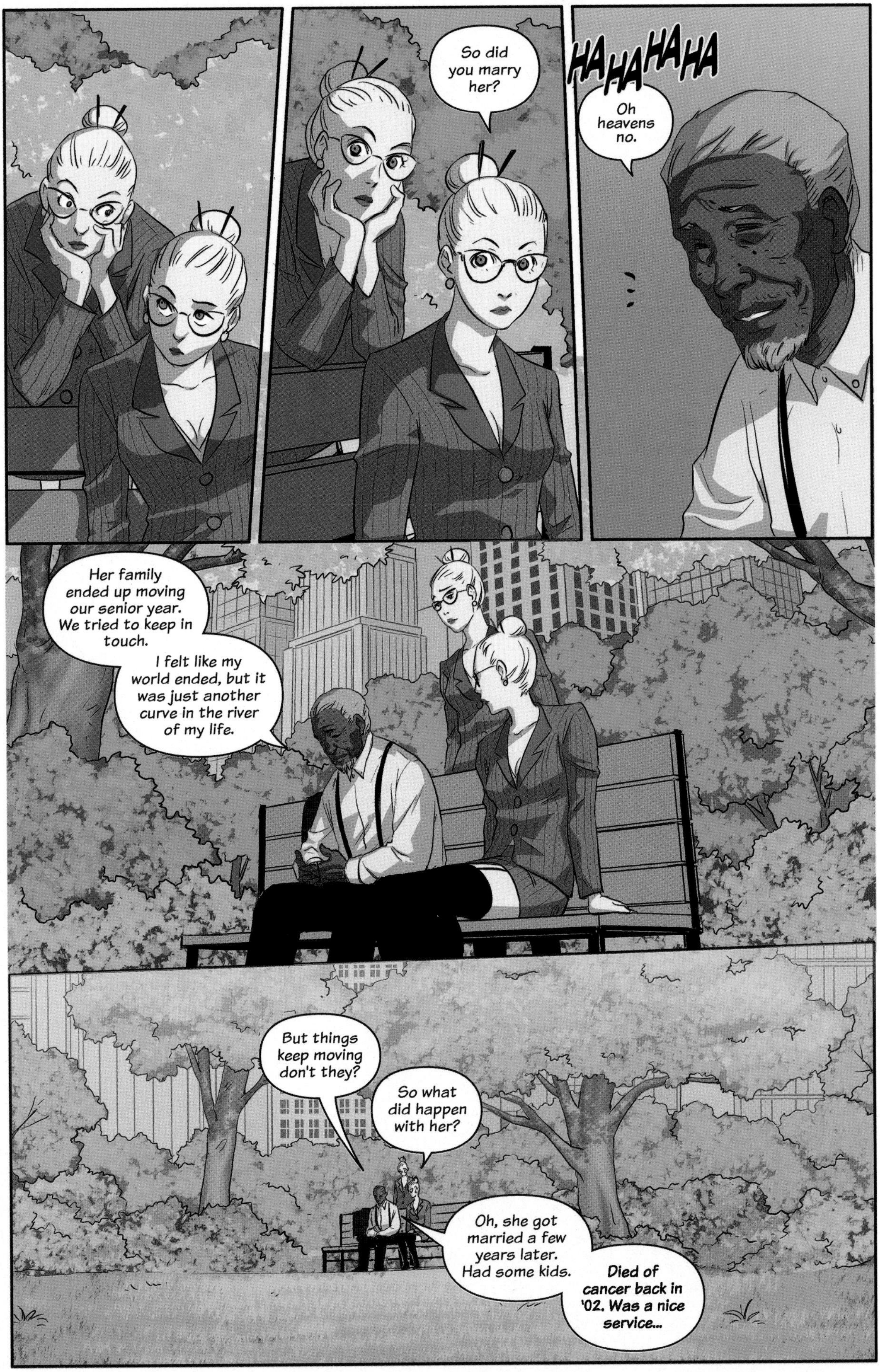
So did you marry her?
HAHAHAHA
Oh heavens no.
Her family ended up moving our senior year. We tried to keep in touch.
I felt like my world ended, but it was just another curve in the river of my life.
But things keep moving don't they?
So what did happen with her?
Oh, she got married a few years later. Had some kids.
Died of cancer back in '02. Was a nice service...

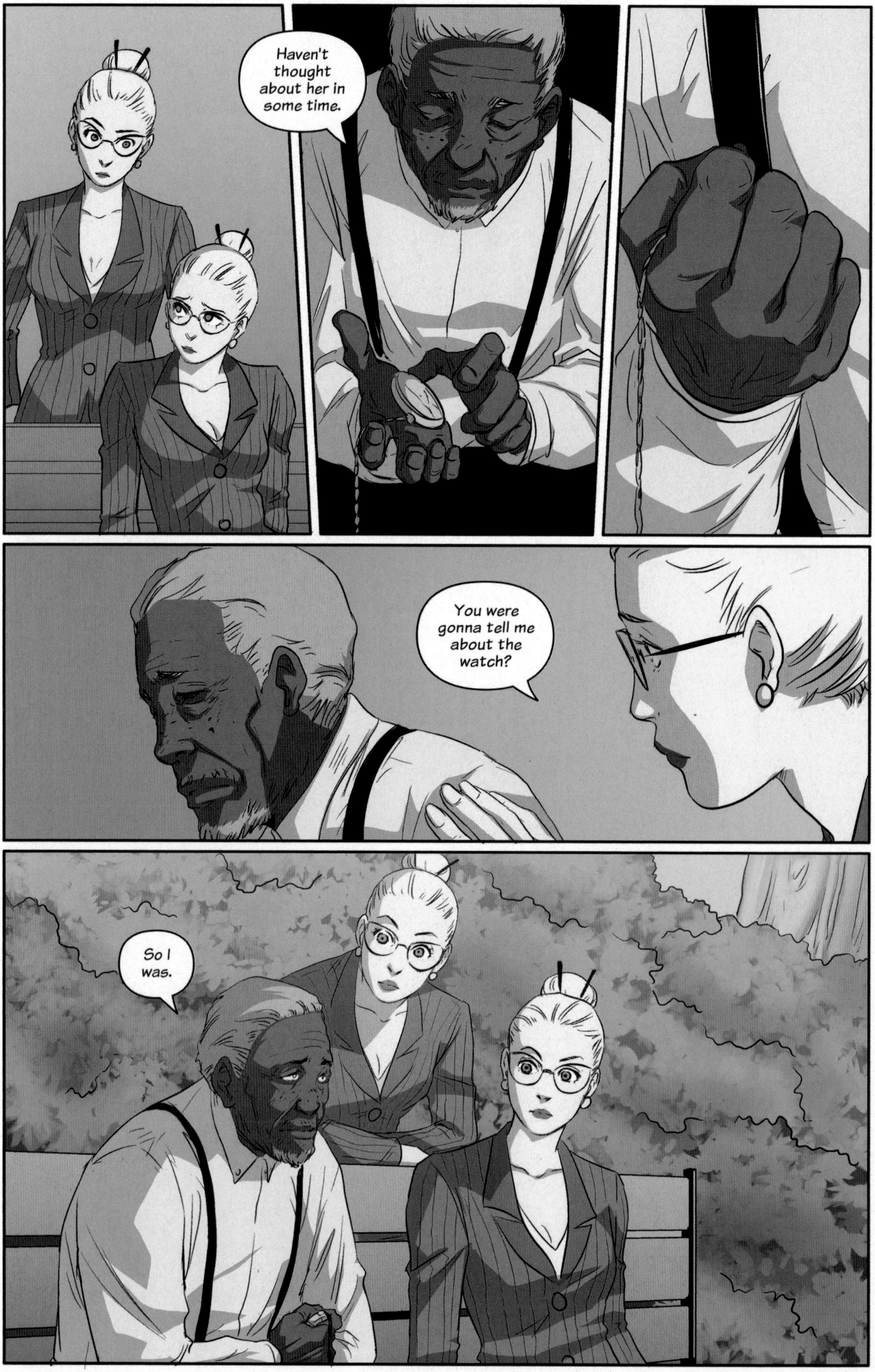
Haven't thought about her in some time.
You were gonna tell me about the watch?
So I was.

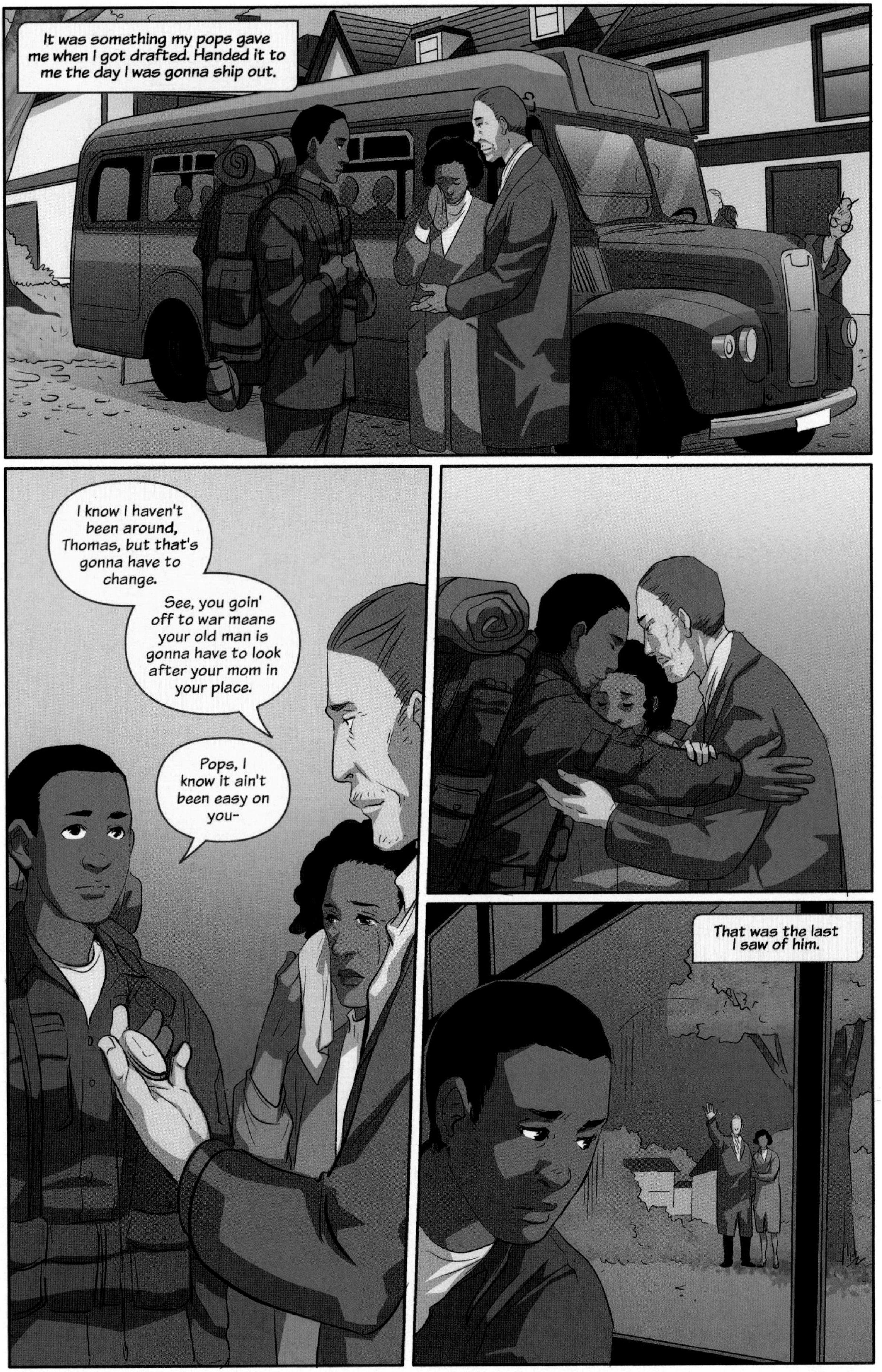
It was something my pops gave me when I got drafted. Handed it to me the day I was gonna ship out.
I know I haven't been around, Thomas, but that's gonna have to change.
See, you goin' off to war means your old man is gonna have to look after your mom in your place.
Pops, I know it ain't been easy on you-
That was the last I saw of him.

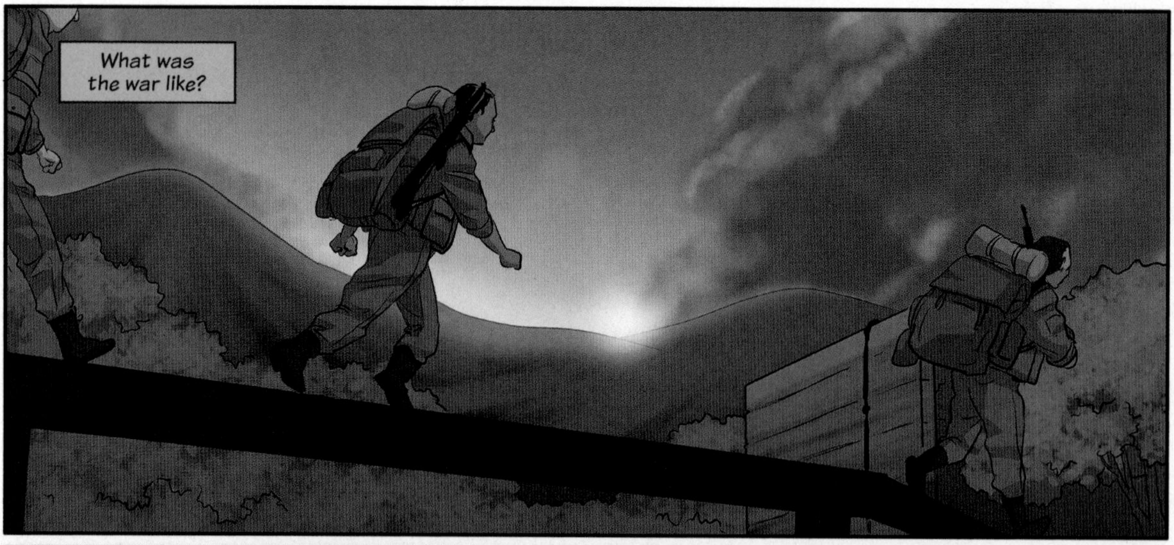
What was
the war like?

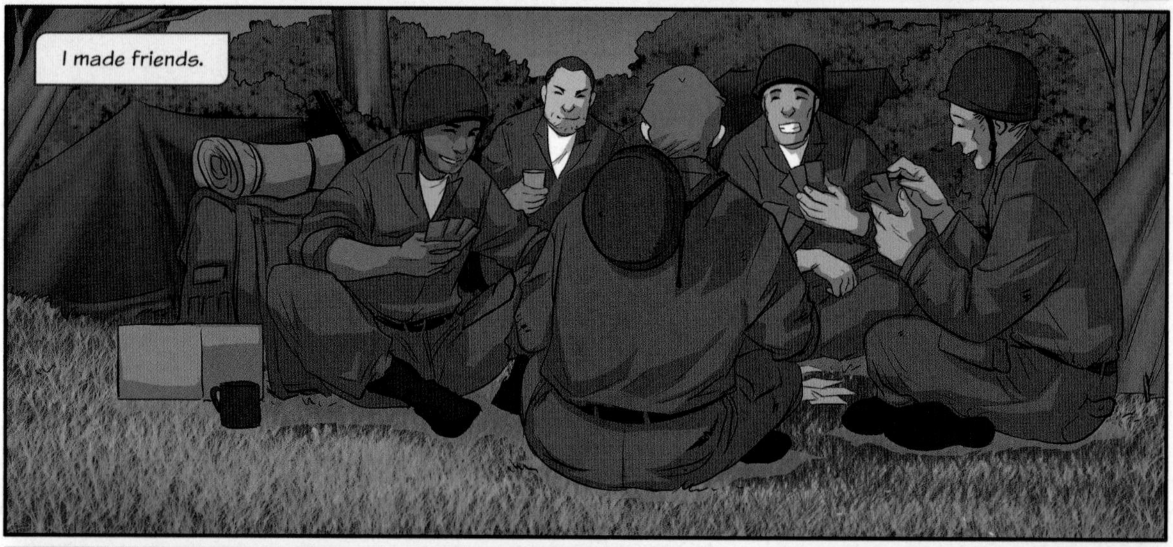
I made friends.

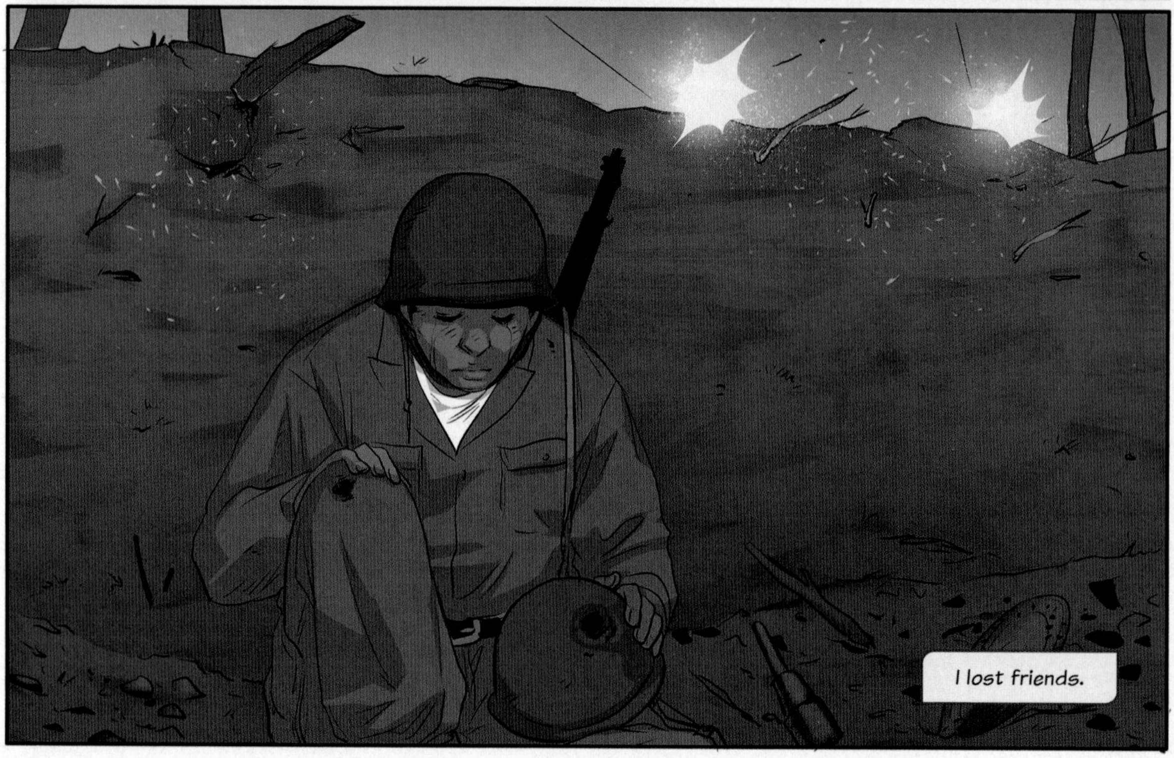
I lost friends.

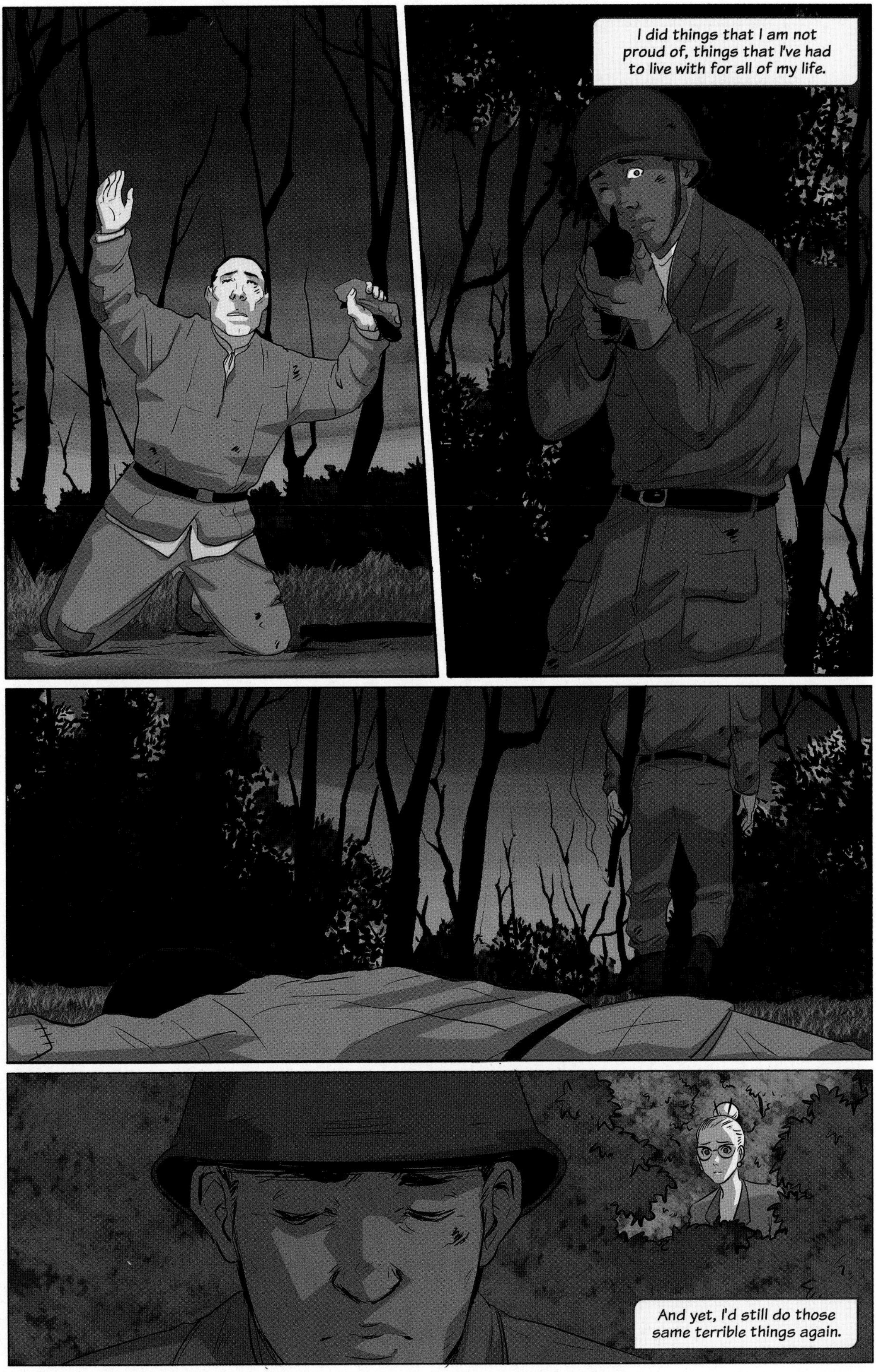
I did things that I am not proud of, things that I've had to live with for all of my life.
And yet, I'd still do those same terrible things again.

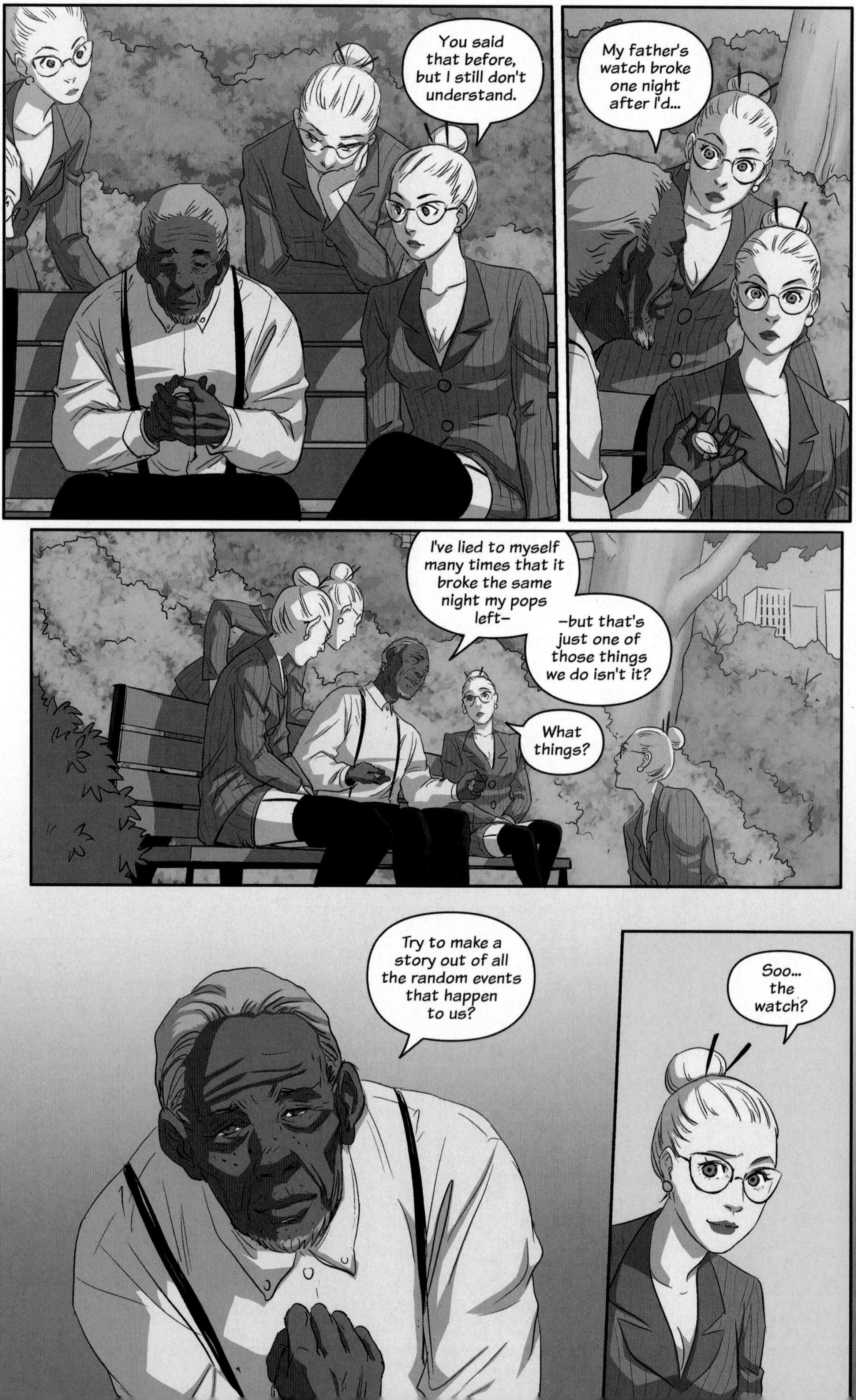
You said that before, but I still don't understand.
My father's watch broke one night after I'd...
I've lied to myself many times that it broke the same night my pops left–
–but that's just one of those things we do isn't it?
What things?
Try to make a story out of all the random events that happen to us?
Soo... the watch?

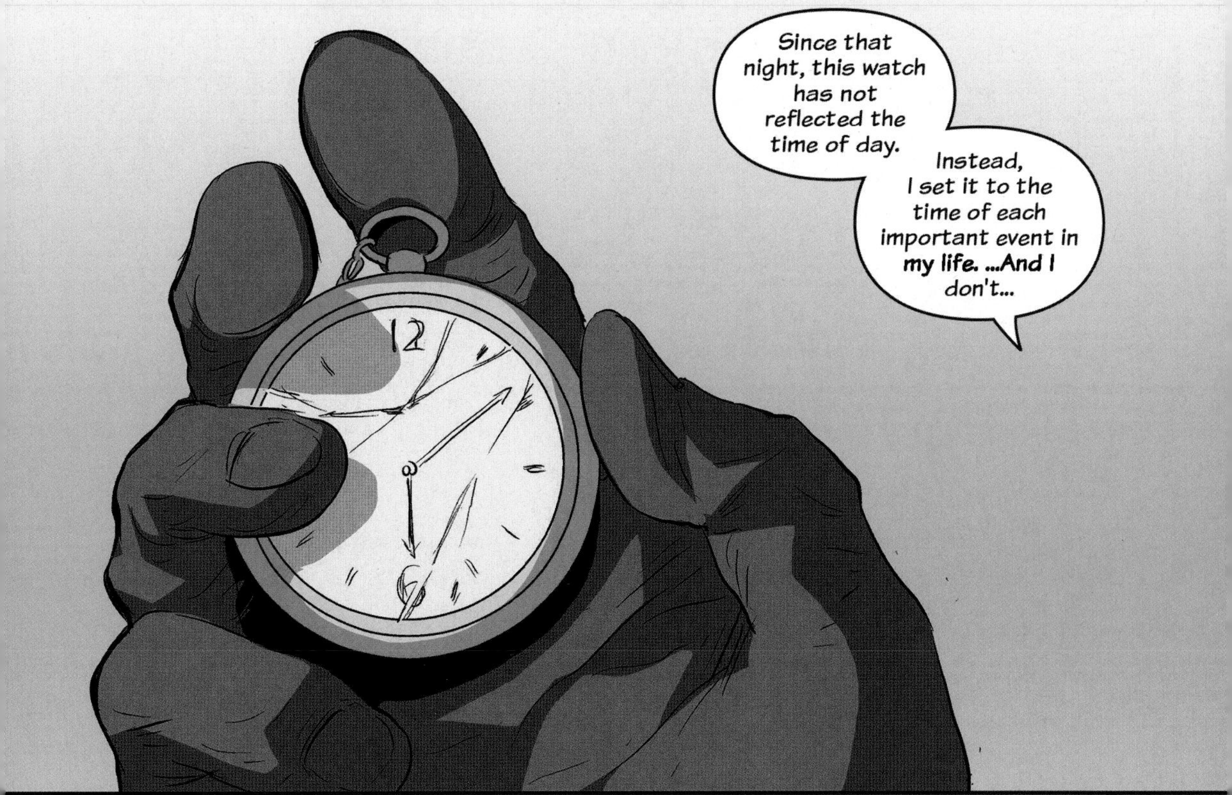
Since that night, this watch has not reflected the time of day.
Instead, I set it to the time of each important event in my life. ...And I don't...

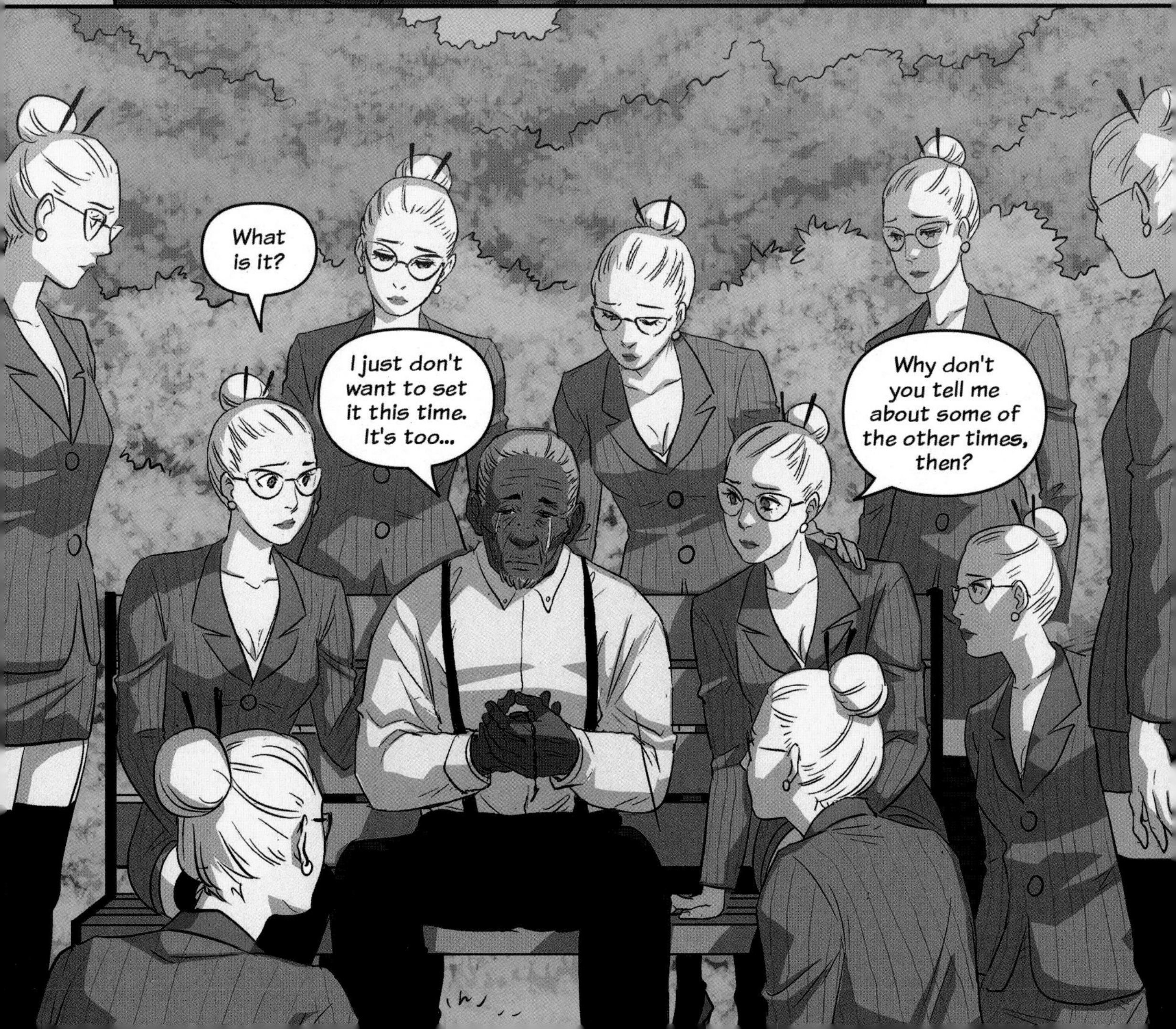
What is it?
I just don't want to set it this time. It's too...
Why don't you tell me about some of the other times, then?

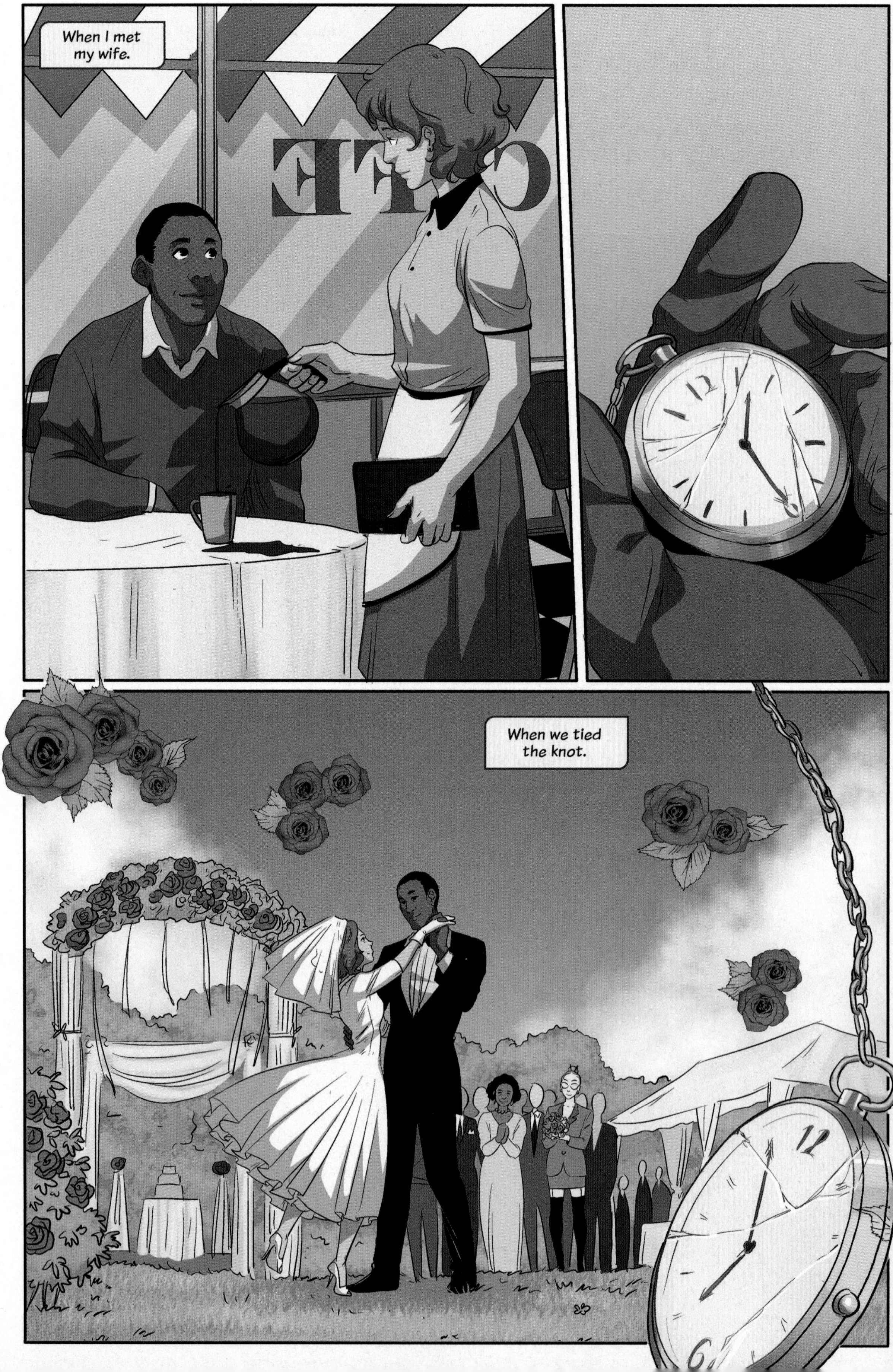
When I met my wife.
When we tied the knot.

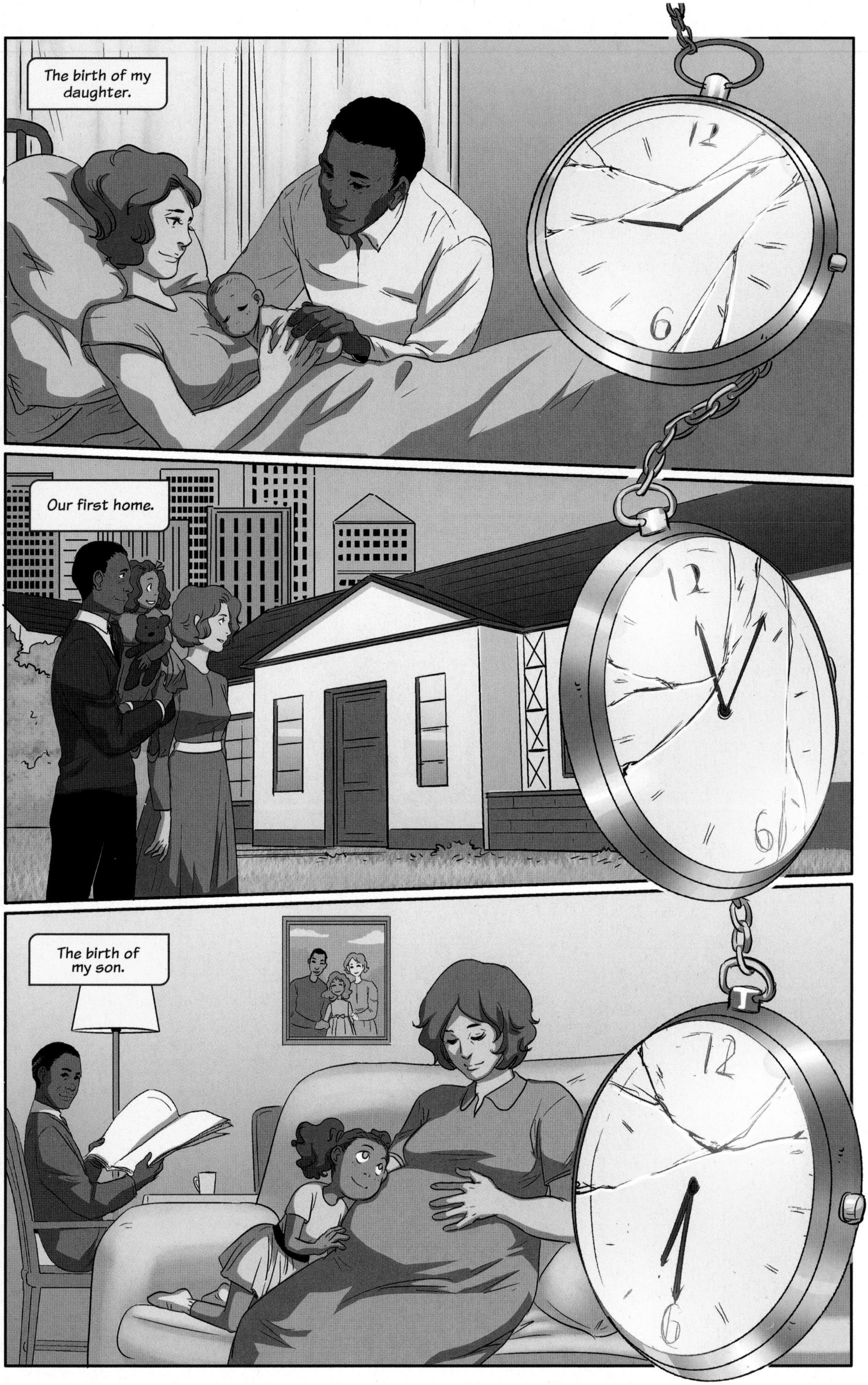

The birth of my daughter.
Our first home.
The birth of my son.

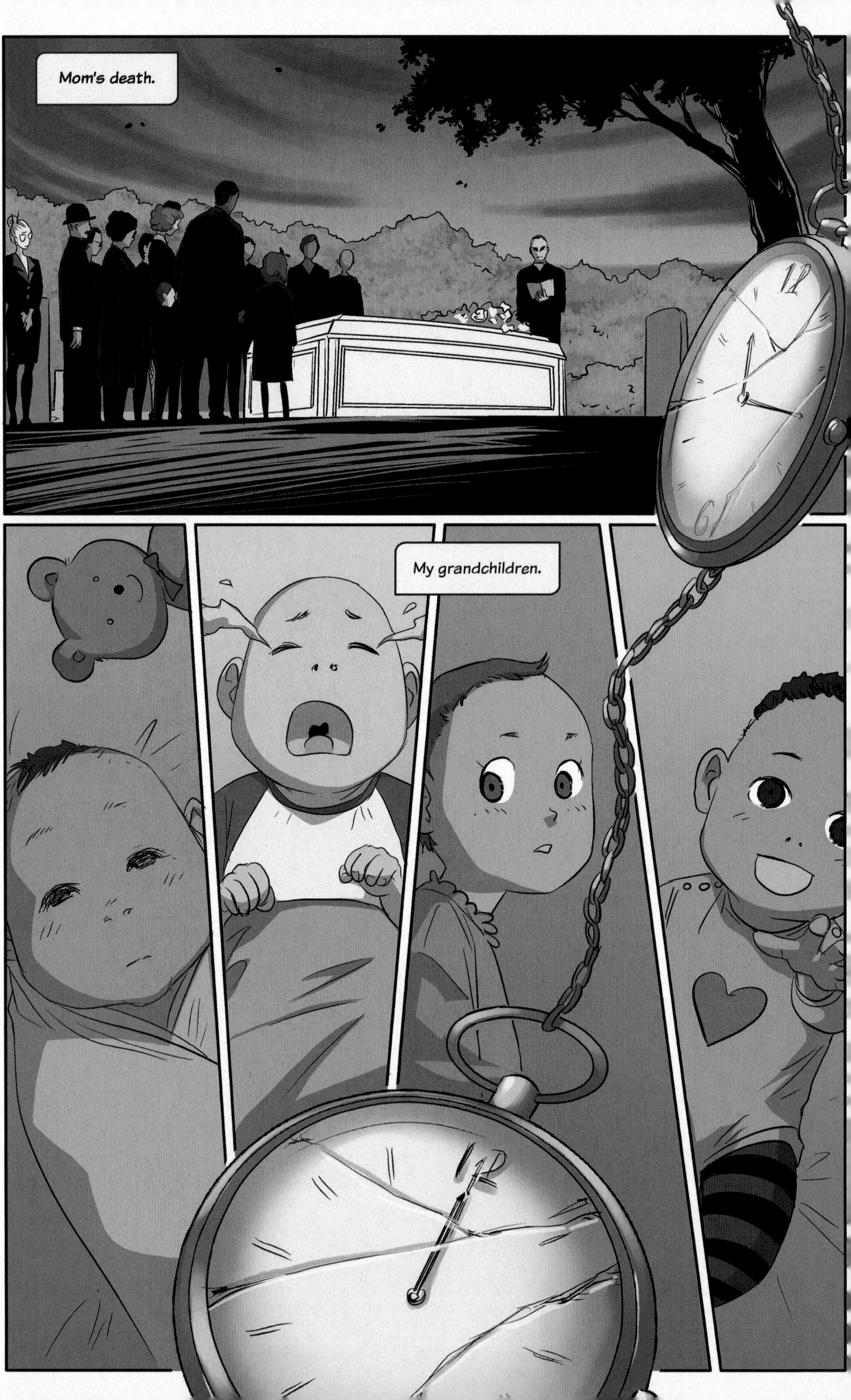
Mom's death.
My grandchildren.

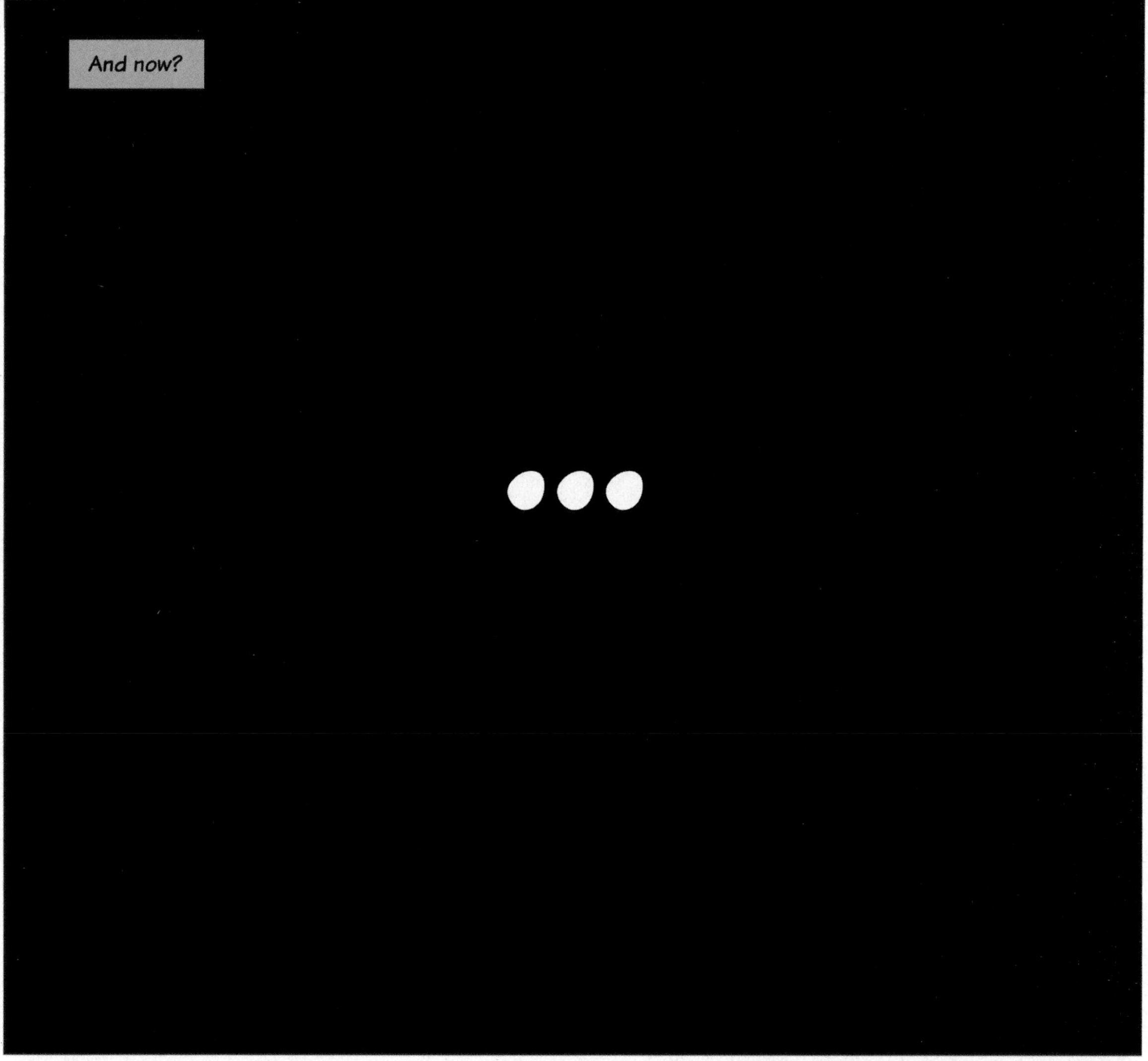
And now?
...

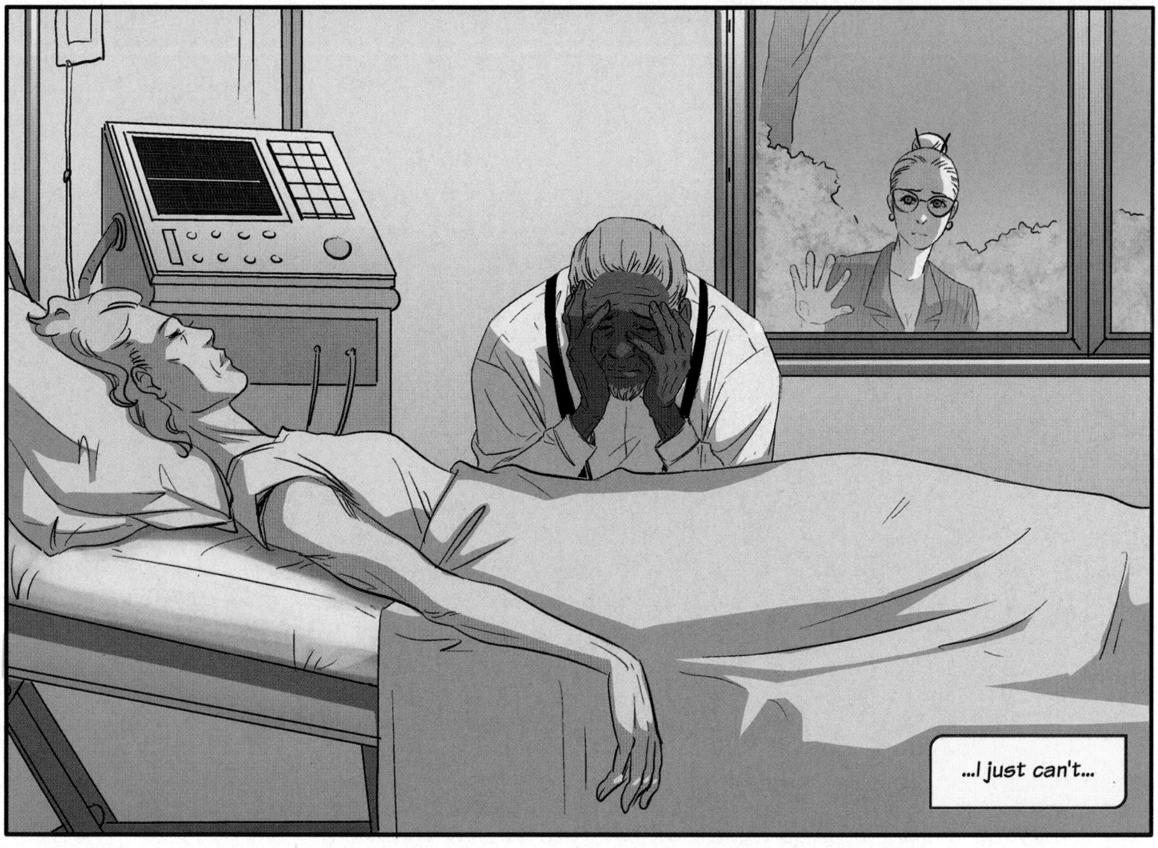
...I just can't...

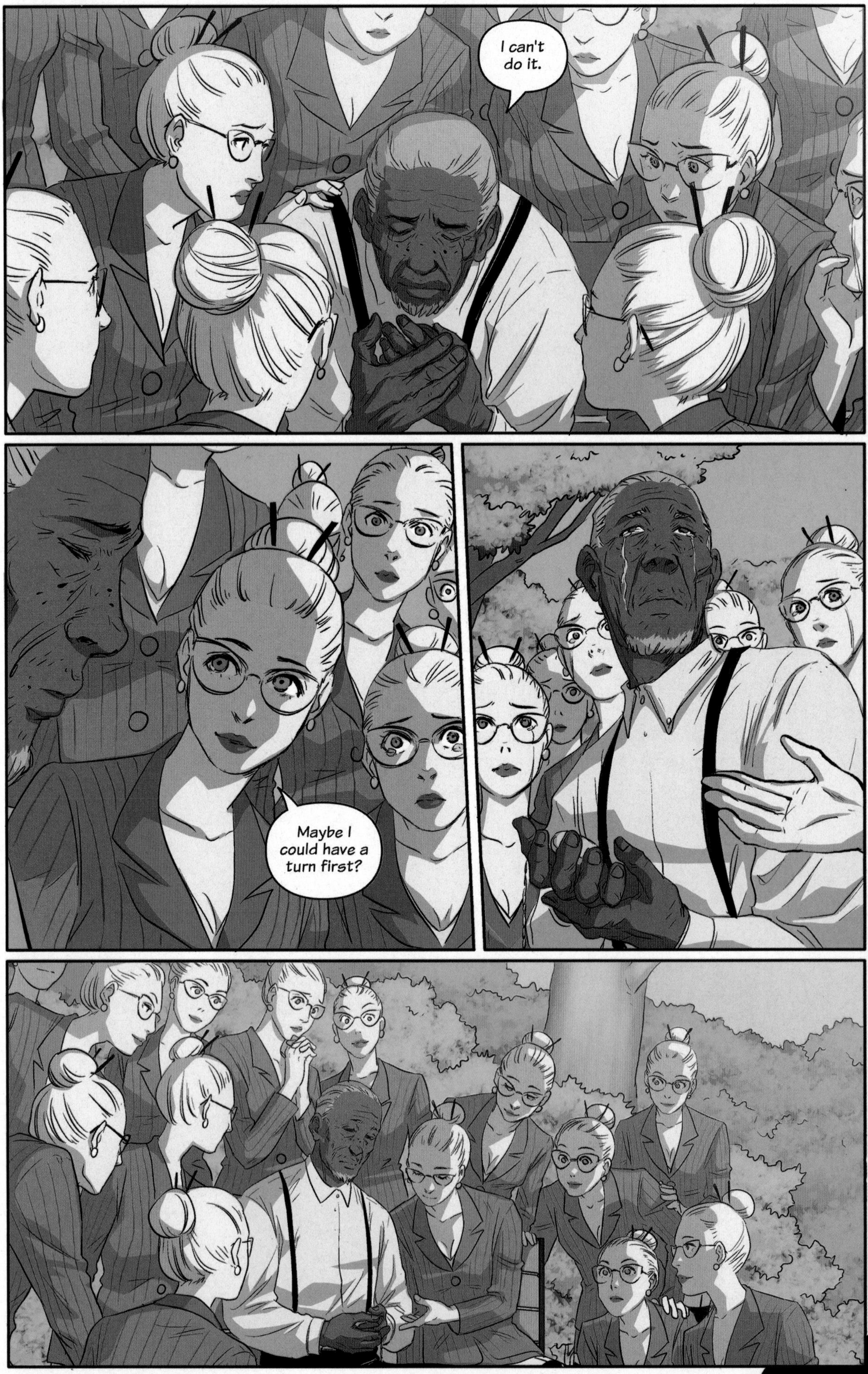
I can't do it.
Maybe I could have a turn first?

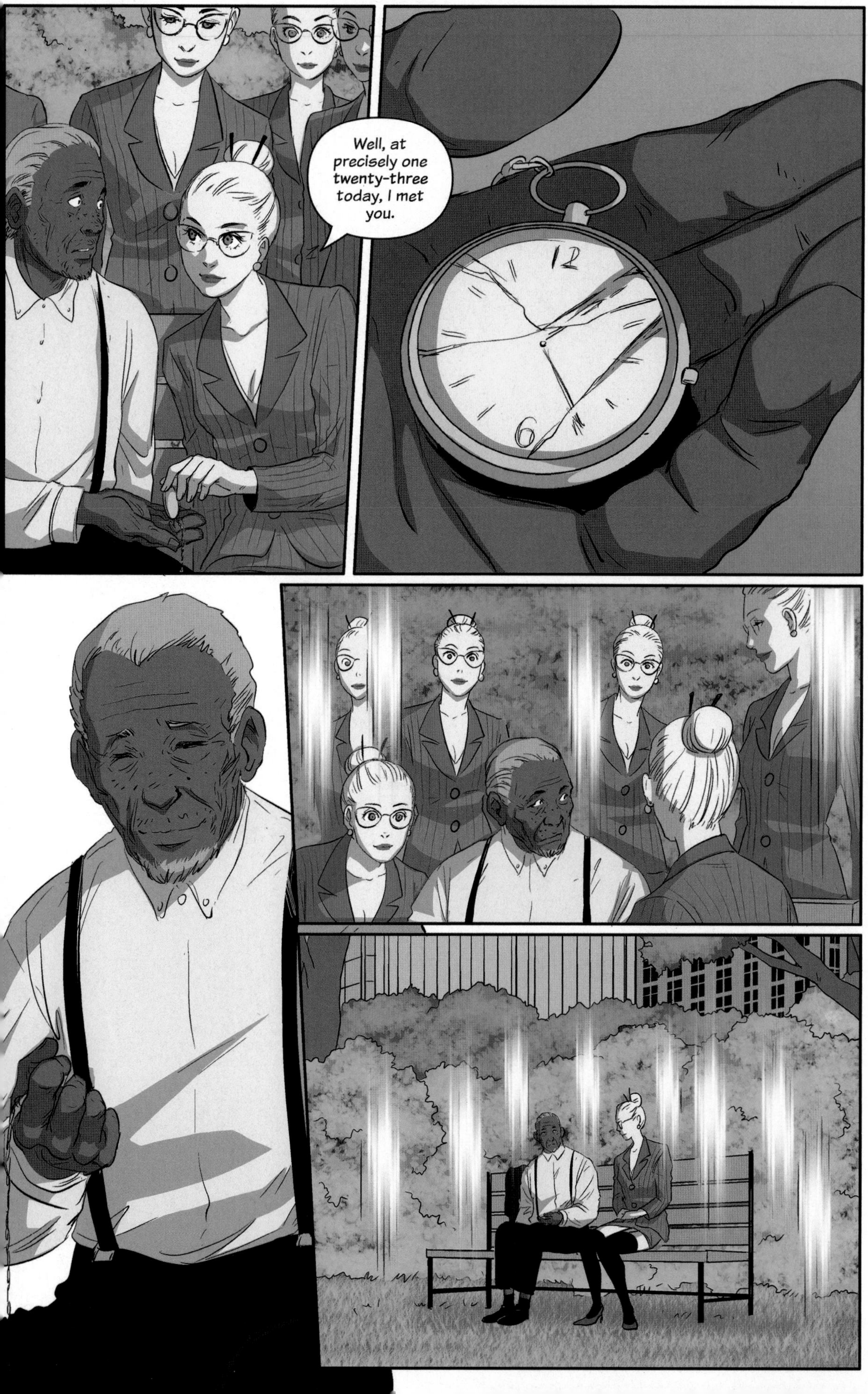
Well, at precisely one twenty-three today, I met you.

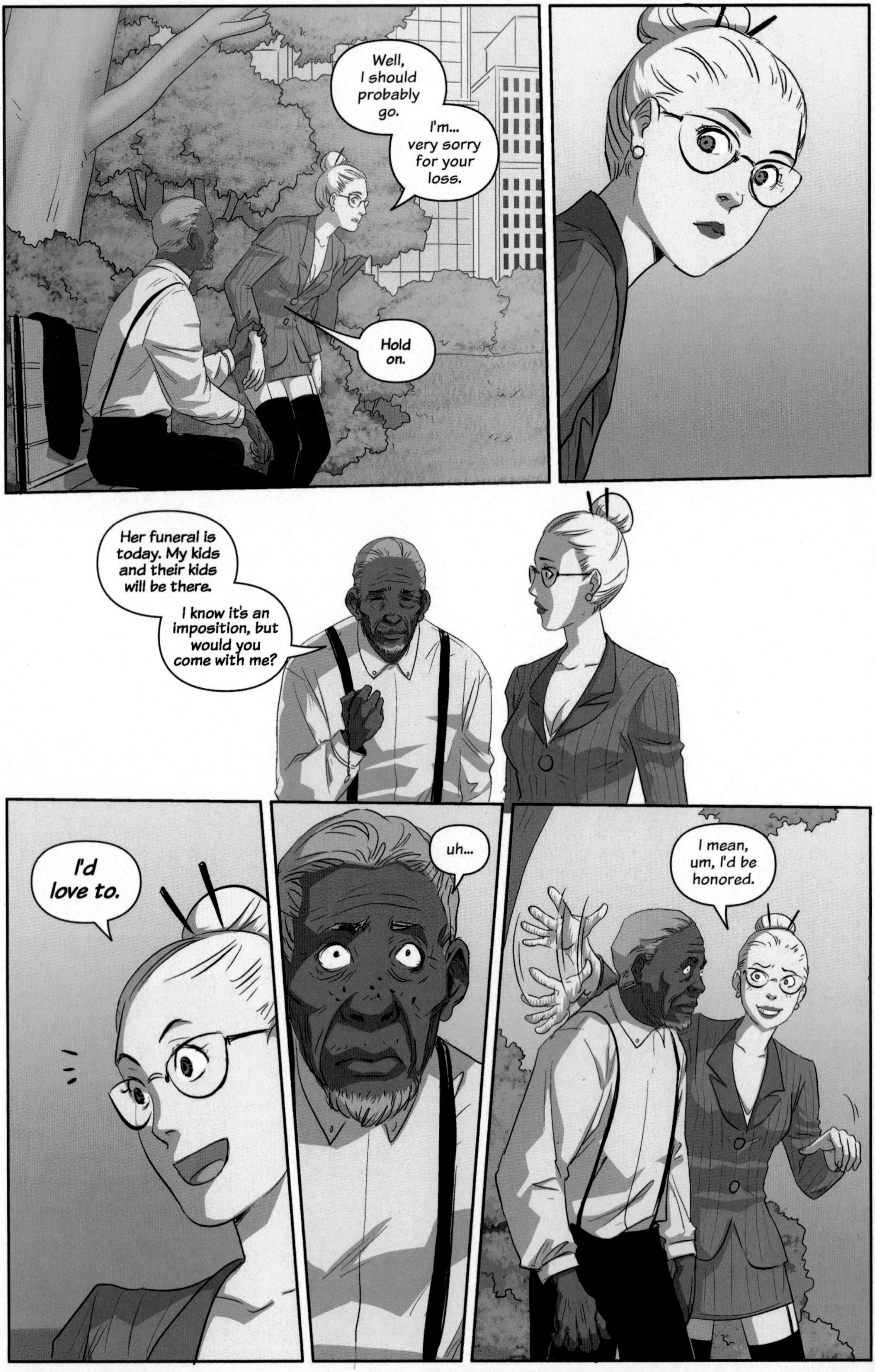
Well, I should probably go.
I'm... very sorry for your loss.
Hold on.
Her funeral is today. My kids and their kids will be there.
I know it's an imposition, but would you come with me?
I'd love to.
uh...
I mean, um, I'd be honored.

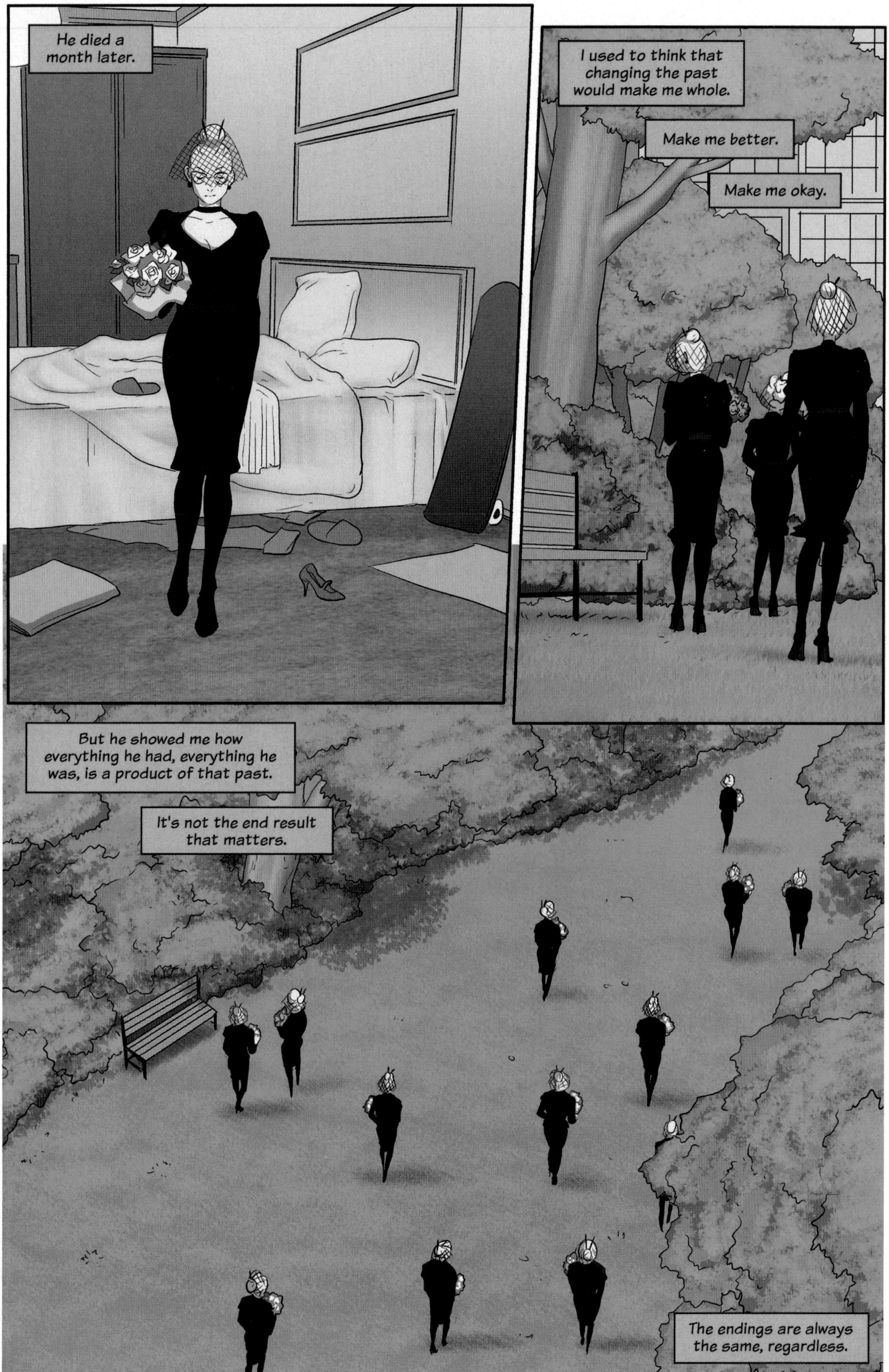

He died a month later.
I used to think that changing the past would make me whole.
Make me better.
Make me okay.
But he showed me how everything he had, everything he was, is a product of that past.
It's not the end result that matters.
The endings are always the same, regardless.

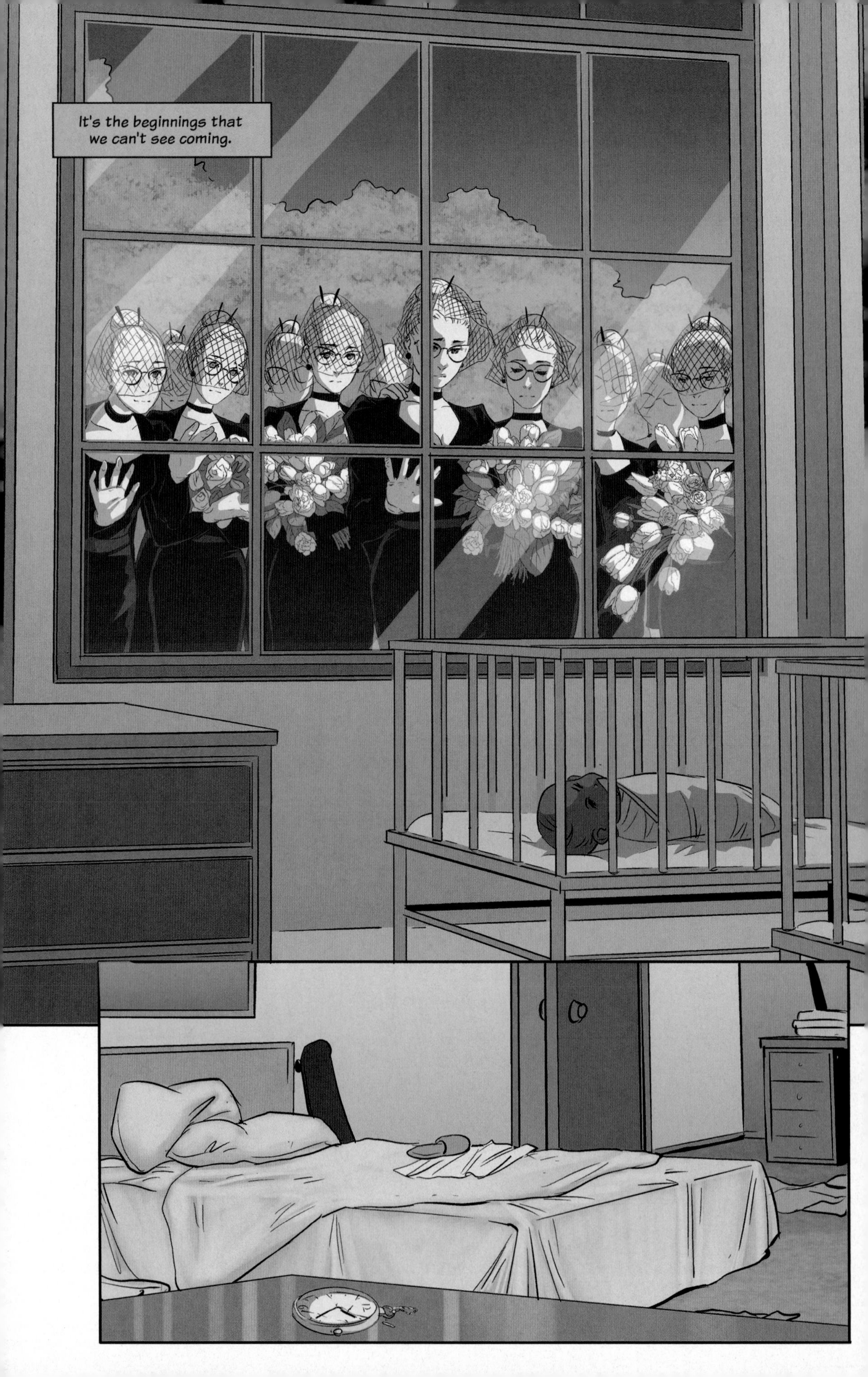
It's the beginnings that we can't see coming.

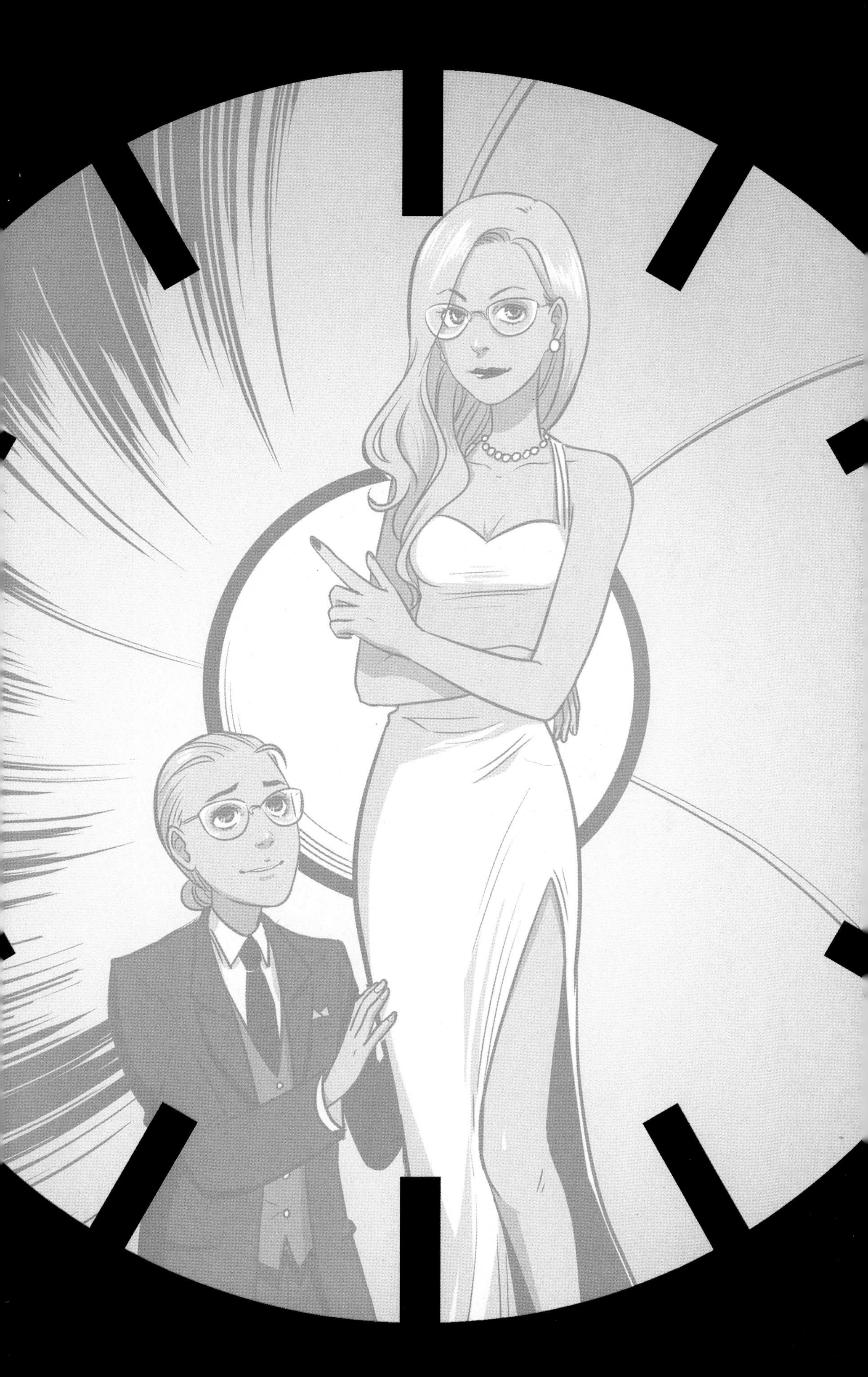

CHAPTER 5

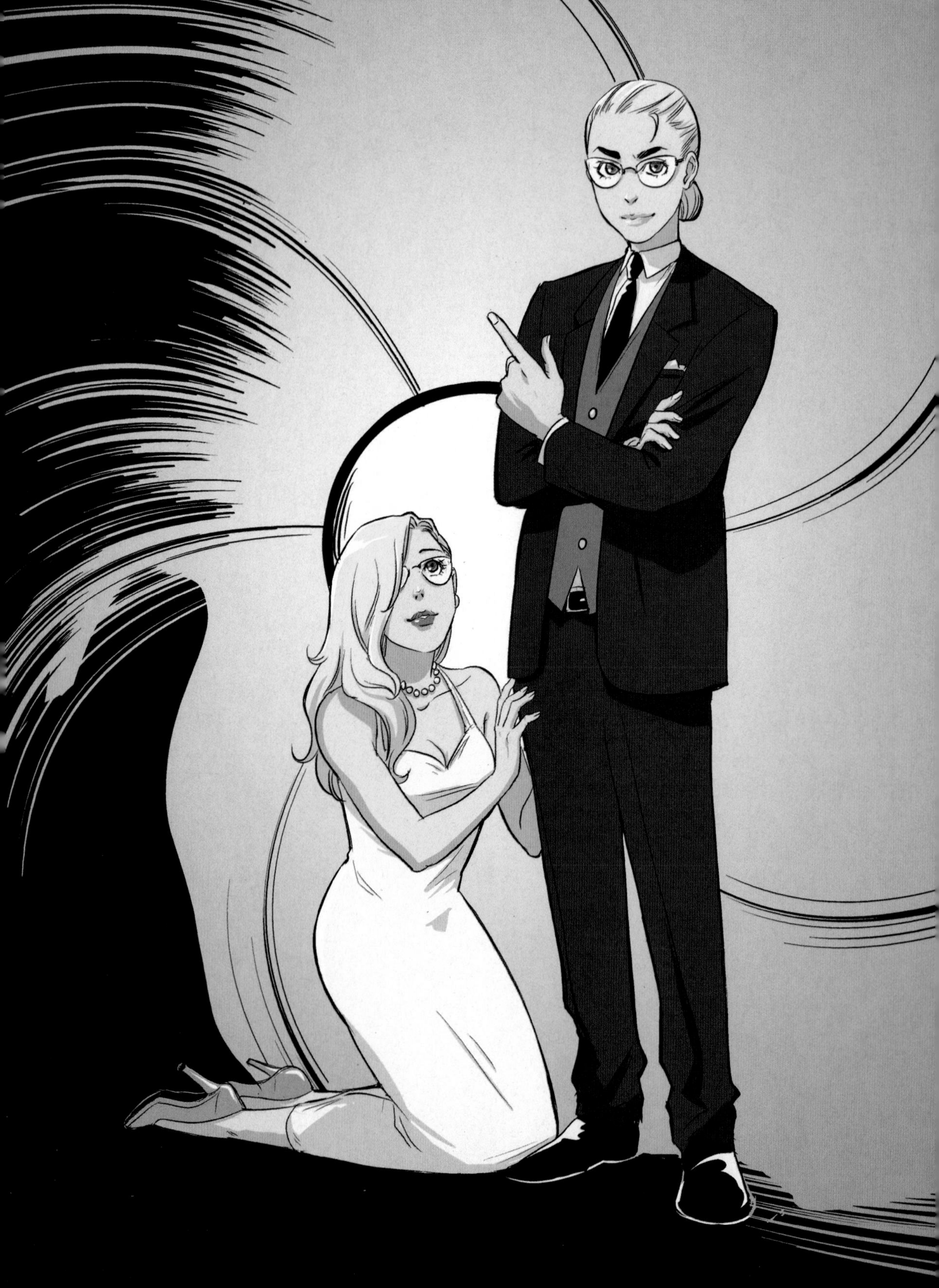

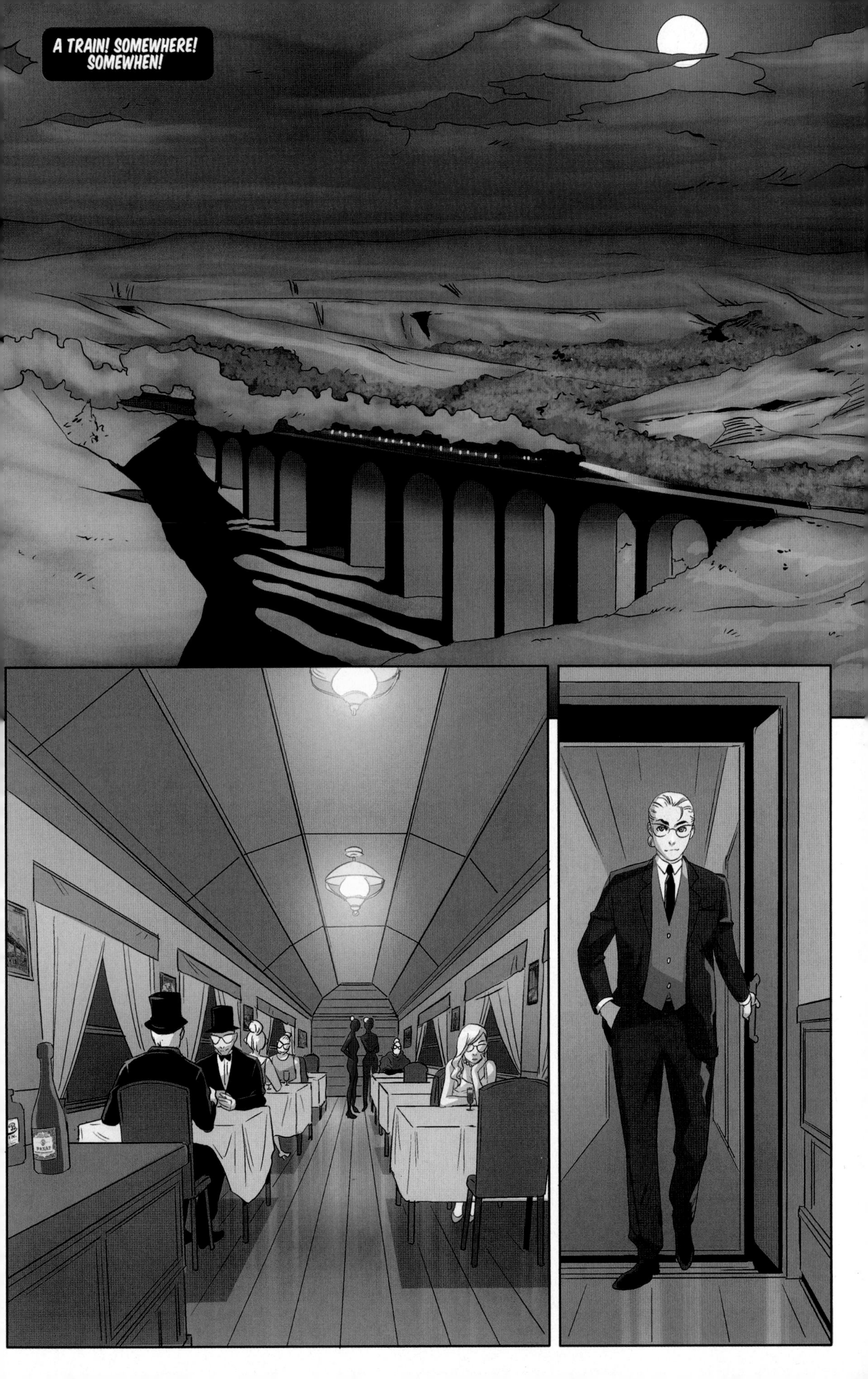
A TRAIN! SOMEWHERE! SOMEWHEN!

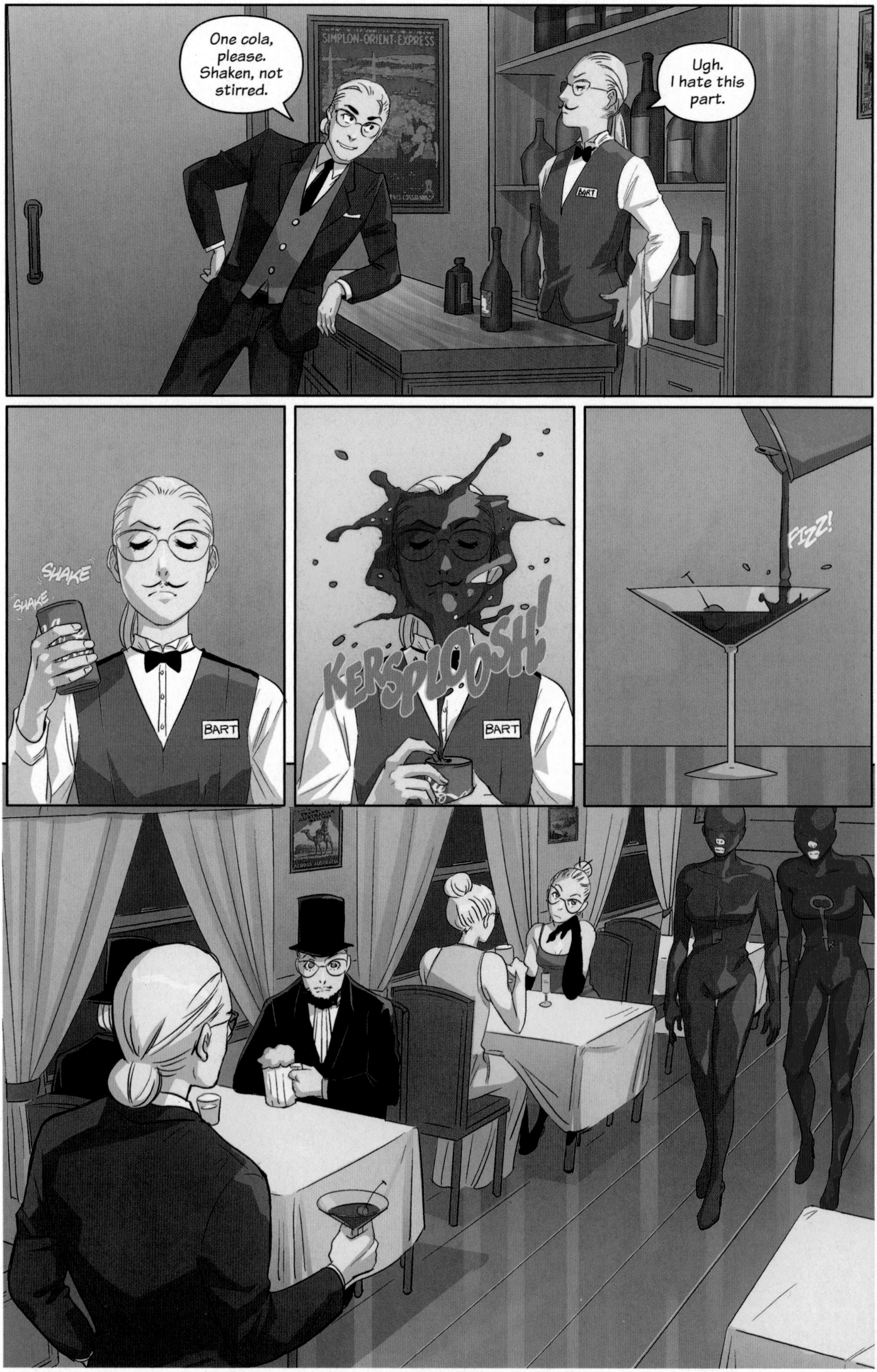
SIMPLON-ORIENT-EXPRESS
One cola, please. Shaken, not stirred.
BART
Ugh. I hate this part.
SHAKE
SHAKE
BART
KERSPLOOSH!
BART
FIZZ!

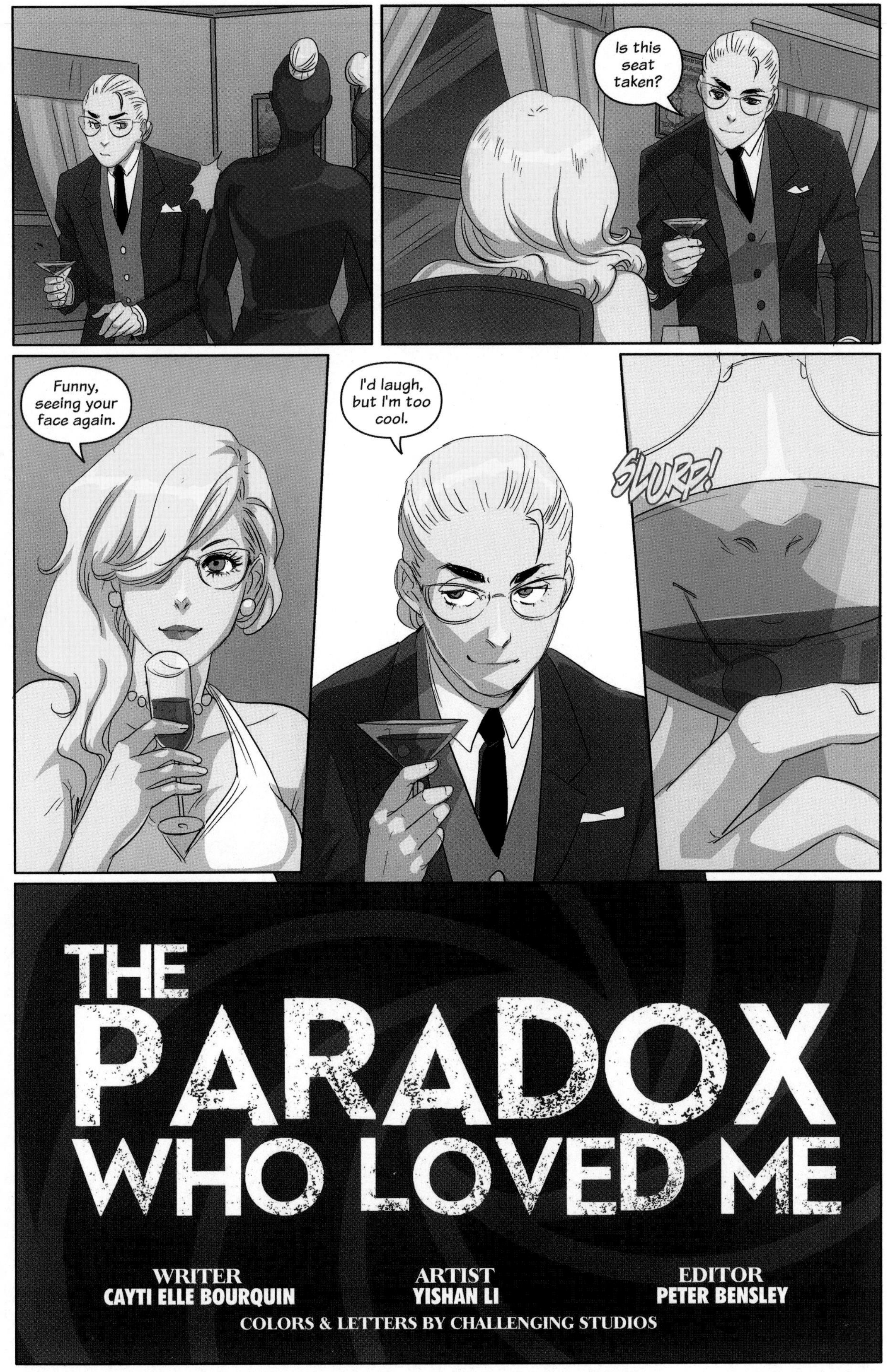
Is this seat taken?
Funny, seeing your face again.
I'd laugh, but I'm too cool.
SLURP!

THE PARADOX WHO LOVED ME

WRITER
CAYTI ELLE BOURQUIN

ARTIST
YISHAN LI

EDITOR
PETER BENSLEY

COLORS & LETTERS BY CHALLENGING STUDIOS

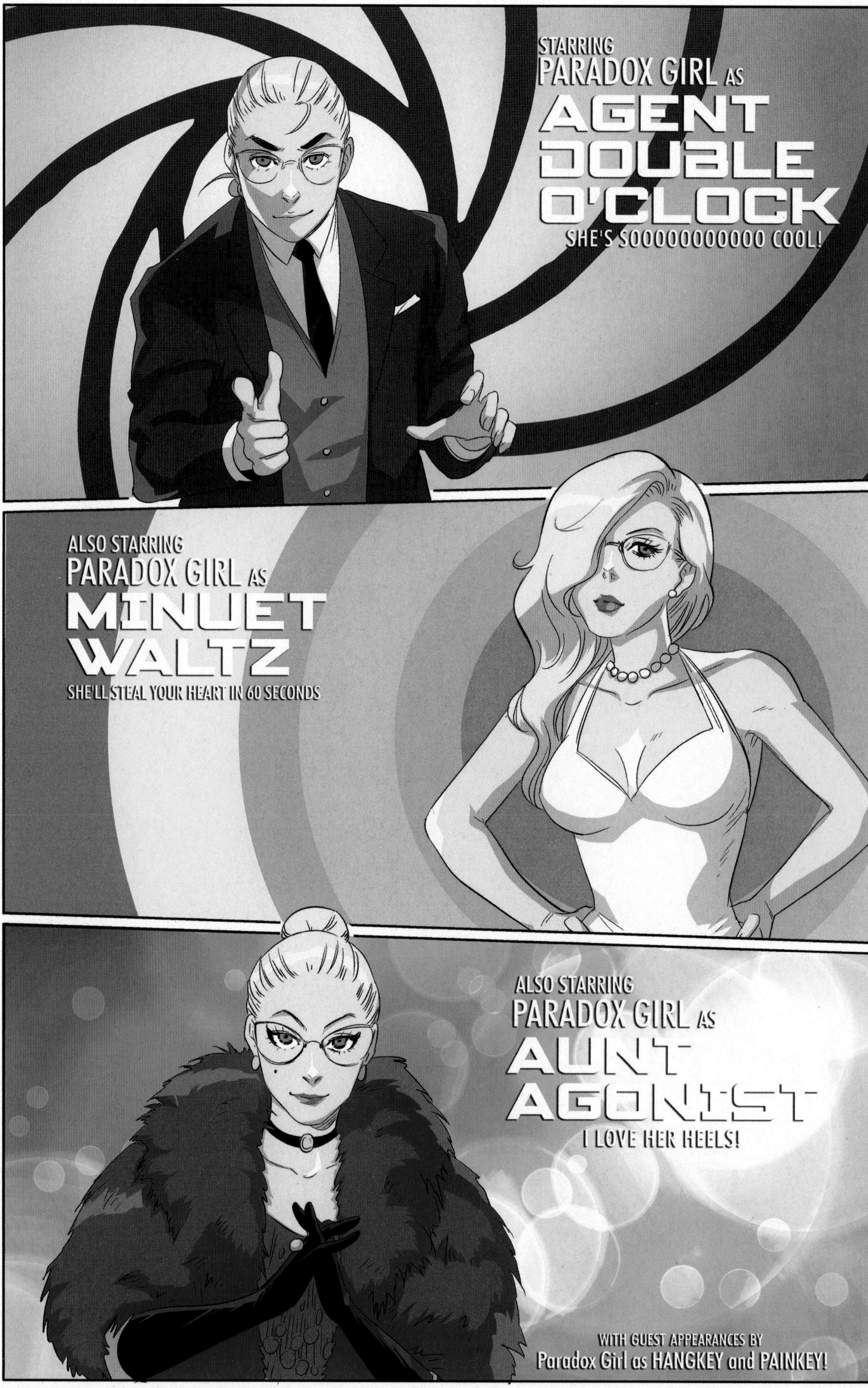
STARRING
PARADOX GIRL AS
AGENT DOUBLE O'CLOCK
SHE'S SOOOOOOOOOOO COOL!
ALSO STARRING
PARADOX GIRL AS
MINUET WALTZ
SHE'LL STEAL YOUR HEART IN 60 SECONDS
ALSO STARRING
PARADOX GIRL AS
AUNT AGONIST
I LOVE HER HEELS!
WITH GUEST APPEARANCES BY
Paradox Girl as HANGKEY and PAINKEY!

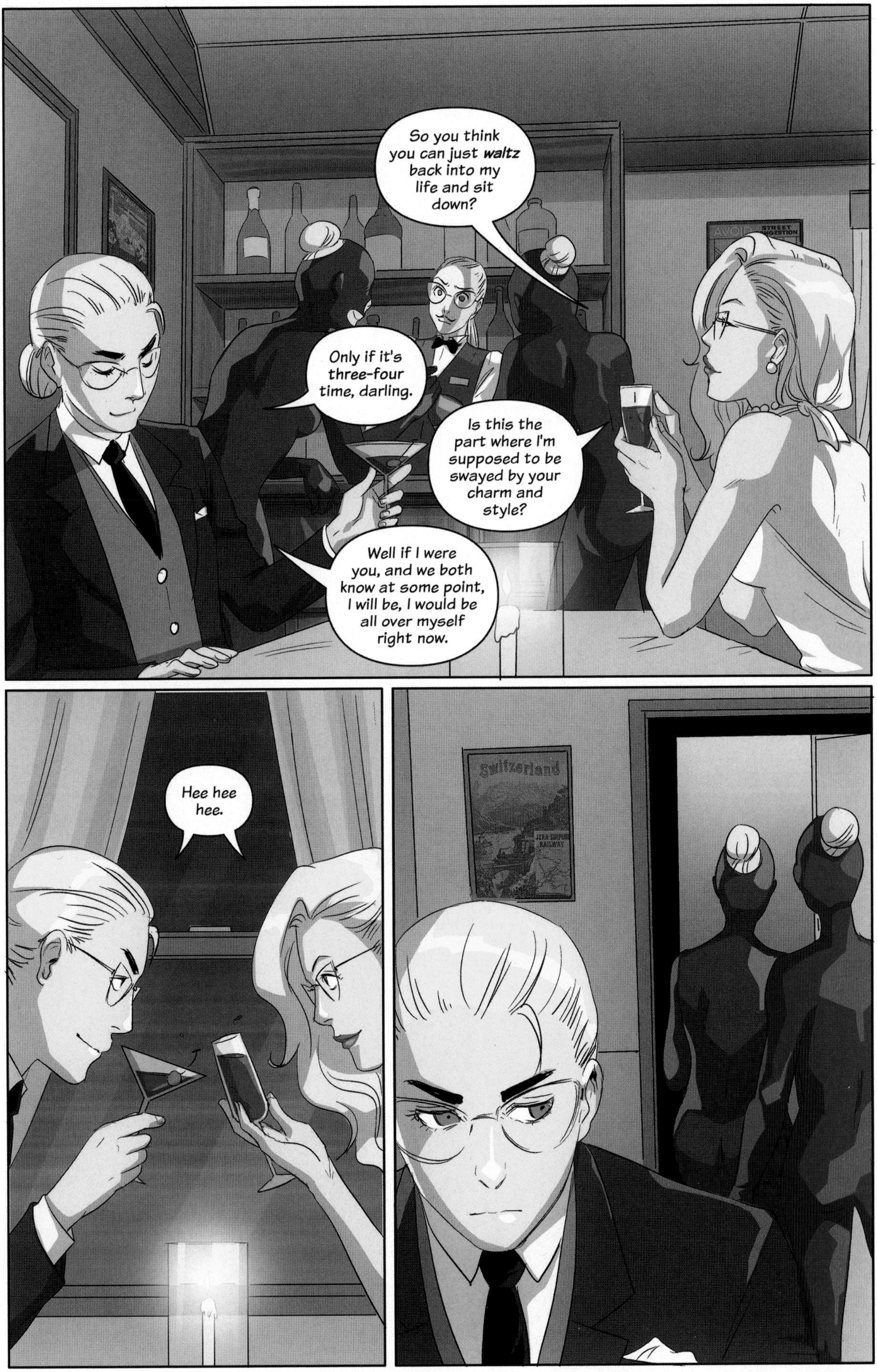
So you think you can just *waltz* back into my life and sit down?
Only if it's three-four time, darling.
Is this the part where I'm supposed to be swayed by your charm and style?
Well if I were you, and we both know at some point, I will be, I would be all over myself right now.
Hee hee hee.
Switzerland

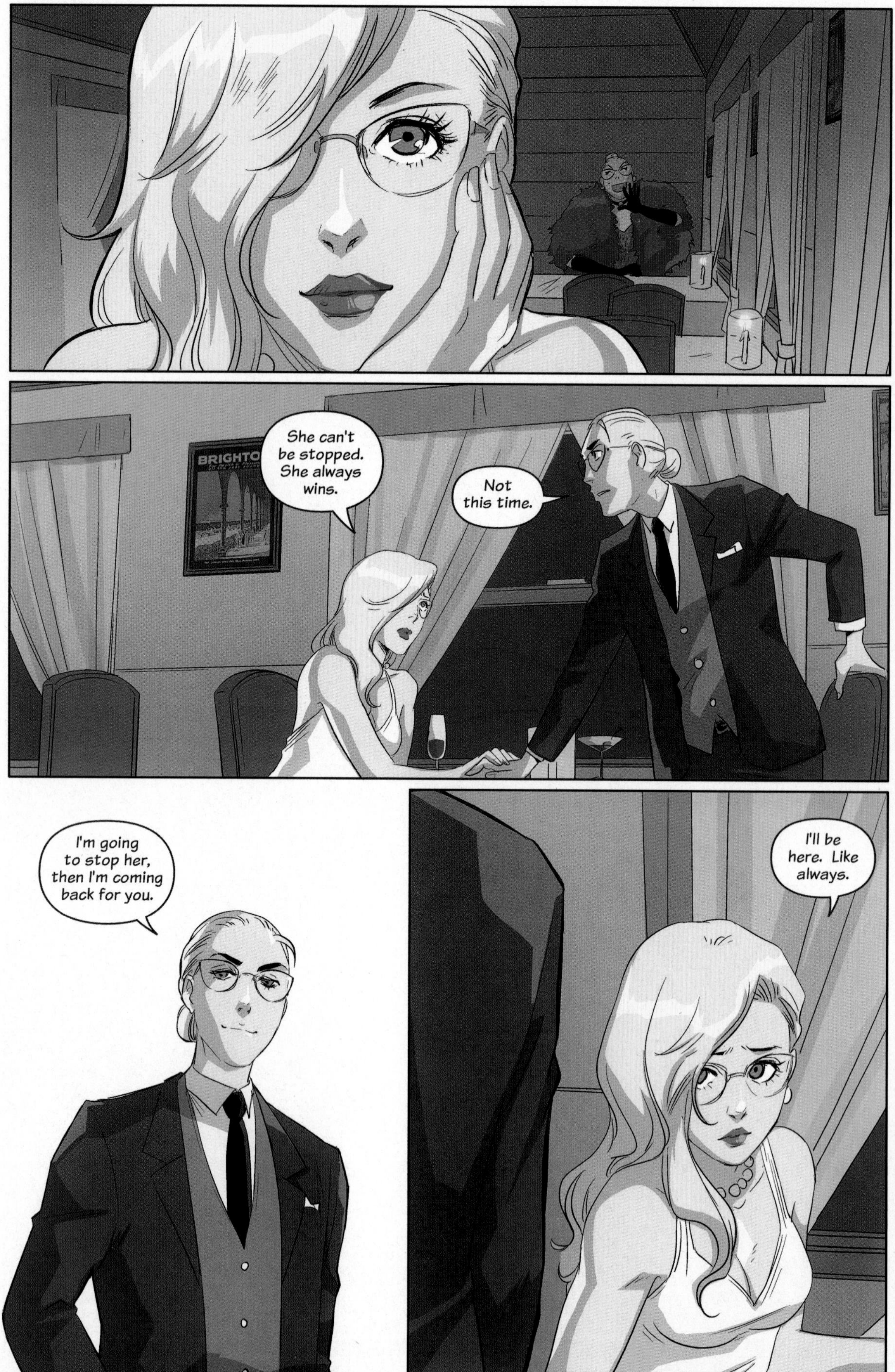
She can't be stopped. She always wins.
Not this time.
I'm going to stop her, then I'm coming back for you.
I'll be here. Like always.

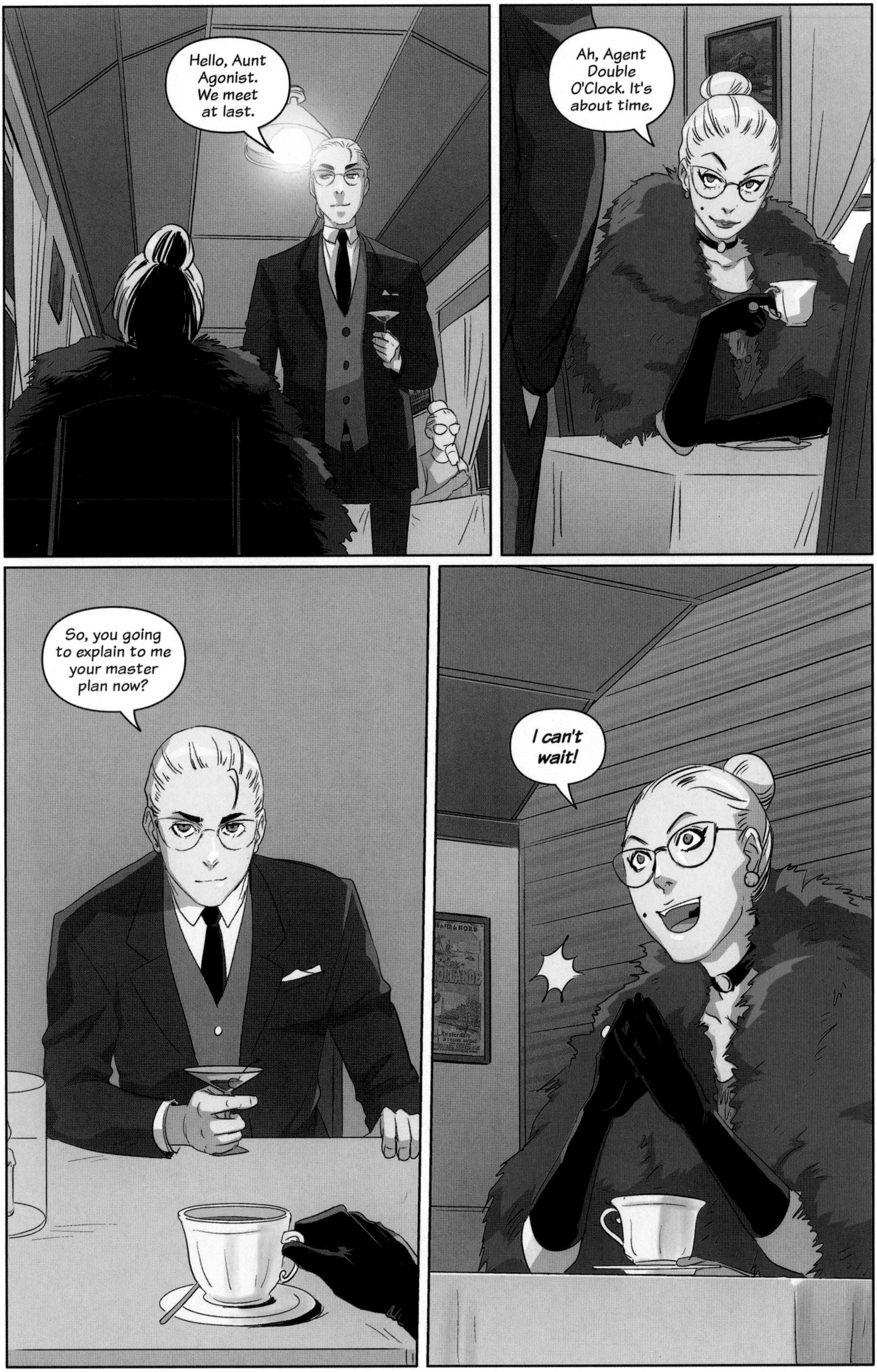
Hello, Aunt Agonist. We meet at last.
Ah, Agent Double O'Clock. It's about time.
So, you going to explain to me your master plan now?
I can't wait!

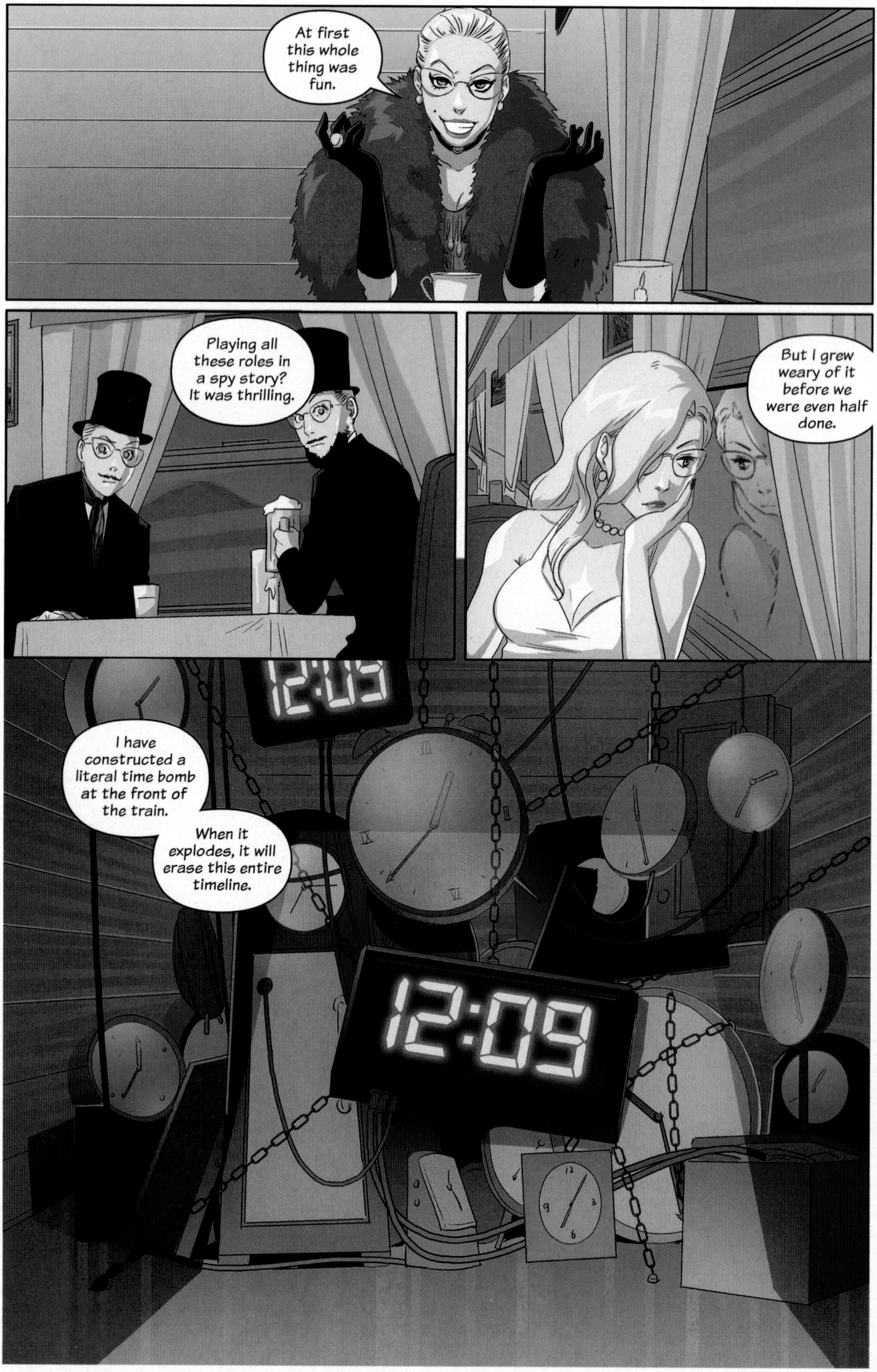
At first this whole thing was fun.
Playing all these roles in a spy story? It was thrilling.
But I grew weary of it before we were even half done.
I have constructed a literal time bomb at the front of the train.
When it explodes, it will erase this entire timeline.
12:09

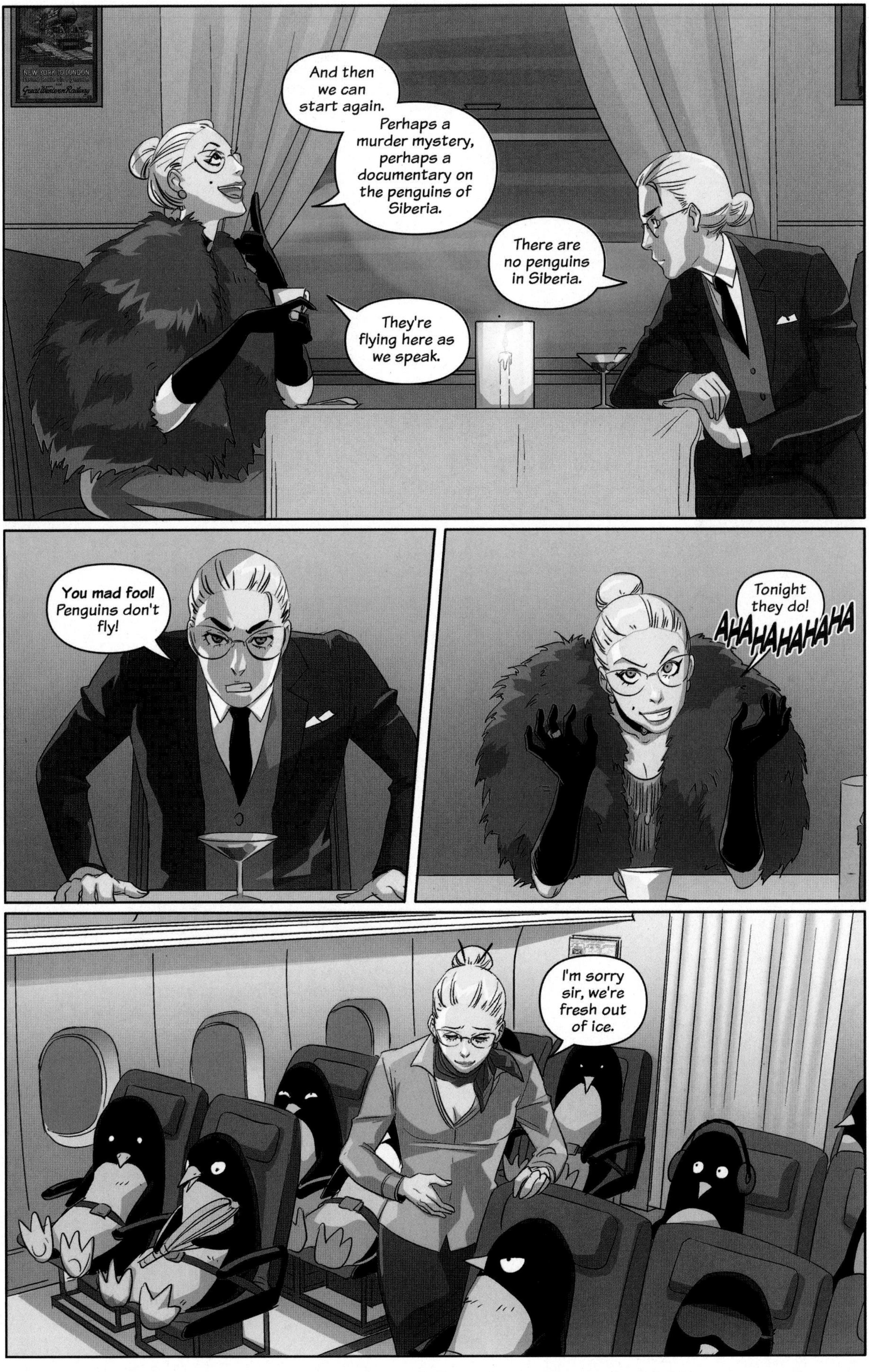
NEW YORK TO LONDON
Great Western Railway
And then we can start again.
Perhaps a murder mystery, perhaps a documentary on the penguins of Siberia.
There are no penguins in Siberia.
They're flying here as we speak.
You mad fool! Penguins don't fly!
Tonight they do!
AHAHAHAHAHA
I'm sorry sir, we're fresh out of ice.

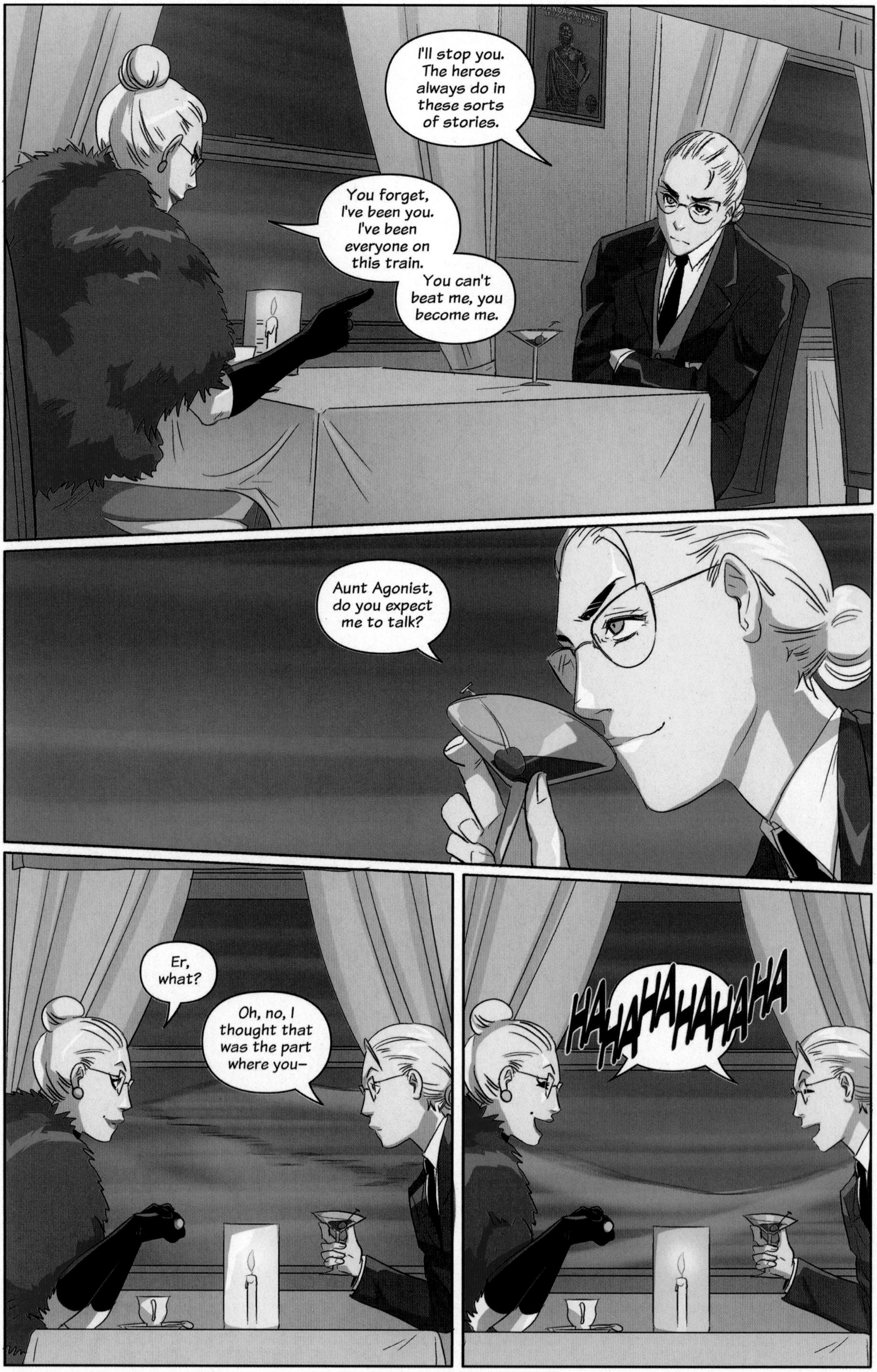
I'll stop you. The heroes always do in these sorts of stories.
You forget, I've been you. I've been everyone on this train.
You can't beat me, you become me.
Aunt Agonist, do you expect me to talk?
Er, what?
Oh, no, I thought that was the part where you—
HAHAHAHAHAHA

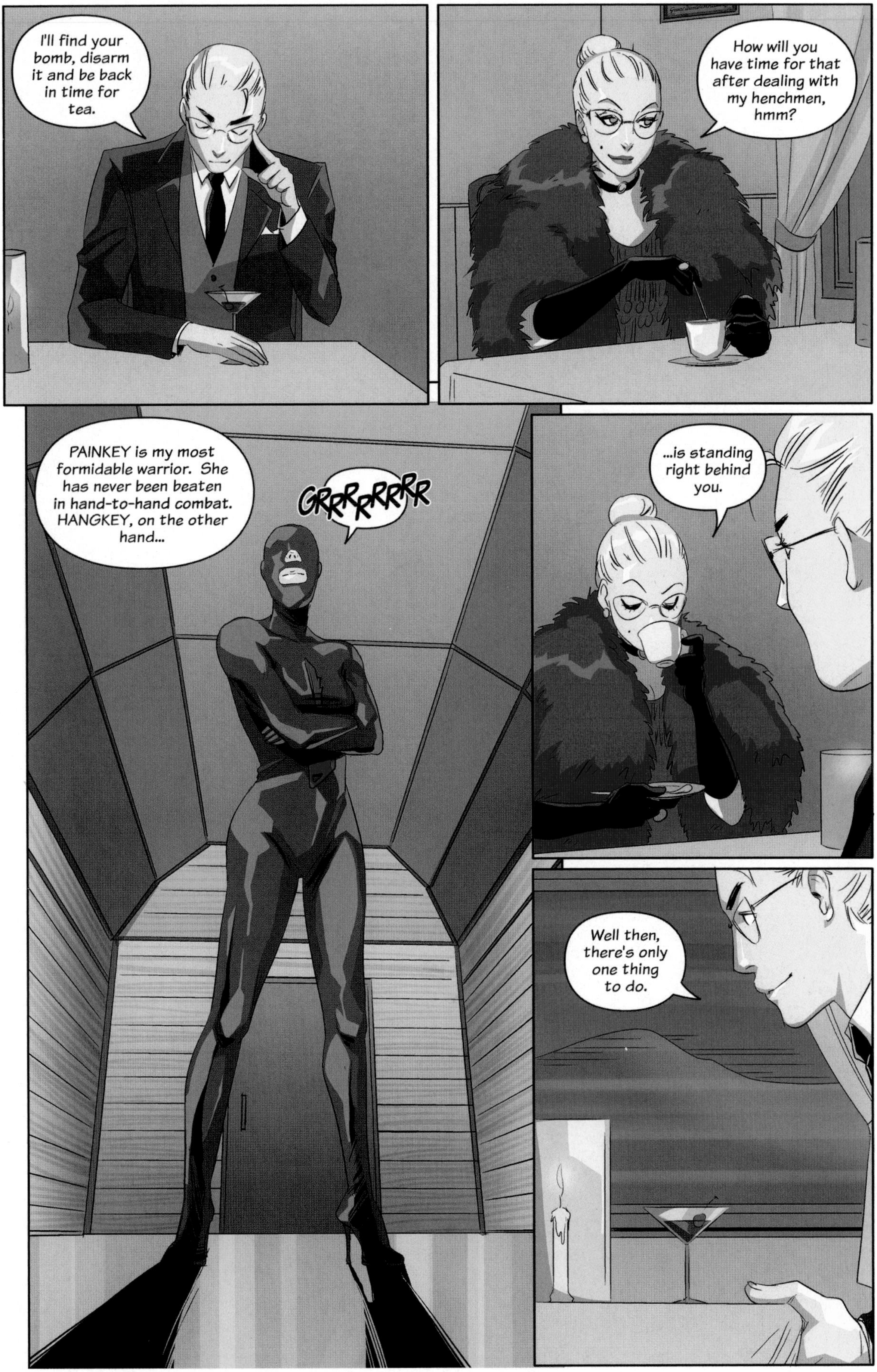
I'll find your bomb, disarm it and be back in time for tea.
How will you have time for that after dealing with my henchmen, hmm?
PAINKEY is my most formidable warrior. She has never been beaten in hand-to-hand combat. HANGKEY, on the other hand...
GRRRRRRR
...is standing right behind you.
Well then, there's only one thing to do.

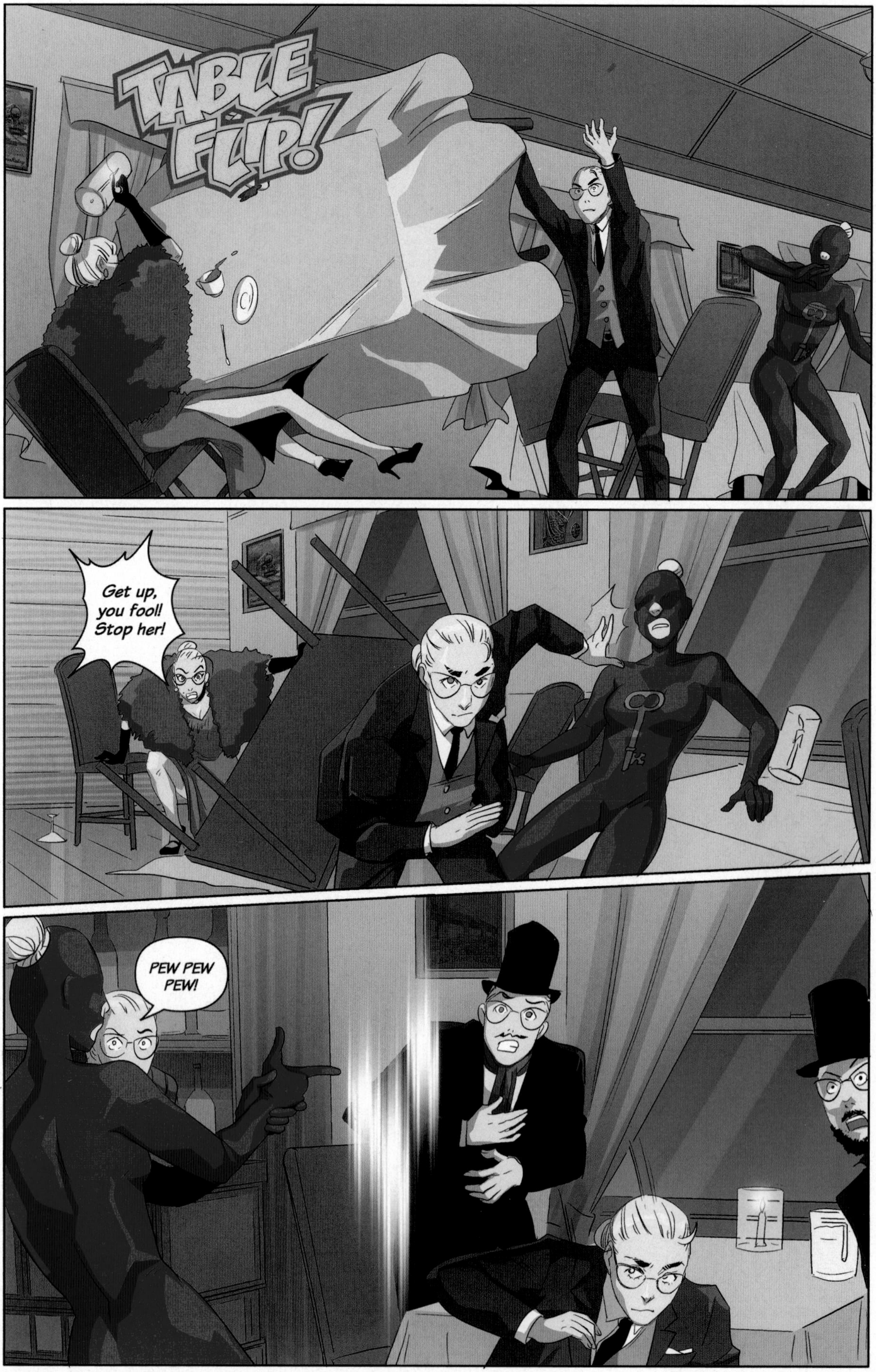
TABLE FLIP!
Get up, you fool! Stop her!
PEW PEW PEW!

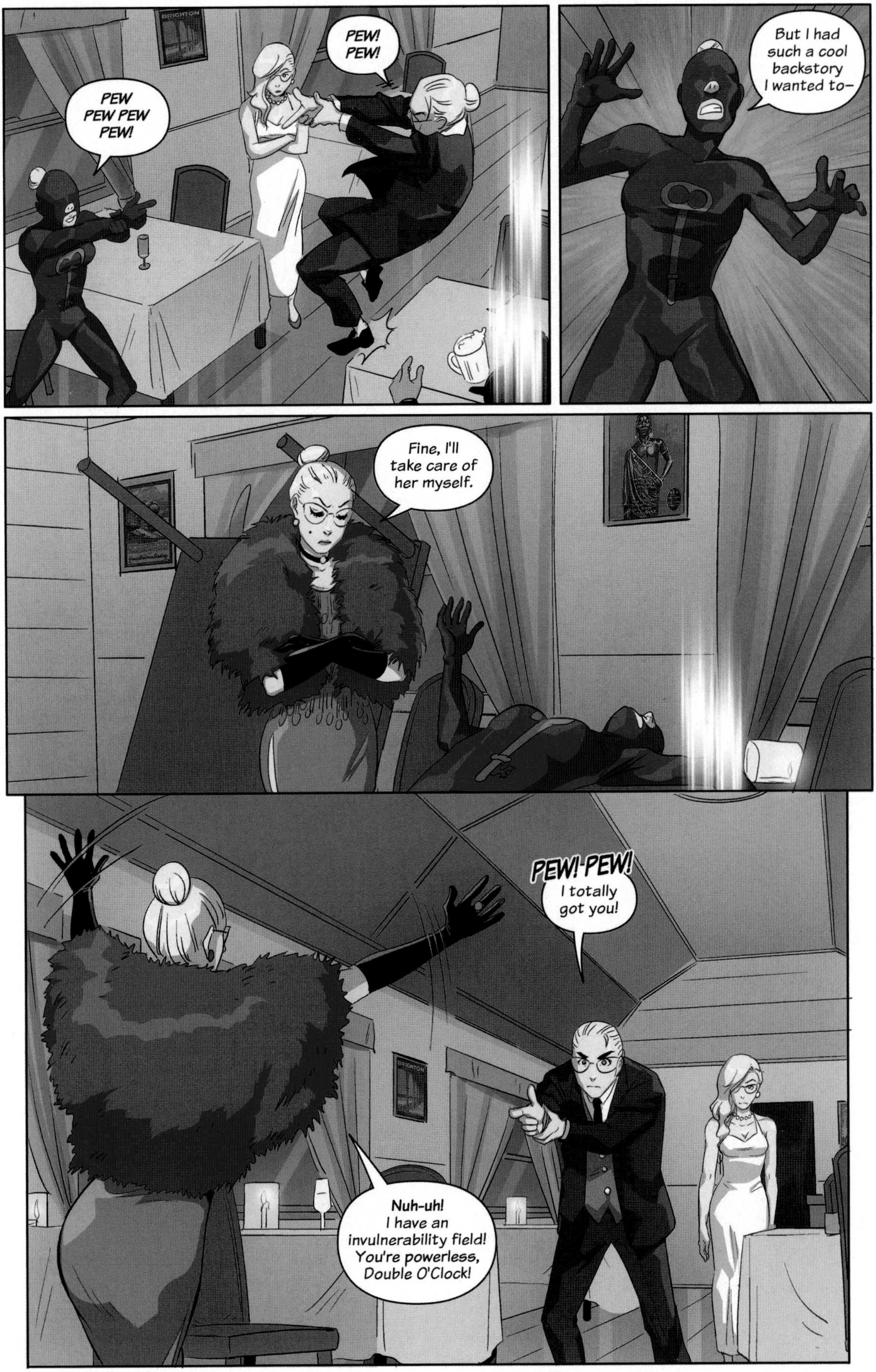
PEW! PEW!
PEW PEW PEW PEW!
BRIGHTON
But I had such a cool backstory I wanted to–
Fine, I'll take care of her myself.
PEW! PEW!
I totally got you!
Nuh-uh! I have an invulnerability field! You're powerless, Double O'Clock!
BRIGHTON

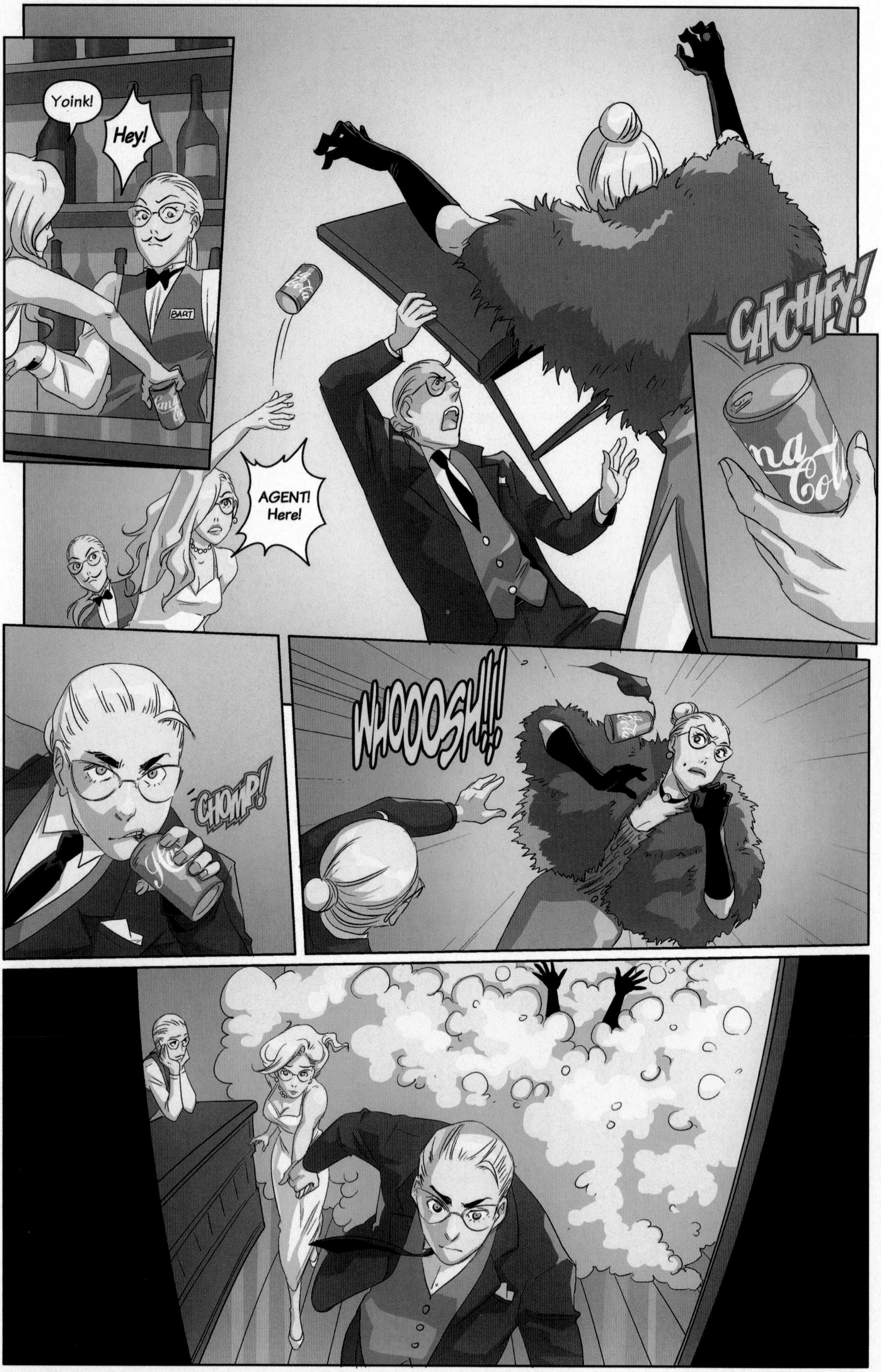
Yoink!
Hey!
BART
AGENT! Here!
CATCHFY!
CHOMP!
WHOOOSH!!!

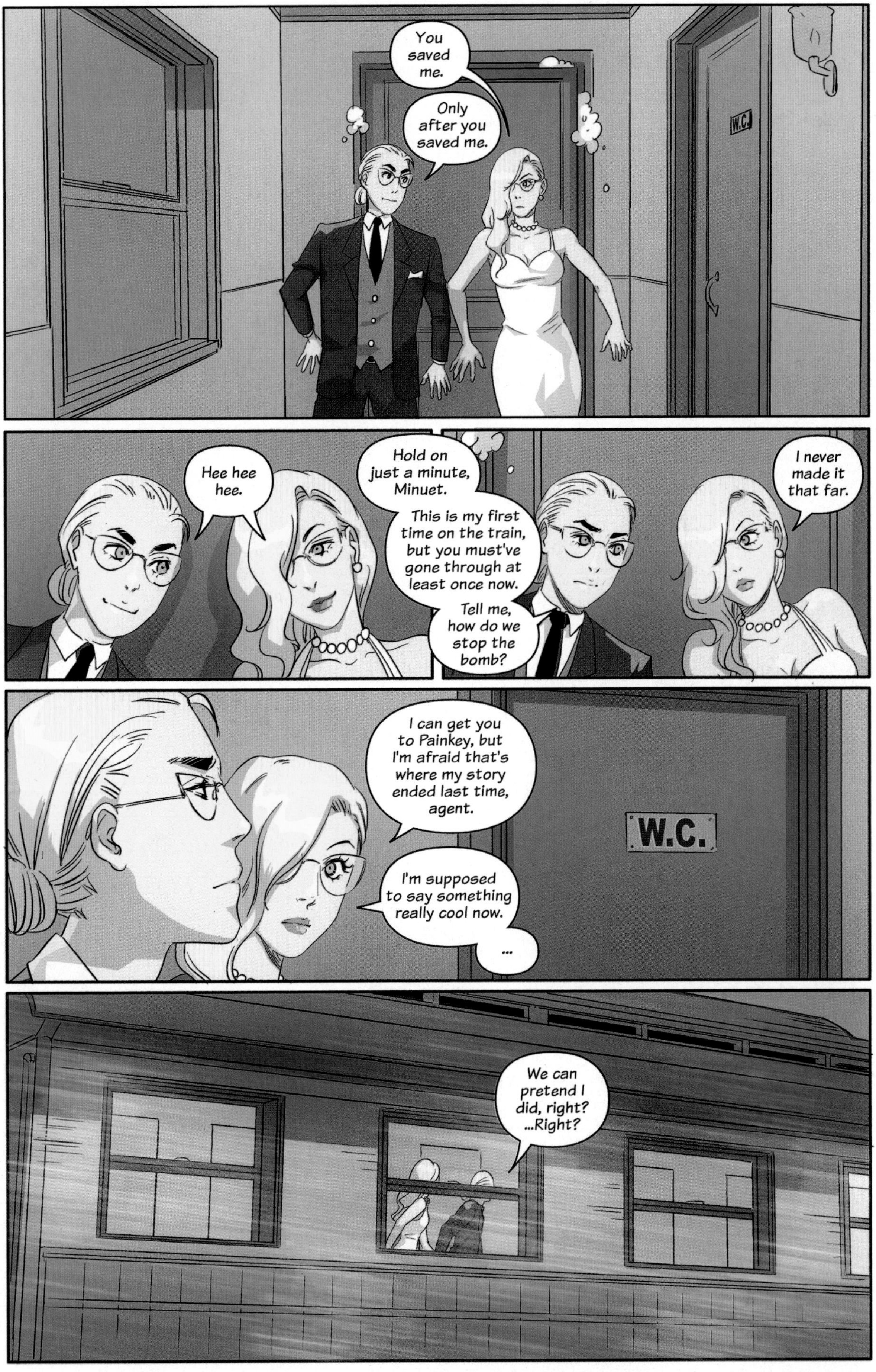
You saved me.
Only after you saved me.
Hee hee hee.
Hold on just a minute, Minuet.
This is my first time on the train, but you must've gone through at least once now.
Tell me, how do we stop the bomb?
I never made it that far.
I can get you to Painkey, but I'm afraid that's where my story ended last time, agent.
W.C.
I'm supposed to say something really cool now.
...
We can pretend I did, right? ...Right?

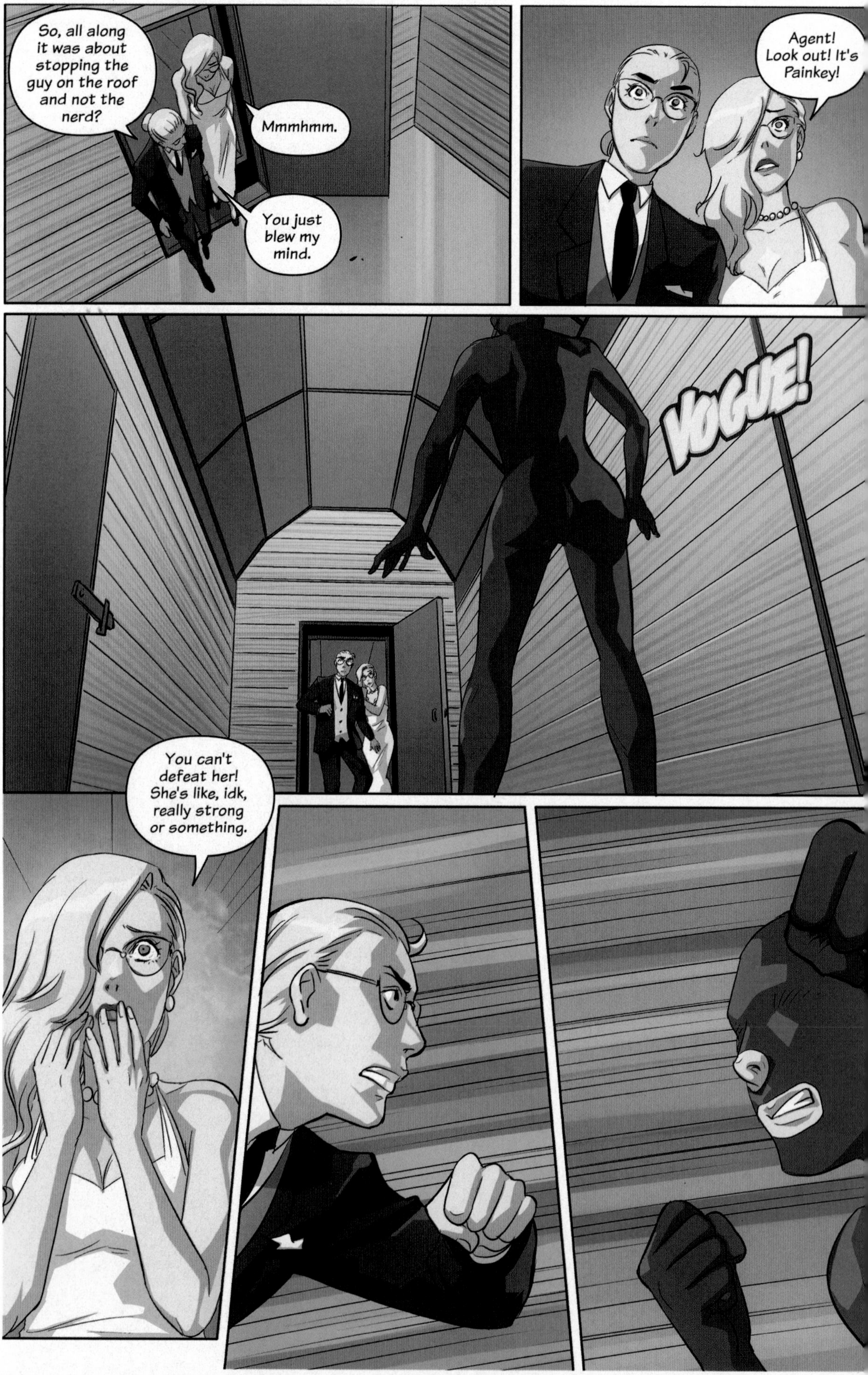
So, all along it was about stopping the guy on the roof and not the nerd?
Mmmhmm.
You just blew my mind.
Agent! Look out! It's Painkey!
VOGUE!
You can't defeat her! She's like, idk, really strong or something.

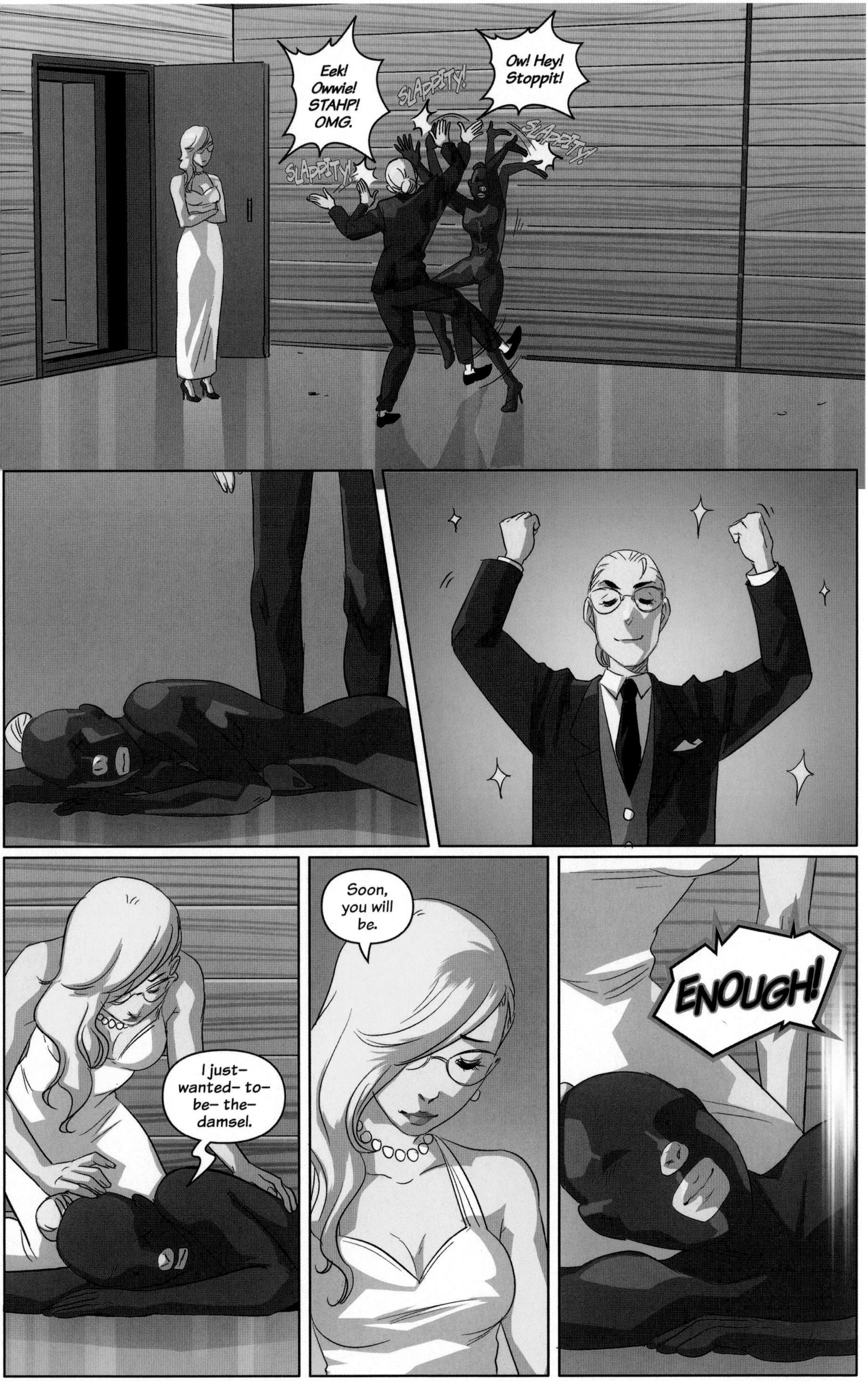
Eek! Owwie! STAHP! OMG.
SLAPPITY!
SLAPPITY!
Ow! Hey! Stoppit!
SLAPPITY!
I just– wanted– to– be– the– damsel.
Soon, you will be.
ENOUGH!

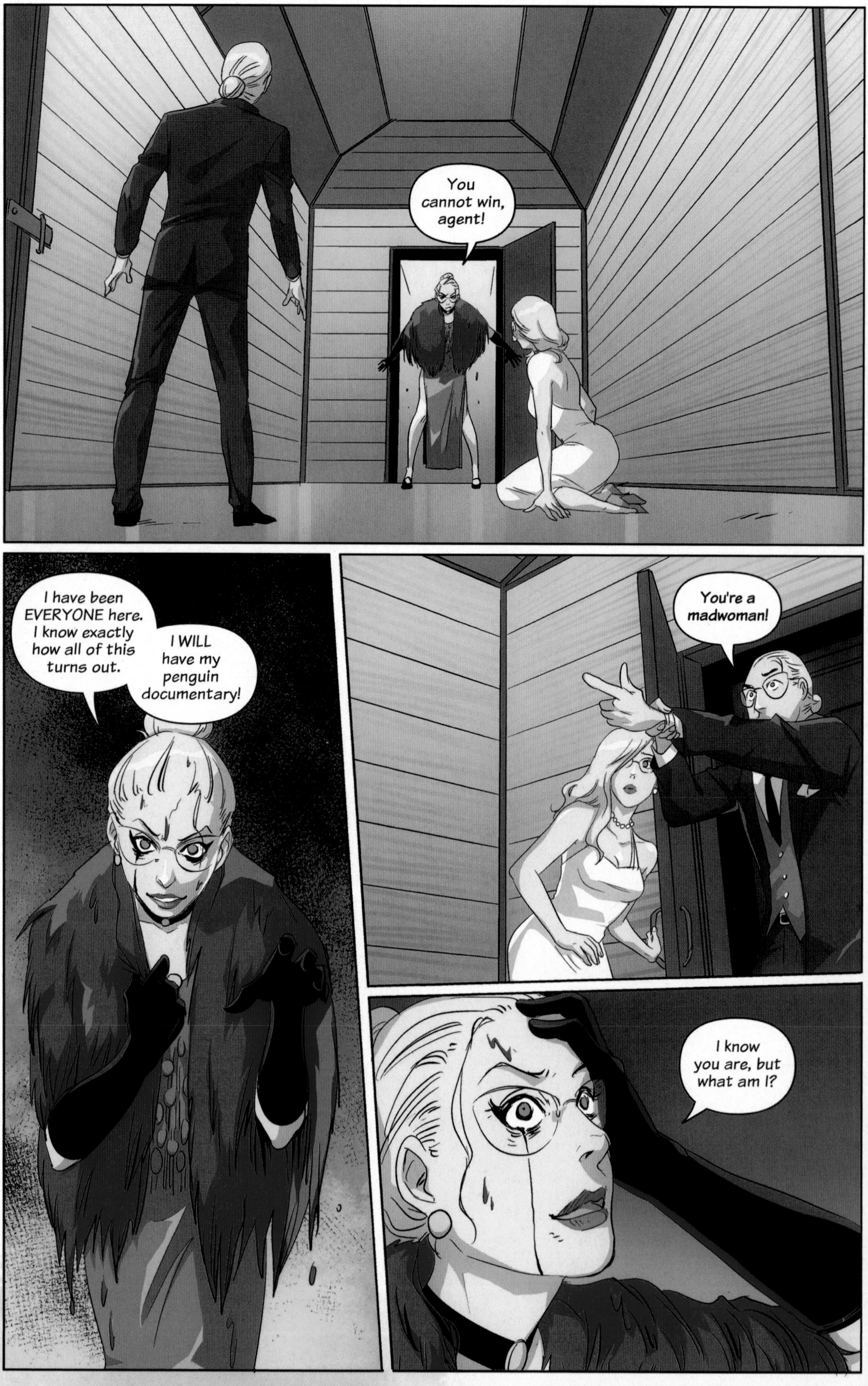
You cannot win, agent!
I have been EVERYONE here. I know exactly how all of this turns out.
I WILL have my penguin documentary!
You're a madwoman!
I know you are, but what am I?

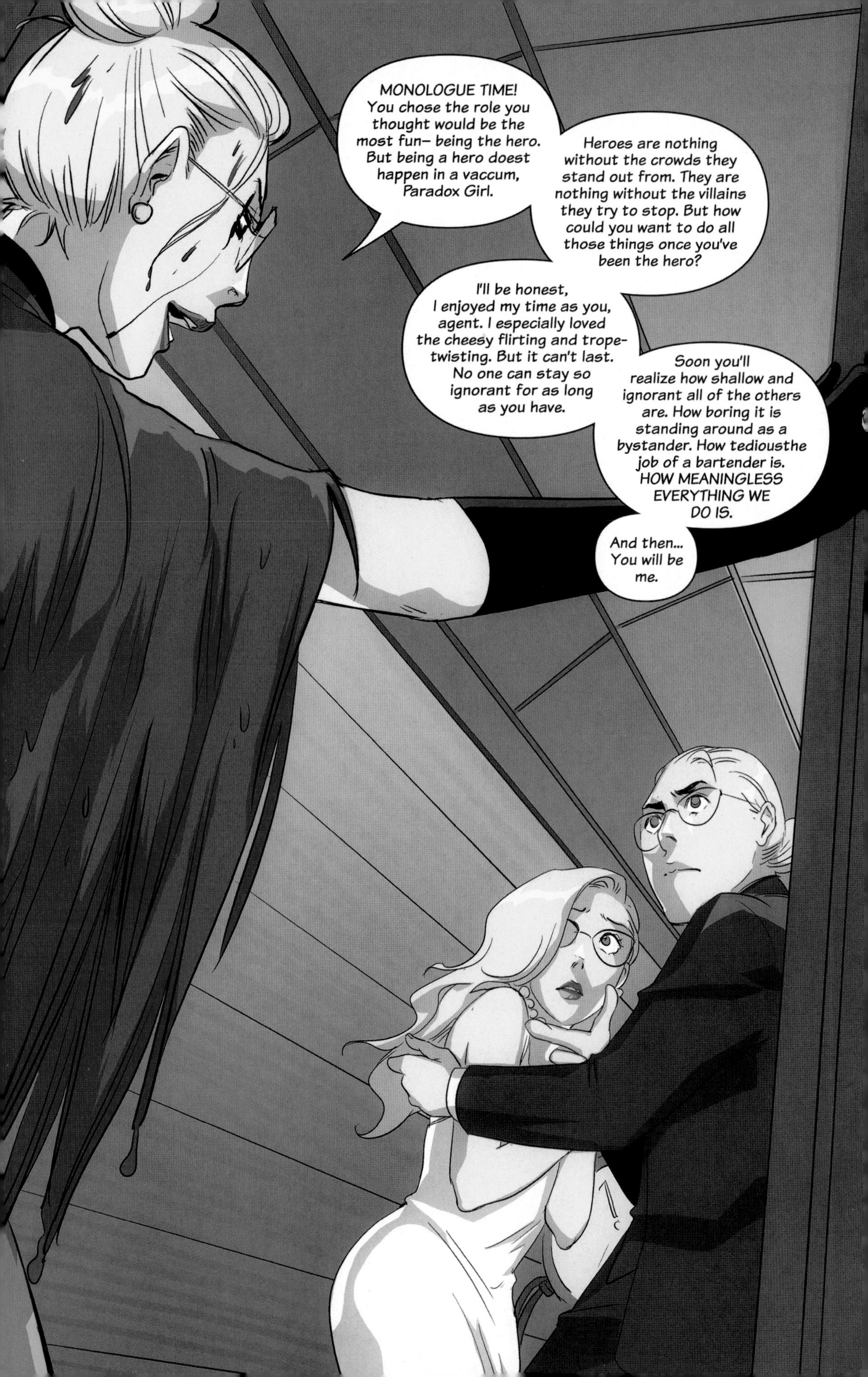
MONOLOGUE TIME! You chose the role you thought would be the most fun– being the hero. But being a hero doest happen in a vaccum, Paradox Girl.
Heroes are nothing without the crowds they stand out from. They are nothing without the villains they try to stop. But how could you want to do all those things once you've been the hero?
I'll be honest, I enjoyed my time as you, agent. I especially loved the cheesy flirting and trope-twisting. But it can't last. No one can stay so ignorant for as long as you have.
Soon you'll realize how shallow and ignorant all of the others are. How boring it is standing around as a bystander. How tediousthe job of a bartender is. HOW MEANINGLESS EVERYTHING WE DO IS.
And then... You will be me.

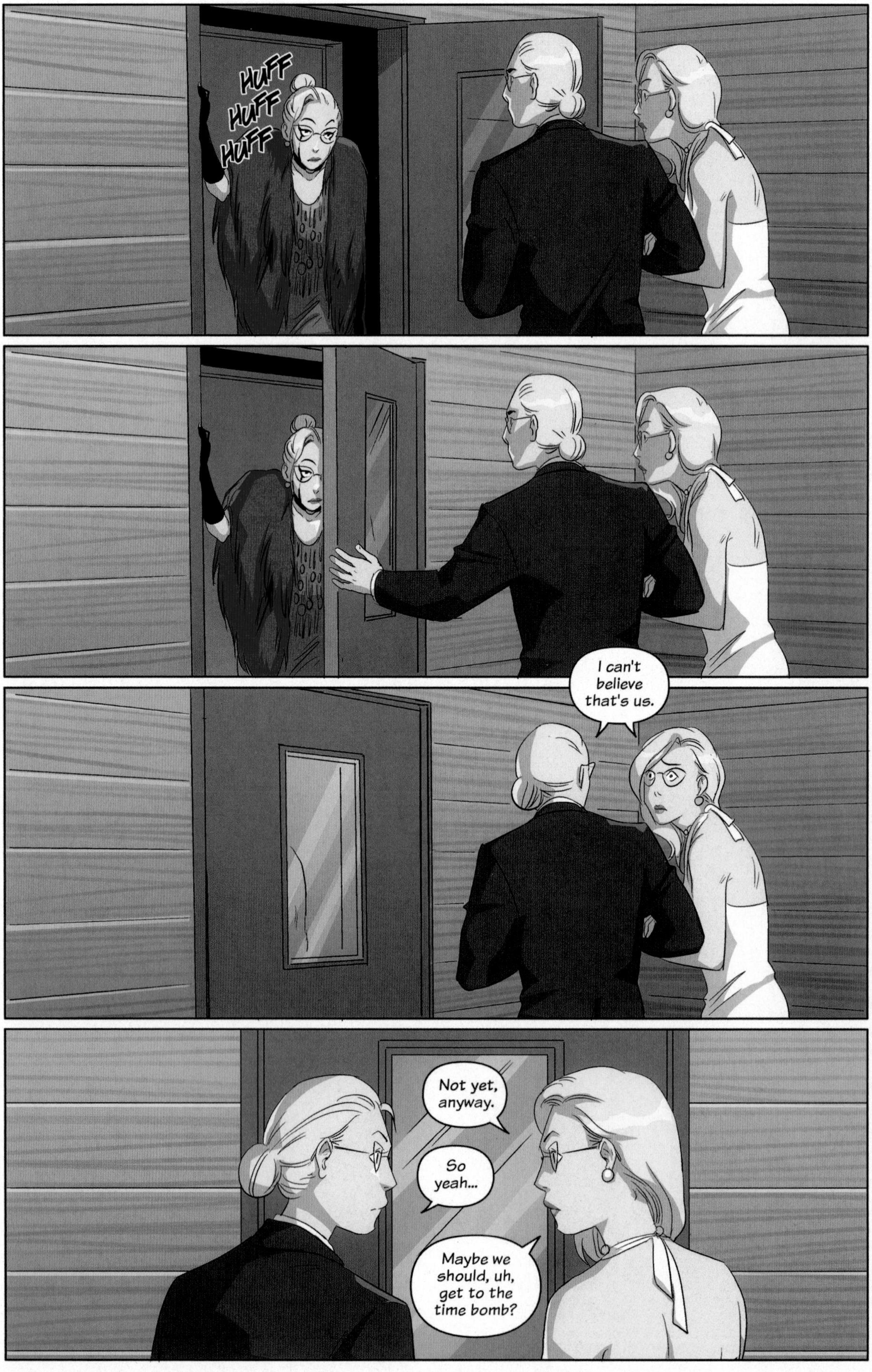
HUFF
HUFF
HUFF
I can't believe that's us.
Not yet, anyway.
So yeah...
Maybe we should, uh, get to the time bomb?

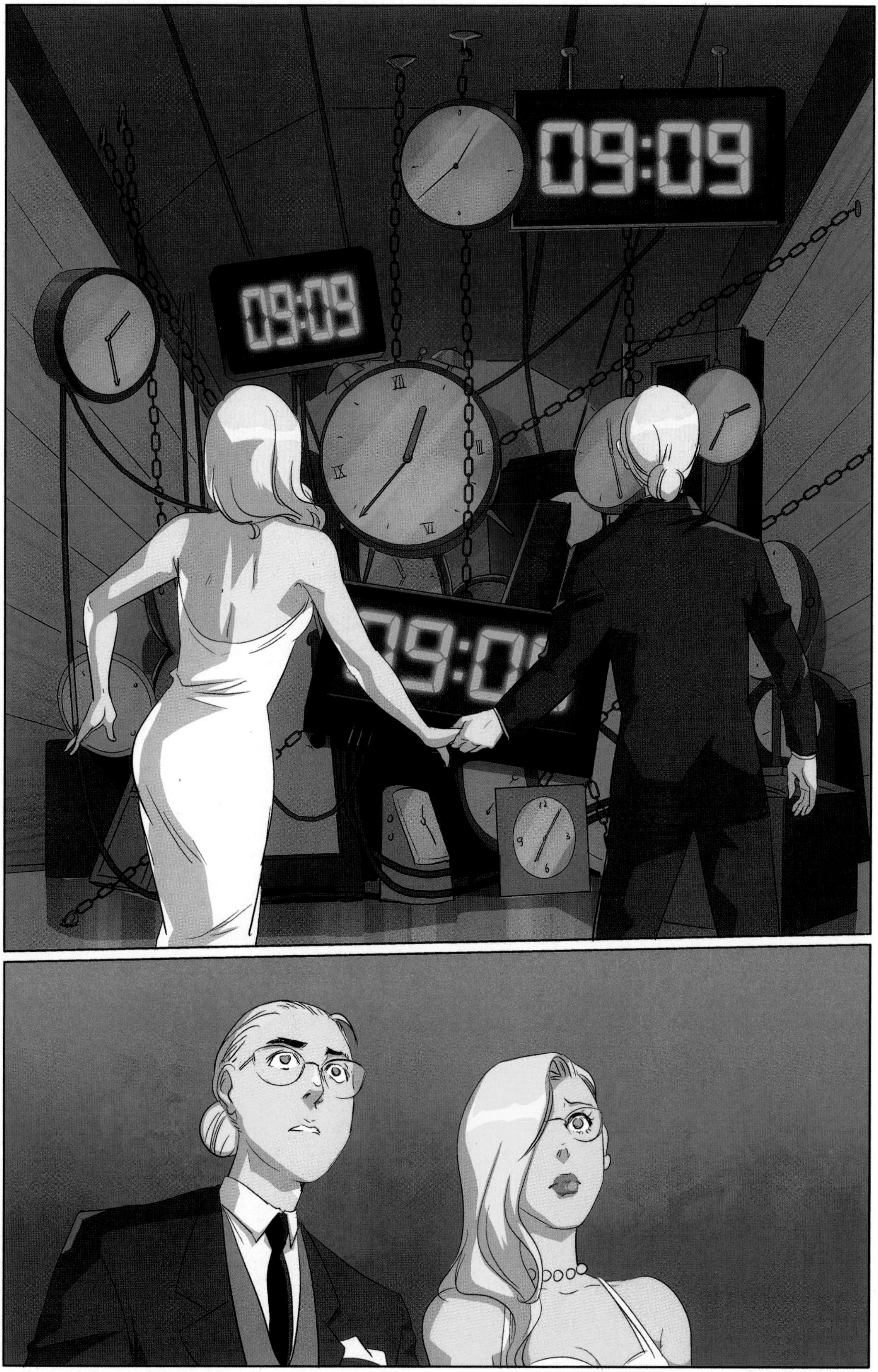
09:09
09:09

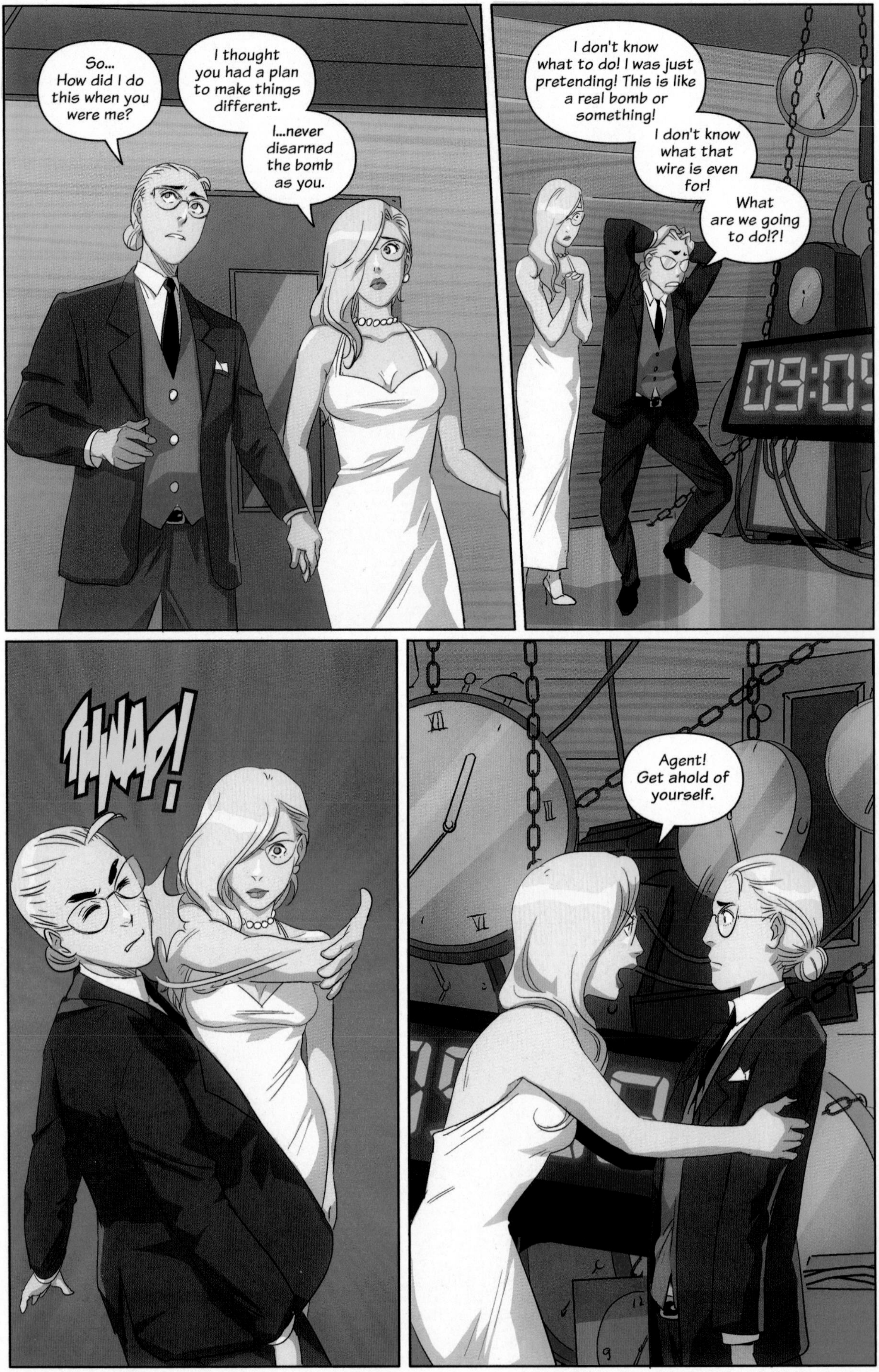
So... How did I do this when you were me?
I thought you had a plan to make things different.
I...never disarmed the bomb as you.
I don't know what to do! I was just pretending! This is like a real bomb or something!
I don't know what that wire is even for!
What are we going to do!?!
09:09
THWAP!
Agent! Get ahold of yourself.

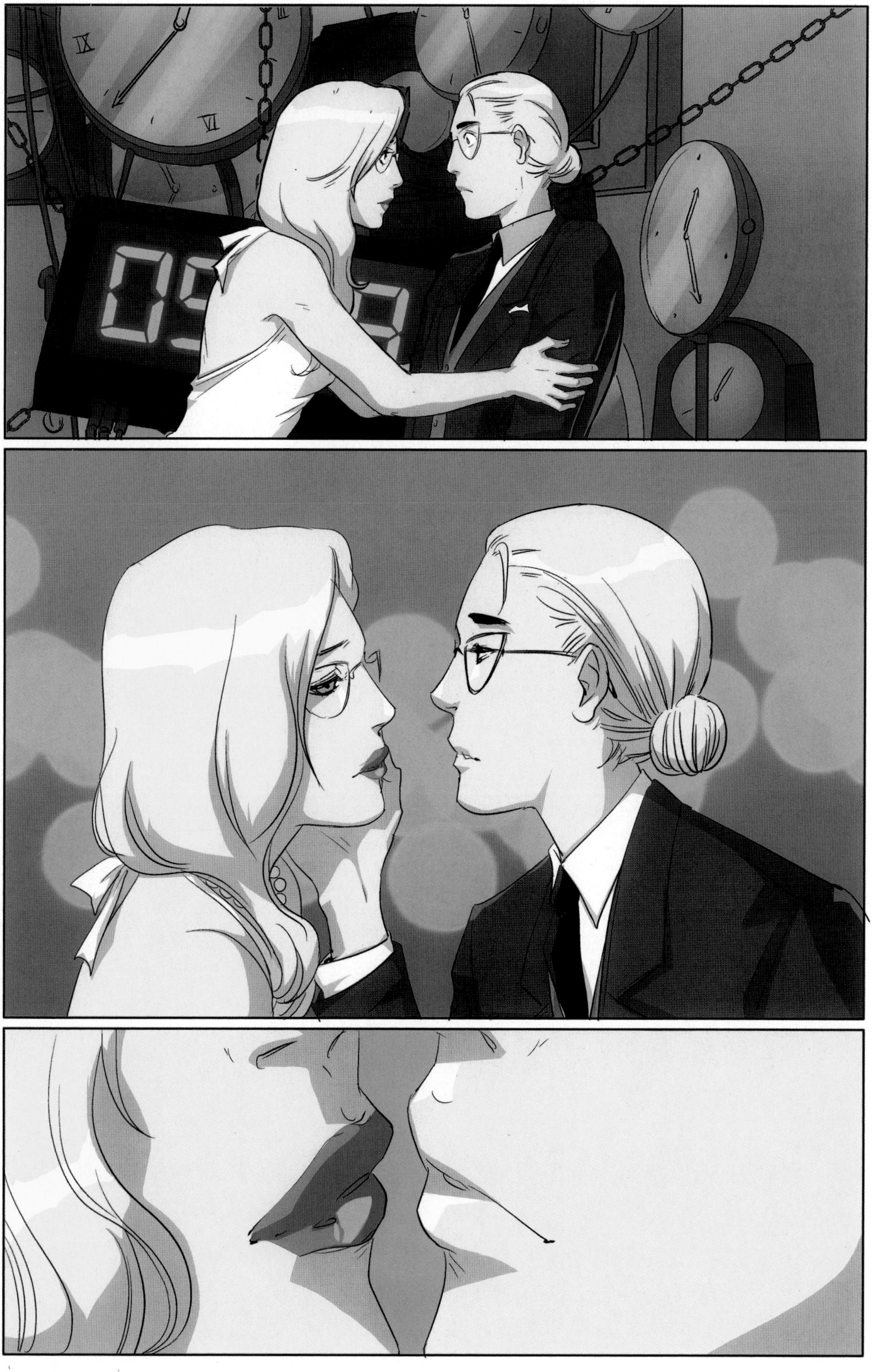

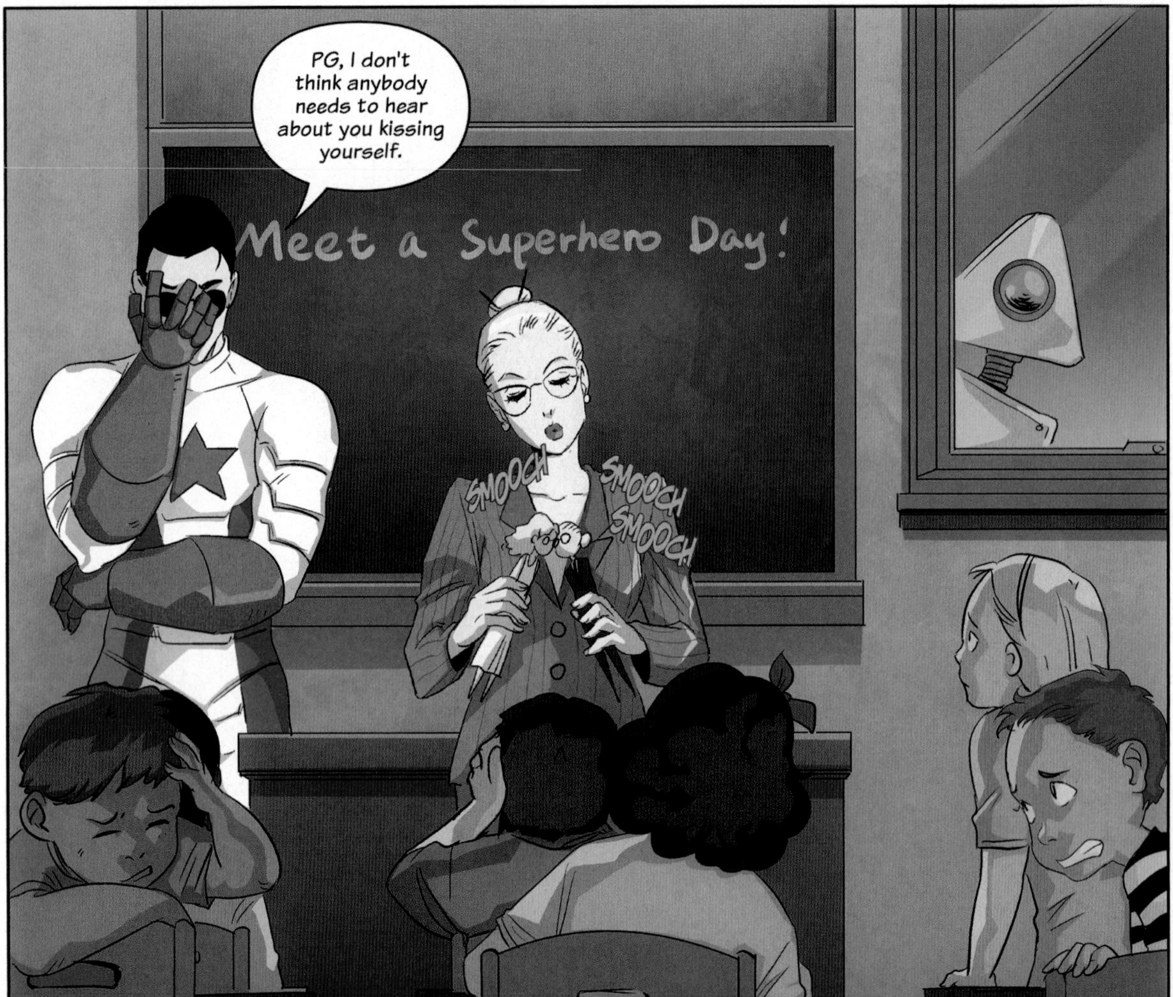
PG, I don't think anybody needs to hear about you kissing yourself.
Meet a Superhero Day!
SMOOCH
SMOOCH
SMOOCH

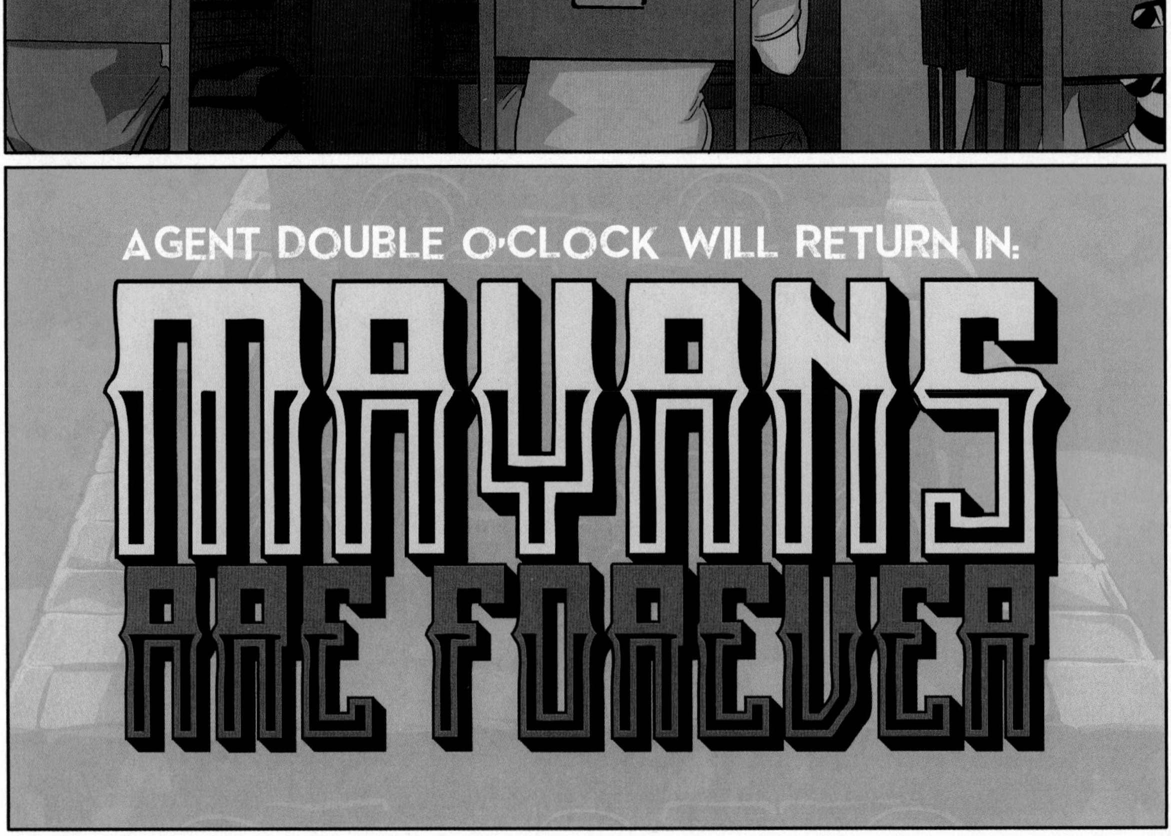
AGENT DOUBLE O-CLOCK WILL RETURN IN:
MAYANS ARE FOREVER

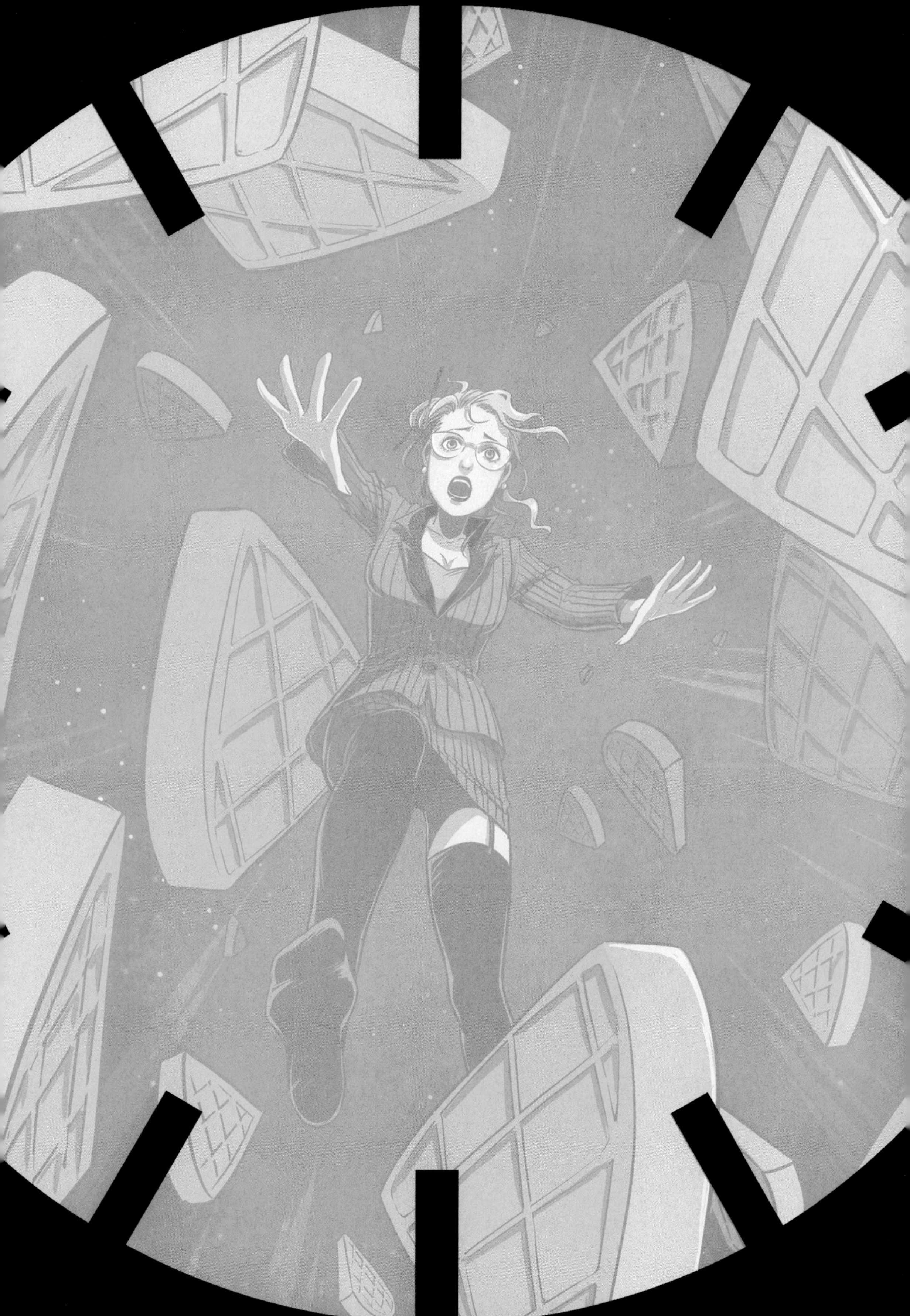

CHAPTER 6

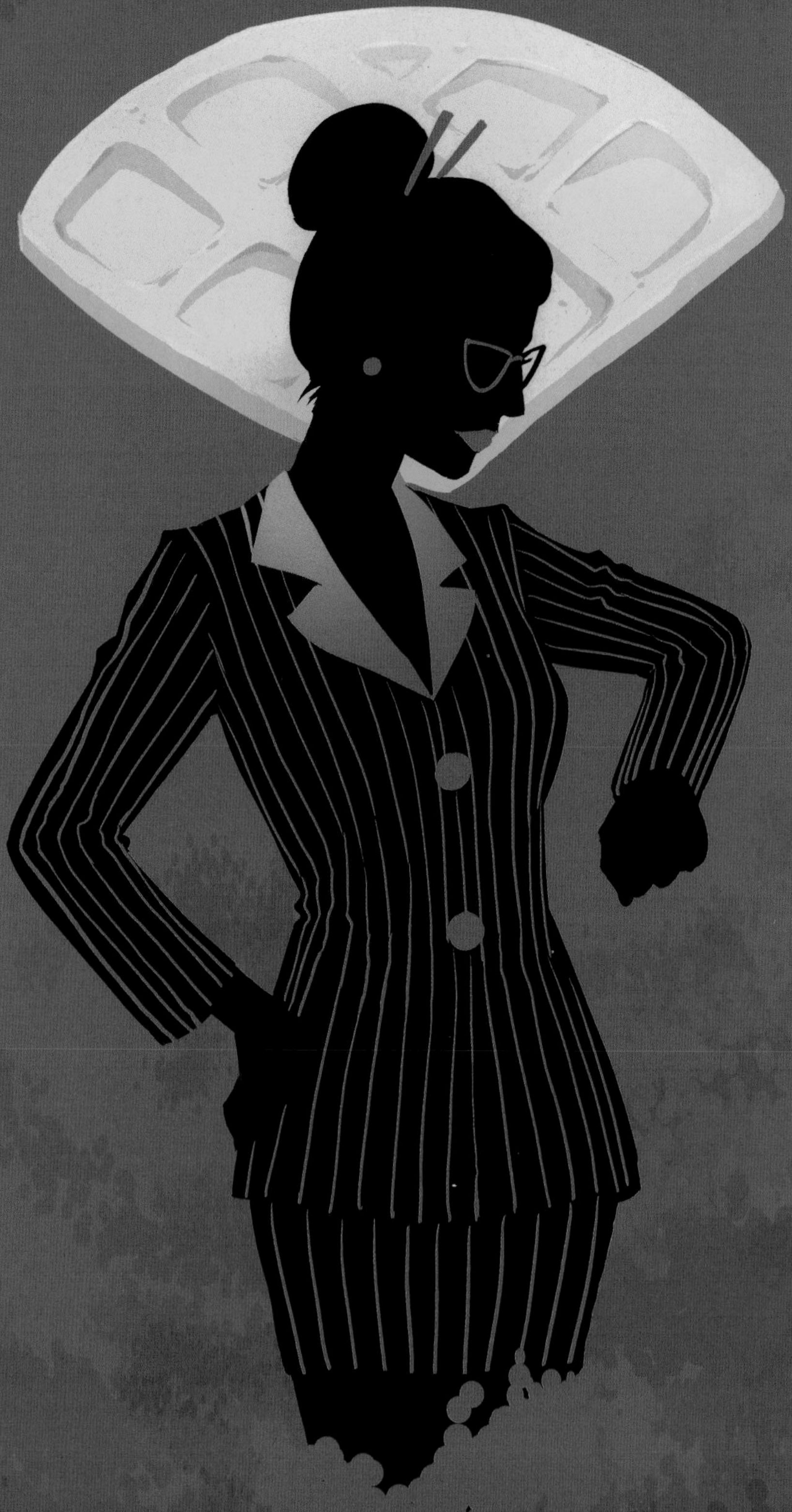

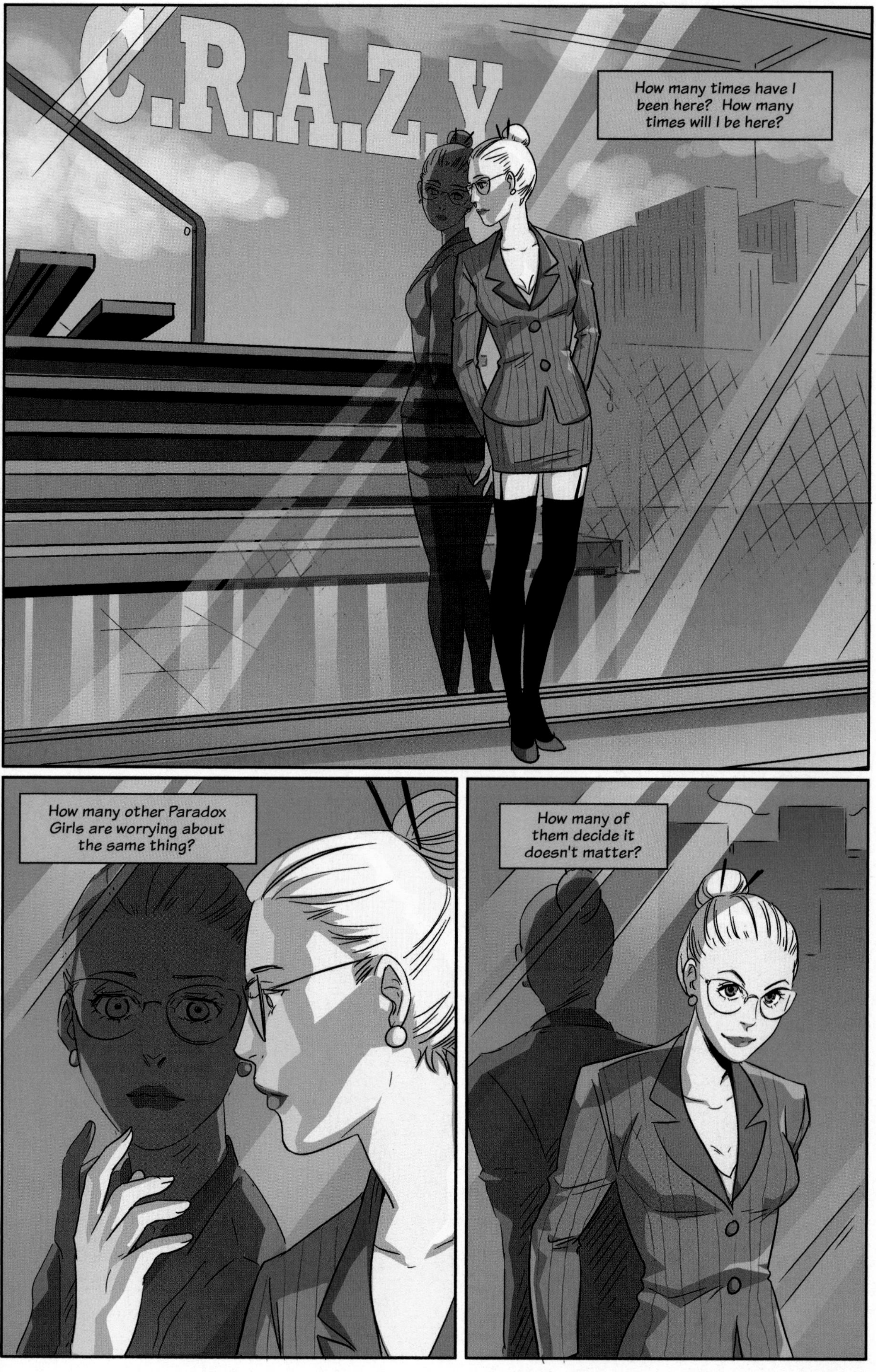
C.R.A.Z.Y
How many times have I been here? How many times will I be here?
How many other Paradox Girls are worrying about the same thing?
How many of them decide it doesn't matter?

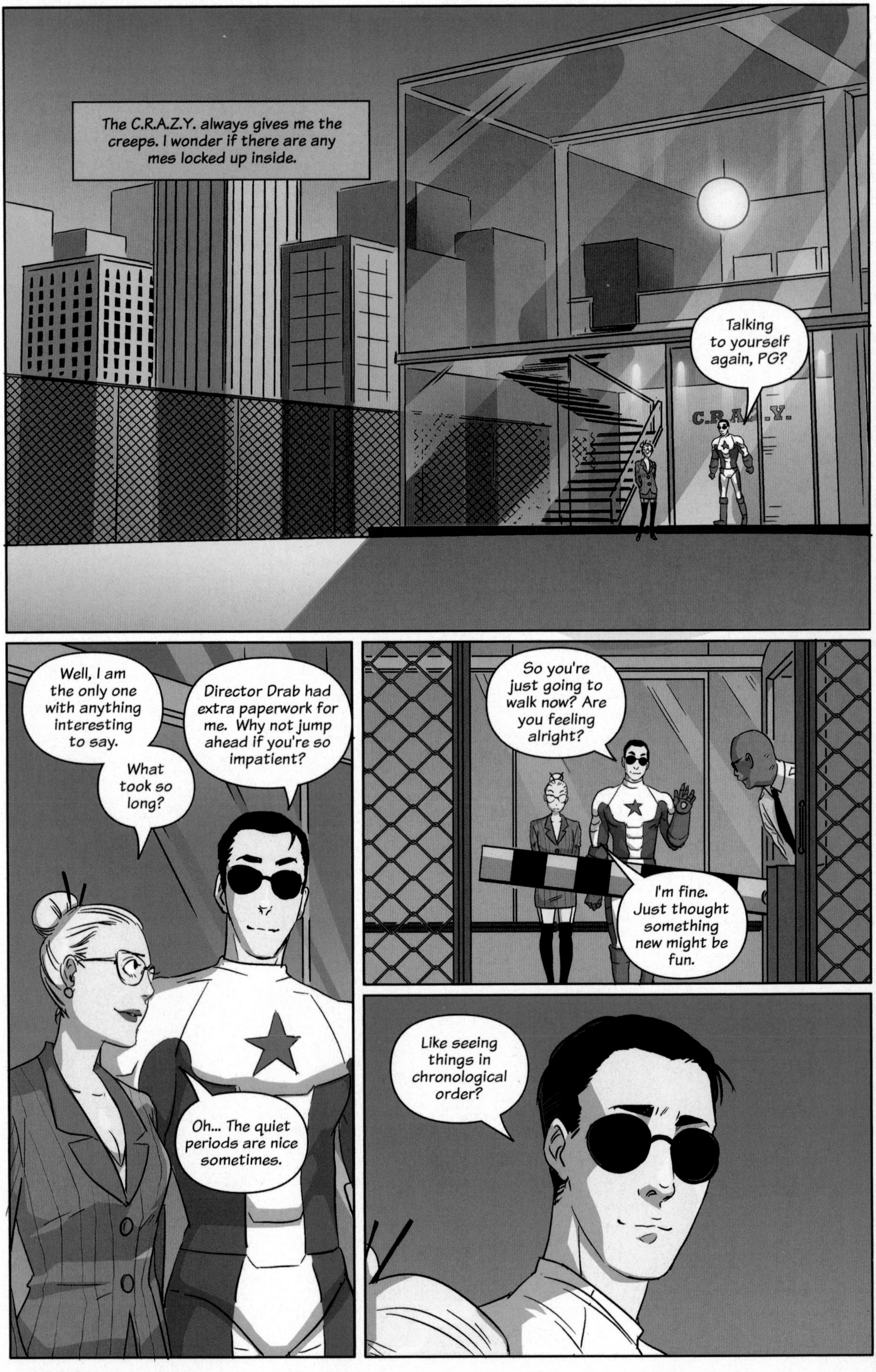
The C.R.A.Z.Y. always gives me the creeps. I wonder if there are any mes locked up inside.
Talking to yourself again, PG?
C.R.A.Z.Y.
Well, I am the only one with anything interesting to say.
What took so long?
Director Drab had extra paperwork for me. Why not jump ahead if you're so impatient?
Oh... The quiet periods are nice sometimes.
So you're just going to walk now? Are you feeling alright?
I'm fine. Just thought something new might be fun.
Like seeing things in chronological order?

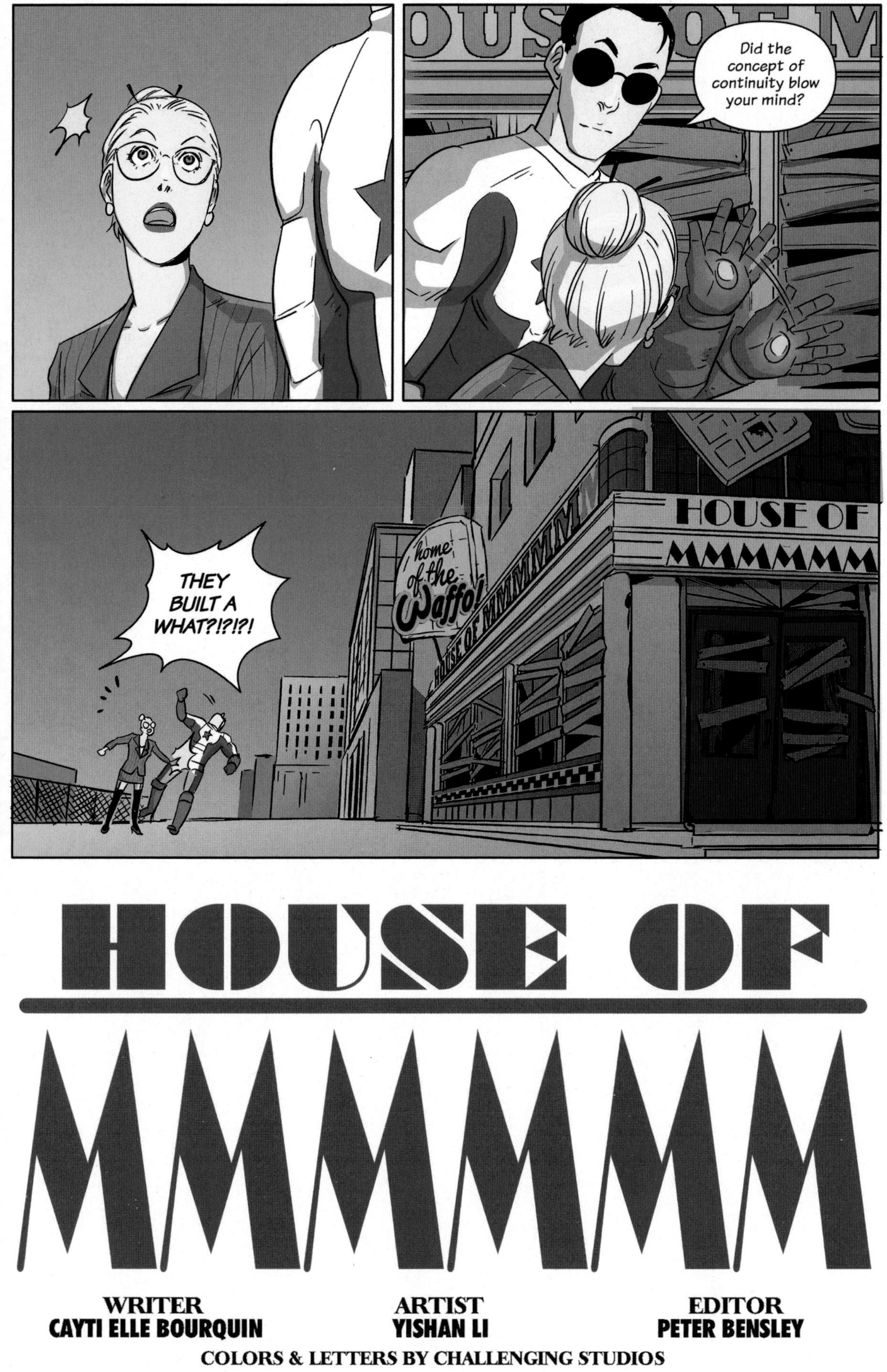
Did the concept of continuity blow your mind?
home of the Waffo!
HOUSE OF
MMMMMM
THEY BUILT A WHAT?!?!?!

HOUSE OF MMMMMM

WRITER
CAYTI ELLE BOURQUIN

ARTIST
YISHAN LI

EDITOR
PETER BENSLEY

COLORS & LETTERS BY CHALLENGING STUDIOS

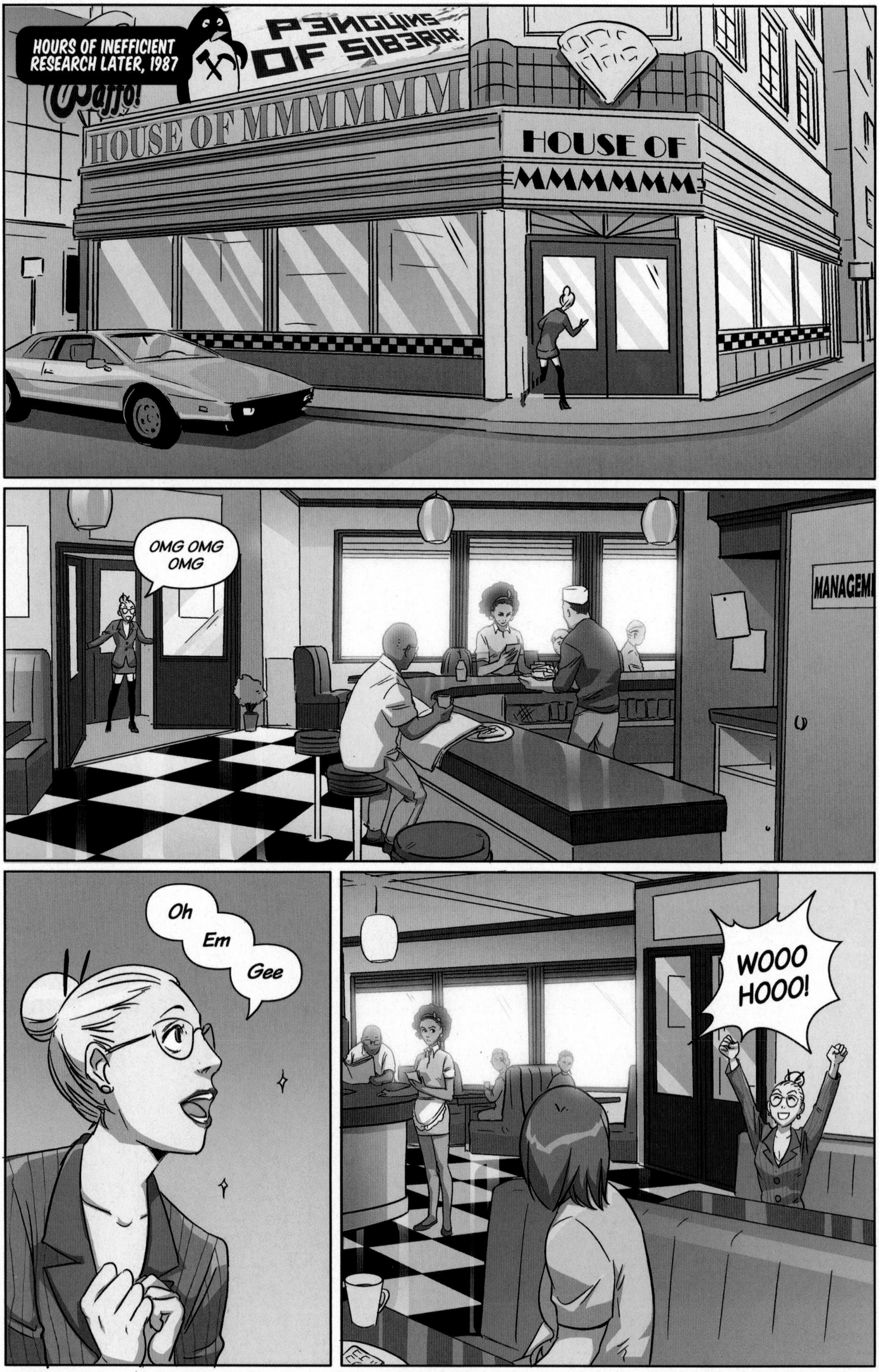
HOURS OF INEFFICIENT RESEARCH LATER, 1987
PENGUINS OF SIBERIA!
HOUSE OF MMMMMMM
HOUSE OF MMMMMM
OMG OMG OMG
MANAGEM
Oh
Em
Gee
WOOO HOOO!

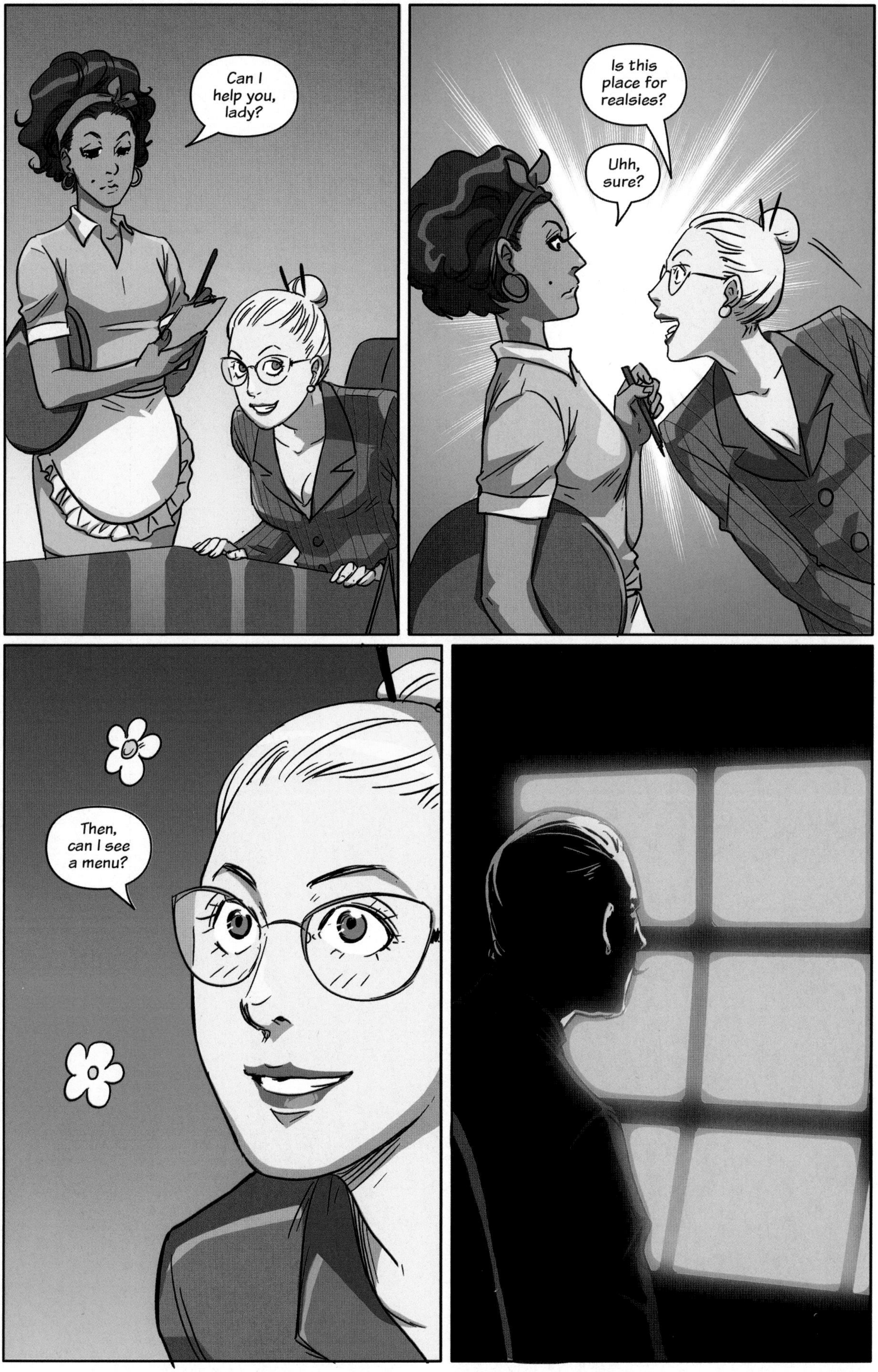
Can I help you, lady?
Is this place for realsies?
Uhh, sure?
Then, can I see a menu?

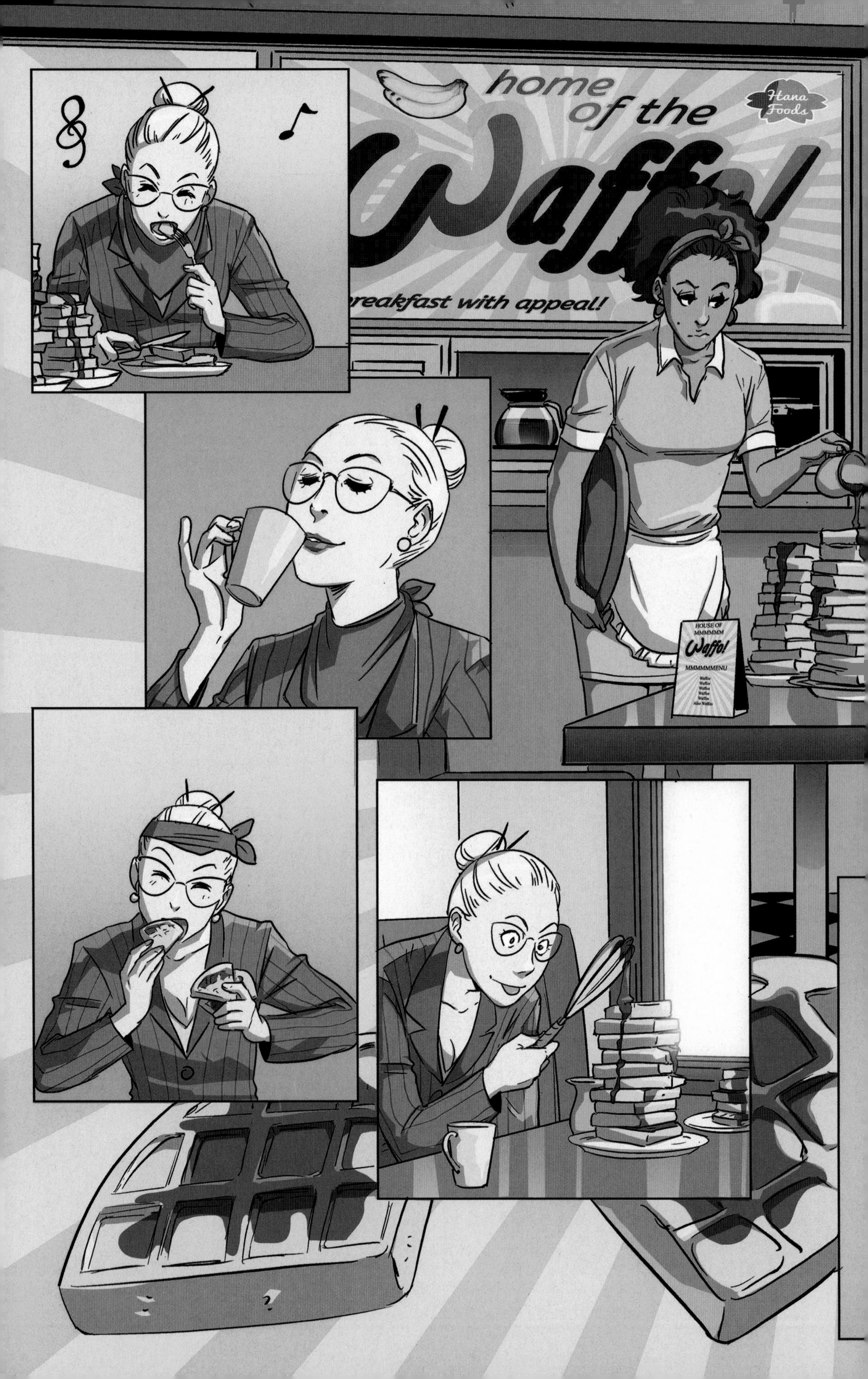
home of the
reakfast with appeal!
Hana Foods
HOUSE OF MMMMMM
Waffo!
MMMMMMMENU
Waffos
Waffos
Waffos
Waffos
Waffos
Also Waffos

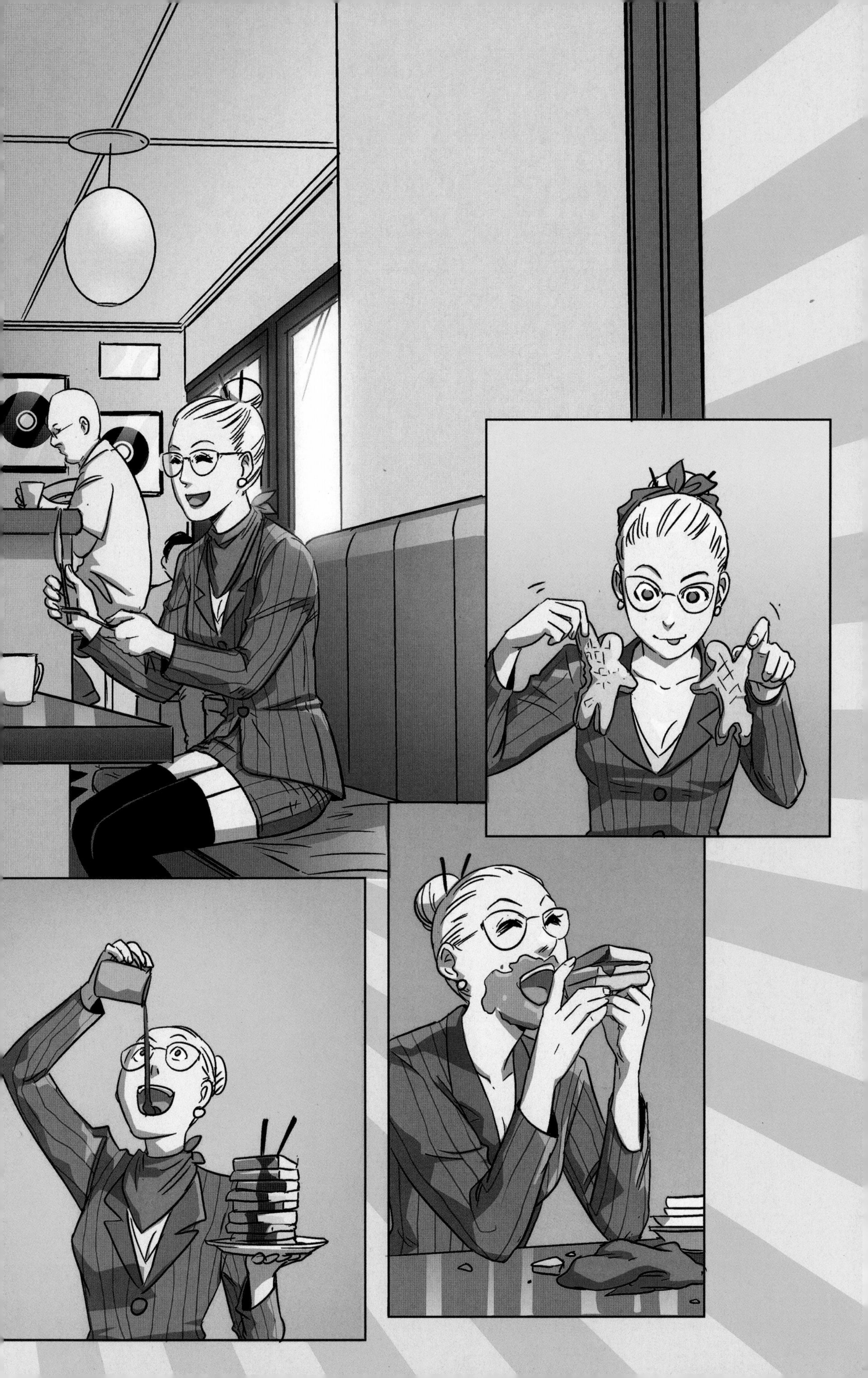

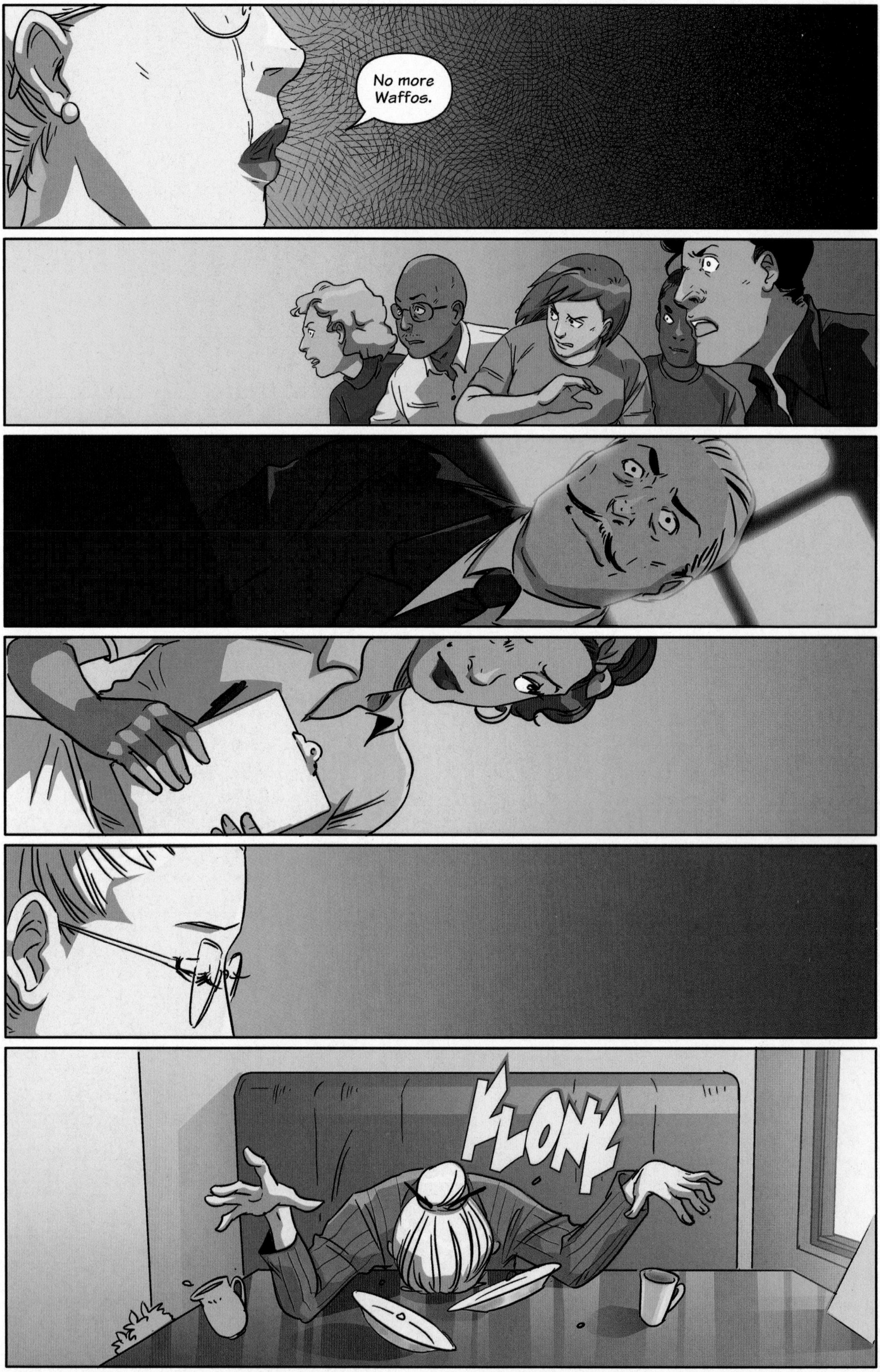
No more Waffos.
KLONK

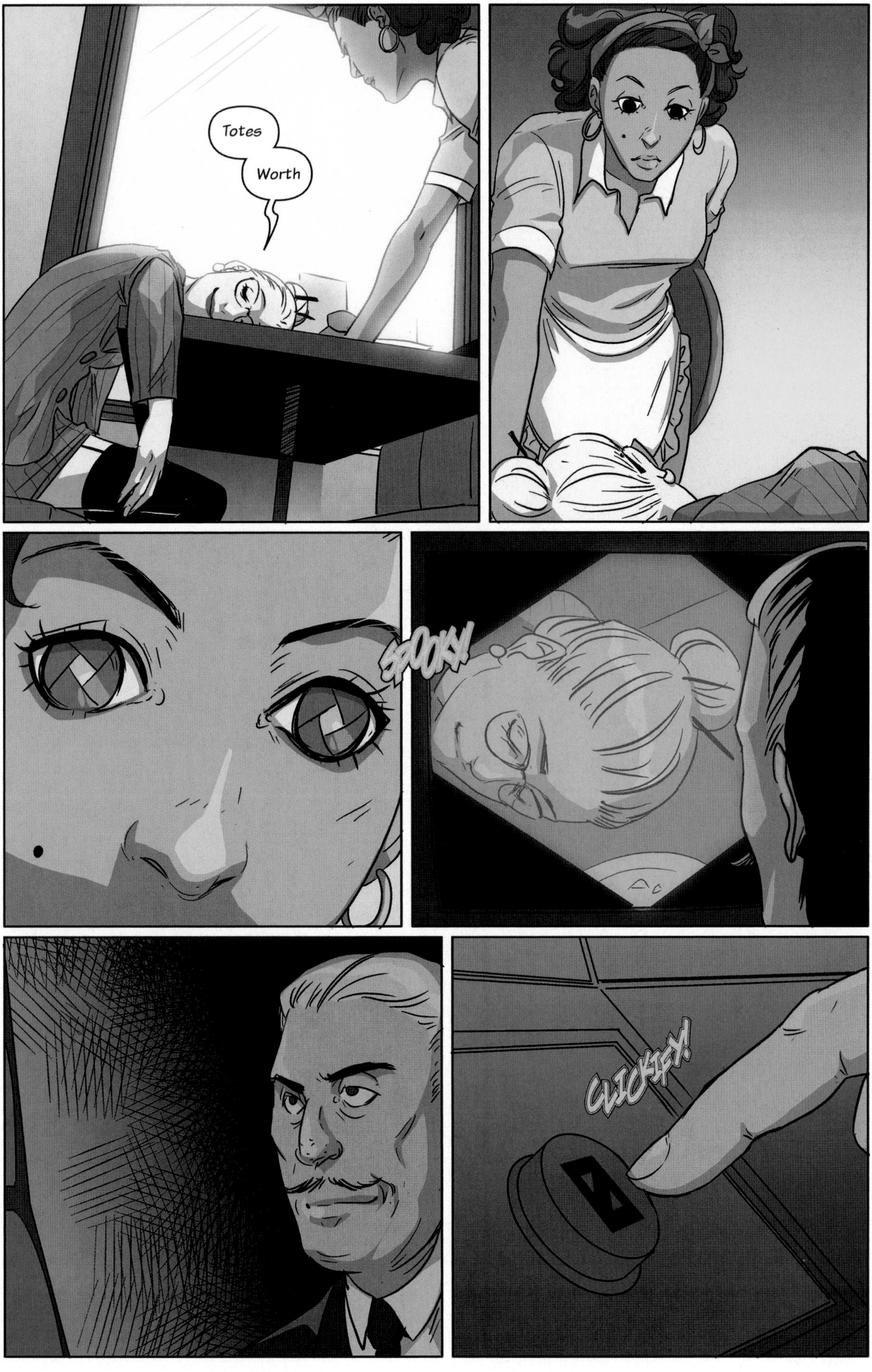
Totes
Worth
SPOOKY!
CLICKIFY!

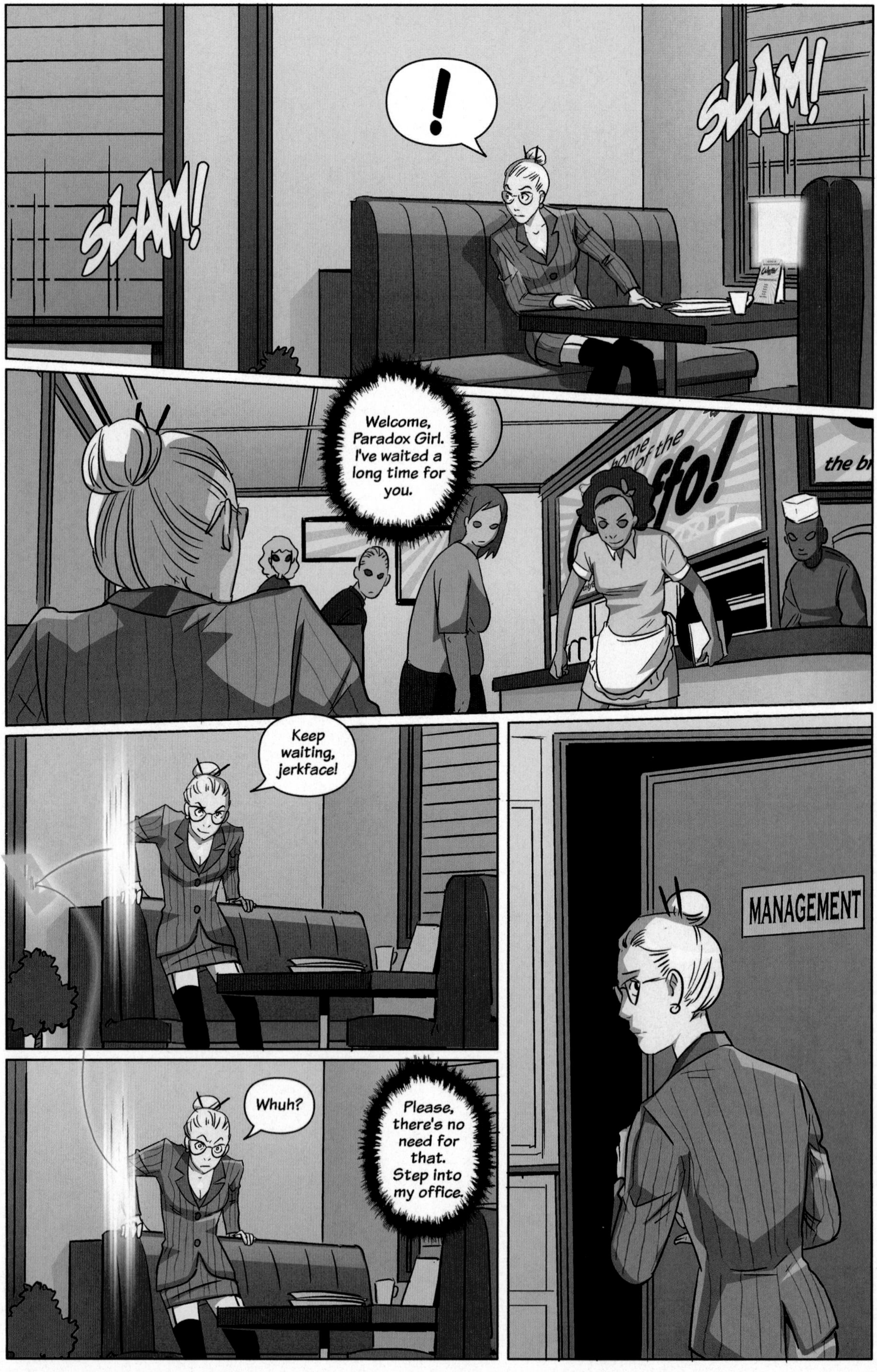
SLAM!
!
SLAM!
Welcome, Paradox Girl. I've waited a long time for you.
Keep waiting, jerkface!
MANAGEMENT
Whuh?
Please, there's no need for that. Step into my office.

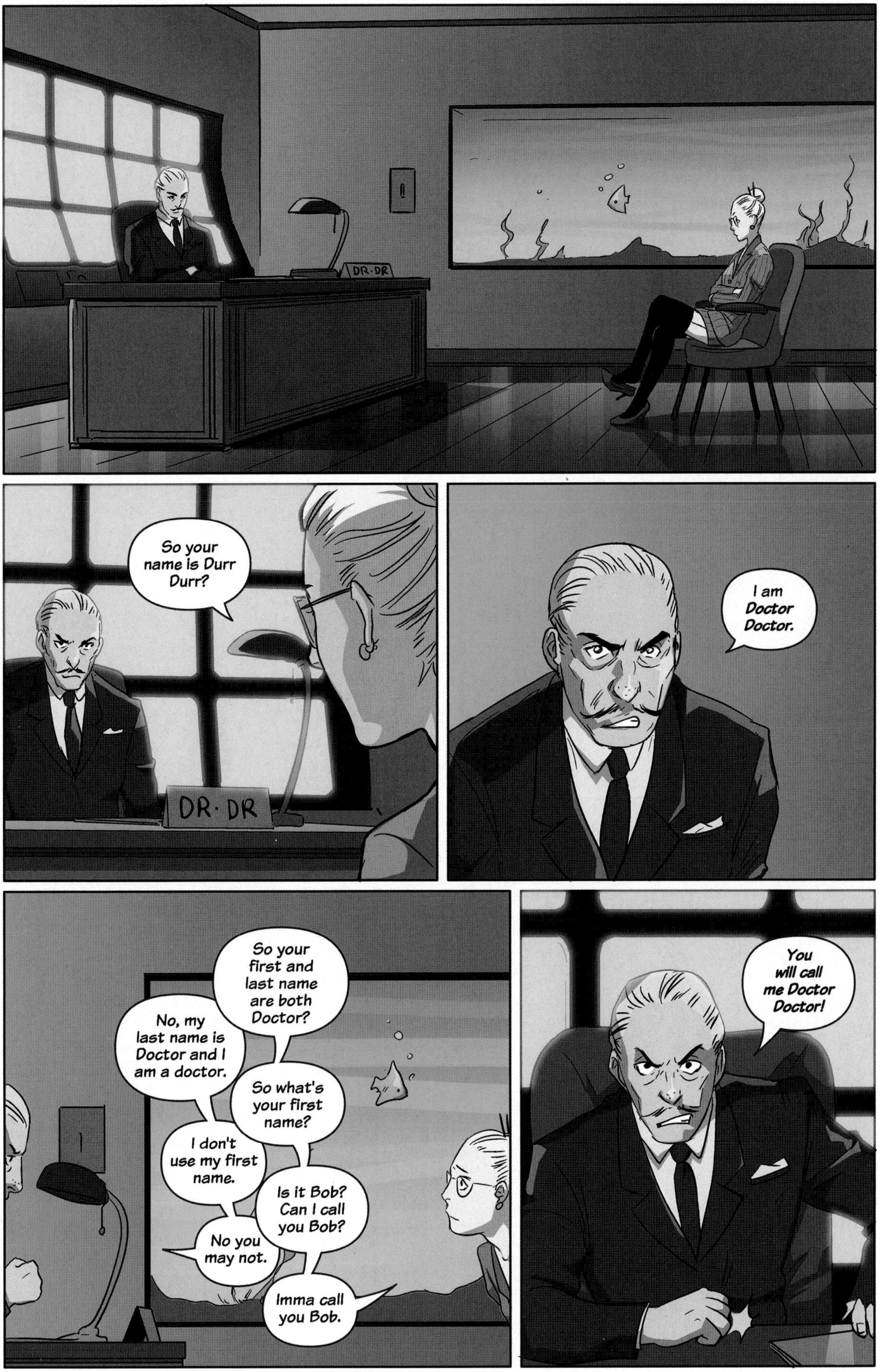
DR·DR
So your name is Durr Durr?
DR·DR
I am Doctor Doctor.
So your first and last name are both Doctor?
No, my last name is Doctor and I am a doctor.
So what's your first name?
I don't use my first name.
Is it Bob? Can I call you Bob?
No you may not.
Imma call you Bob.
You will call me Doctor Doctor!

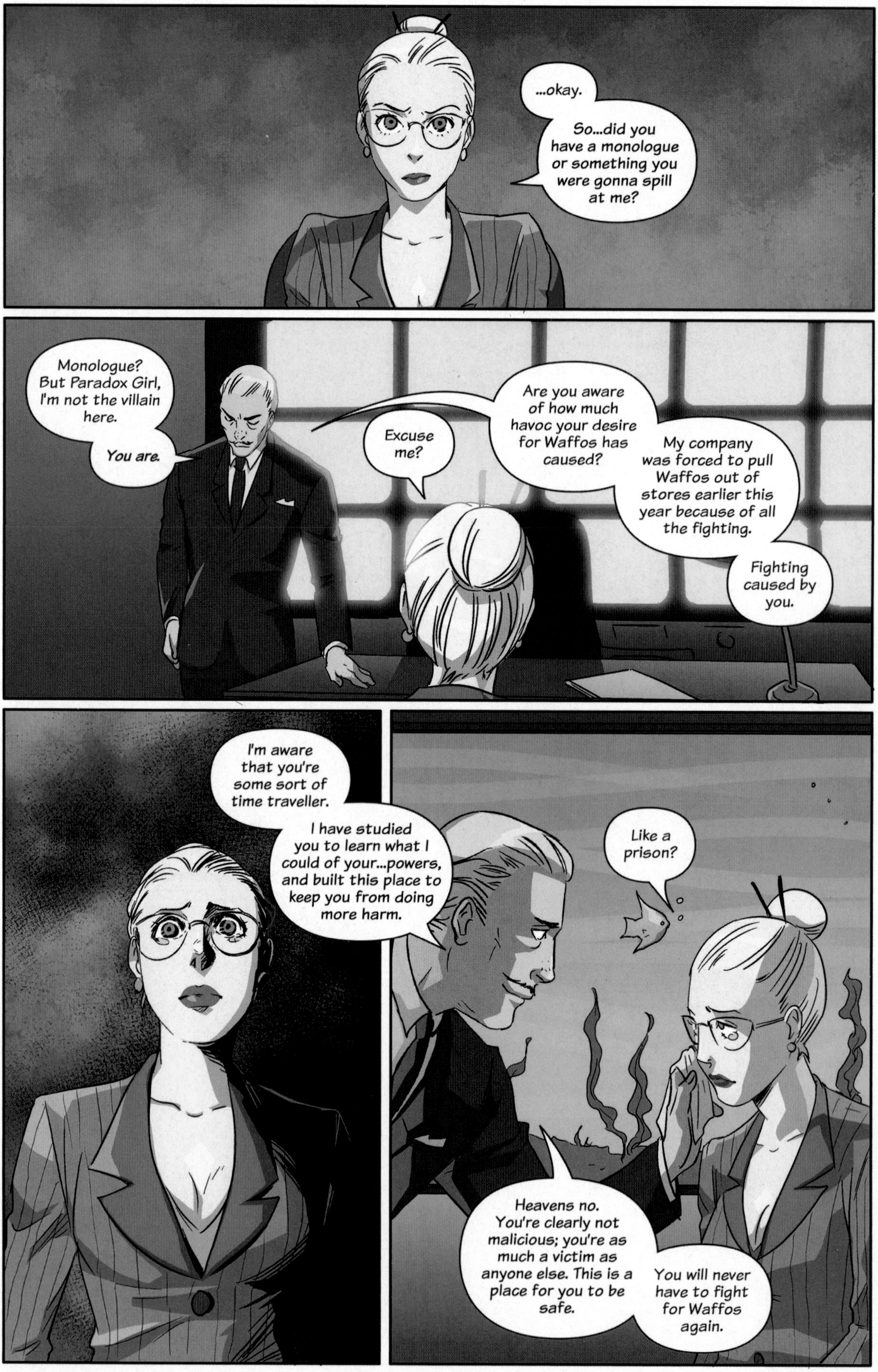
...okay.
So...did you have a monologue or something you were gonna spill at me?
Monologue? But Paradox Girl, I'm not the villain here.
You are.
Excuse me?
Are you aware of how much havoc your desire for Waffos has caused?
My company was forced to pull Waffos out of stores earlier this year because of all the fighting.
Fighting caused by you.
I'm aware that you're some sort of time traveller.
I have studied you to learn what I could of your...powers, and built this place to keep you from doing more harm.
Like a prison?
Heavens no. You're clearly not malicious; you're as much a victim as anyone else. This is a place for you to be safe.
You will never have to fight for Waffos again.

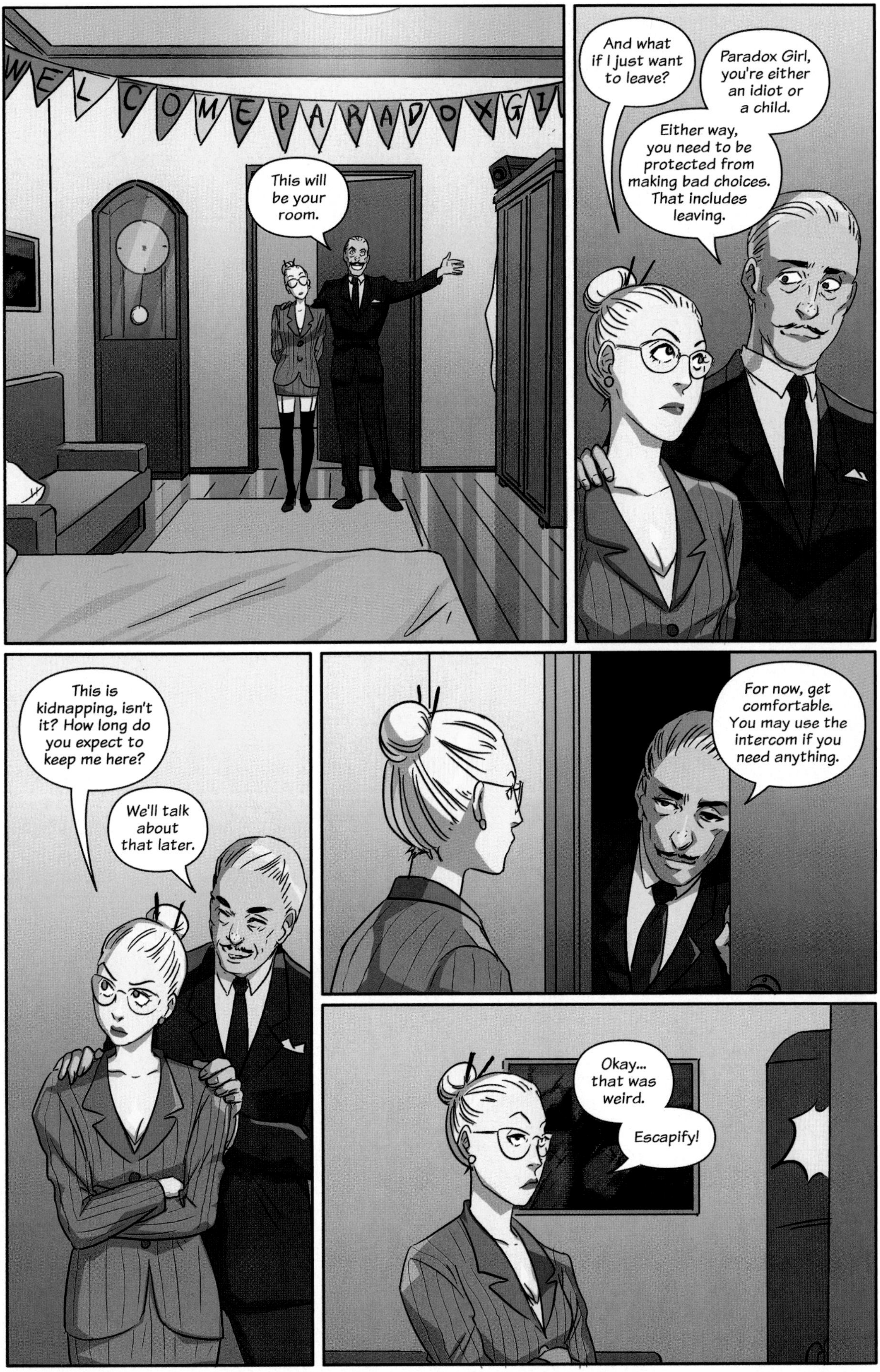
WELCOME PARADOX GI
This will be your room.
And what if I just want to leave?
Paradox Girl, you're either an idiot or a child.
Either way, you need to be protected from making bad choices. That includes leaving.
This is kidnapping, isn't it? How long do you expect to keep me here?
We'll talk about that later.
For now, get comfortable. You may use the intercom if you need anything.
Okay... that was weird.
Escapify!

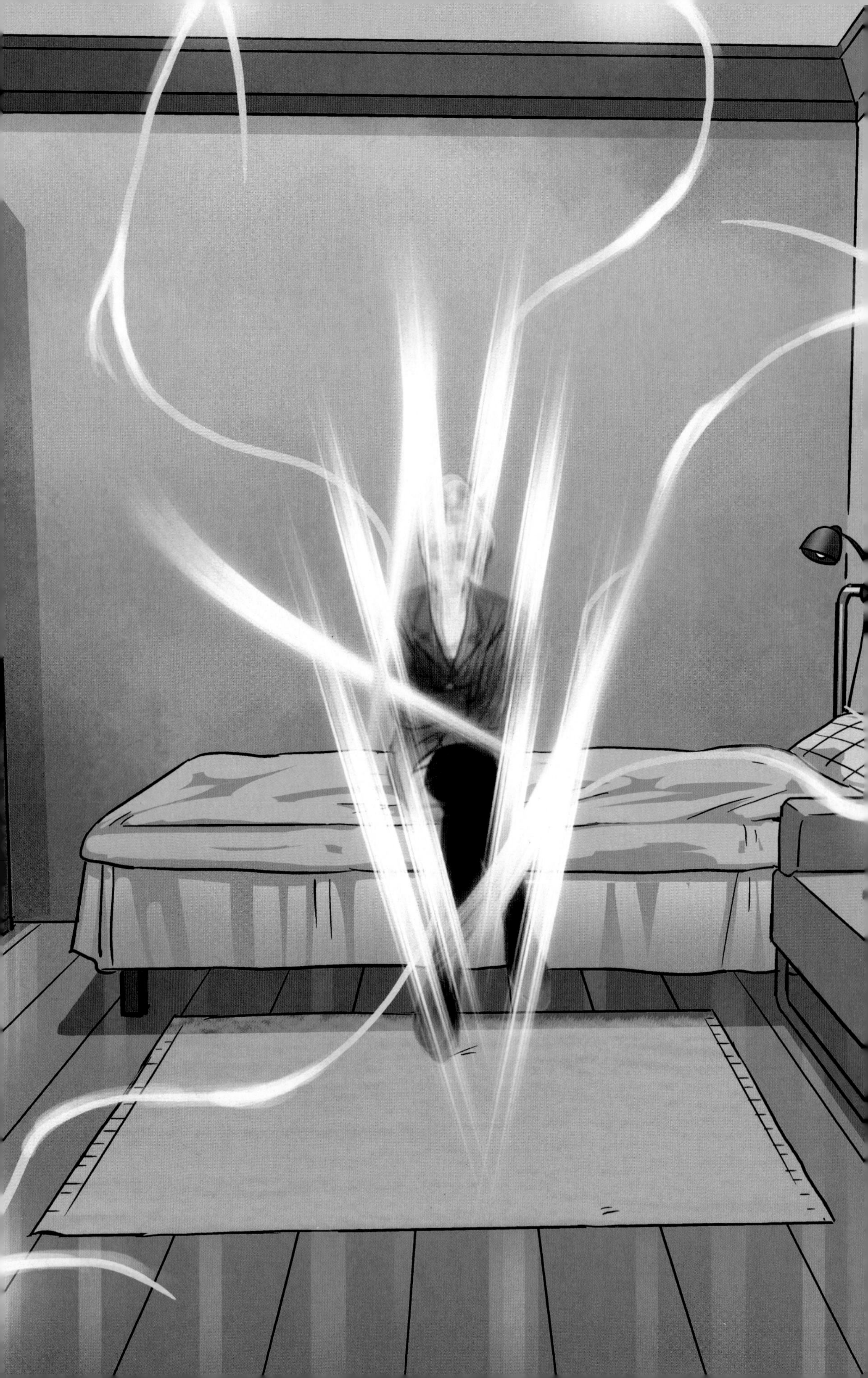

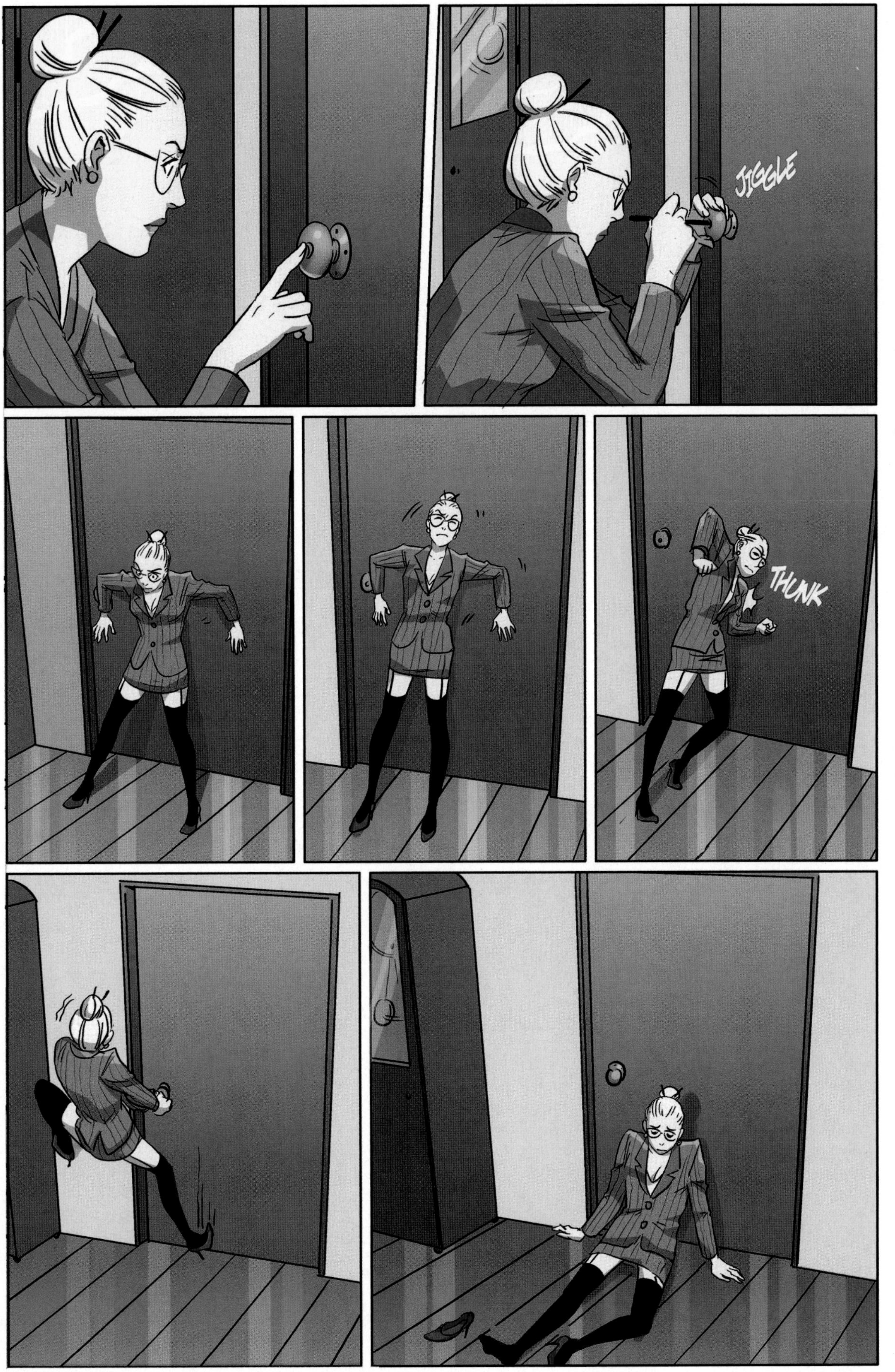
JIGGLE
THUNK

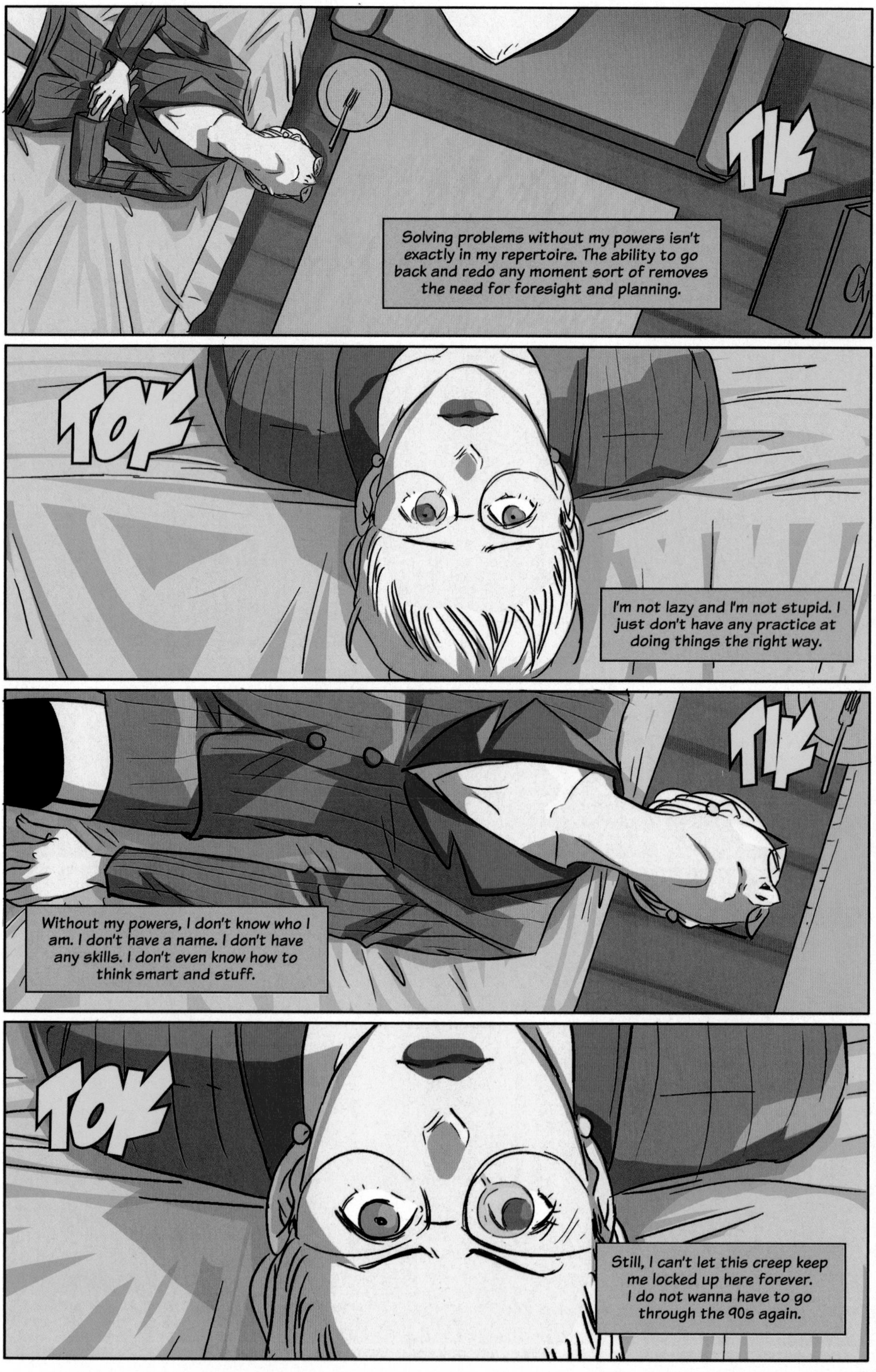
TIK
Solving problems without my powers isn't exactly in my repertoire. The ability to go back and redo any moment sort of removes the need for foresight and planning.
TOK
I'm not lazy and I'm not stupid. I just don't have any practice at doing things the right way.
TIK
Without my powers, I don't know who I am. I don't have a name. I don't have any skills. I don't even know how to think smart and stuff.
TOK
Still, I can't let this creep keep me locked up here forever. I do not wanna have to go through the 90s again.

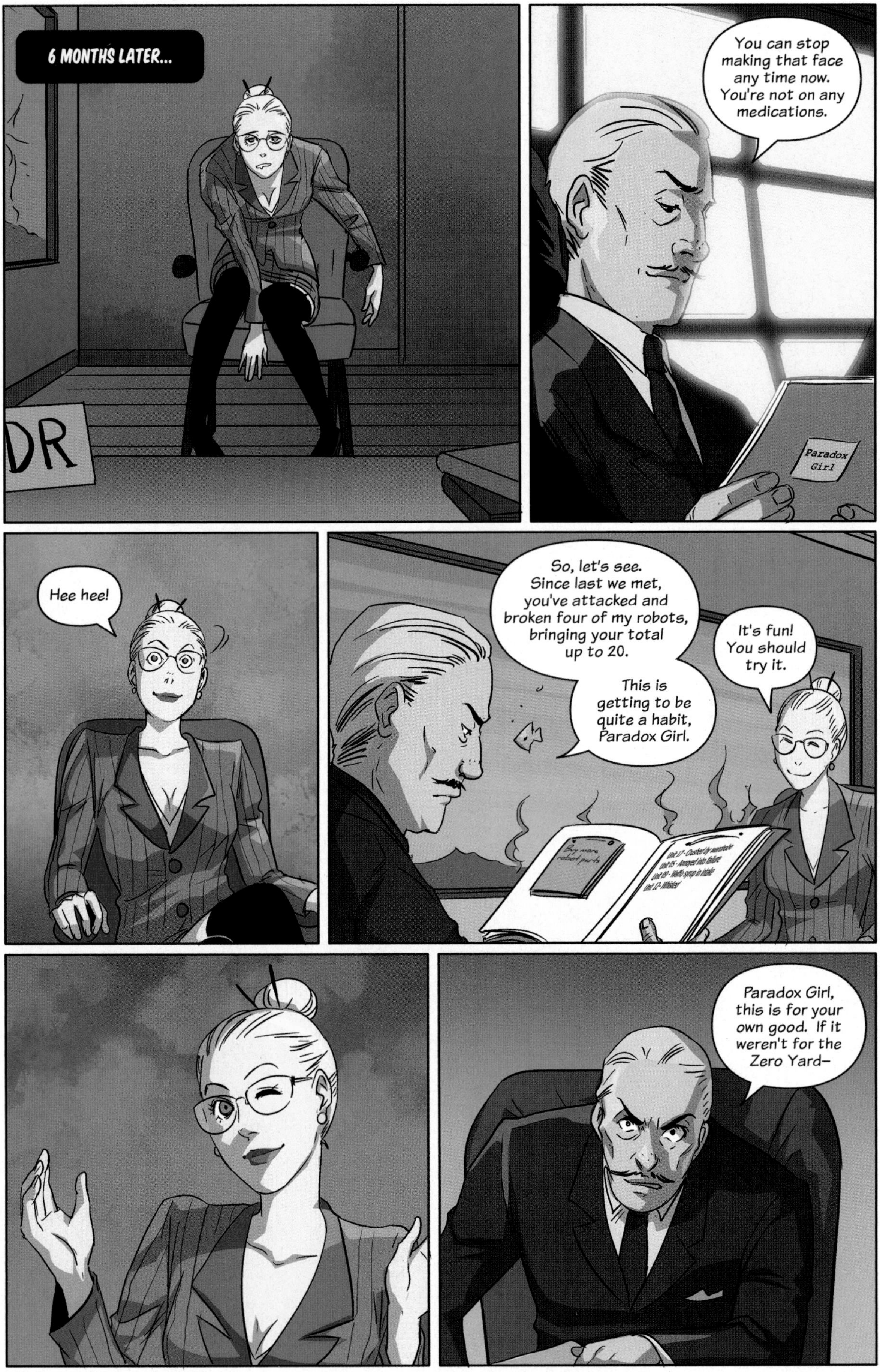
6 MONTHS LATER...
DR
You can stop making that face any time now. You're not on any medications.
Paradox Girl
Hee hee!
So, let's see. Since last we met, you've attacked and broken four of my robots, bringing your total up to 20.
This is getting to be quite a habit, Paradox Girl.
It's fun! You should try it.
Paradox Girl, this is for your own good. If it weren't for the Zero Yard–

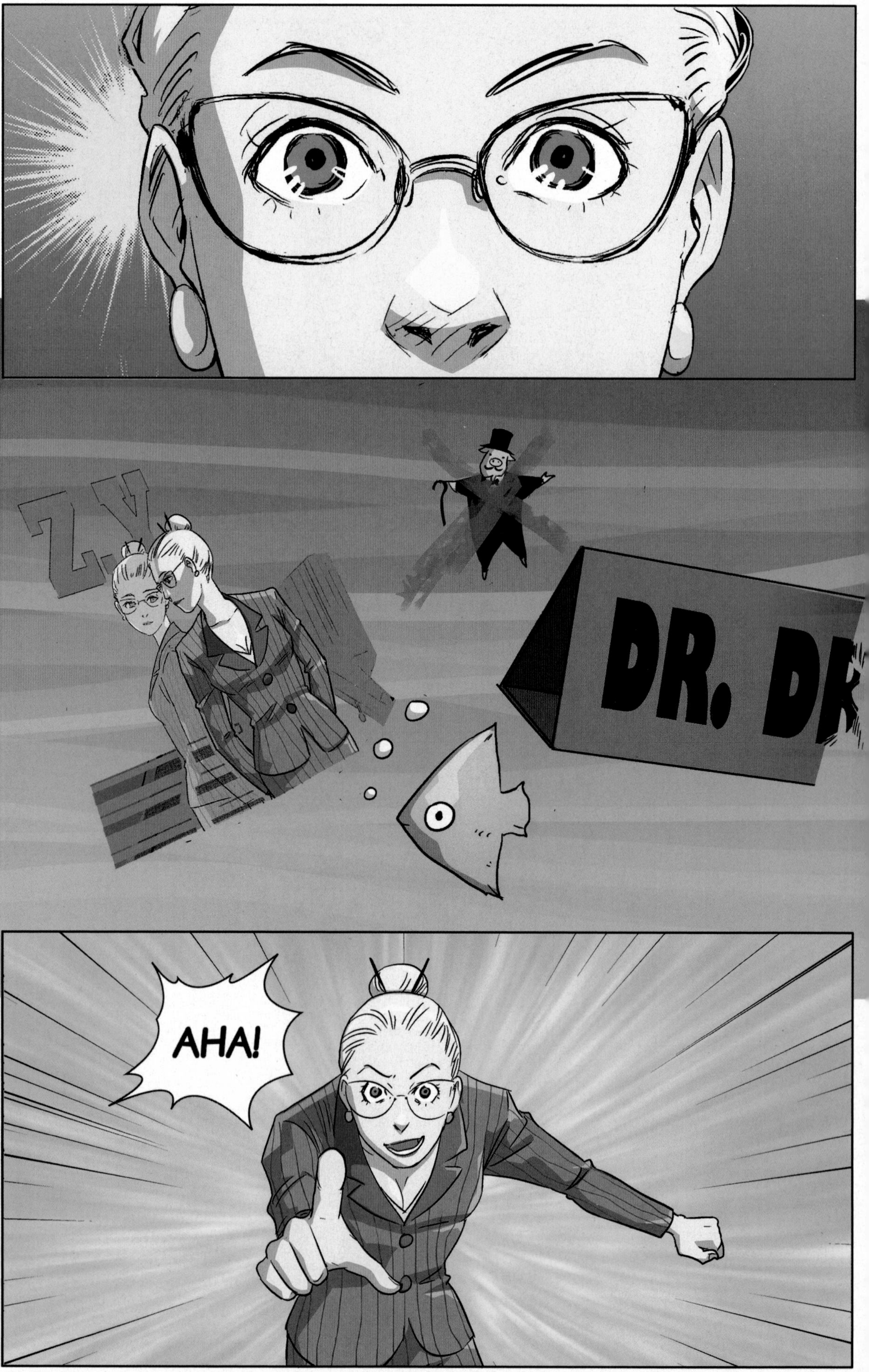
Z.V
DR. DR
AHA!

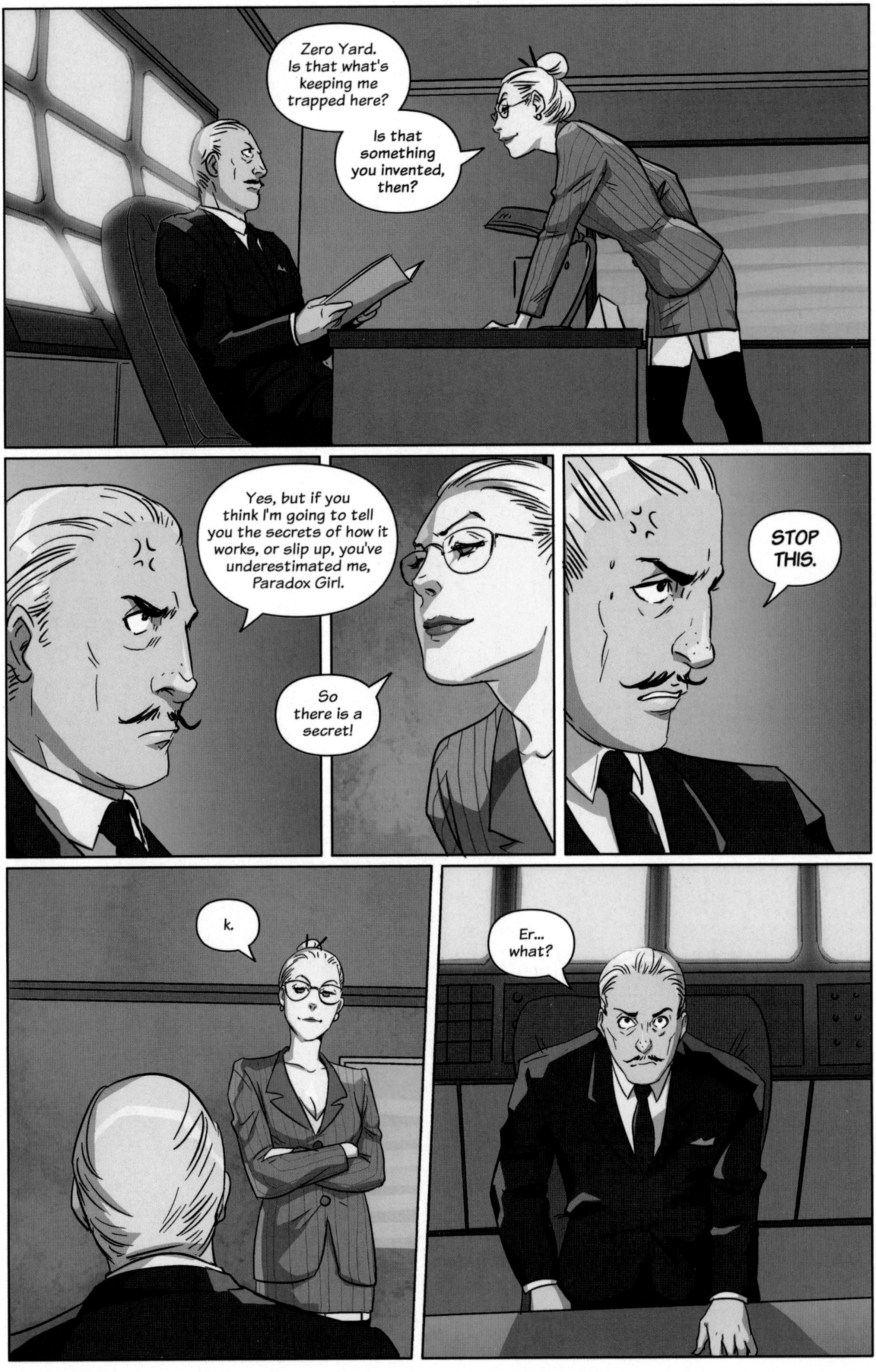

Zero Yard. Is that what's keeping me trapped here?
Is that something you invented, then?
Yes, but if you think I'm going to tell you the secrets of how it works, or slip up, you've underestimated me, Paradox Girl.
So there is a secret!
STOP THIS.
k.
Er... what?

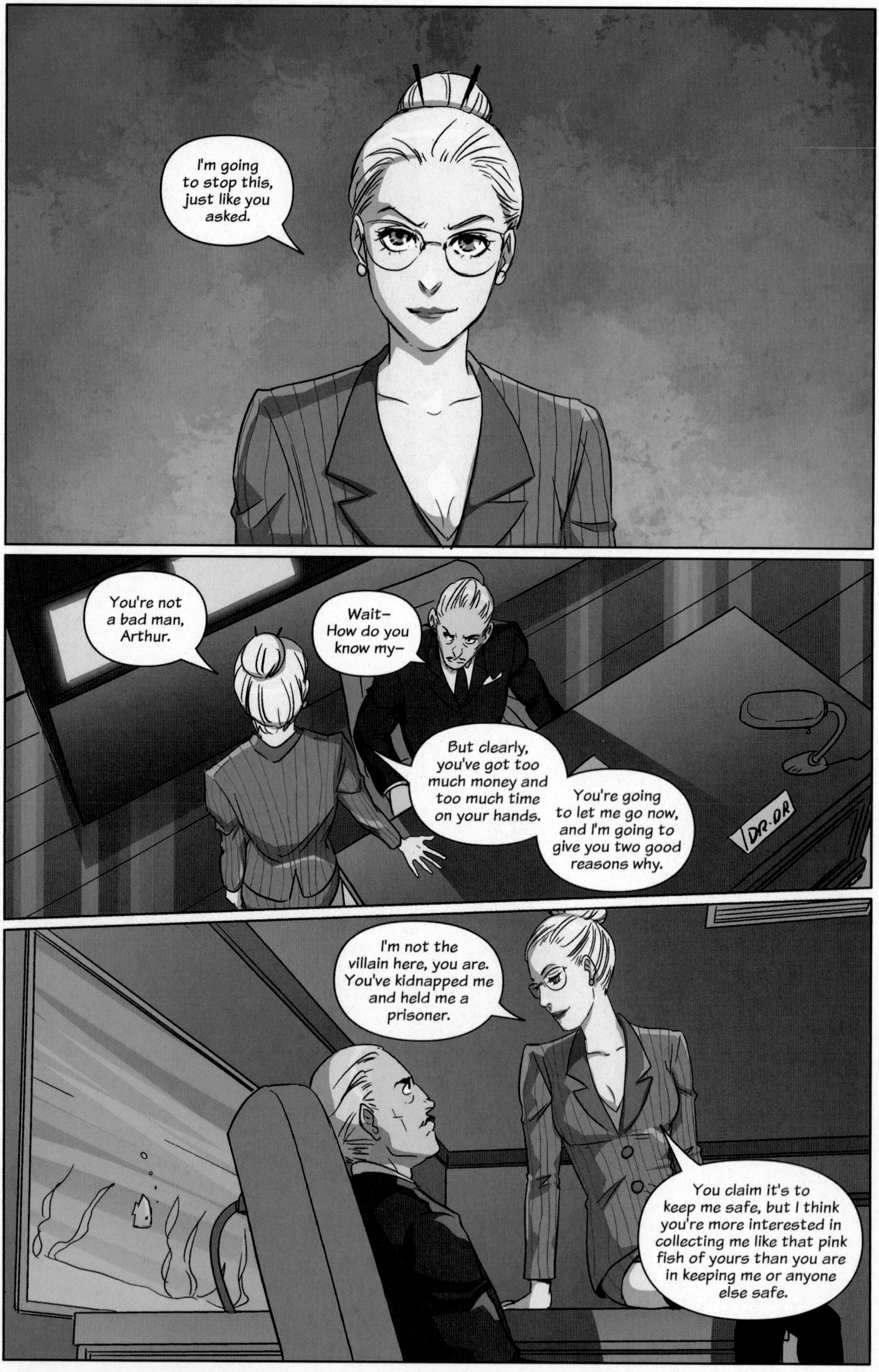
I'm going to stop this, just like you asked.
You're not a bad man, Arthur.
Wait— How do you know my—
But clearly, you've got too much money and too much time on your hands.
You're going to let me go now, and I'm going to give you two good reasons why.
DR. DR
I'm not the villain here, you are. You've kidnapped me and held me a prisoner.
You claim it's to keep me safe, but I think you're more interested in collecting me like that pink fish of yours than you are in keeping me or anyone else safe.

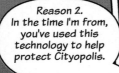

Reason 2.
In the time I'm from, you've used this technology to help protect Cityopolis.

You're not using it for selfish aims, you're helping people.

You're *Director Arthur Drab* and you have a staff of people— not robots— who respect the work that you do.

And since I know that's you—I know we must've gone through this already, and inevitably you let me go.

Besides, you end up having a wife and a handful of kids, and future you wouldn't like you messing that up just to watch me eat Waffos.

CLICKIFY!

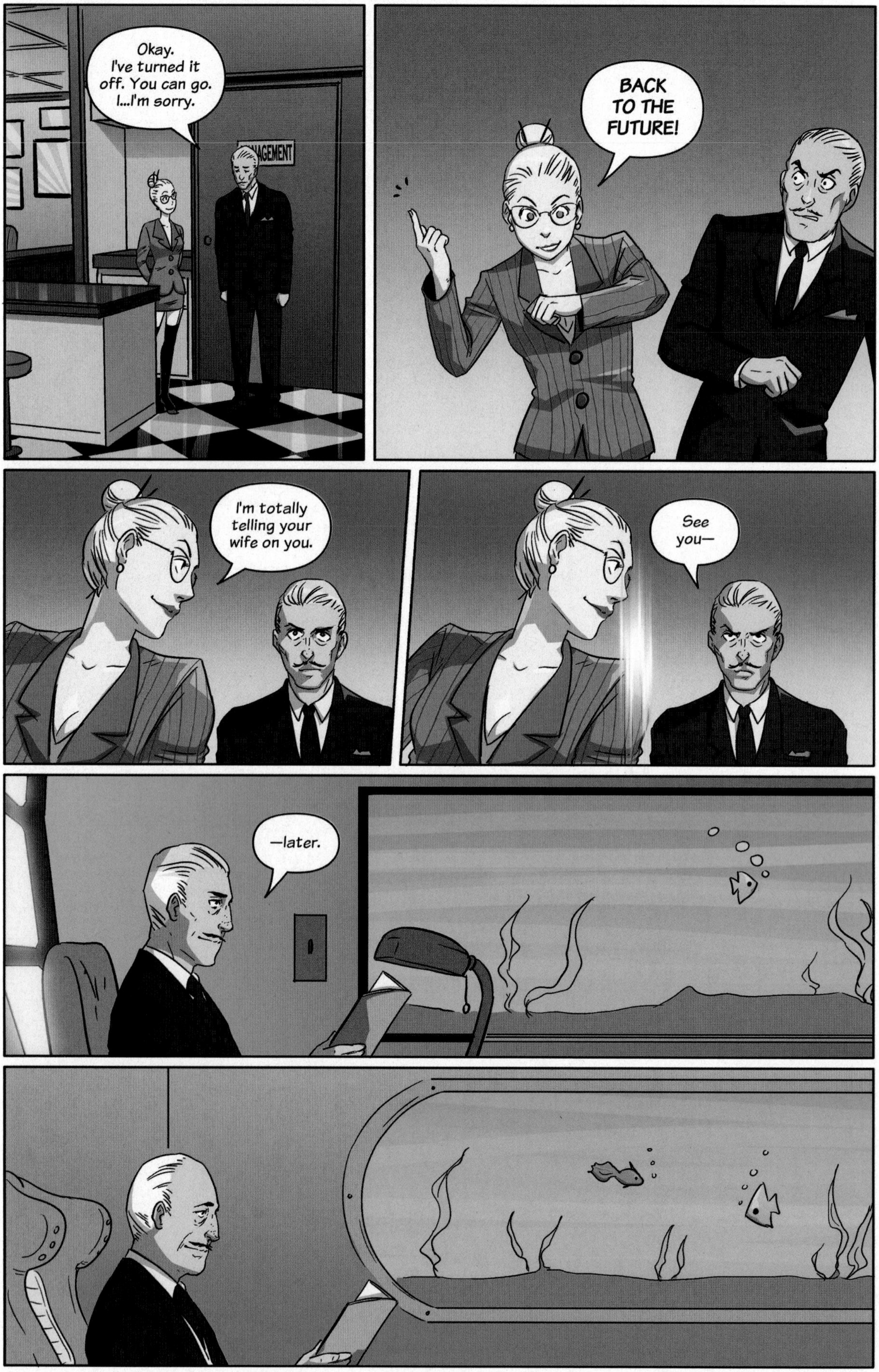
MANAGEMENT
Okay. I've turned it off. You can go. I...I'm sorry.
BACK TO THE FUTURE!
I'm totally telling your wife on you.
See you—
—later.

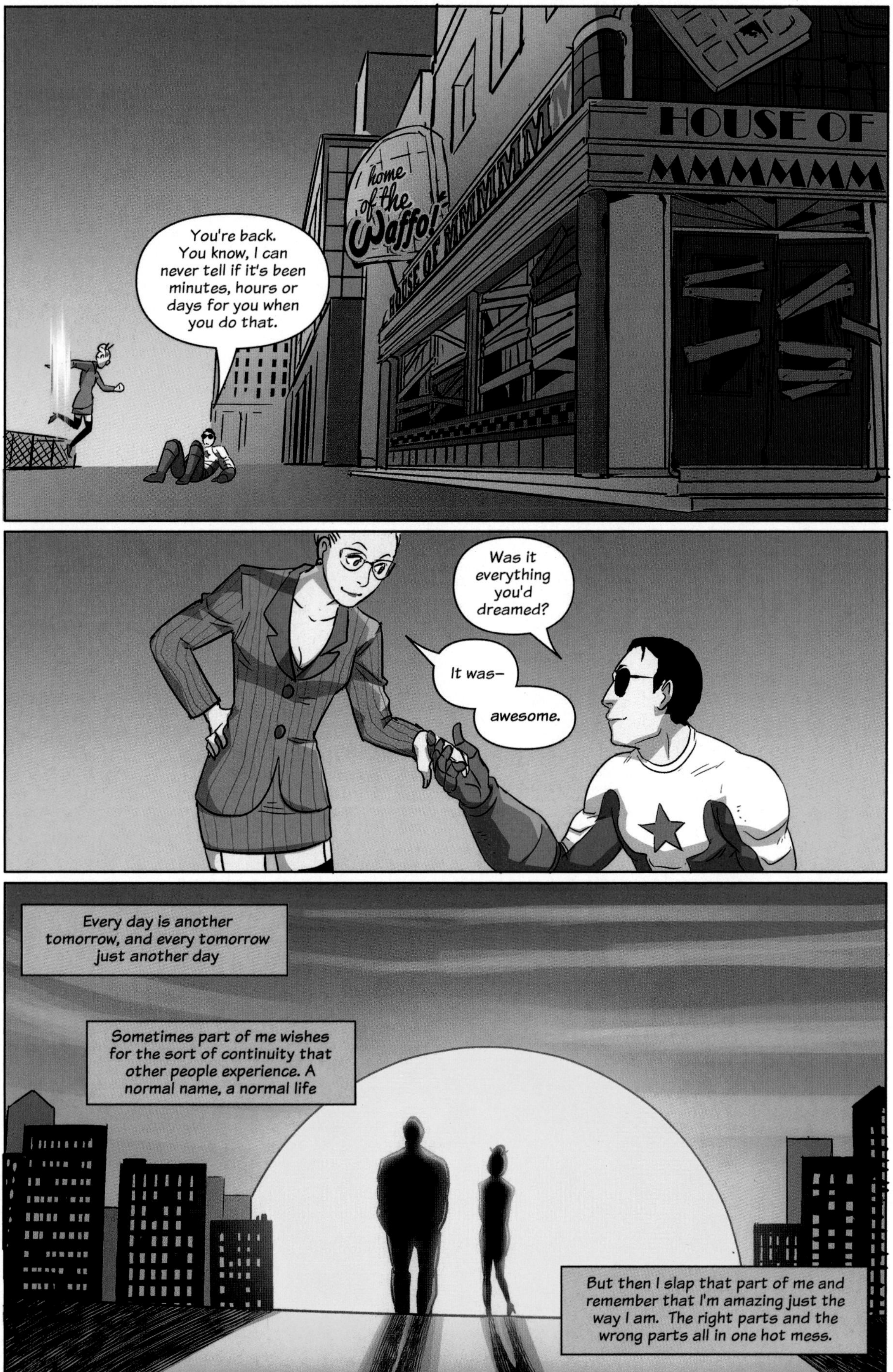
HOUSE OF
MMMMMM
home of the Waffo!
HOUSE OF MMMMMM
You're back. You know, I can never tell if it's been minutes, hours or days for you when you do that.
Was it everything you'd dreamed?
It was–
awesome.
Every day is another tomorrow, and every tomorrow just another day
Sometimes part of me wishes for the sort of continuity that other people experience. A normal name, a normal life
But then I slap that part of me and remember that I'm amazing just the way I am. The right parts and the wrong parts all in one hot mess.

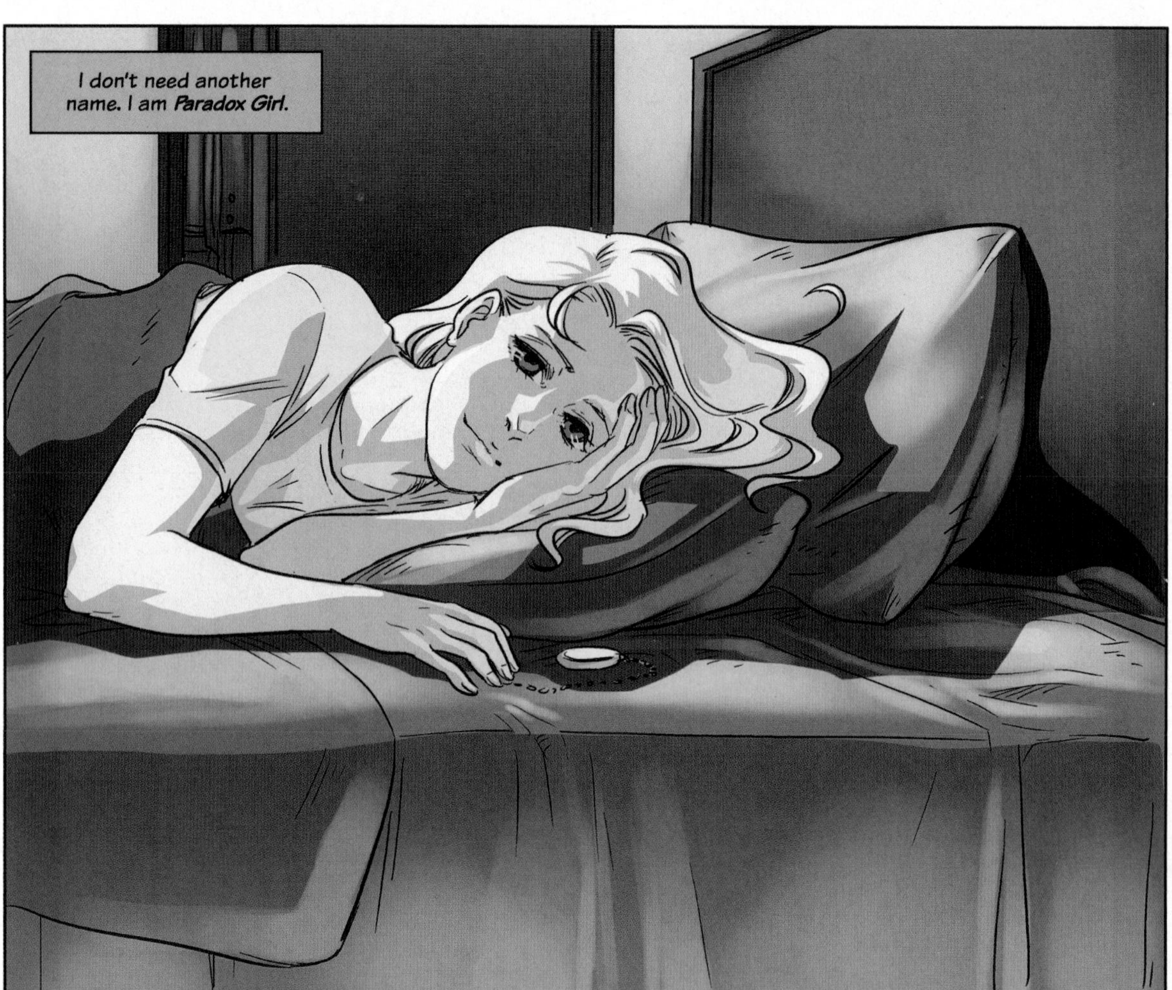
I don't need another name. I am *Paradox Girl*.

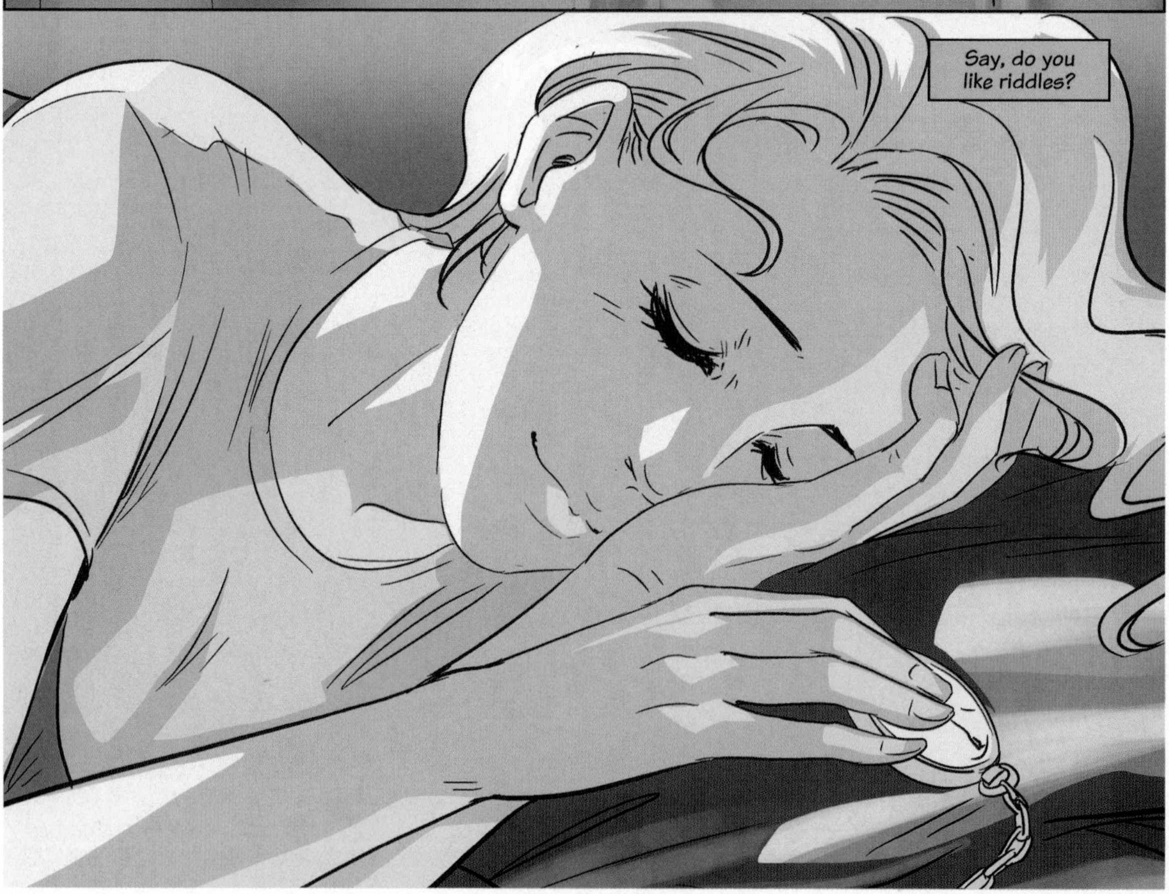
Say, do you like riddles?

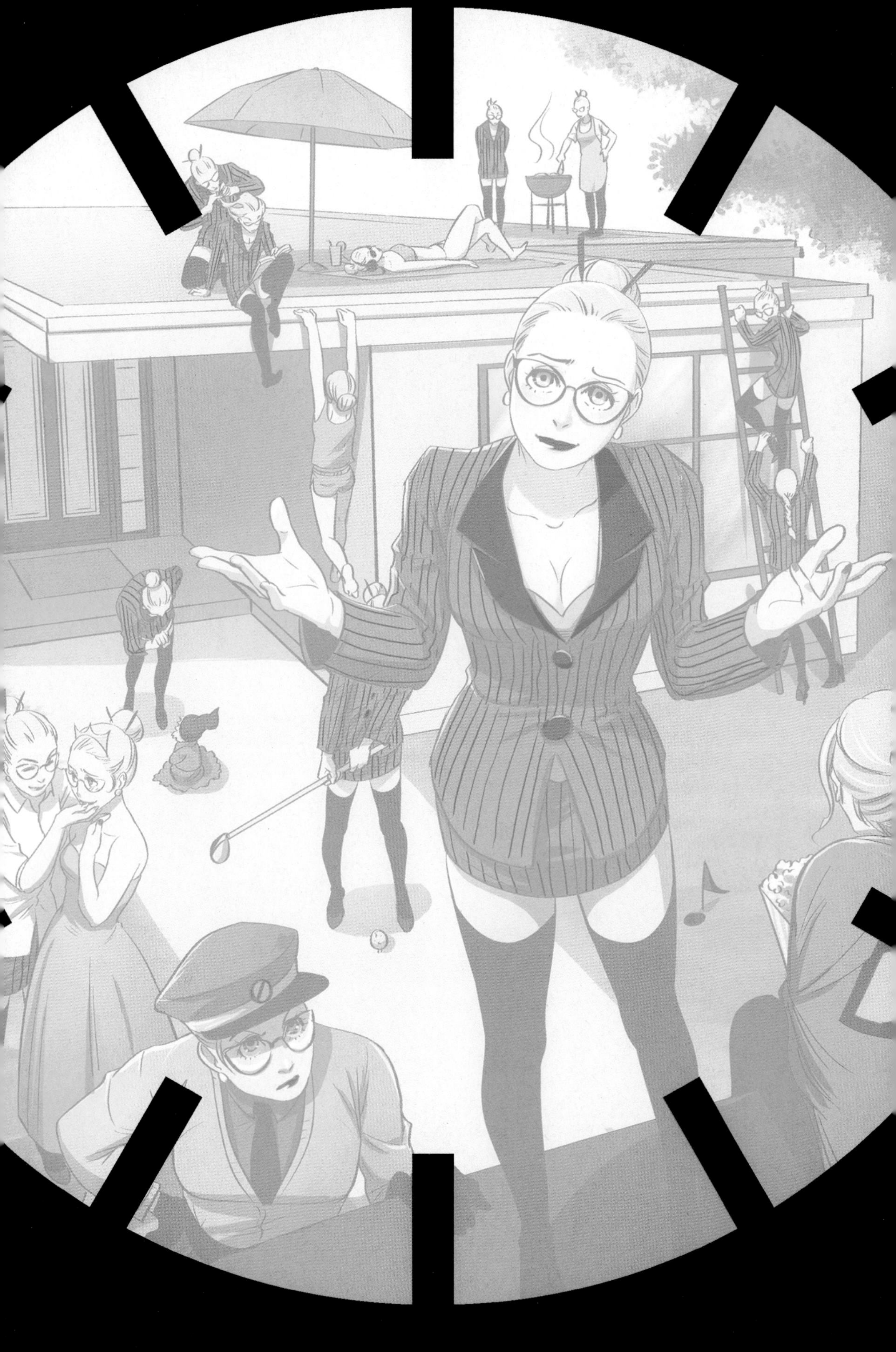

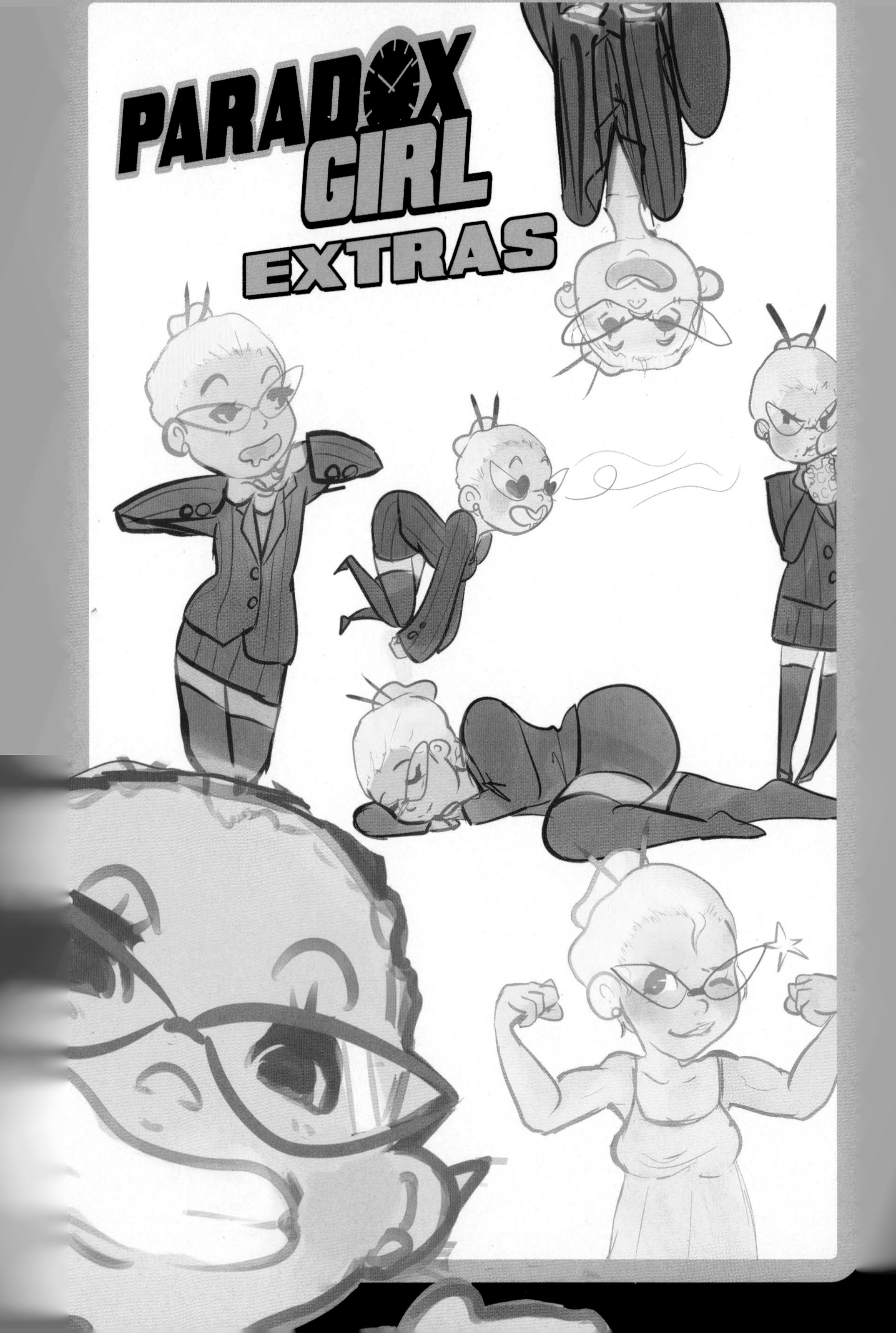
PARADOX GIRL
EXTRAS

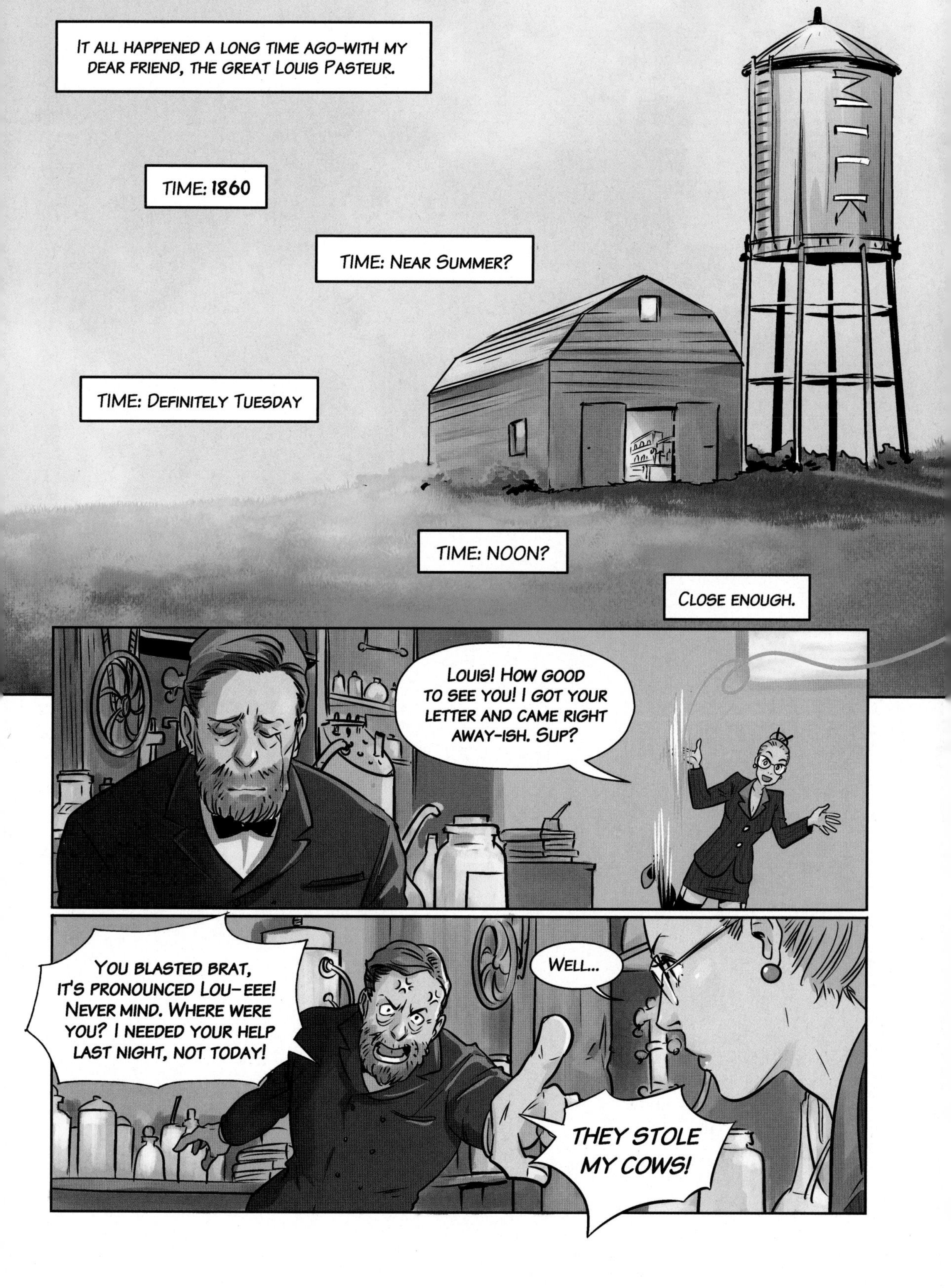

MILK
IT ALL HAPPENED A LONG TIME AGO-WITH MY DEAR FRIEND, THE GREAT LOUIS PASTEUR.
TIME: 1860
TIME: NEAR SUMMER?
TIME: DEFINITELY TUESDAY
TIME: NOON?
CLOSE ENOUGH.
LOUIS! HOW GOOD TO SEE YOU! I GOT YOUR LETTER AND CAME RIGHT AWAY-ISH. SUP?
YOU BLASTED BRAT, IT'S PRONOUNCED LOU-EEE! NEVER MIND. WHERE WERE YOU? I NEEDED YOUR HELP LAST NIGHT, NOT TODAY!
WELL...
THEY STOLE MY COWS!

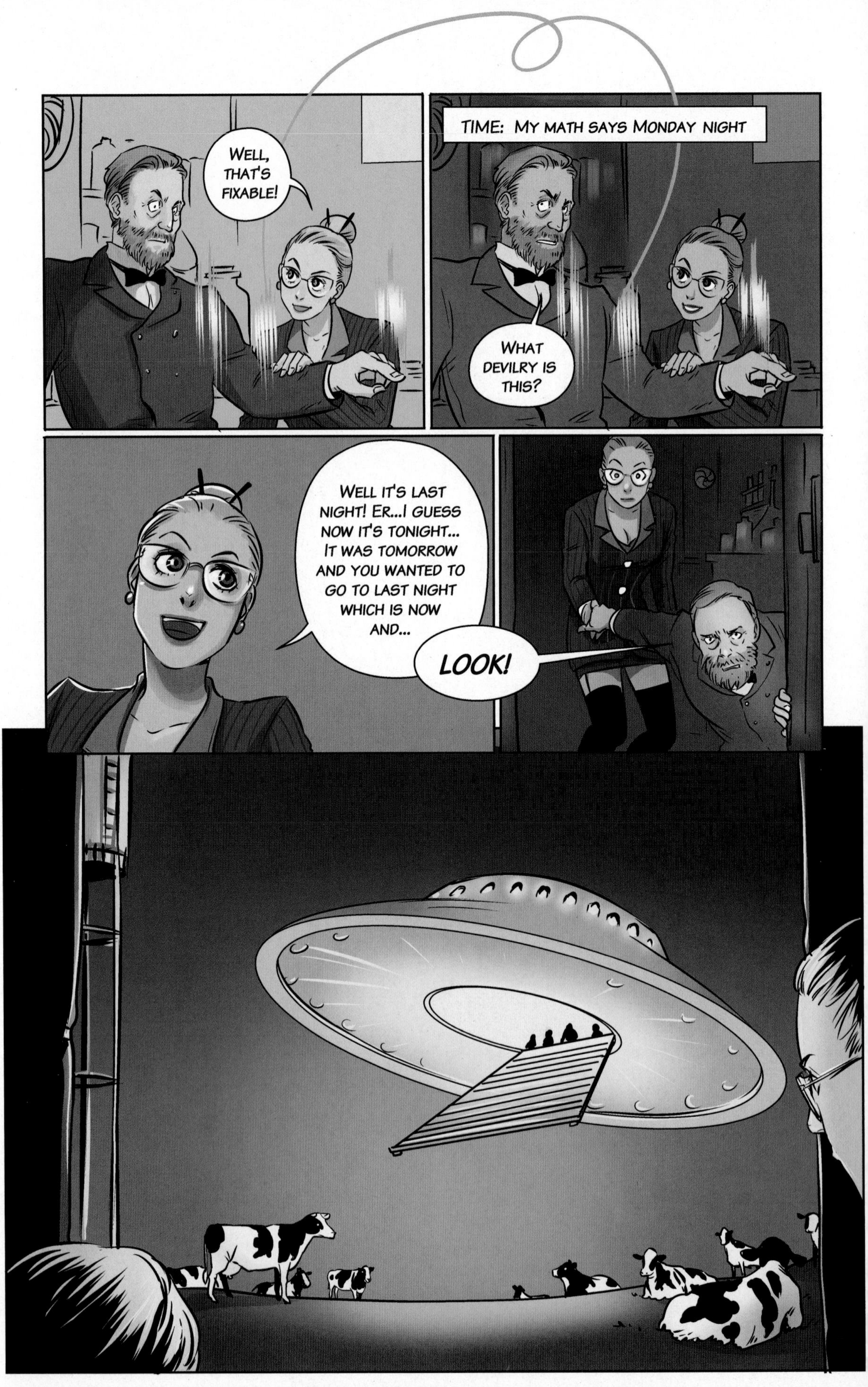
WELL, THAT'S FIXABLE!
TIME: MY MATH SAYS MONDAY NIGHT
WHAT DEVILRY IS THIS?
WELL IT'S LAST NIGHT! ER...I GUESS NOW IT'S TONIGHT... IT WAS TOMORROW AND YOU WANTED TO GO TO LAST NIGHT WHICH IS NOW AND...
LOOK!

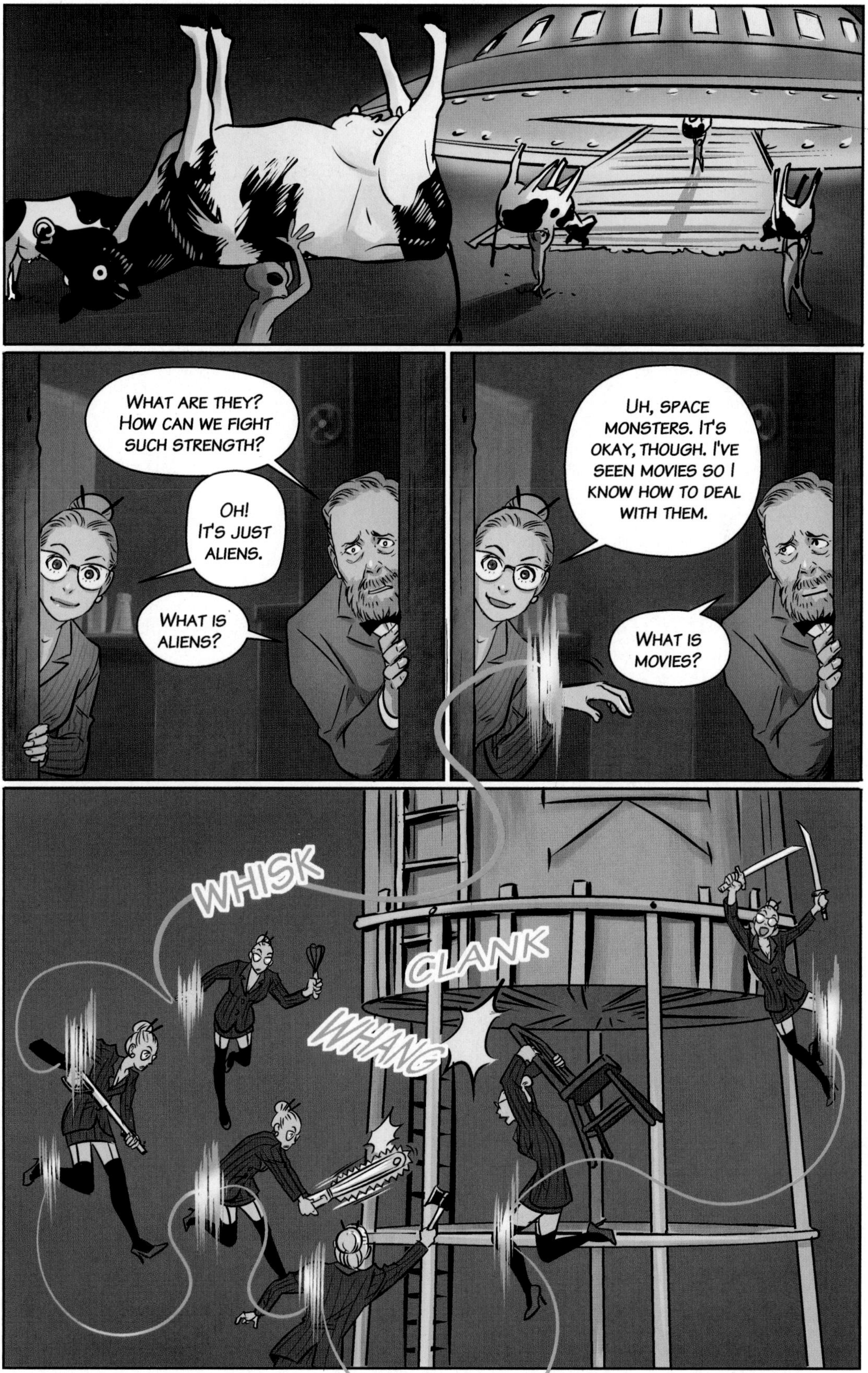
WHAT ARE THEY? HOW CAN WE FIGHT SUCH STRENGTH?
OH! IT'S JUST ALIENS.
WHAT IS ALIENS?
UH, SPACE MONSTERS. IT'S OKAY, THOUGH. I'VE SEEN MOVIES SO I KNOW HOW TO DEAL WITH THEM.
WHAT IS MOVIES?
WHISK
CLANK
WHANG

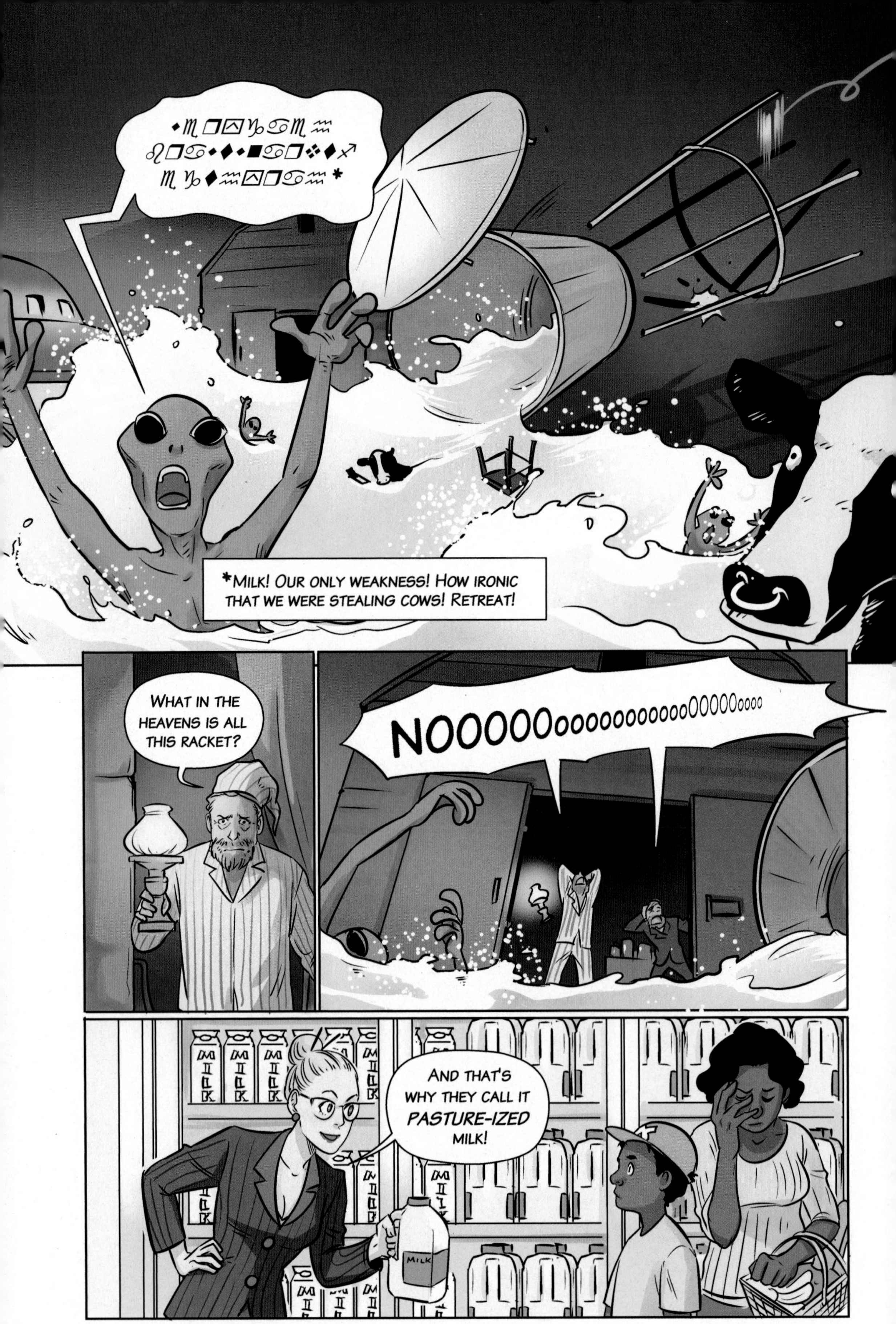
*MILK! OUR ONLY WEAKNESS! HOW IRONIC THAT WE WERE STEALING COWS! RETREAT!
WHAT IN THE HEAVENS IS ALL THIS RACKET?
NOOOOOoooooooooooooOOOOOoooo
AND THAT'S WHY THEY CALL IT *PASTURE-IZED* MILK!
MILK

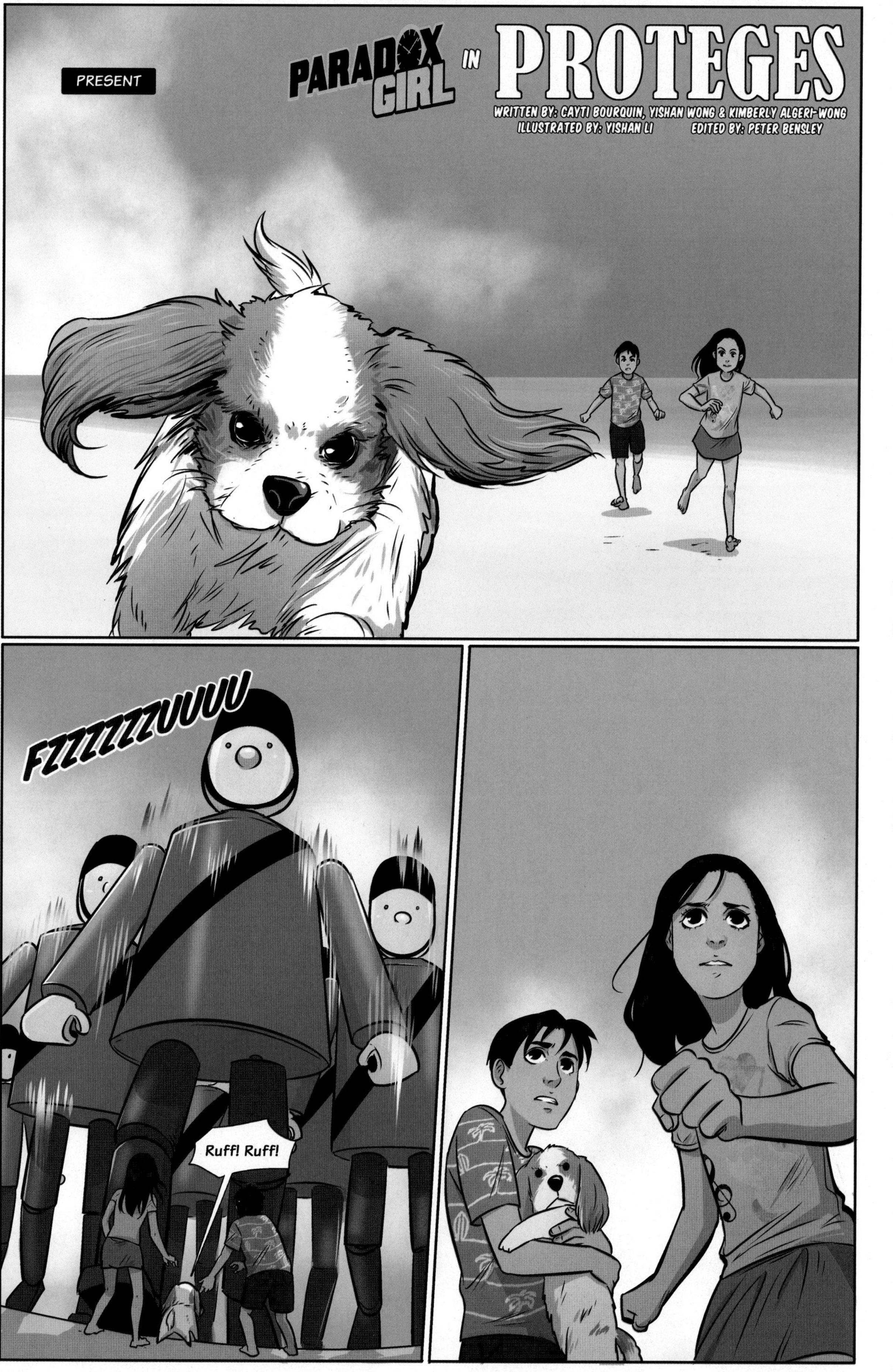
PRESENT
PARADOX GIRL in PROTEGES
WRITTEN BY: CAYTI BOURQUIN, YISHAN WONG & KIMBERLY ALGERI-WONG
ILLUSTRATED BY: YISHAN LI
EDITED BY: PETER BENSLEY
FZZZZZZUUUU
Ruff! Ruff!

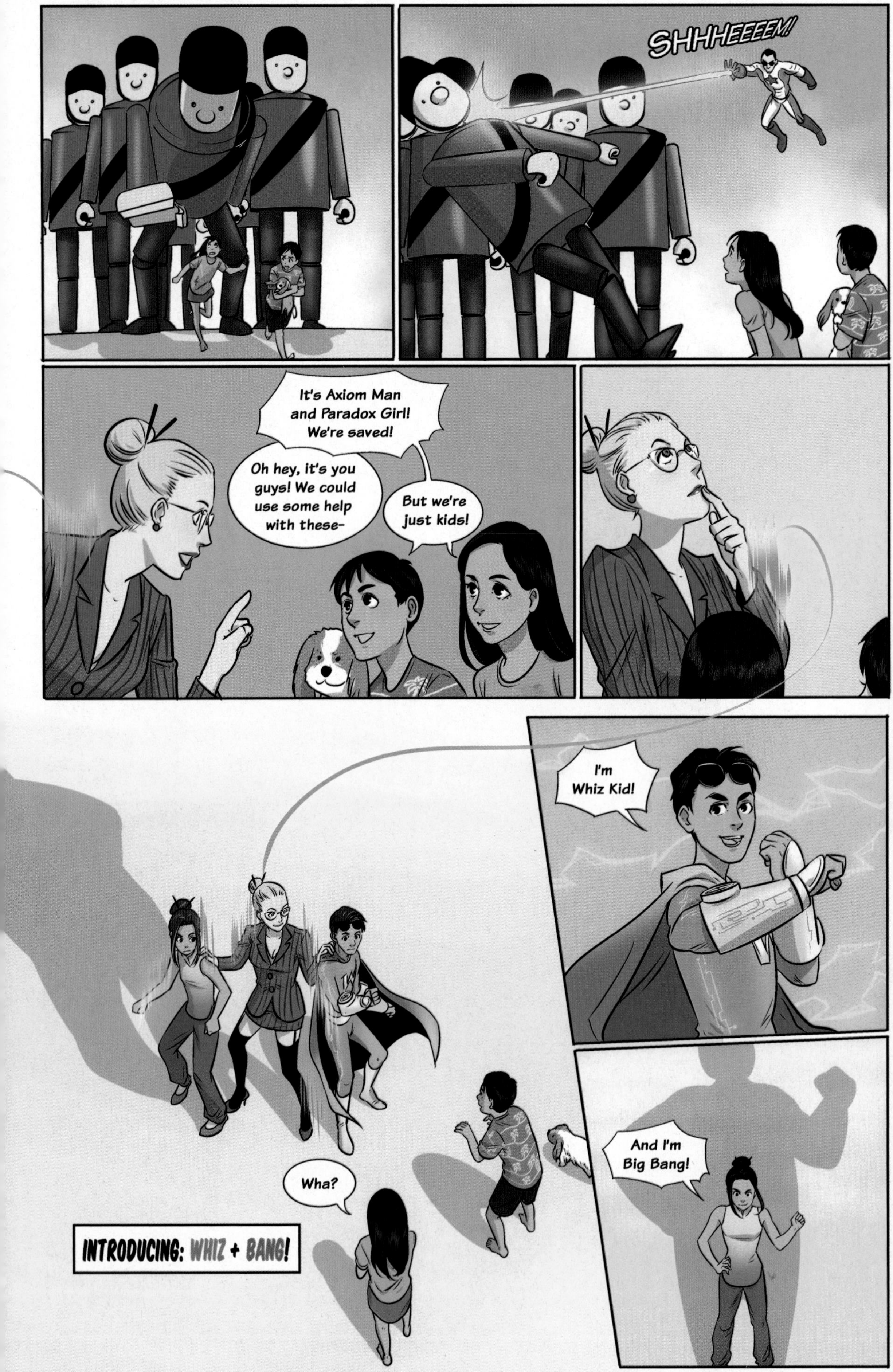
SHHHEEEEM!
It's Axiom Man and Paradox Girl! We're saved!
Oh hey, it's you guys! We could use some help with these-
But we're just kids!
I'm Whiz Kid!
And I'm Big Bang!
Wha?
INTRODUCING: WHIZ + BANG!

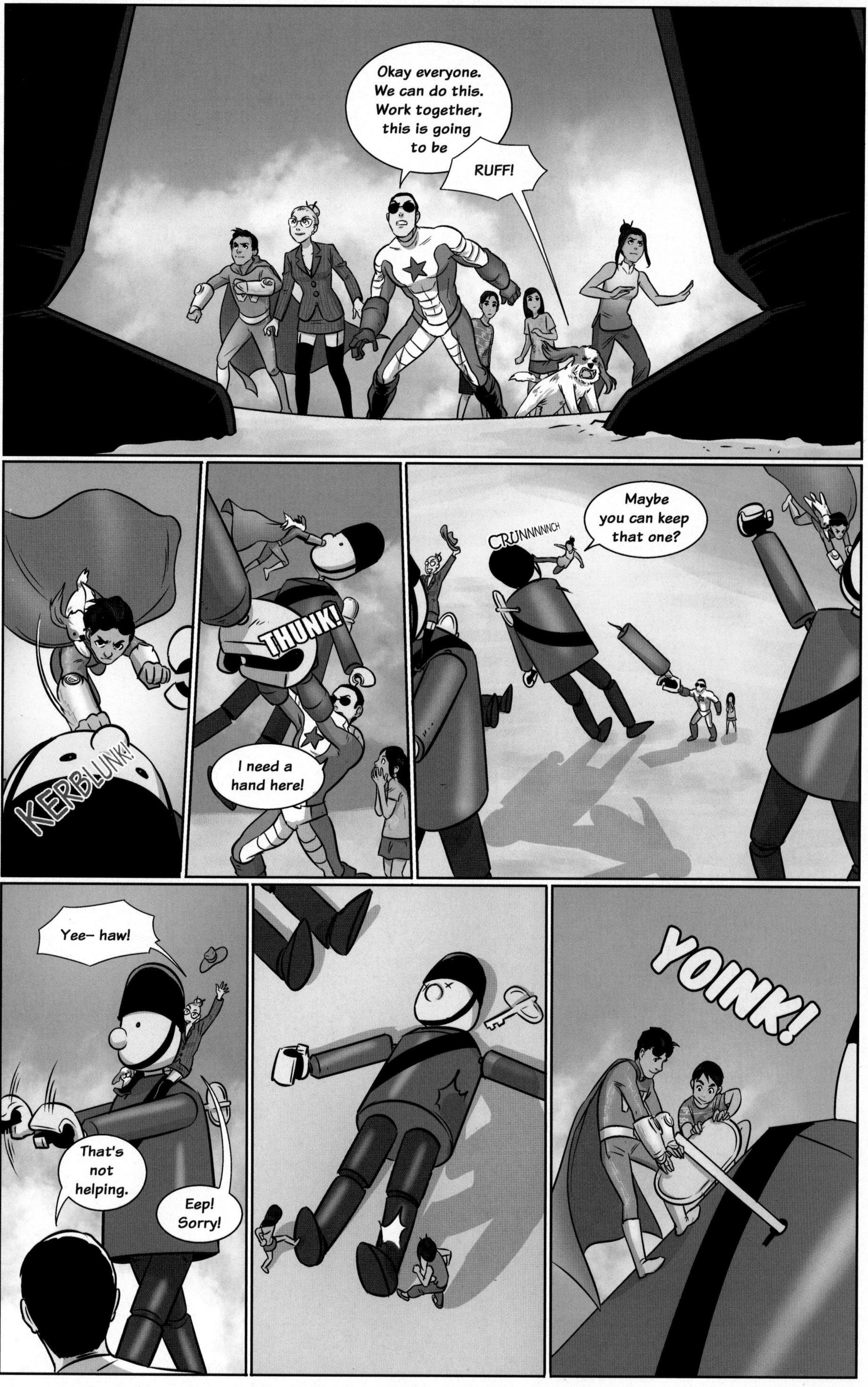
Okay everyone. We can do this. Work together, this is going to be
RUFF!
KERBLUNK!
THUNK!
I need a hand here!
CRUNNNNNCH
Maybe you can keep that one?
Yee- haw!
That's not helping.
Eep! Sorry!
YOINK!

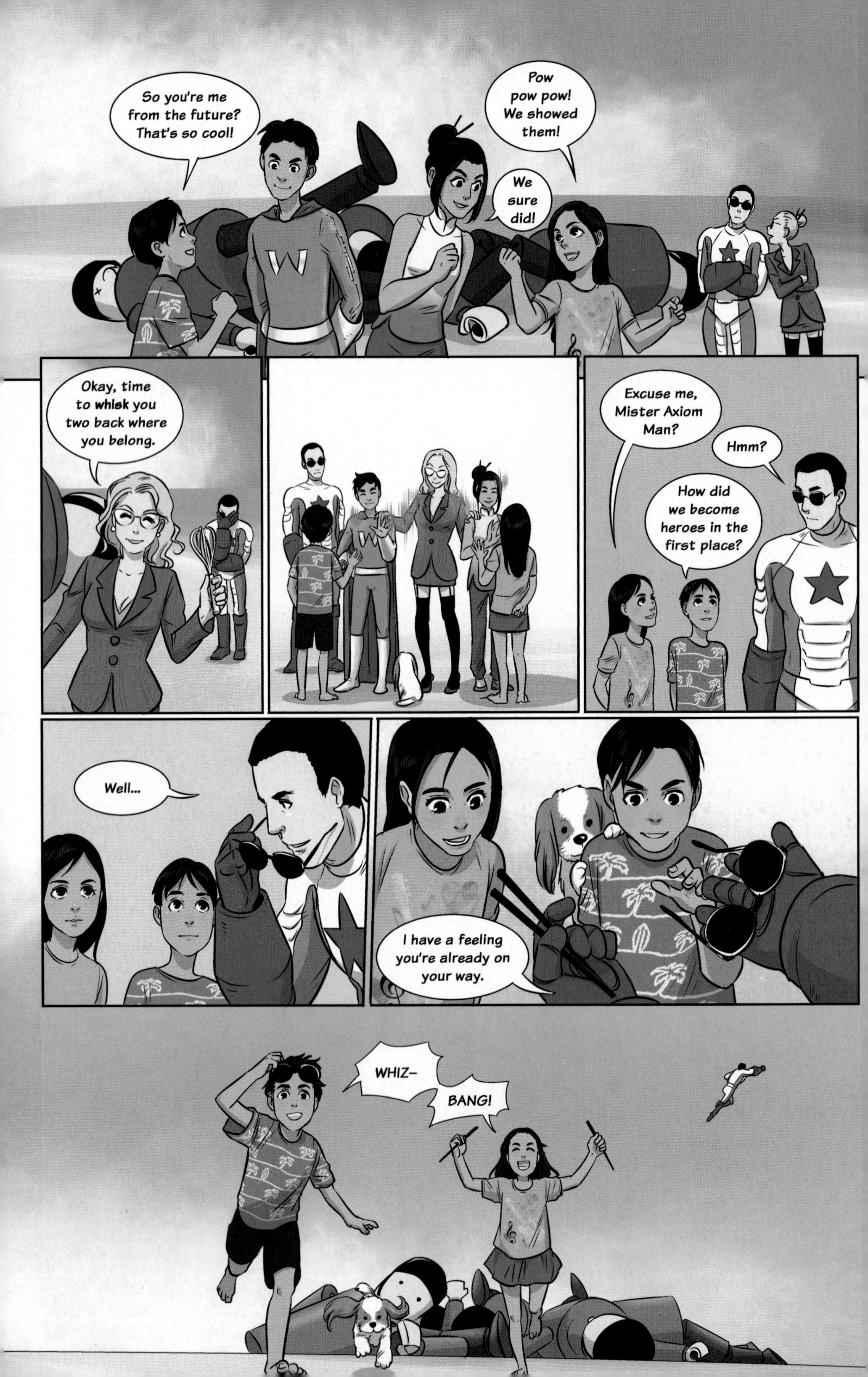
So you're me from the future? That's so cool!
Pow pow pow! We showed them!
We sure did!
Okay, time to whisk you two back where you belong.
Excuse me, Mister Axiom Man?
Hmm?
How did we become heroes in the first place?
Well...
I have a feeling you're already on your way.
WHIZ-
BANG!

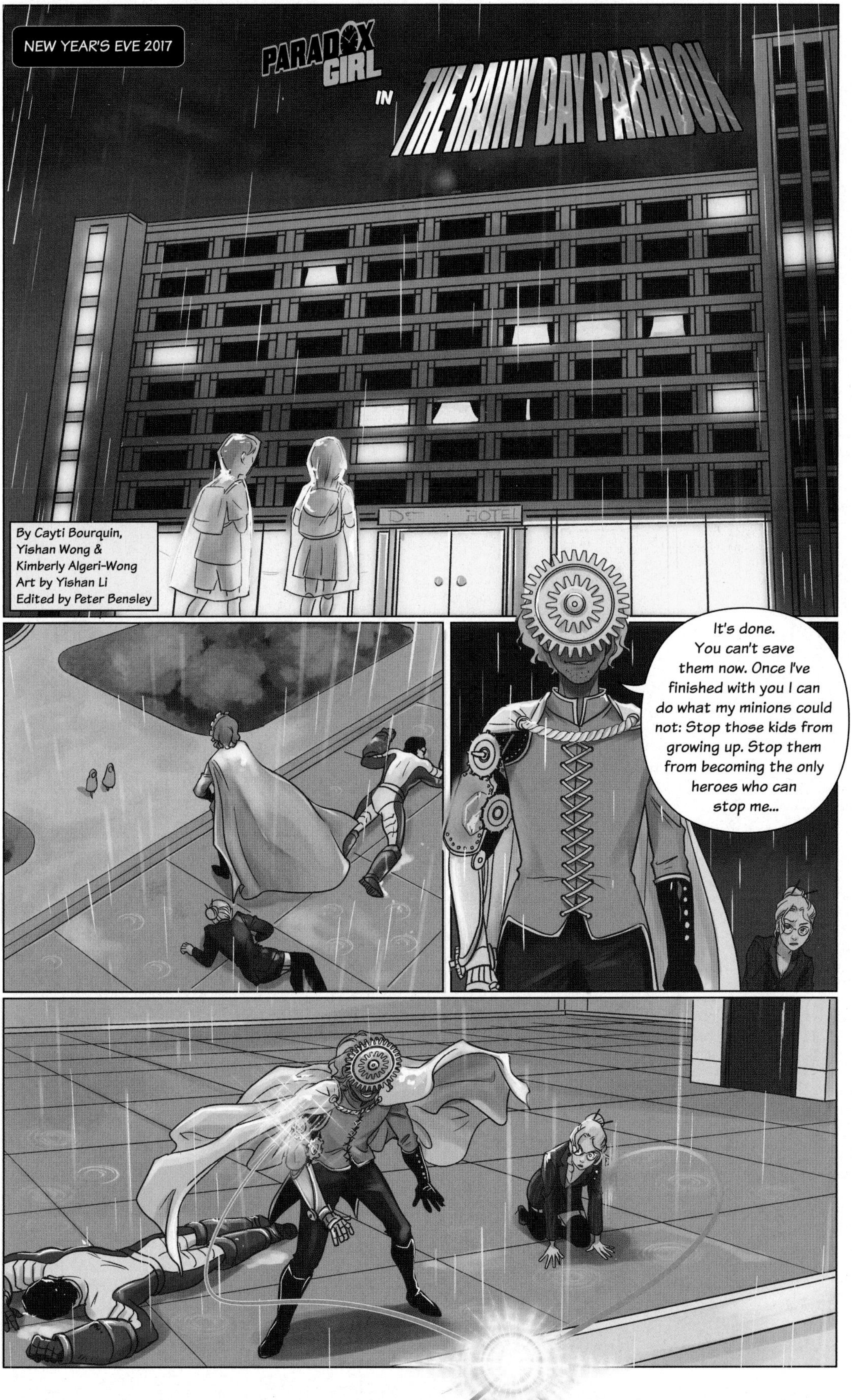
NEW YEAR'S EVE 2017
PARADOX GIRL
IN
THE RAINY DAY PARADOX
By Cayti Bourquin,
Yishan Wong &
Kimberly Algeri-Wong
Art by Yishan Li
Edited by Peter Bensley
It's done. You can't save them now. Once I've finished with you I can do what my minions could not: Stop those kids from growing up. Stop them from becoming the only heroes who can stop me...

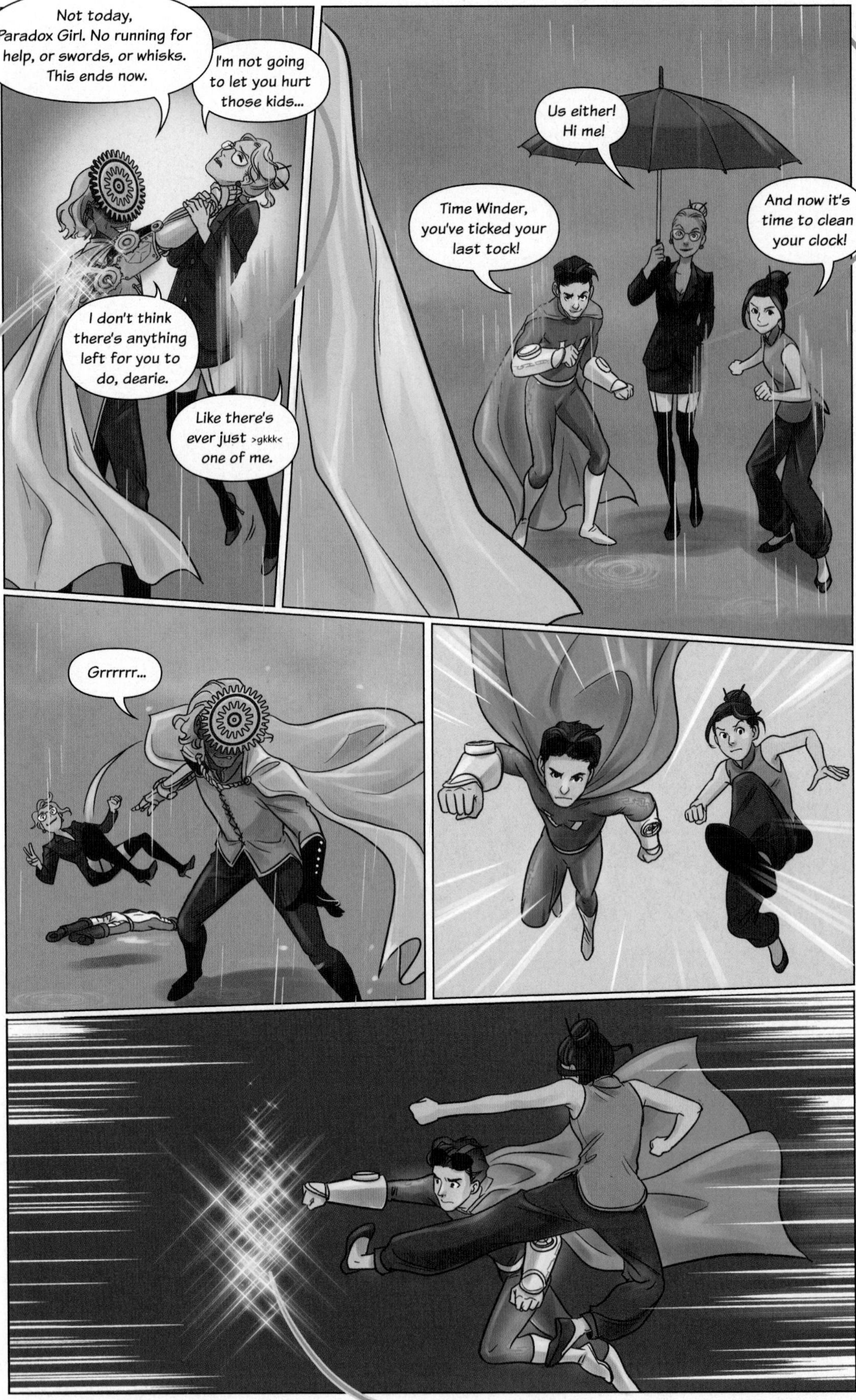
Not today, Paradox Girl. No running for help, or swords, or whisks. This ends now.
I'm not going to let you hurt those kids...
I don't think there's anything left for you to do, dearie.
Like there's ever just >gkkk< one of me.
Us either! Hi me!
Time Winder, you've ticked your last tock!
And now it's time to clean your clock!
Grrrrrr...

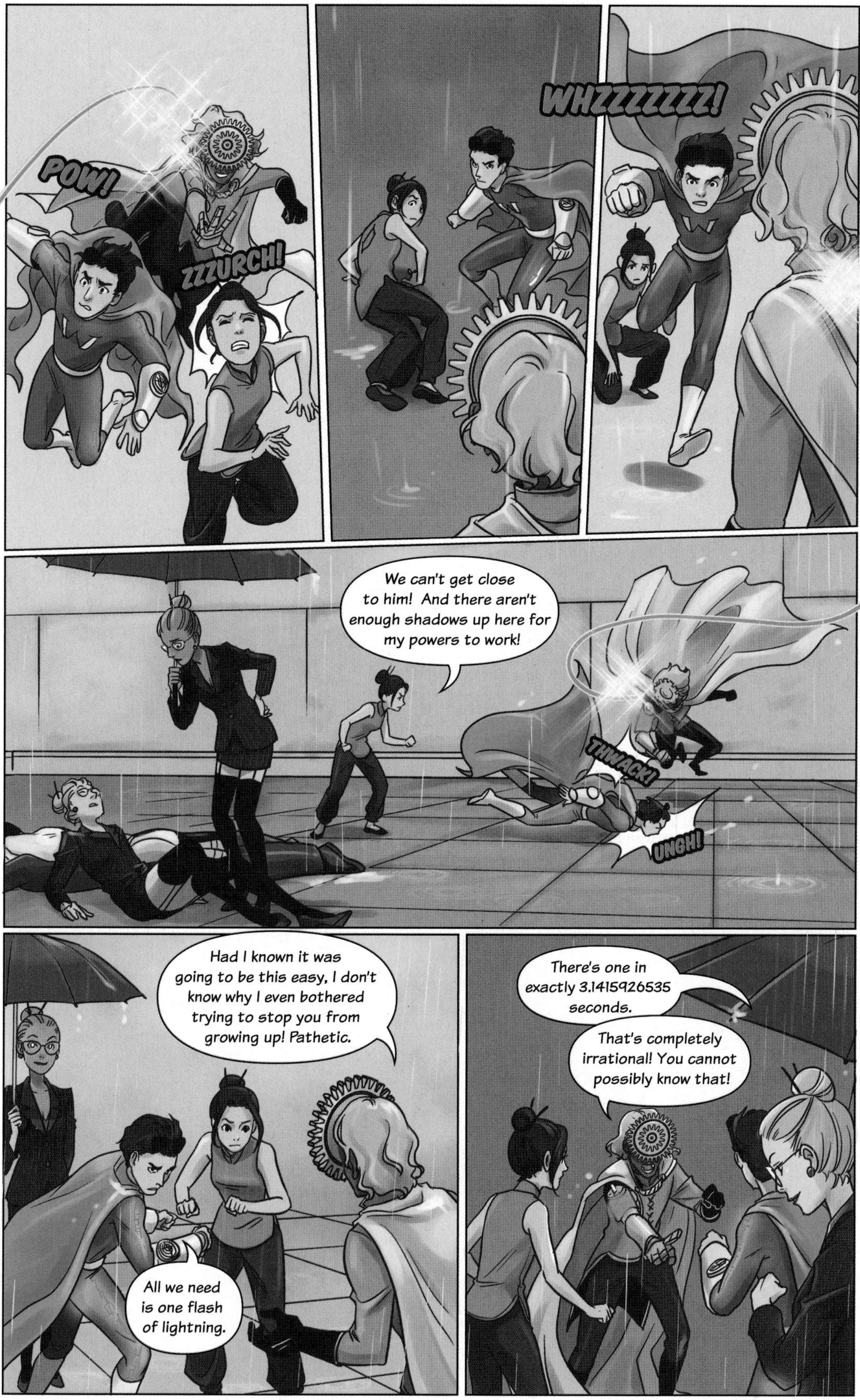
POW!
ZZZURCH!
WHZZZZZZZZ!
We can't get close to him! And there aren't enough shadows up here for my powers to work!
THWACK!
UNGH!
Had I known it was going to be this easy, I don't know why I even bothered trying to stop you from growing up! Pathetic.
All we need is one flash of lightning.
There's one in exactly 3.1415926535 seconds.
That's completely irrational! You cannot possibly know that!

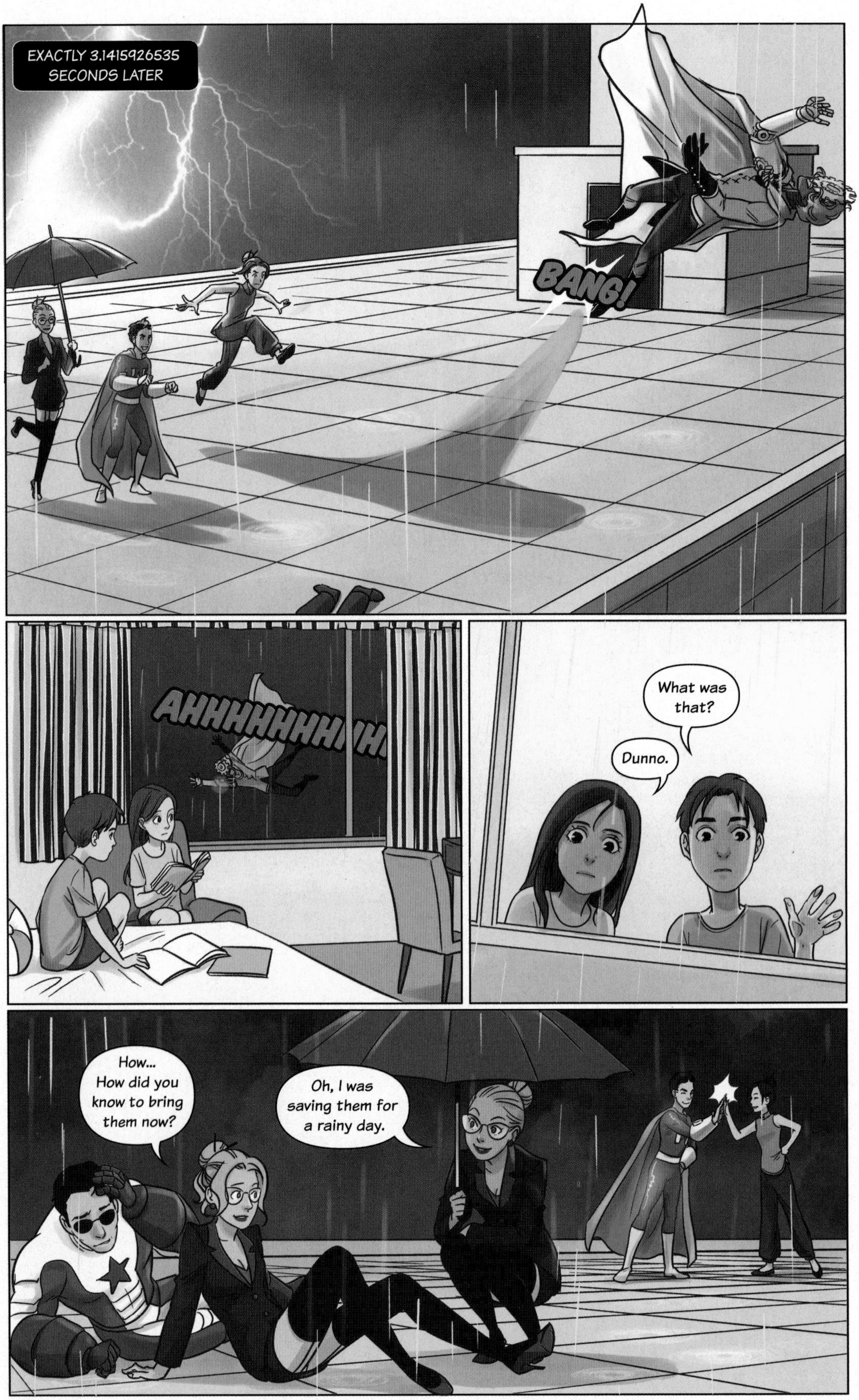
EXACTLY 3.1415926535 SECONDS LATER
BANG!
AHHHHHHHHH
What was that?
Dunno.
How... How did you know to bring them now?
Oh, I was saving them for a rainy day.

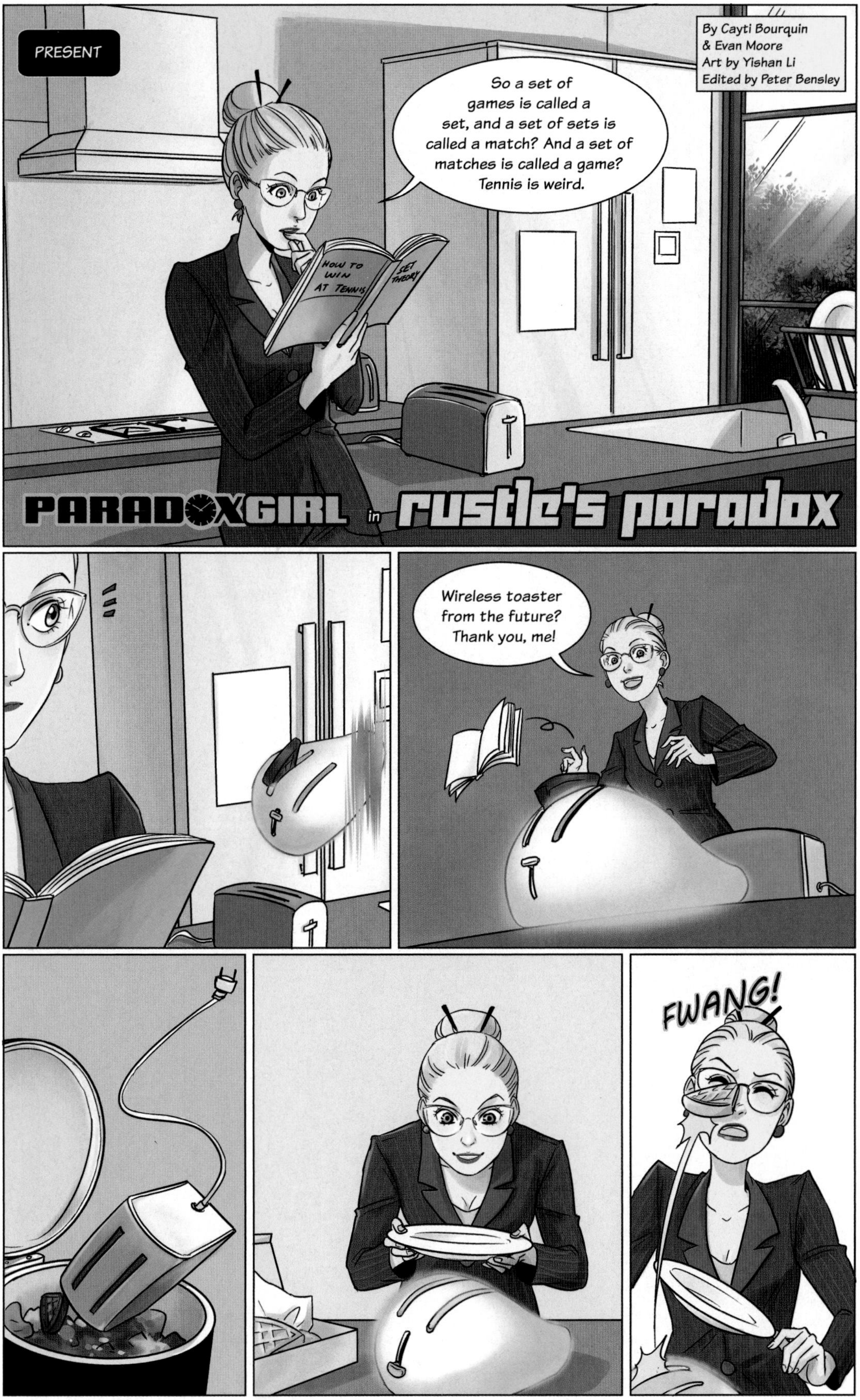
PRESENT
By Cayti Bourquin
& Evan Moore
Art by Yishan Li
Edited by Peter Bensley
So a set of games is called a set, and a set of sets is called a match? And a set of matches is called a game? Tennis is weird.
HOW TO WIN AT TENNIS
SET THEORY
PARADOXGIRL in rustle's paradox
Wireless toaster from the future? Thank you, me!
FWANG!

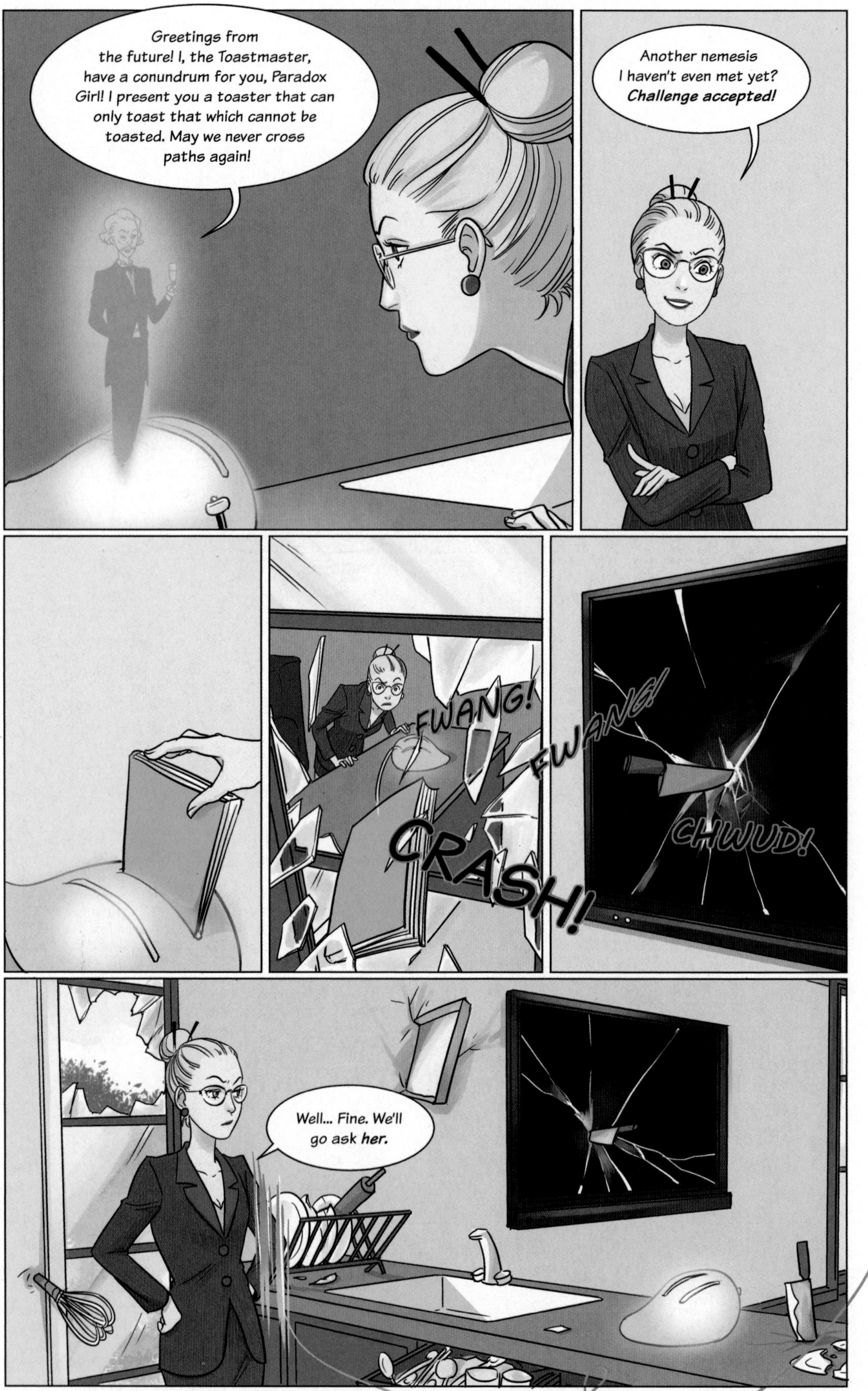
Greetings from the future! I, the Toastmaster, have a conundrum for you, Paradox Girl! I present you a toaster that can only toast that which cannot be toasted. May we never cross paths again!
Another nemesis I haven't even met yet? **Challenge accepted!**
FWANG!
FWANG!
CRASH!
CHWUD!
Well... Fine. We'll go ask **her.**

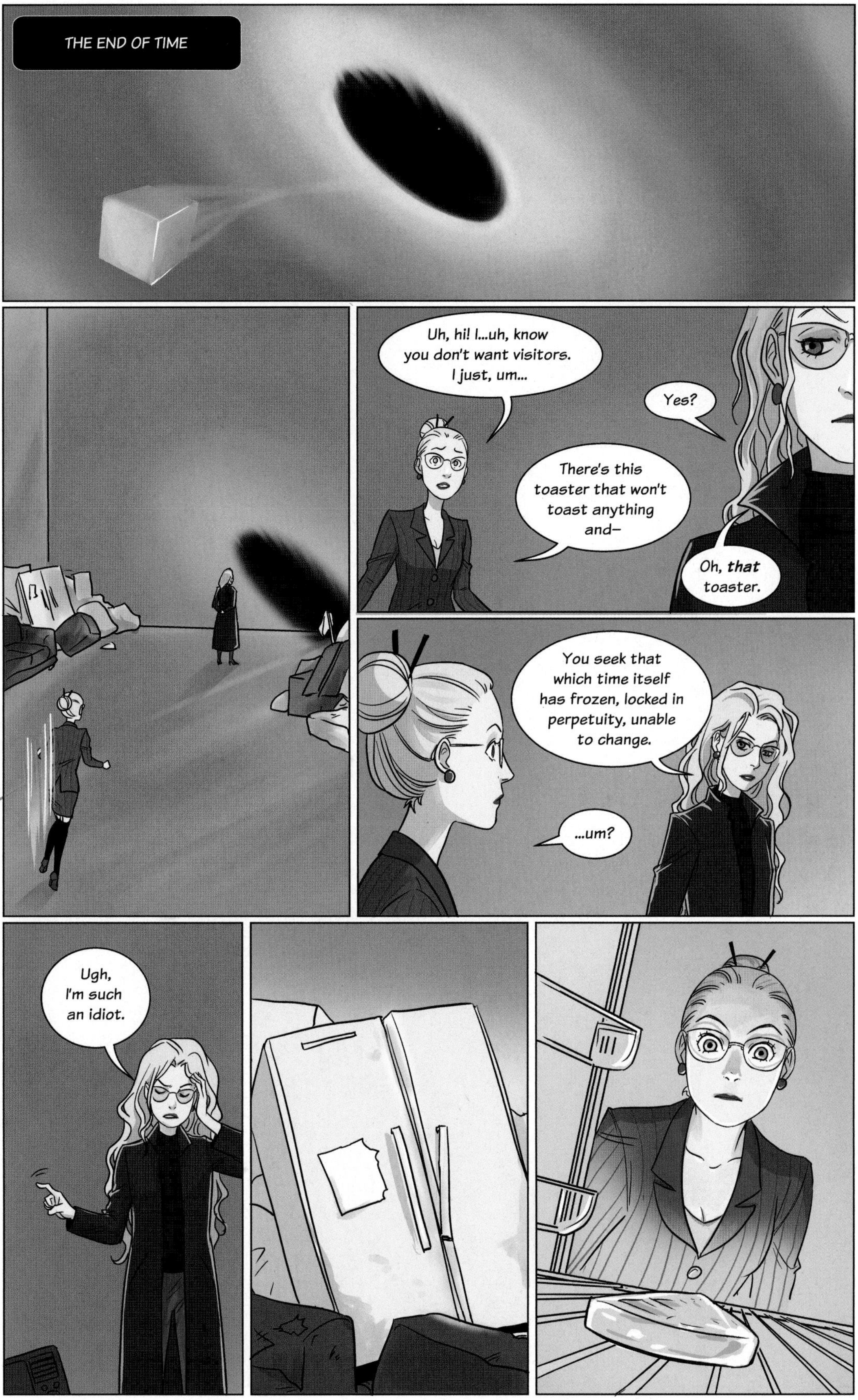
THE END OF TIME
Uh, hi! I...uh, know you don't want visitors. I just, um...
Yes?
There's this toaster that won't toast anything and—
Oh, **that** toaster.
You seek that which time itself has frozen, locked in perpetuity, unable to change.
...um?
Ugh, I'm such an idiot.

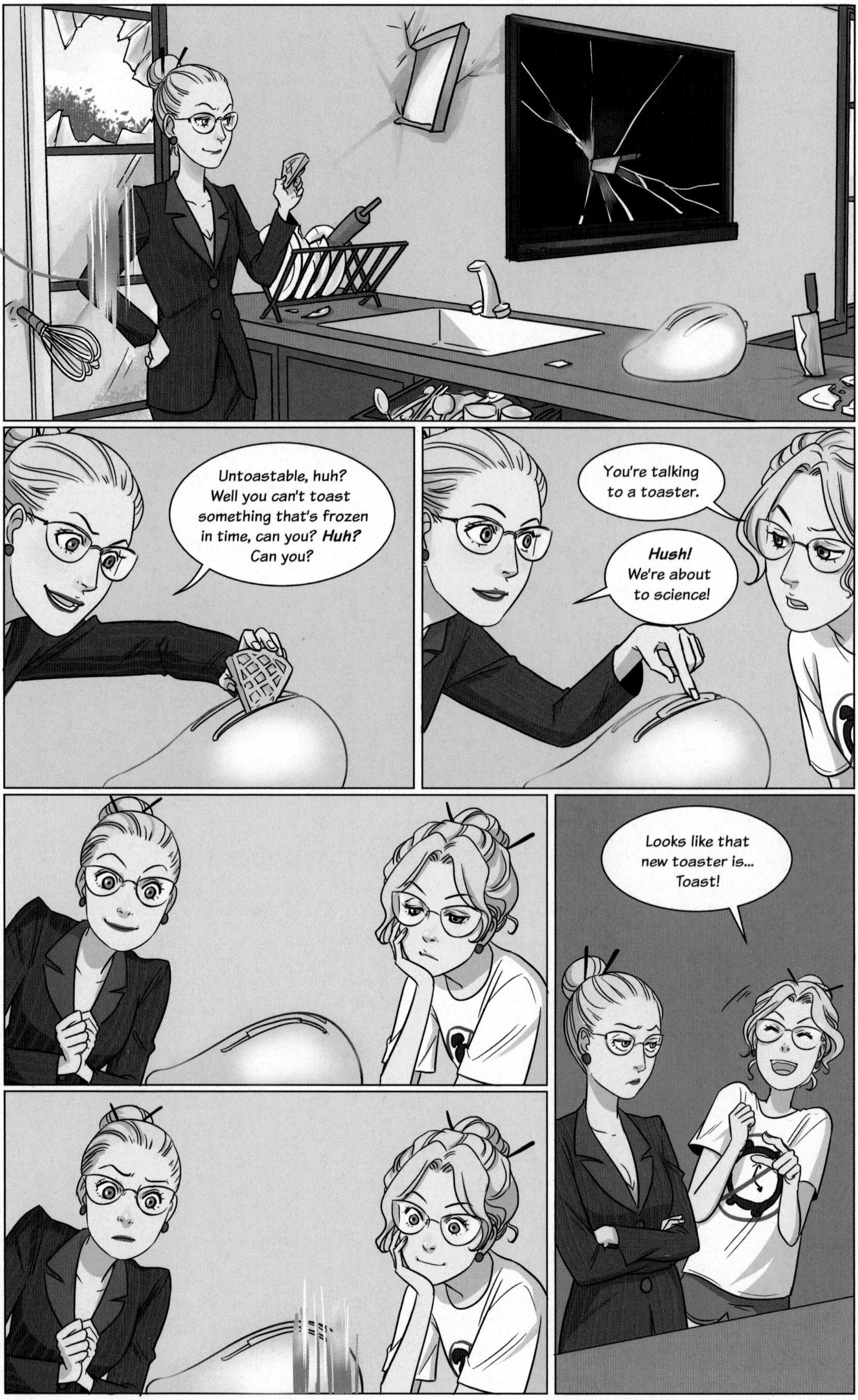

Untoastable, huh? Well you can't toast something that's frozen in time, can you? **Huh?** Can you?
You're talking to a toaster.
Hush! We're about to science!
Looks like that new toaster is... Toast!

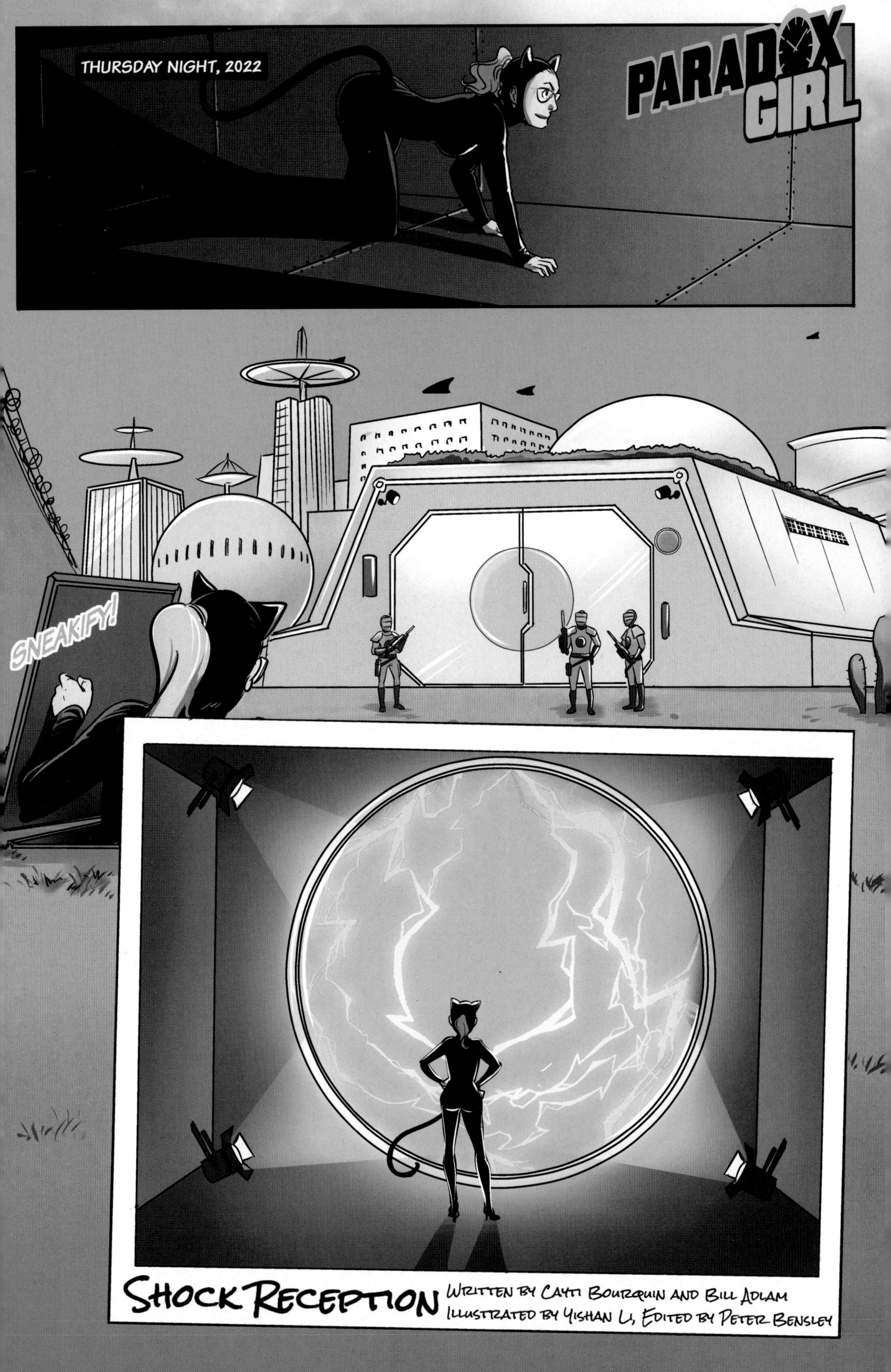
THURSDAY NIGHT, 2022
PARADOX GIRL
SNEAKIFY!
SHOCK RECEPTION
WRITTEN BY CAYTI BOURQUIN AND BILL ADLAM
ILLUSTRATED BY YISHAN LI, EDITED BY PETER BENSLEY

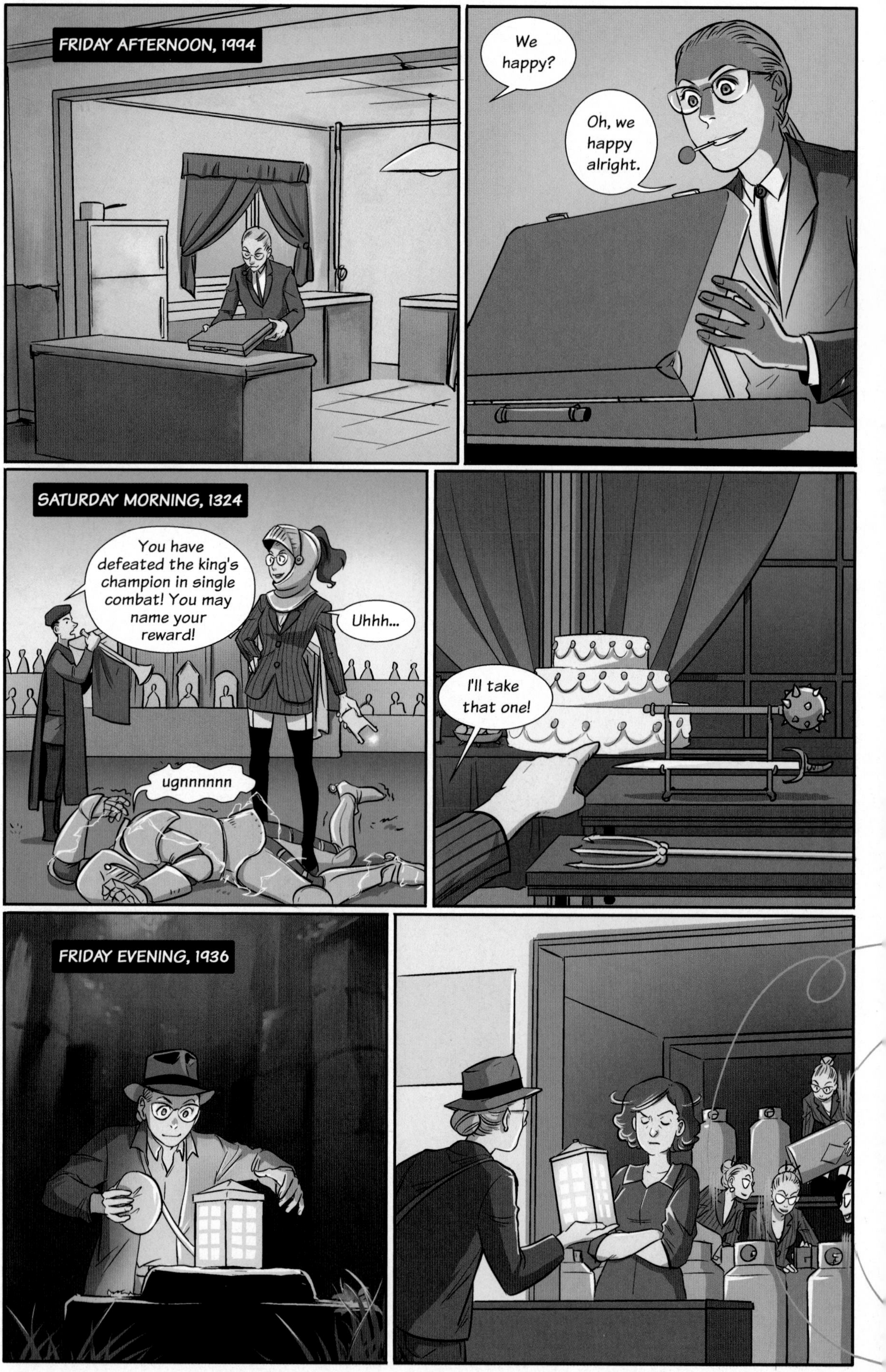
FRIDAY AFTERNOON, 1994
We happy?
Oh, we happy alright.
SATURDAY MORNING, 1324
You have defeated the king's champion in single combat! You may name your reward!
Uhhh...
ugnnnnnn
I'll take that one!
FRIDAY EVENING, 1936

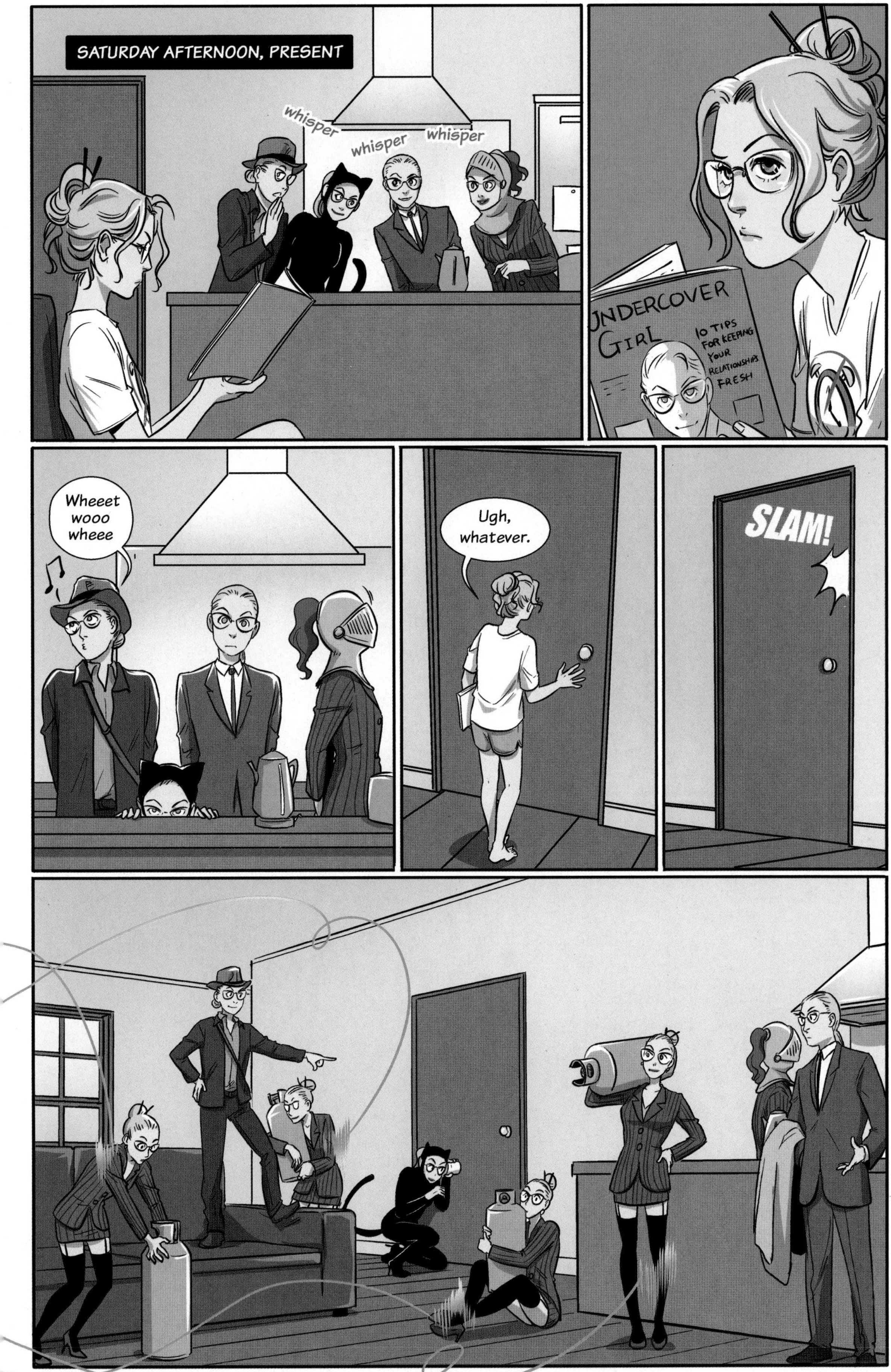
SATURDAY AFTERNOON, PRESENT
whisper
whisper
whisper
UNDERCOVER GIRL
10 TIPS FOR KEEPING YOUR RELATIONSHIPS FRESH
Wheeet wooo wheee
Ugh, whatever.
SLAM!

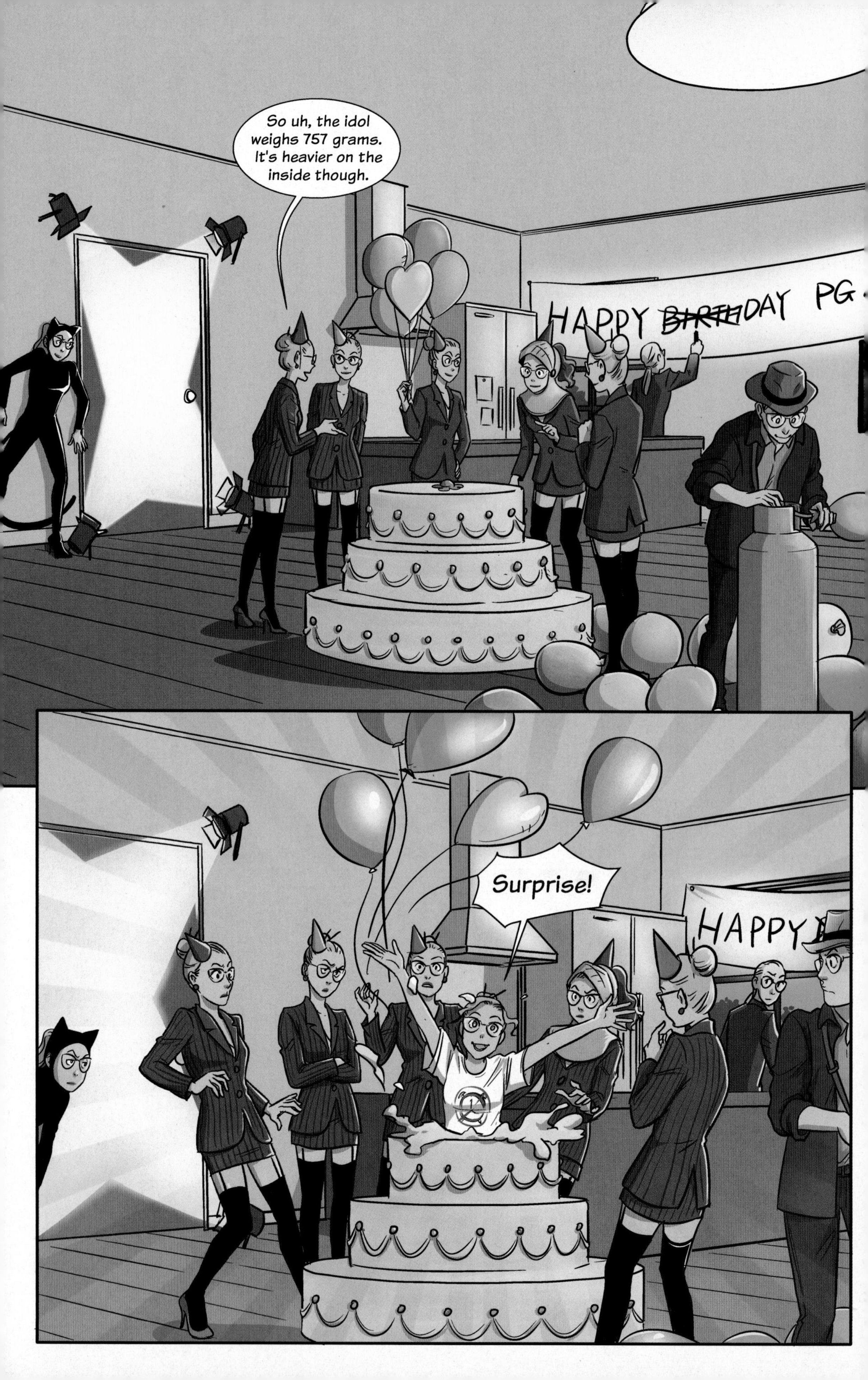
So uh, the idol weighs 757 grams. It's heavier on the inside though.
HAPPY ~~BIRTH~~DAY PG
Surprise!
HAPPY

COVER GALLERY

ART BY YISHAN LI

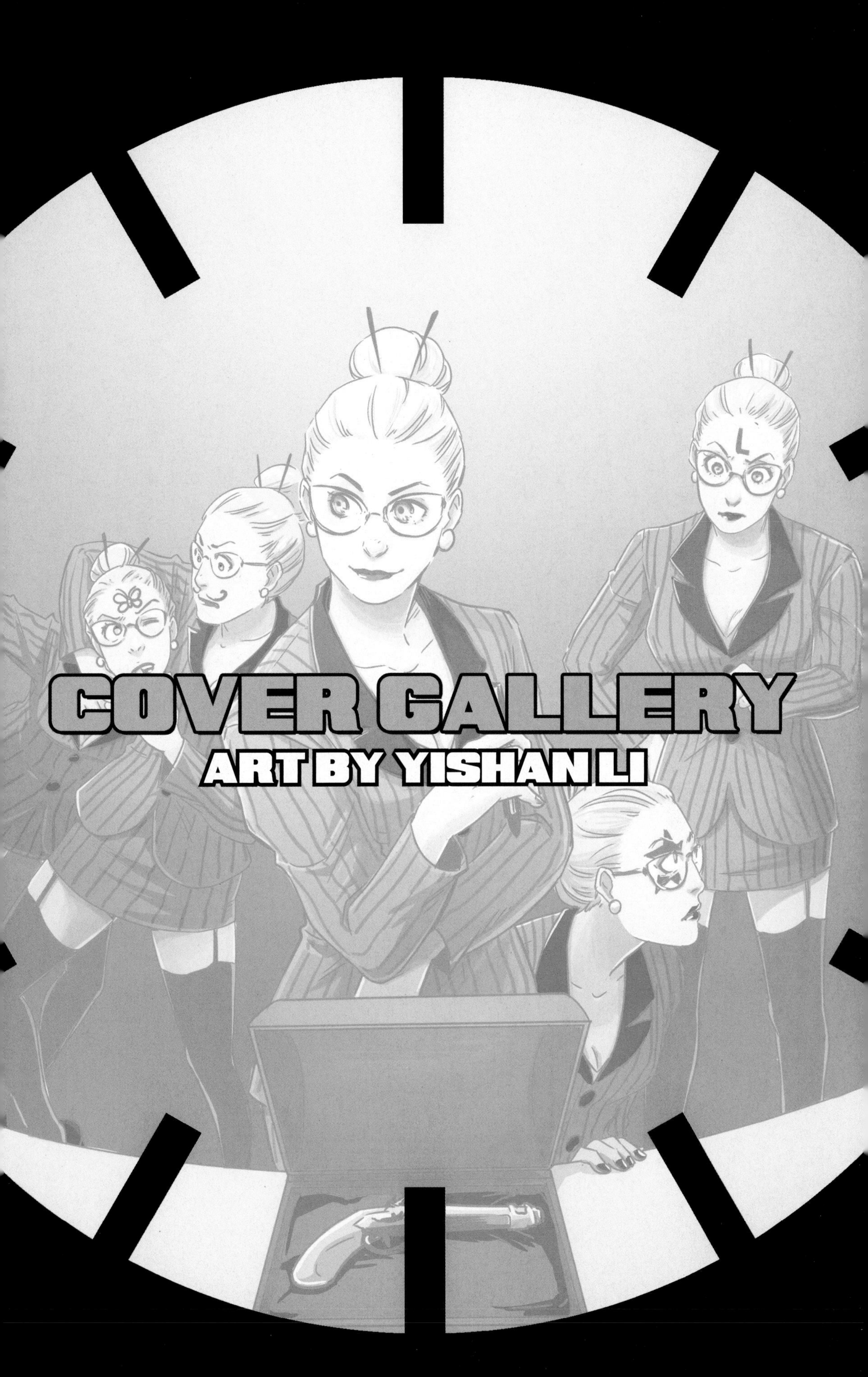

ISSUE 1 COVER A

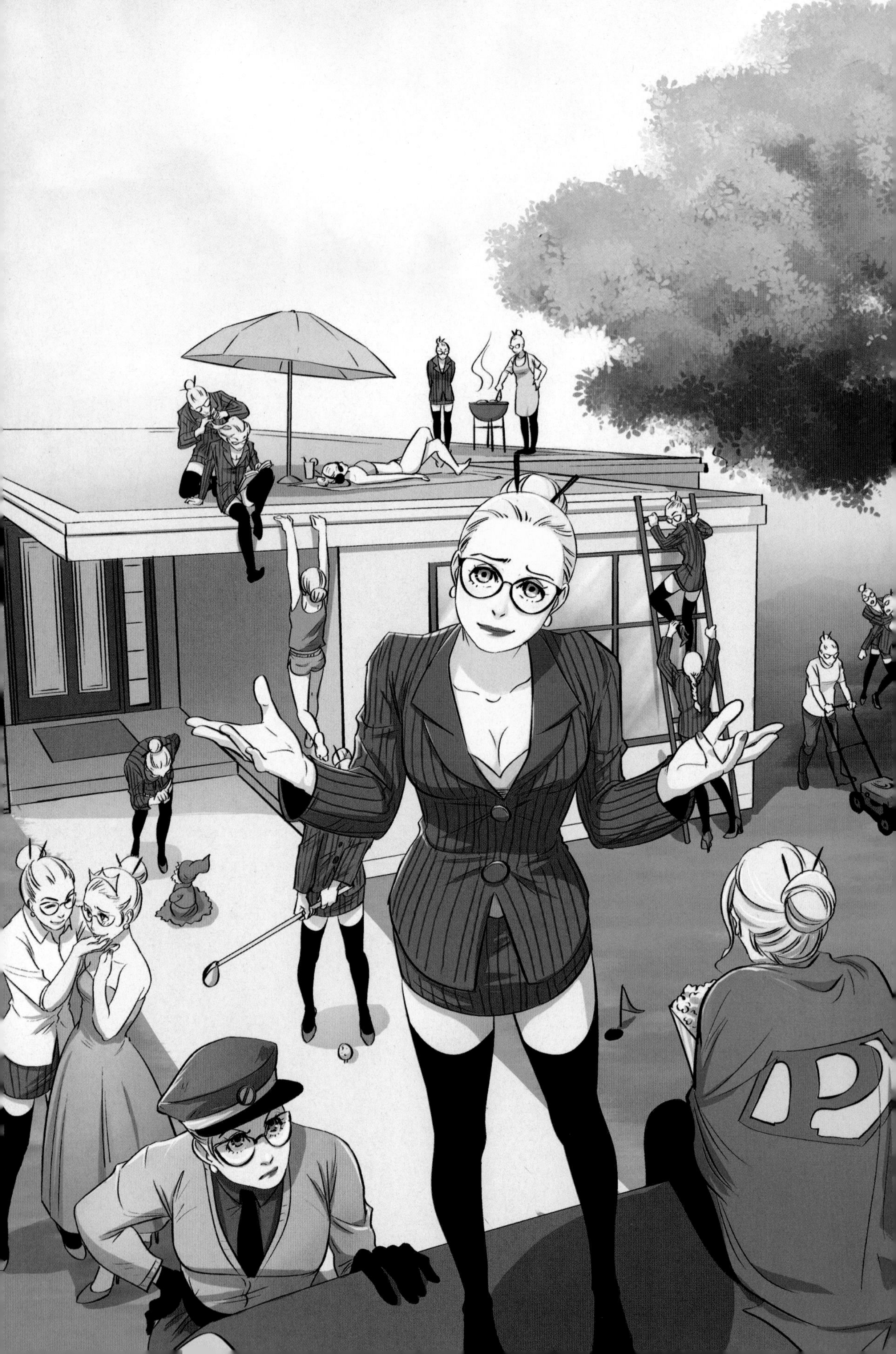

ISSUE 1 COVER B

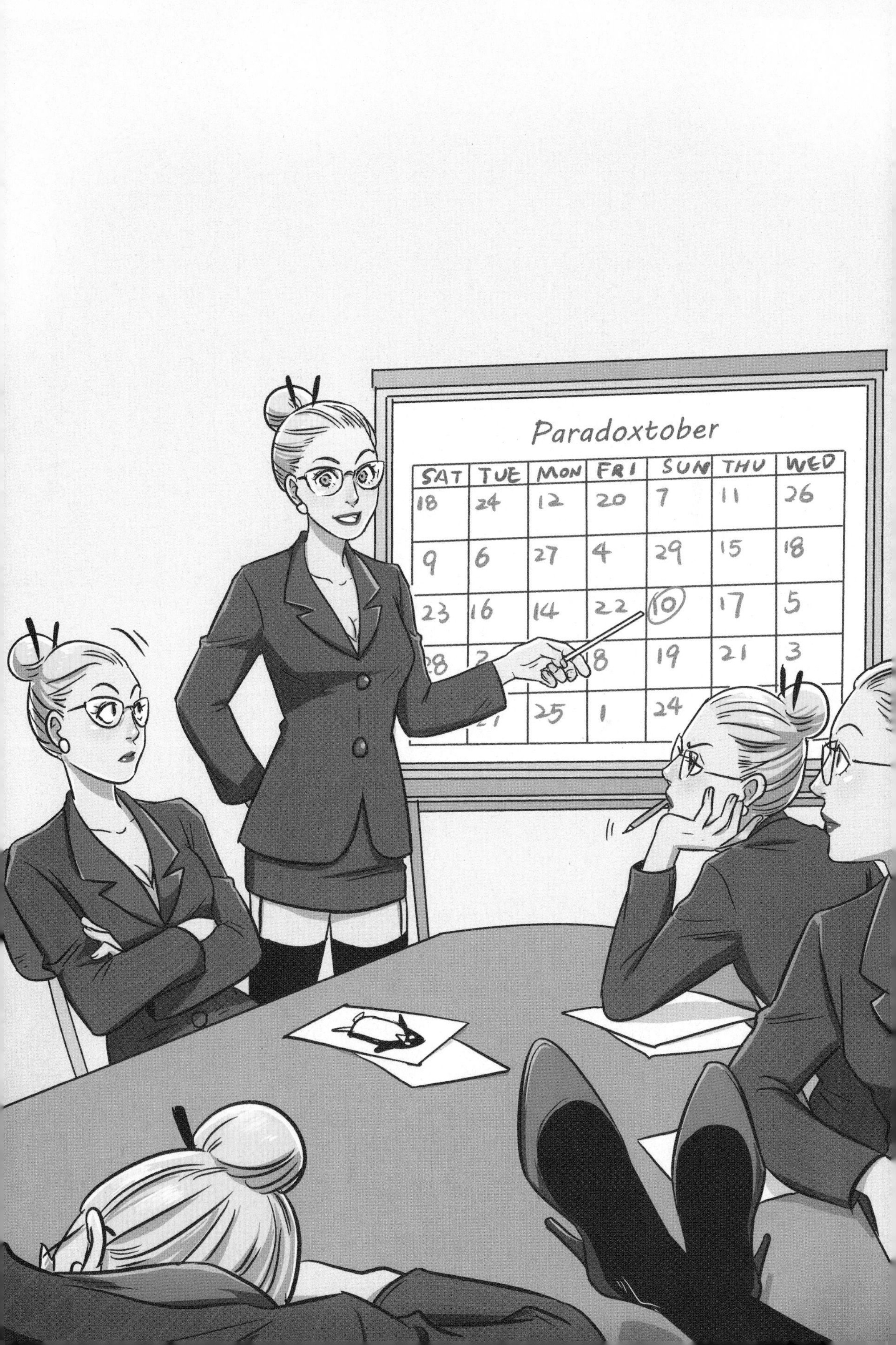

Paradoxtober
SAT TUE MON FRI SUN THU WED
18 24 12 20 7 11 26
9 6 27 4 29 15 18
23 16 14 22 10 17 5
19 21 3
25 1 24

ISSUE 2 COVER A

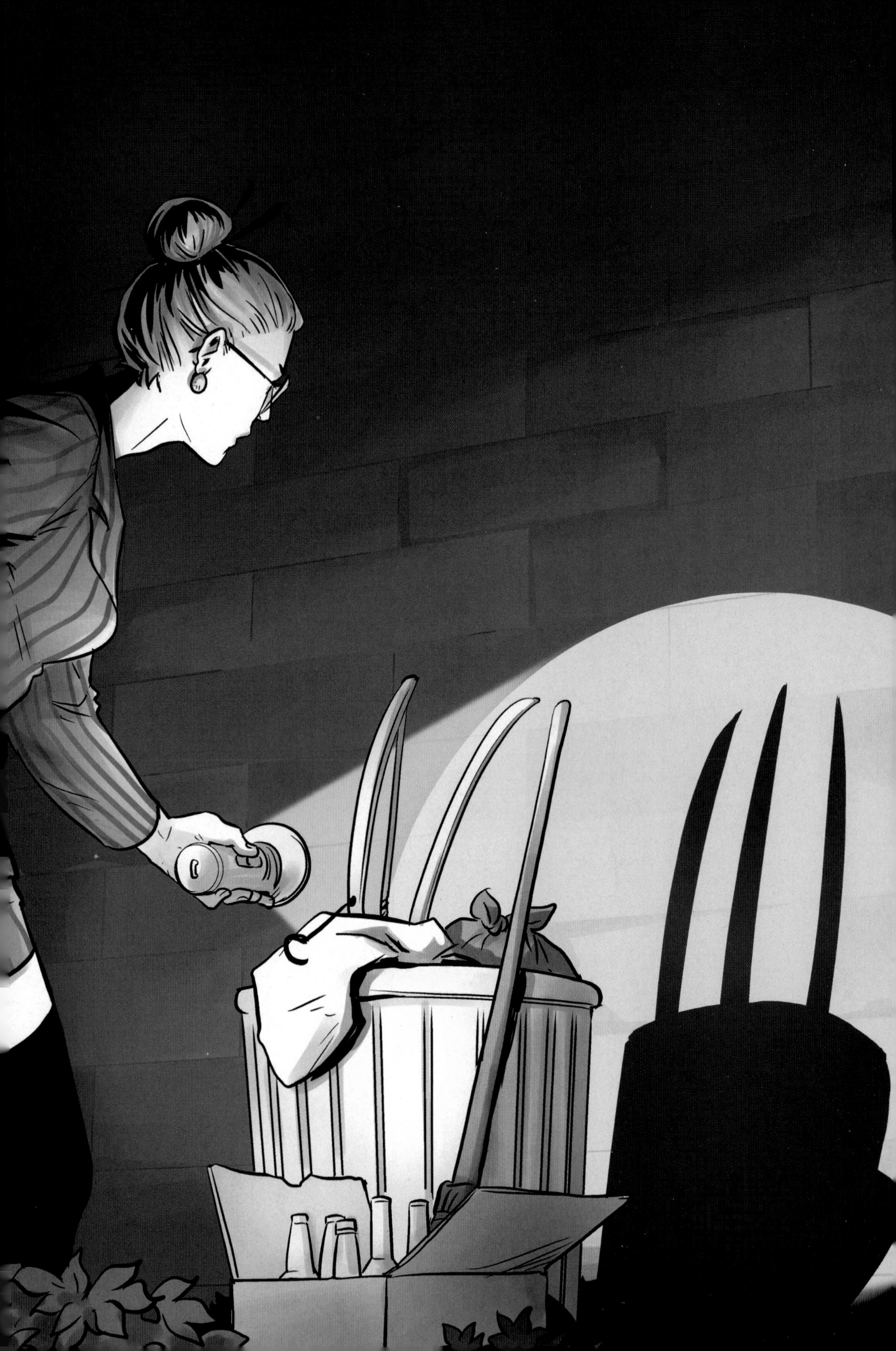

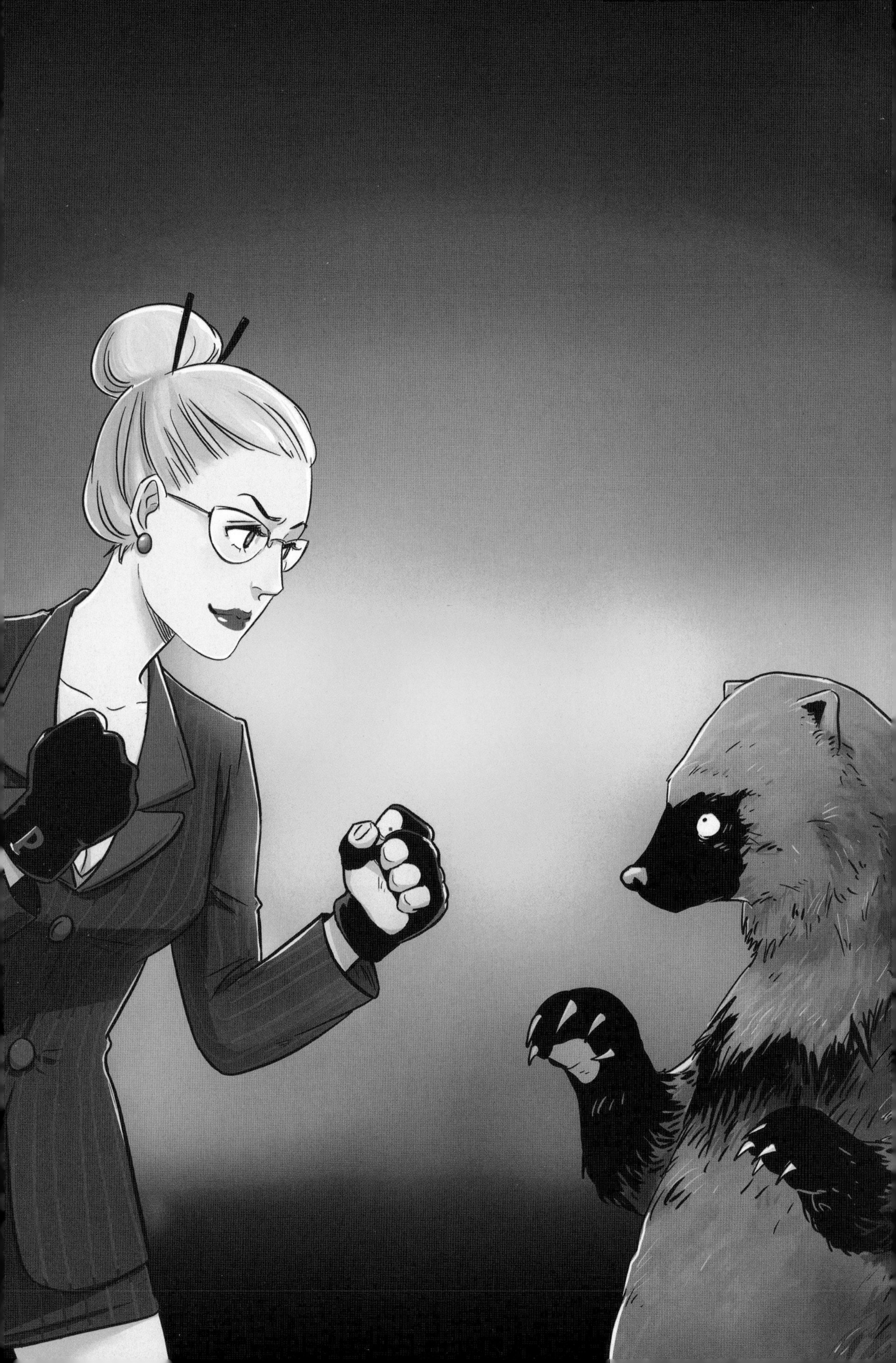

ISSUE 3 COVER A

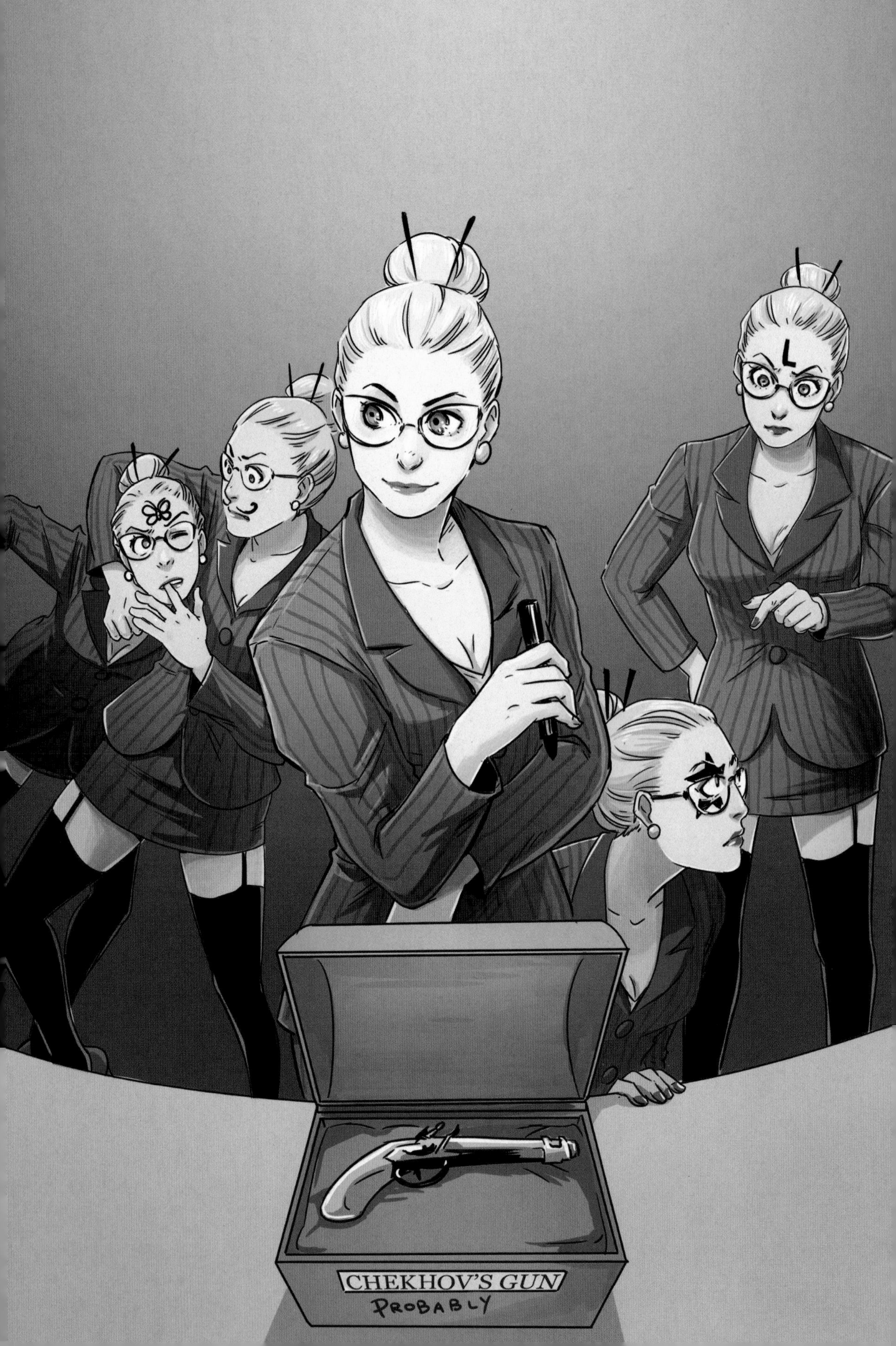
CHEKHOV'S GUN
PROBABLY

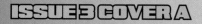

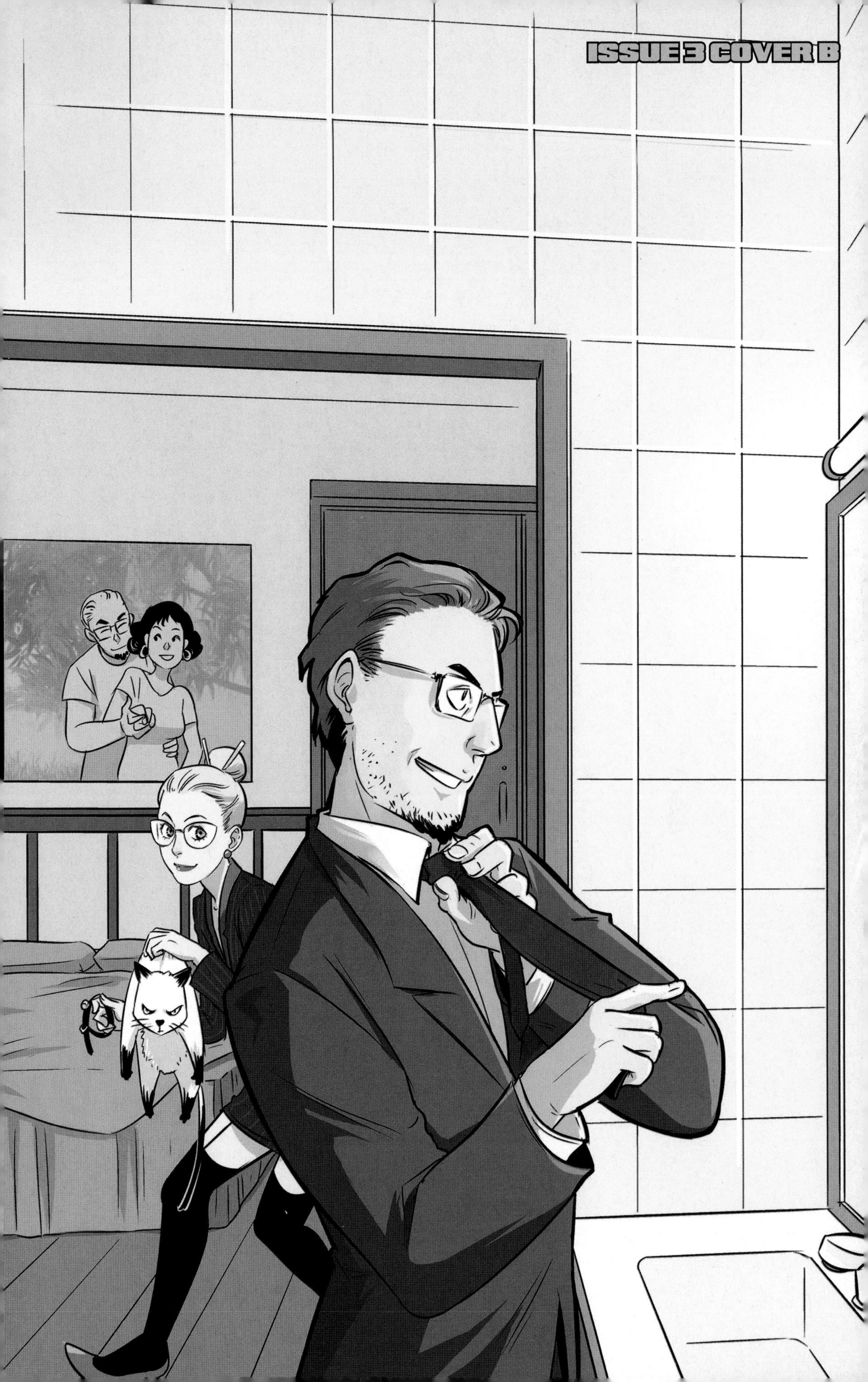

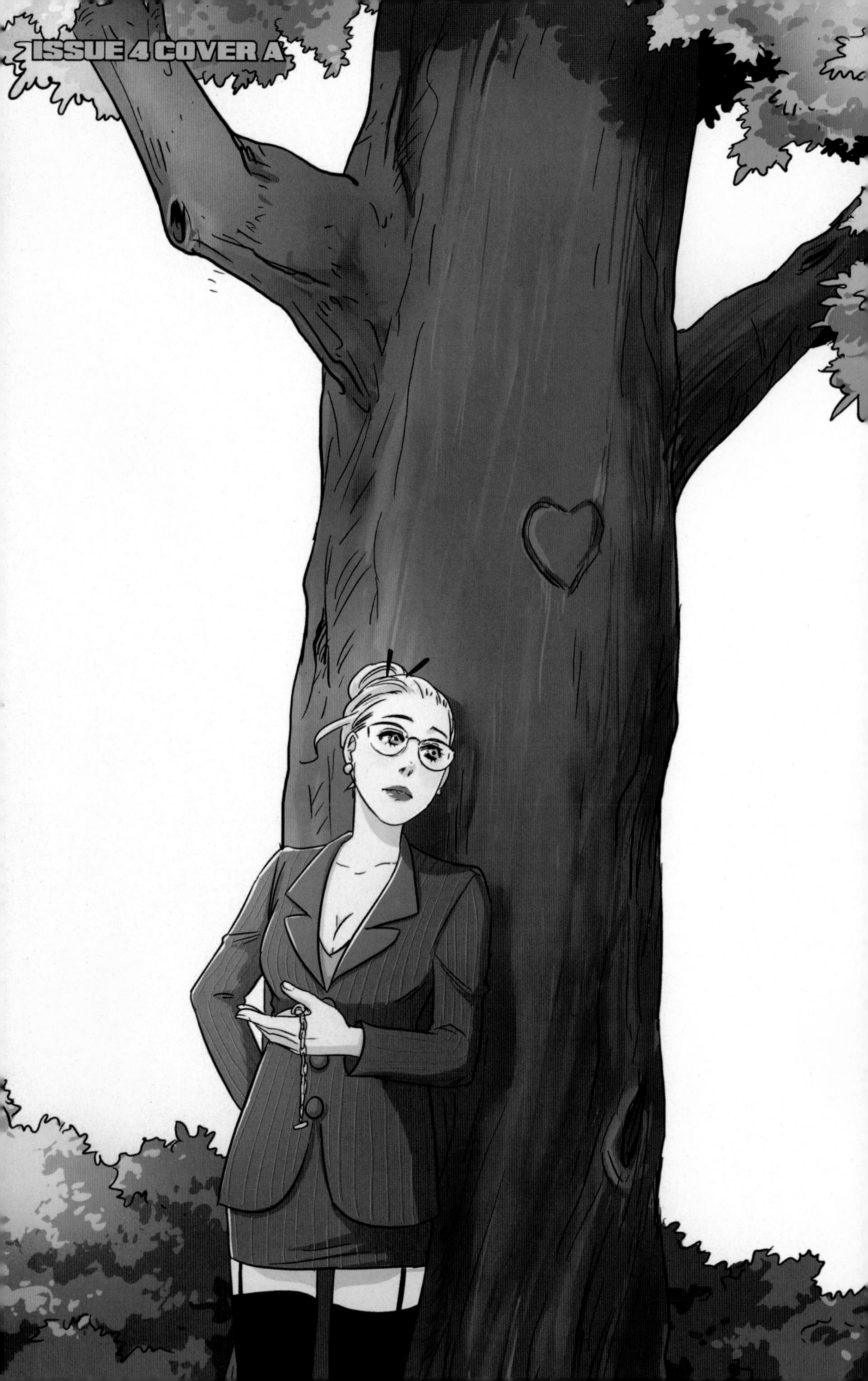
ISSUE 4 COVER A

ISSUE 4 COVER B

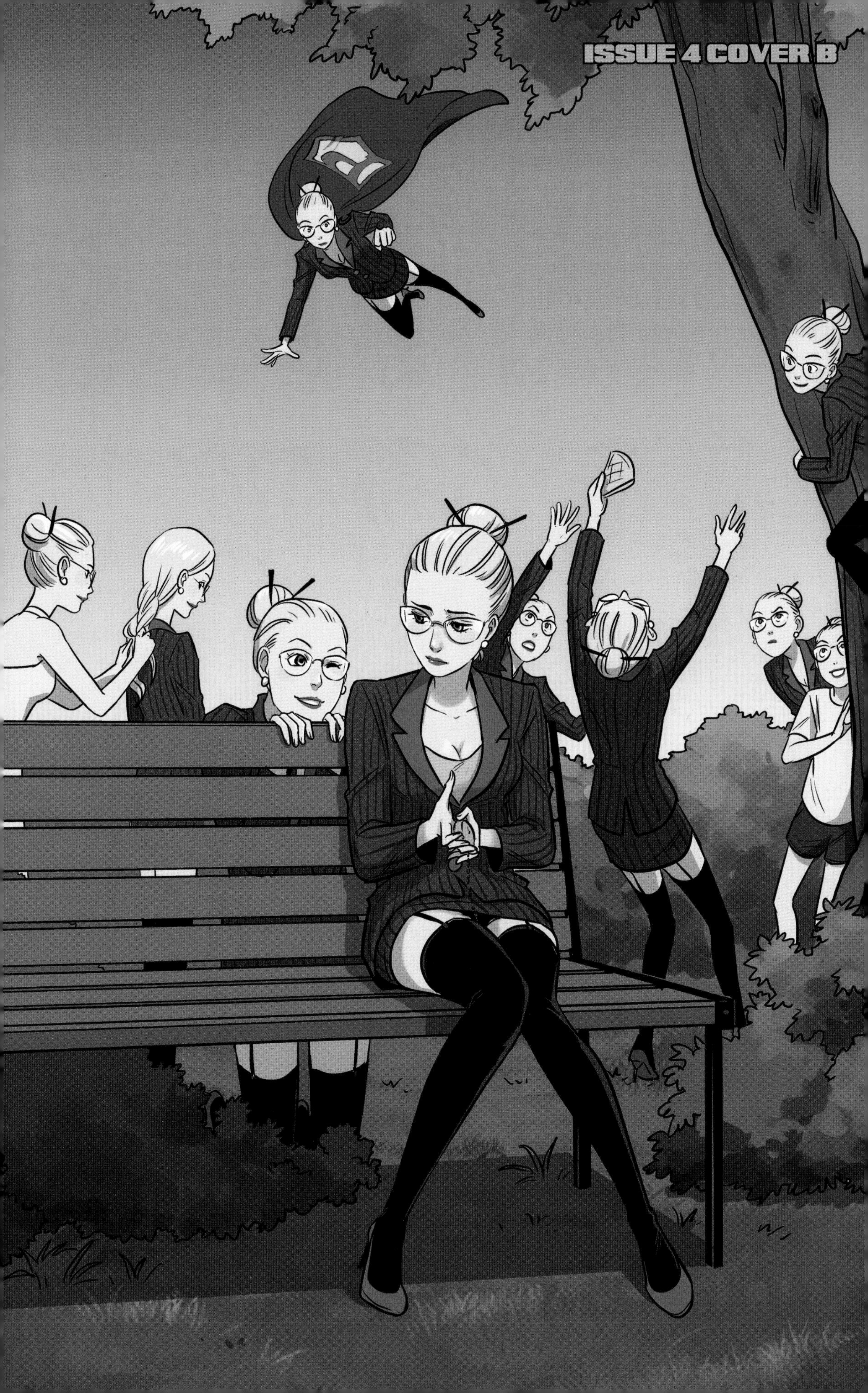

ISSUE 5 COVER A

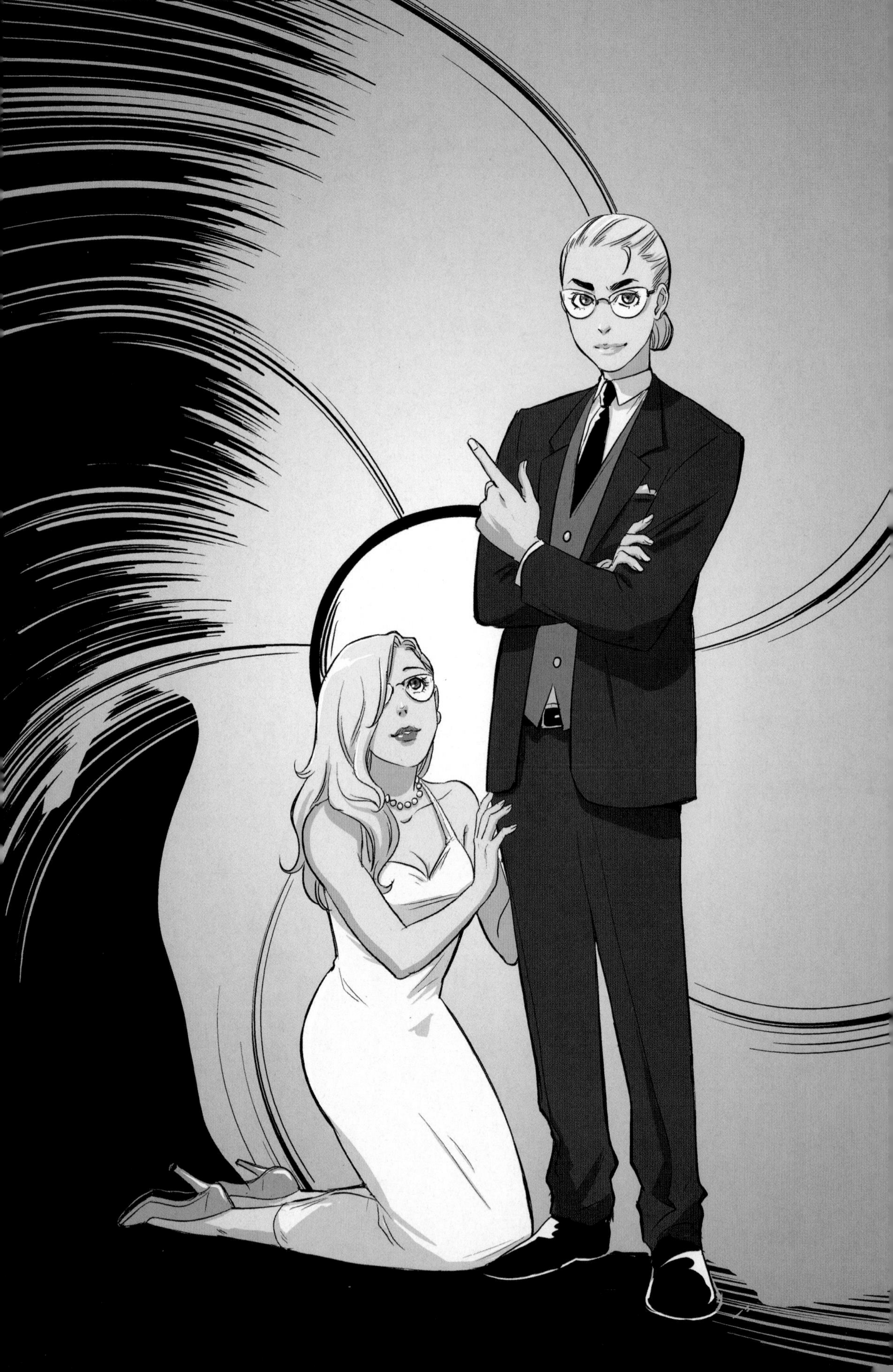

ISSUE 5 COVER B

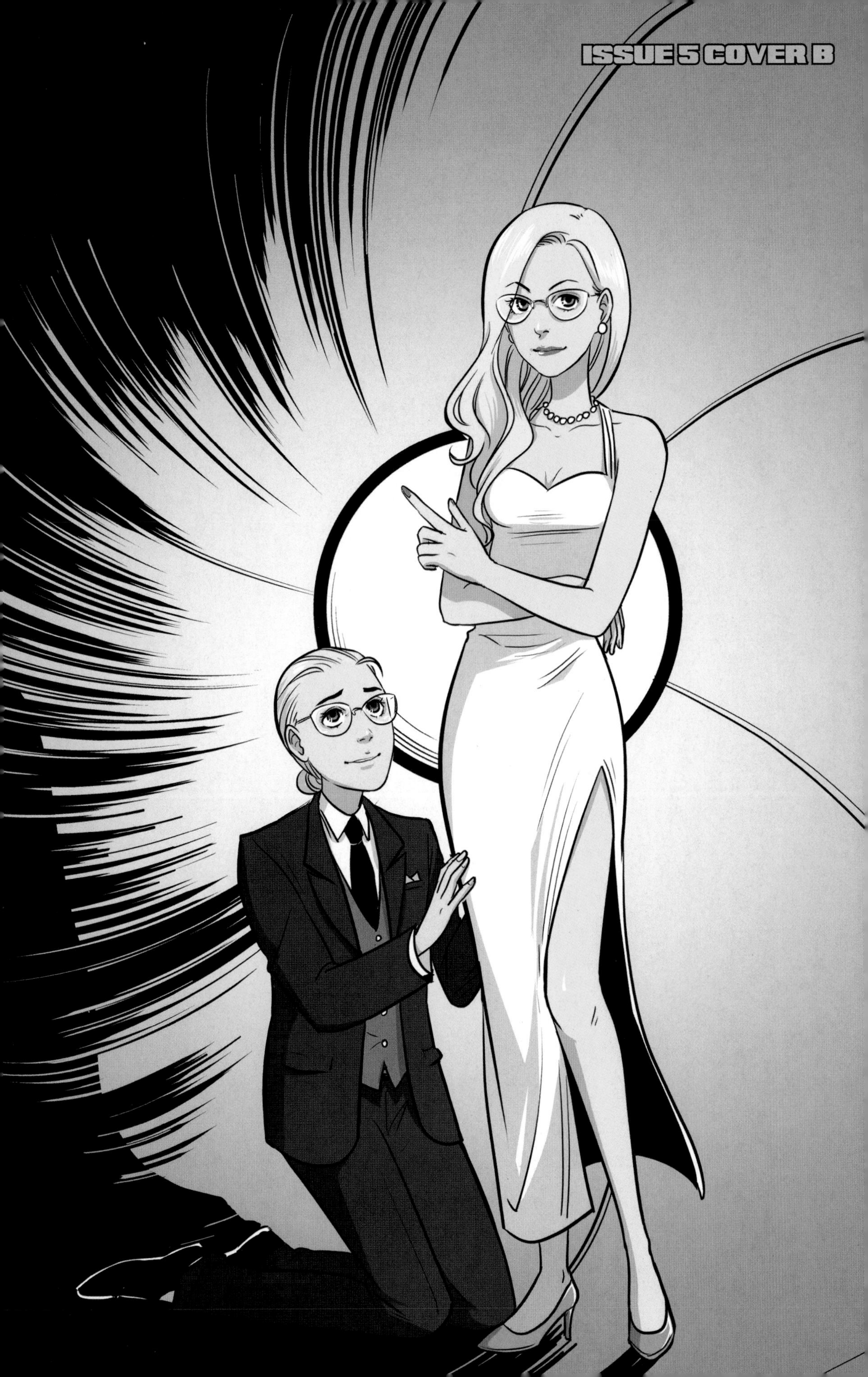

ISSUE 6 COVER A

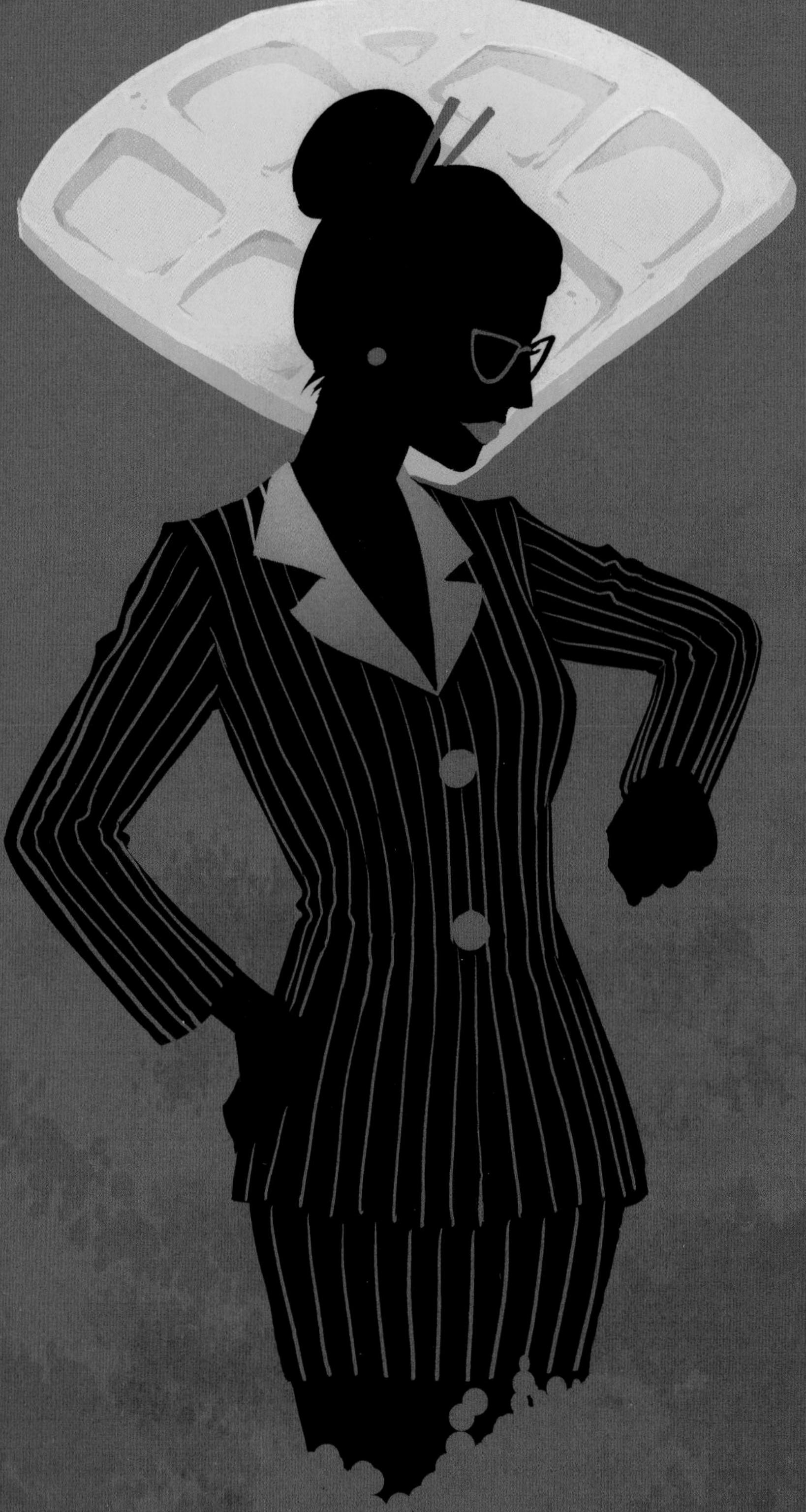

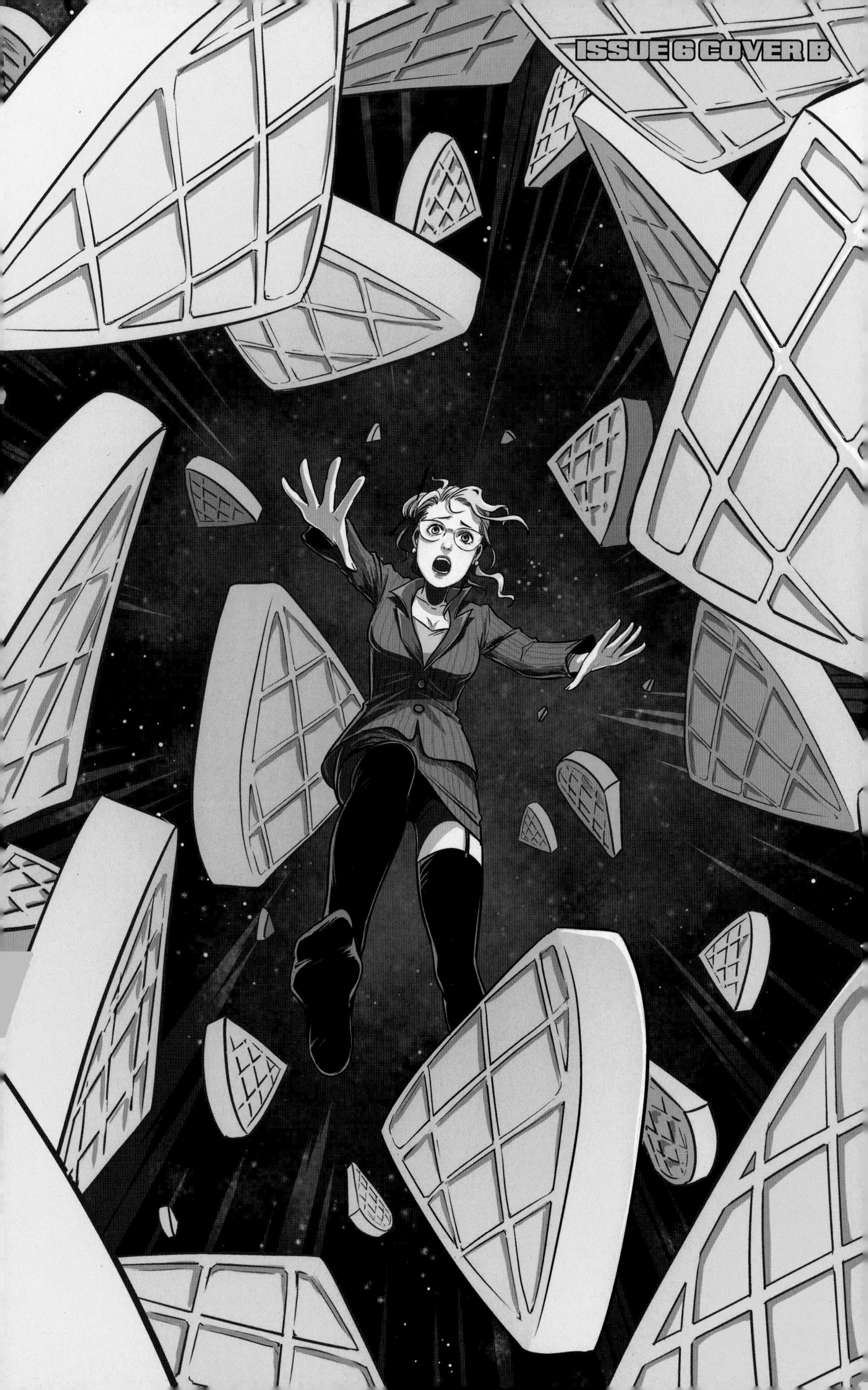

ISSUE 6 COVER B

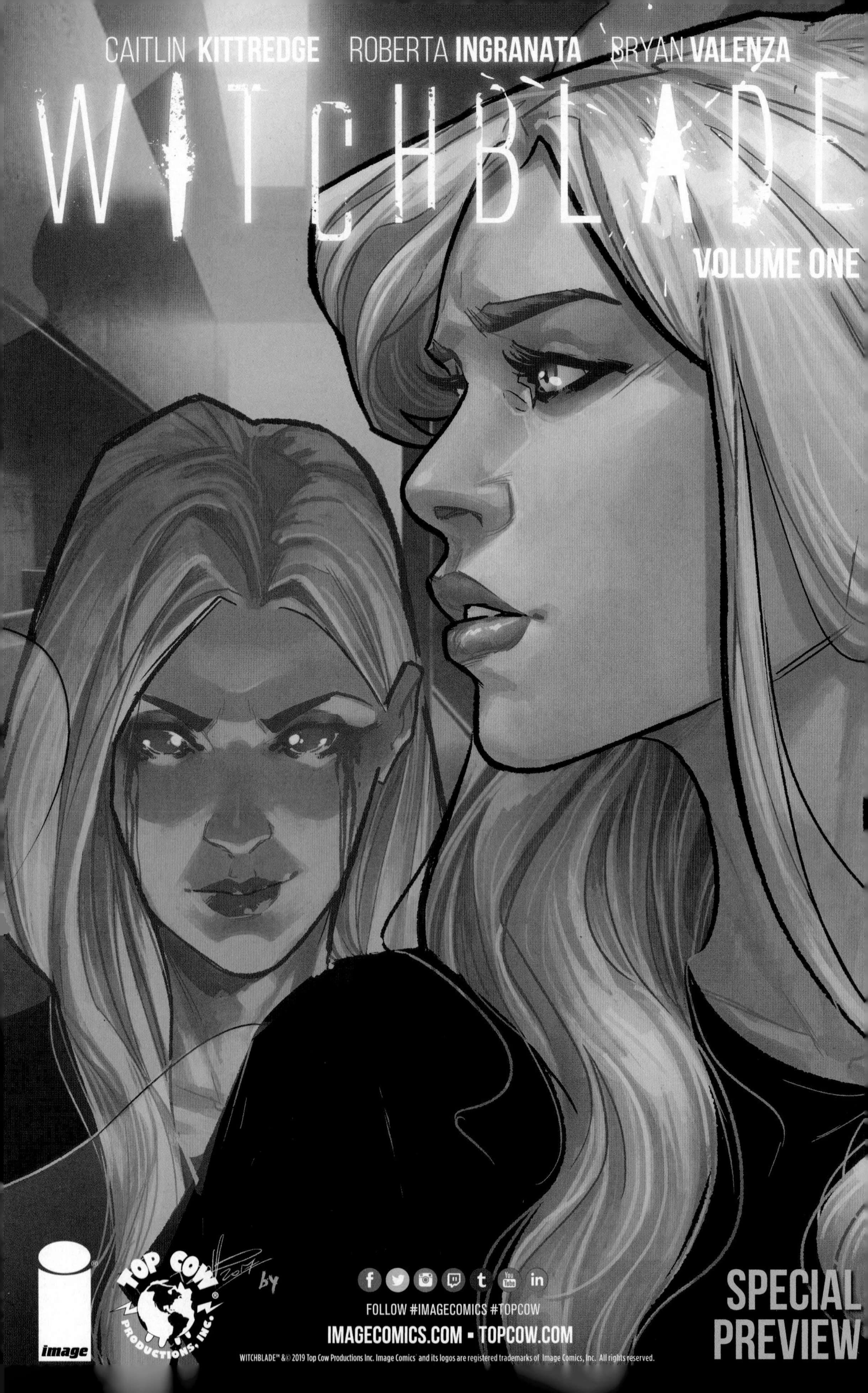
CAITLIN KITTREDGE ROBERTA INGRANATA BRYAN VALENZA
WITCHBLADE
VOLUME ONE
FOLLOW #IMAGECOMICS #TOPCOW
IMAGECOMICS.COM - TOPCOW.COM
WITCHBLADE™ &© 2019 Top Cow Productions Inc. Image Comics® and its logos are registered trademarks of Image Comics, Inc. All rights reserved.
SPECIAL PREVIEW

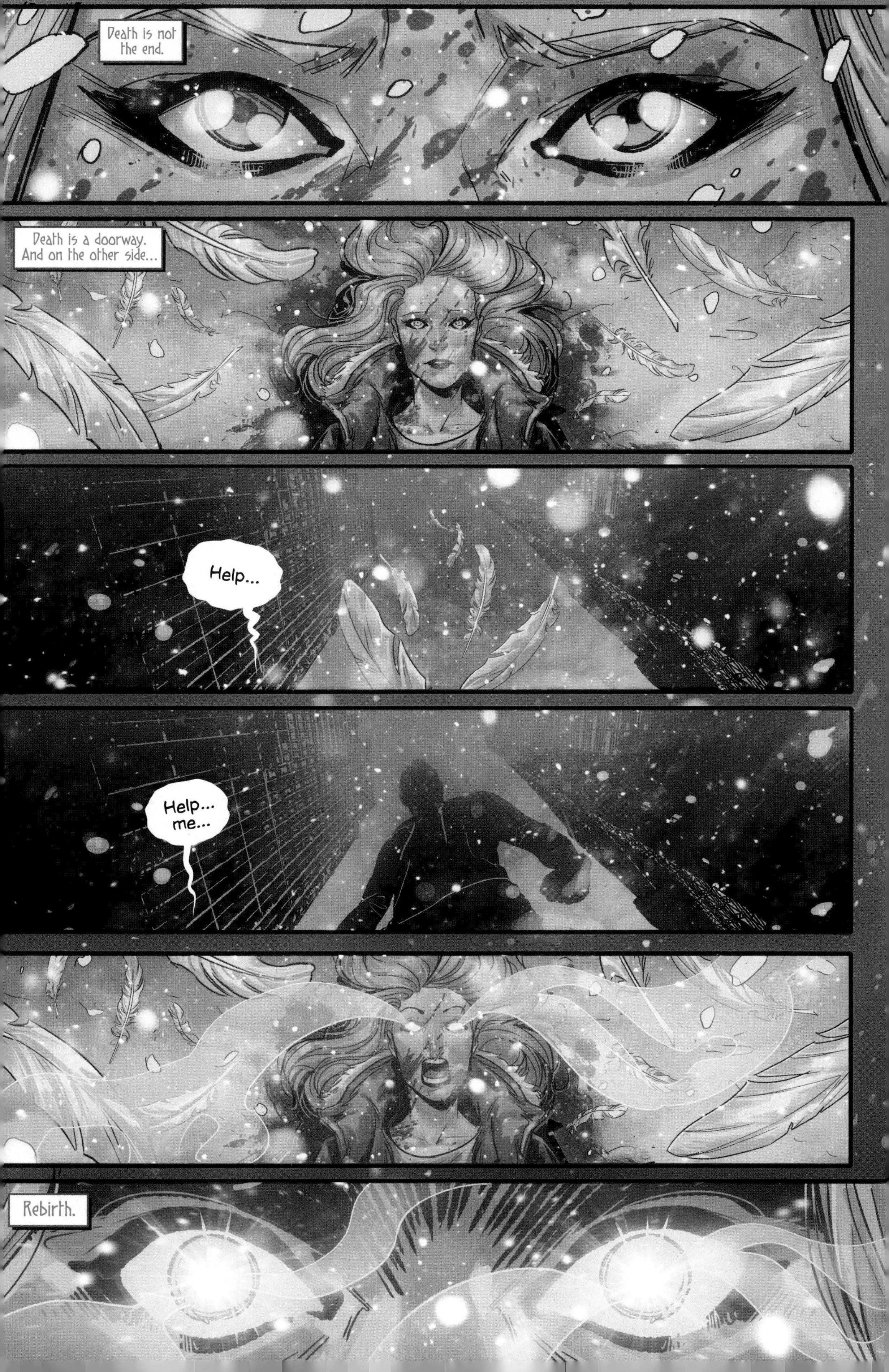
Death is not the end.
Death is a doorway. And on the other side...
Help...
Help... me...
Rebirth.

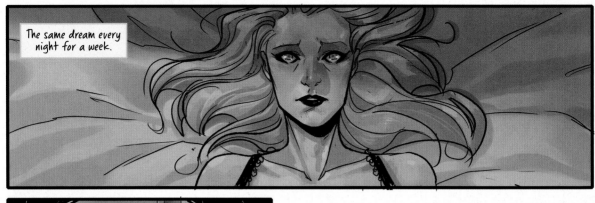

The same dream every night for a week.

Brooklyn, New York
24 hours earlier

You'd think my subconscious would get bored.

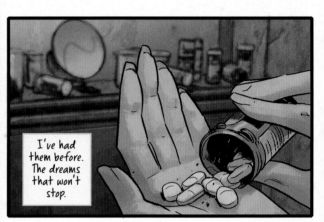

I've had them before. The dreams that won't stop.

But not for a long time. I thought it was over.

It's never over, though. Not for me.

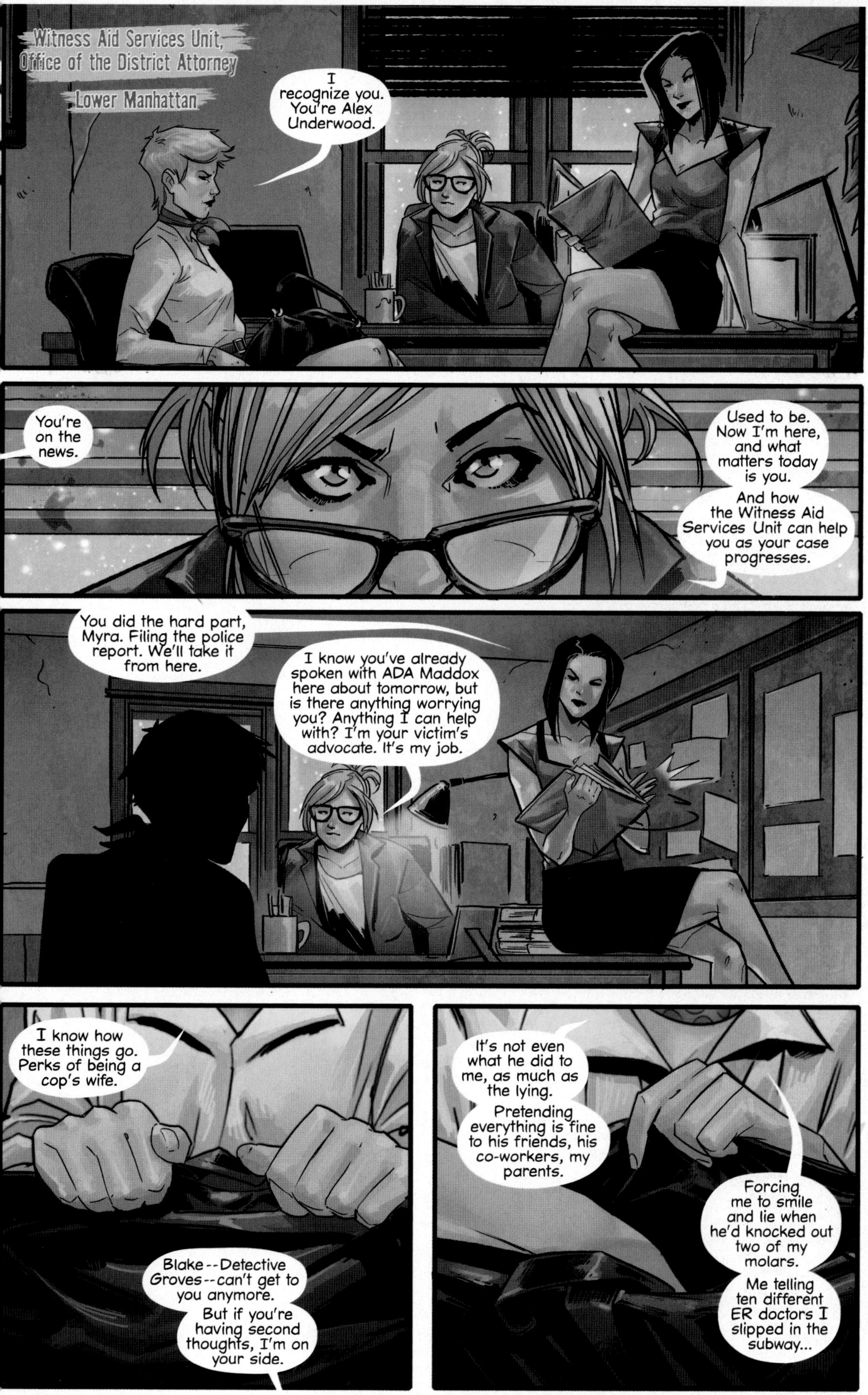
Witness Aid Services Unit, Office of the District Attorney
Lower Manhattan
I recognize you. You're Alex Underwood.
You're on the news.
Used to be. Now I'm here, and what matters today is you.
And how the Witness Aid Services Unit can help you as your case progresses.
You did the hard part, Myra. Filing the police report. We'll take it from here.
I know you've already spoken with ADA Maddox here about tomorrow, but is there anything worrying you? Anything I can help with? I'm your victim's advocate. It's my job.
I know how these things go. Perks of being a cop's wife.
Blake--Detective Groves--can't get to you anymore.
But if you're having second thoughts, I'm on your side.
It's not even what he did to me, as much as the lying.
Pretending everything is fine to his friends, his co-workers, my parents.
Forcing me to smile and lie when he'd knocked out two of my molars.
Me telling ten different ER doctors I slipped in the subway...

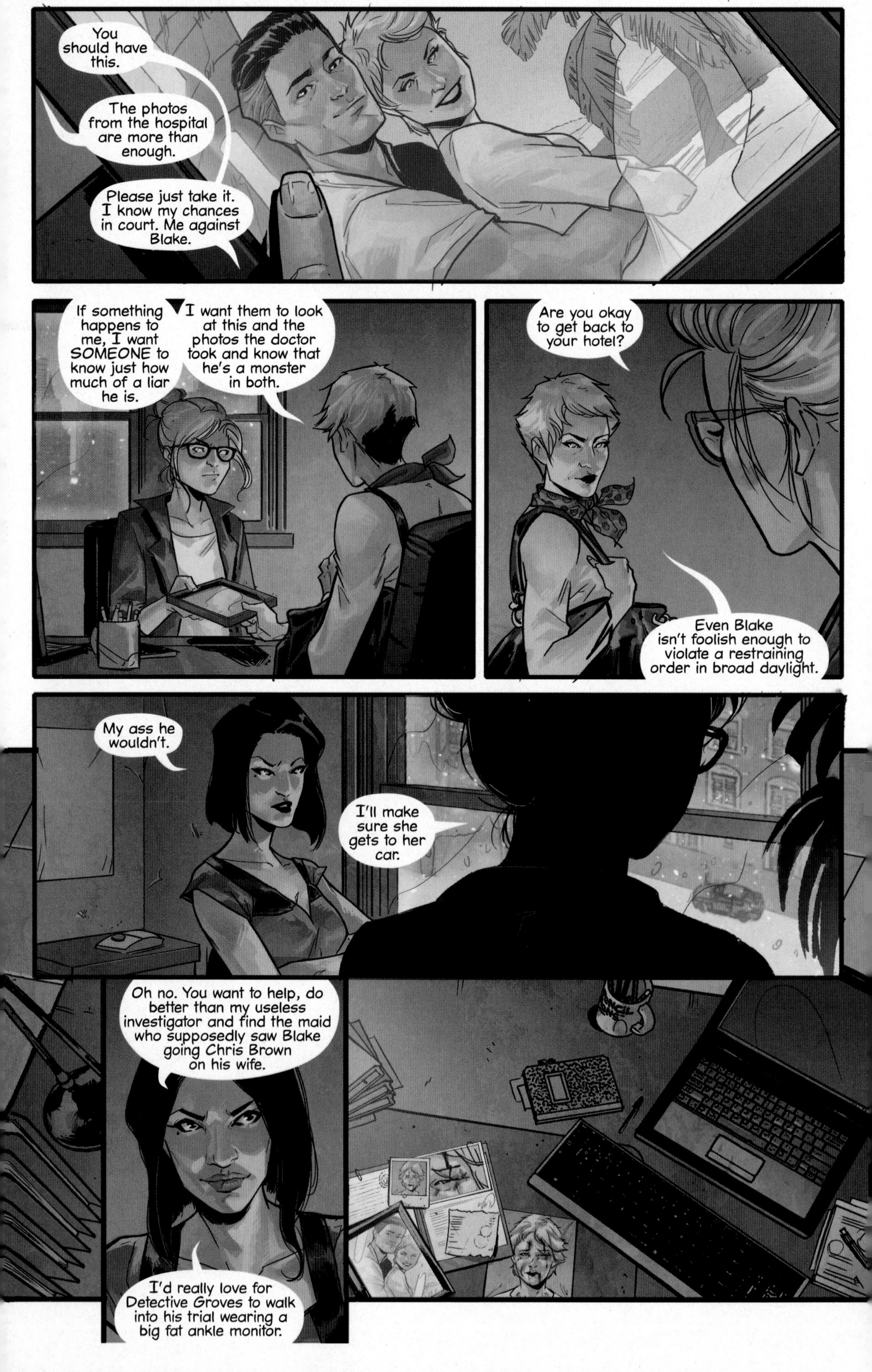
You should have this.
The photos from the hospital are more than enough.
Please just take it. I know my chances in court. Me against Blake.
If something happens to me, I want SOMEONE to know just how much of a liar he is.
I want them to look at this and the photos the doctor took and know that he's a monster in both.
Are you okay to get back to your hotel?
Even Blake isn't foolish enough to violate a restraining order in broad daylight.
My ass he wouldn't.
I'll make sure she gets to her car.
Oh no. You want to help, do better than my useless investigator and find the maid who supposedly saw Blake going Chris Brown on his wife.
I'd really love for Detective Groves to walk into his trial wearing a big fat ankle monitor.

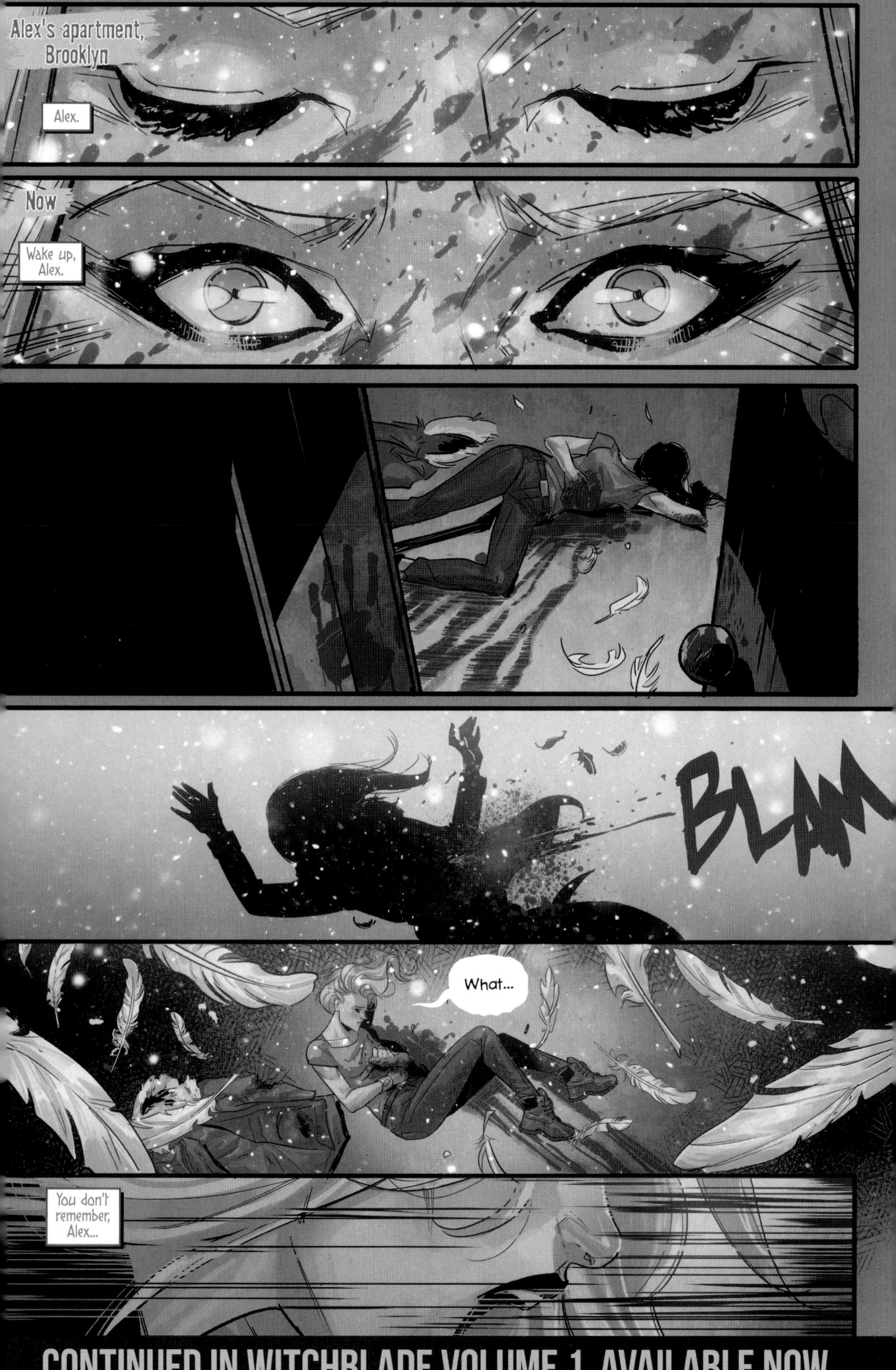
Alex's apartment, Brooklyn
Alex.
Now
Wake up, Alex.
BLAM
What...
You don't remember, Alex...

CONTINUED IN WITCHBLADE VOLUME 1, AVAILABLE NOW

The Top Cow essentials checklist: